NEW FORCES IN OLD CHINA

ARTHUR JUDSON BROWN

NEW FORCES IN OLD CHINA

AN INEVITABLE AWAKENING

BIBLIOBAZAAR

New Forces in Old China

To my Friends in China

Preface

THE object of this book is to describe the operation upon and within old, conservative, exclusive China of the three great transforming forces of the modern world—Western trade, Western politics and Western religion. These forces are producing stupendous changes in that hitherto sluggish mass of humanity. The full significance of these changes both to China and to the world cannot be comprehended now. There is something fascinating and at the same time something appalling in the spectacle of a nation numbering nearly one-third of the human race slowly and majestically rousing itself from the torpor of ages under the influence of new and powerful revolutionary forces. No other movement of our age is so colossal, no other is more pregnant with meaning. In the words of D. C. Bougler, "The grip of the outer world has tightened round China. It will either strangle her or galvanize her into fresh life."

The immediate occasion of this volume was the invitation of the faculty of Princeton Theological Seminary to deliver a series of lectures on China on the Student Lectureship Foundation and to publish them in book form. This will account in part for the style of some passages. I have, however, added considerable material which was not included in the lectures, while some articles that were contributed to the Century Magazine, the American Monthly Review of Reviews and other magazines have been inserted in their proper place in the discussion. The materials were gathered not only in study and correspondence but in an extended tour of Asia in the years 1901 and 1902. In that tour, advantage was taken of every opportunity to confer with Chinese of all classes, foreign consuls, editors, business men and American, German and British officials, as well as with missionaries of all denominations. Everywhere I was cordially received, and, as I look at my voluminous note-books, I am very grateful to the men of all faiths and nationalities who so generously aided me in my search for information.

No one system of spelling Chinese names has been followed for the simple reason that no one has been generally accepted. The Chinese characters represent words and ideas rather than letters and can only be phonetically reproduced in English. Unfortunately, scholars differ widely as to this phonetic spelling, while each nationality works in its own peculiarities wherever practicable. And so we have Manchuria, Mantchuria and Manchouria; Kiao-chou, Kiau-Tshou, Kiao-Chau, Kiau-tschou and Kiao-chow; Chinan and Tsi-nan; Ychou, Ichow and I-chou; Tsing-tau and Ching-Dao; while Mukden is confusingly known as Moukden, Shen-Yang, Feng-tien-fu and Sheng-king. As some authors follow one system, some another and some none at all, and as usage varies in different parts of the Empire, an attempt at uniformity would have involved the correction of quotations and the changing of forms that have the sanction of established usage as, for example, the alteration of Chefoo to Chi-fu or Tshi-fu. I have deemed it wise, as a rule, to omit the aspirate (e. g, Tai-shan instead of T'ai-shan) as unintelligible to one who does not speak Chinese. Few foreigners except missionaries can pronounce Chinese names correctly anyway. Besides, no matter what the system of spelling, the pronunciation differs, the Chinese themselves in various parts of the Empire pronouncing the name of the Imperial City Beh-ging, Bay-ging, Bai-ging and Bei-jing, while most foreigners pronounce it Pe-kin or Pi-king. I have followed the best obtainable advice in using the hyphen between the different parts of many proper names. For the rest I join the perplexed reader who devoutly hopes that the various commit-tees that are at work on the Romanization of the Chinese language may in time agree among themselves and evolve a system that a plain, wayfaring man can understand without provocation to wrath.

156 Fifth Avenue,
     New York City.

Preface to the Second Edition

THE author gratefully acknowledges the kindness with which his book has been received not only in this country but in England and China. In this edition he has corrected a number of errors that appeared in the first edition and has availed himself of later statistical information. He is under special obligations to the Rev. W. A. P. Martin, D. D., LL. D., of Wuchang, and the Rev. Arthur H. Smith, D. D. LL. D., of Pang-chwang, for valuable counsel. These distinguished authorities on China have been so kind as to study the book with painstaking care and to give the author the benefit of their suggestions. All these suggestions have been incorporated in this edition to the great improvement of its accuracy.

The result of the Russia-Japan War is noticeably accelerating the new movement in China. The Chinese have been as much startled and impressed by the Japanese victory as the rest of the world and they are more and more disposed to follow the path which the Japanese have so successfully marked out. The considerations presented in this book are therefore even more true to-day than when they were first published. The problem of the future is plainly the problem of China and no thoughtful person can afford to be indifferent to the vast transformation which is taking place as the result of the operation of the great formative forces of the modern world.

156 Fifth Avenue,
New York City.

CONTENTS

PART I
OLD CHINA AND ITS PEOPLE

PART II
THE COMMERCIAL FORCE AND THE
ECONOMIC REVOLUTION

PART III
THE POLITICAL FORCE AND THE
NATIONAL PROTEST

PART IV
THE MISSIONARY FORCE AND THE
CHINESE CHURCH

PART V
THE FUTURE OF CHINA AND OUR RELATION TO IT

PART I

OLD CHINA AND ITS PEOPLE

I

THE ANCIENT EMPIRE

HE must be dead to all noble thoughts who can tread the venerable continent of Asia without profound emotion. Beyond any other part of the earth, its soil teems with historic associations. Here was the birthplace of the human race. Here first appeared civilization. Here were born art and science, learning and philosophy. Here man first engaged in commerce and manufacture. And here emerged all the religious teachers who have most powerfully influenced mankind, for it was in Asia in an unknown antiquity that the Persian Zoroaster taught the dualism of good and evil; that the Indian Gautama 600 years before Christ declared that self-abnegation was the path to a dreamless Nirvana; that less than a century later the Chinese Lao-tse enunciated the mysteries of Taoism and Confucius uttered his maxims regarding the five earthly relations of man, to be followed within another century by the bold teaching of Mencius that kings should rule in righteousness. In Asia it was 1,000 years afterwards that the Arabian Mohammed proclaimed himself as the authoritative prophet. There the God and Father of us all revealed Himself to Hebrew sage and prophet in the night vision and the angelic form and the still, small voice; and in Asia are the village in which was cradled and the great altar of the world on which was crucified the Son of God.

We of the West boast of our national history. But how brief is our day compared with the succession of world powers which Asia has seen.

Chaldea began the march of kingdoms 2,200 years before Christ. Its proud king, Chedor-laomer, ruled from the Persian Gulf to the sources of the Euphrates, and from the Zagros Mountains to the Mediterranean. Then Egypt arose to rule not only over the northeastern part of Africa, but over half of Arabia and all of the preceding territory of Chaldea. Assyria followed, stretching from the Black Sea nearly half-way down the Persian Gulf and from the Mediterranean to the eastern boundary of modern Persia. Babylon, too, was once a world power whose monarch sat

"High on a throne of royal state, which far
Outshone the wealth of Ormus or of Ind."[1]

Persia was mightier still. Two thousand years before America was heard of, while France and Germany, England and Spain, were savage wildernesses, Persia was the abode of civilization and culture, of learning and eloquence. Her empire extended from the Indus to the Danube and from the Oxus to the Nile, embracing twenty satrapies each one of whose governors was well-nigh a king. Alexander the Great, too, at the head of his invincible army, swept over vast areas of Asia, capturing cities, unseating rulers, and bringing well-nigh all the civilized world under his dominion. And was not Rome also an Asiatic power, for it stretched not only from the firths of Scotland on the north to the deserts of Africa on the south, but from the Atlantic Ocean on the west to the River Euphrates on the east.

Altogether it is a majestic but awful procession, overwhelming us by its grandeur and yet no less by its horror. It is a kaleidoscope on a colossal scale, whose pieces appear like fragments of a broken universe. Empires rise and fall. Thrones are erected and overturned. The mightiest creations of man vanish. Yea, they have all waxed "old as doth a garment," and "as a vesture" are they "changed."

But were these ancient nations the last of Asia? Has that mighty continent nothing more to contribute to the world than the memories of a mighty past? It is impossible to believe that this is all. The historic review gives a momentum which the mind cannot easily overcome. As we look towards the Far East, we can

---

1   Milton, "Paradise Lost," Book II.

plainly see that the evolution is incomplete. Whatever purpose the Creator had in mind has certainly not yet been accomplished. More than two-thirds of those innumerable myriads have as yet never heard of those high ideals of life and destiny which God Himself revealed to men. It is incredible that a wise God should have made such a large part of the world only to arrest its development at its present unfinished stage, inconceivable that He should have made and preserved so large a part of the human race for no other and higher purpose than has yet been achieved.

Within this generation, a new Asiatic power has suddenly appeared in a part of Asia far removed from the region in which the wise men of old lived and studied, and the might of that nation is even now checking the progress of huge and haughty Russia. But brilliant as has been the meteoric career of Japan, there is another race in Asia, which, though now moving more sluggishly, has possibilities of development that may in time make it a dominant factor in the future of the world. Great forces are now operating on that race and it is the purpose of this book to give some account of those forces and to indicate the stupendous transformation which they are slowly but surely producing.

The magnitude of China is almost overwhelming. In spite of all that I had read, I was amazed by what I saw. To say that the Empire has an area of 4,218,401 square miles is almost like saying that it is 255,000,000,000 miles to the North Star; the statement conveys no intelligible idea. The mind is only confused by such enormous figures. But it may help us to remember that China is one-third larger than all Europe, and that if the United States and Alaska could be laid upon China there would be room left for several Great Britains. Extending from the fifty-fourth parallel of latitude southward to the eighteenth, the Empire has every variety of climate from arctic cold to tropic heat. It is a land of vast forests, of fertile soil, of rich minerals, of navigable rivers. The very fact that it has so long sustained such a vast population suggests the richness of its resources. There are said to be 600,000,000 acres of arable soil, and so thriftily is it cultivated that many parts of the Empire are almost continuous gardens and fields. Four hundred and nineteen thousand square miles are believed to be underlaid with coal. Baron von Richthofen thinks that 600,000,000,000 tons of it are anthracite, and that the single Province of Shen-si could supply the entire world for a thousand years. When we add to this supply of coal the apparently inexhaustible deposits of iron ore, we have the two products on which material greatness largely depends.

The population proves to be even greater than was supposed, for while 400,000,000 was formerly believed to be a maximum estimate, the general census recently taken by the Chinese Government for the purpose of assessing the war tax places the population of the Empire at 426,000,000. This, however, includes 8,500,000 in Manchuria, 2,580,000 in Mongolia, 6,430,020 in Tibet and 1,200,000 in Chinese Turkestan. Some of these regions are only nominally Chinese. Those on the western frontier were until comparatively recent years almost as unknown as the poles. Sven Hedin's description of those that he traversed is wonderfully fascinating. Only a daring spirit, the explorer of the type that is born, not made, could have pierced those vast solitudes and wrested from them the secret of their existence. That Hedin had no money for such a costly quest could not deter this Viking of the Northland. Kings headed the subscription and others so eagerly followed that ample funds were soon in hand. Princes helped with equipment and counsel. The Czar made all Russian railways free highways, and every local official and nomad chieftain exerted himself to aid the expedition. Hedin does not claim to give anything more than an ordered diary of his travels, together with a description of the lands he explored and the peoples he found. But what a diary it is! It takes the reader away from the whirl of crowded cities and clanging trolley-cars into the boundless, wind-swept desert and the solitude of majestic mountains where the lonely traveller wanders with his camels through untrodden wildernesses or floats down the interminable stretches of unknown rivers, while night after night he sleeps in his tiny tent or under the open sky. The author failed to reach the long-sought Lassa, the suspicious Dalai Lama refusing to be deceived or cajoled and sternly sending the inquisitive traveller out of the country. But the expedition of three years and three days was rich in other disclosures of ruined cities and great watercourses and lofty plateaus and majestic mountain ranges. The population is sparse in those desolate wastes, and the scattered inhabitants are wild and uncouth and free.

Manchuria, however, is far from being the barren country that so many imagine it to be. It is, in many respects, like Canada, a region embracing about 370,000 square miles and of almost boundless agricultural and mineral wealth. The population, save in the southern parts, is not yet dense but it is rapidly increasing.

But in central and eastern China, the conditions are very different. Here the population can only be indicated by a figure so large that it is almost impossible for us to comprehend it. Consider that the eighteen provinces alone, with an area about equal to that part of the United States east of the Mississippi River, have eight times the population of that part of our country.

"There are twice as many people in China as on the four continents—Africa, North and South America and Oceanica. Every third person who toils under the sun and sleeps under God's stars is a Chinese. Every third child born into the world looks into the face of a Chinese mother. Every third pair given in marriage plight their troth in a Chinese cup of wine. Every third orphan weeping through the day every third widow wailing through the night are in China. Put them in rank, joining hands, and they will girdle the globe ten times at the equator with living, beating human hearts. Constitute them pilgrims and let two thousand go past every day and night under the sunlight and under the solemn stars, and you must hear the ceaseless tramp, tramp, of the weary, pressing, throbbing throng for five hundred years."[2]

There is something amazing in the immensity of the population. Great cities are surprisingly numerous. In America, a city of nearly a million inhabitants is a wonderful place and all the world is supposed to know about it. But while Canton and Tientsin are tolerably familiar names, how many in the United States ever heard of Hsiang-tan-hsien ? Yet Hsiang-tan-hsien is said to have 1,000,000 inhabitants, while within comparatively short distances are other great cities and innumerable villages. In the Swatow region, within a territory a hundred and fifty miles long and fifty miles wide, there are no less than ten walled cities of from 40,000 to 250,000 inhabitants, besides hundreds of towns and villages ranging from a few hundred to 25,000 or 30,000 people. Men never tire of writing about the population adjacent to New York, Boston and Chicago. But in five weeks' constant journeying through the interior of the Shantung Province, there was hardly an

2   The Rev. J. T. Gracey, D. D., "China in Outline," p. 10.

hour in which multitudes were not in sight. There are no scattered farmhouses as in America, but the people live in villages and towns, the latter strongly walled and even the former often have a mud wall. As the country is comparatively level, it was easy to count them, and as a rule there were a dozen or more in plain view. I recall a memorable morning. It was Friday, June 28, 1901. We had risen early, and by daylight we had breakfasted, and started our carts and litters. In our enjoyment of the cool, delicious morning air, we walked for several li. Just before the sun rose, we crossed a low ridge and from its crest, I counted no less than thirty villages in front of us, while behind there were about as many more, the average population being apparently about 500 each. For days at a time, my road lay through the narrow, crowded street of what seemed to be an almost continuous village, the intervening farms being often hardly more than a mile in width.

Imagine half the population of the United States packed into the single state of Missouri and an idea of the situation will be obtained, for with an area almost equal to that of Missouri, Shantung has no less than 38,247,900 inhabitants. It is the most densely populated part of China. But the Province of Shan-si is as thickly settled as Hungary. Fukien and Hupeh have about as many inhabitants to the square mile as England. Chih-li is as populous as France and Yun-nan as Bulgaria.

The density of China's population may be better realized by a glance at the following detailed comparison between the population of Chinese provinces and the population of similar areas in the United States:

Provinces	Area Square miles	Population
Hupeh,	71,410	35,280,685
Ohio and Indiana	76,670	5,864,720
Honan,	67,940	35,316,800
Cheh-kiang,	36,670	1
Kentucky,	40,000	1,858,635
Kiang-si,	6819,47580	26 532,125
Virginia and West Virginia,	64}77600	7,fi50S282
Michigan and Wisconsin,	111,880	22,876 340
Georgia,	50,g80	1,837 353

Shantung,	62 000	4 7øø 945
Shan-si,	81 830	12 200 456
Illinois,	S6,000	3,826,8S 1
Shen-si,	776 8240	1 058,910
Ran-su,	Icc.q80	10~385~376
California,	155,9	1,208,130
Sze-chuen,	218,480	68 724,890
Ohio, Ind., Ill., Ky.,	173s430	11 350,219
Ngan-hwei,	54,810	23,670,314
New York,	47,600	5,997,853
Klang-su,	38,600	13,980,235
Pennsylvania,	44,985	5,258,014
Kwan-tung and Hainan,	gg,g70	31,865,251
Kansas,	81,700	I,427,o96
Kwang-si,	77,200	5,142,330
Minnesota,	79,205	x,301,826
Hunan,	83,380	22,169,673
Louisiana,	45,000	Iw1

Perhaps the most thoroughly typical city in China is Canton. The approach by way of the West River from Hongkong gives the traveller a view of some of the finest scenery in China. The green rice-fields, the villages nestling beneath the groves, the stately palm-trees, the quaint pagodas, the broad, smooth reaches of the river reflecting the glories of sunset and moon-rises and the noble hills in the background combine to form a scene worth journeying far to see.

But Canton itself is unique among the world's great cities, and the most sated traveller cannot fail to find much that will interest him. After much journeying in China, we thought we had seen its typical places, but no one has seen China until he has visited Canton. With an estimated population of 1,800,000, it is the metropolis of the Empire. The number of people per acre may be less than in some parts of the East Side in New York, for the houses are only one story in height. But the crowding is amazing. The streets are mere alleys from four to eight feet wide, lined with open-front shops, so filled overhead with perpendicular signs and cross coverings of bamboo poles and mattings that they are in as perpetual shade as an African forest, and so choked with people that men often had to back into a shop to let our chairs pass. No wheeled vehicle can enter those corkscrew streets and we saw no animal of any kind save two cows that were being led to slaughter.

And the hubbub! Such shouting and yelling cannot be heard anywhere else in the world. Our chair coolies were in a constant state of objurgation in clearing a way. Everybody seemed to be bellowing to everybody else and when two chairs met, the din shattered the atmosphere. A foreigner excites a surprising amount of curiosity, considering the number that visit Canton. Troops of boys followed us and there was a good deal of what sounded like cat-calling. But it was all good-natured, or appeared to be.

The unpretentious shop-fronts often beckon to mysteries that are well worth penetrating—tobacco factories where coolies stamp the leaves with bare feet; tea, gold, dye and embroidery shops where designs of exquisite delicacy are exhibited; silk-weaving factories where fine fabrics are made on the simplest of looms; feather shops where breastpins and other ornaments are made of tiny bits of feathers on a silver base—a work requiring almost incredible nicety of vision and such strain upon the eyes that the operators often become blind by forty. Another curiosity is a shop where crickets are reared for fighting as the Filipino fights cocks and the Anglo-Saxon fights dogs. The Chinese gamble on the result and a good fighting cricket is sometimes sold for $100. The attendant put a couple in a jar for our alleged amusement and they began fighting fiercely. But I promptly stopped the melee as I did not enjoy such sport.

The river is one of the sights of China. It is crowded with boats of all sizes. The owner of each lives on it with his family, the babies having ropes tied to them so that if they tumble into the water, they can be pulled out.

Altogether, it is a remarkable city. Viewed from the famous Five-Story Pagoda, on a high part of the old city wall, it is a swarming hive of humanity. As one looks out on those myriads of toiling, struggling, sorrowing men and women, he is conscious of a new sense of the pathos and the tragedy of human life. If I may adapt the words of the Rev. Dr. Richard S. Storrs on the heights above Naples, at the Church of San Mar-tino, on the way to St. Elmo—I suppose that every one who has ever stood on the balcony of that lofty pagoda "has noticed, as I remember to have noticed, that all the sounds coming up from that populous city, as they reached the upper air, met and mingled on the minor key. There were the voices of traffic, and the voices of command, the voices of affection and the voices of rebuke, the shouts of sailors, and the cries of itinerant venders in the street, with the chatter and the laugh of childhood; but they all came up into this incessant moan in the air. That is the voice of the world in the upper air, where there are spirits to hear it. That is the cry of the world for help."[3]

3   "Address on Foreign Missions," pp. 178, 179.

II
DO WE RIGHTLY VIEW THE CHINESE

TOO much has been made of the peculiarities of the Chinese, ignoring the fact that many customs and traits that appear peculiar to us are simply the differences developed by environment. Eliza Scidmore affirms that "no one knows or ever really will know the Chinese, the most comprehensible, inscrutable, contradictory, logical, illogical people on earth." But a Chinese gentleman, who was educated in the United States, justly retorts: "Behold the American as he is, as I honestly found him—great, small, good, bad, self-glorious, egotistical, intellectual, supercilious, ignorant, superstitious, vain and bombastic. In truth," he adds, "so very remarkable, so contradictory, so incongruous have I found the American that I hesitate."[4]

The Chinese are, indeed, very different from western peoples in some of their customs.

"They mount a horse on the right side instead of the left. The old men play marbles and fly kites, while children look gravely on. They shake hands with themselves instead of with each other. What we call the surname is written first and the other name afterwards. A coffin is a very acceptable present to a rich parent in good health. In the north they sail and pull their wheelbarrows in place of merely pushing them.

China is a country where the roads have no carriages and the ships have no keels; where the needle points to the south, the place

---

4   "As a Chinaman Saw Us," pp. 1, 2.

of honour is on the left hand, and the seat of intellect is supposed to lie in the stomach; where it is rude to take off your hat, and to wear white clothes is to go into mourning. Can one be astonished to find a literature without an alphabet and a language without a grammar?"[5]

It would never occur to us to commit suicide in order to spite another. But in China such suicides occur every day, because it is believed that a death on the premises is a lasting curse to the owner. And so the Chinese drowns himself in his enemy's well or takes poison on his foe's door-step. Only a few months ago, a rich Chinese murdered an employee in a British colony, and knowing that inexorable British law would not be satisfied until some one was punished, he hired a poor Chinese named Sack Chum to confess to having committed the murder and to permit himself to be hung, the real murderer promising to give him a good funeral and to care for his family. An Englishman who thought this an incredible story wrote a letter of inquiry to an intelligent Chinese merchant of his acquaintance and received the following reply:

"Nothing strange to Chinamen. Sack Chum, old man, no money, soon die. Every day in China such thing. Chinaman not like white man—not afraid to die. Suppose some one pay his funeral, take care his family. 'I die,' he say. Chinaman know Sack Chum, we suppose, sell himself to men who kill Ah Chee. Somebody must die for them. Sack Chum say he do it. All right. Police got him. What for they want more?"

These things appear odd from our view-point and there are many other peculiarities that are equally strange to us. But it may be wholesome for us to remember that some of our customs impress the Chinese no less oddly. The Frankfurter Zeitung, Germany, prints the following from a Chinese who had seen much of the Europeans and Americans in Shanghai:

"We are always told that the countries of the foreign devils are grand and rich; but that cannot be true, else what do they all come here for? It is here that they grow rich. They jump around and kick balls as if they were paid to do it. Again you will find them making long tramps into the country; but that is probably a religious duty, for when they tramp they wave sticks in the air, nobody knows why.

5   Temple Bar, quoted in Smith's "Rex Christus," p. 115.

They have no sense of dignity, for they may be found walking with women. Yet the women are to be pitied, too. On festive occasions they are dragged around a room to the accompaniment of the most hellish music."

A Chinese resident in America wrote to his friends at home a letter from which the following extract is taken:

"What is queerer still, men will stroll out in company with their wives in broad daylight without a blush. And will you believe that men and women take hold of each other's hands by way of salutation? Oh, I have seen it myself more than once. After all, what can you expect of folk who have been brought up in barbarous countries on the very verge of the world? They have not been taught the maxims of our sages; they never heard of the Rites; how can they know what good manners mean? We often think them rude and insolent when I'm sure they don't mean it they're ignorant, that's all."[6]

A call that I made upon a high official in an interior city developed a curious interest. He was a pale, thin man, apparently an opium smoker and a mandarin of the old school. But he was intelligent enough to ask me not only about "the twenty-story buildings of New York," but "the differences between the various Protestant sects," and in particular about "the Mormons and their strength!" Who could have imagined that the Latter Day Saints of Utah could be known to a Chinese nobleman of Chih-li? Verily, our own idiosyncrasies are known afar.

It will thus be seen that mutual recriminations regarding national peculiarities are not likely to be convincing to either party. Human nature is much the same the world over. From this viewpoint at least we may discreetly remember that

> "There is so much bad in the best of us,
> And so much good in the worst of us,
> That it hardly behoves any of us
> To talk about the rest of us."

I do not mean to give an exaggerated impression of the virtues of the Chinese or what Mrs. Isabella Bird Bishop calls "a milk-and-

---

6   Smith, "Rex Christus," p. 116.

water idea" of heathenism. Undoubtedly, they have grave defects. Official corruption is well-nigh universal. A correspondent of the North China Herald reports a well-informed Chinese gentleman of the Province of Chih-li as expressing the conviction that one-half the land tax never reaches the Government. "But that is not all," said he.

"There are other sources of income for the hsien official. Thus here in this county, thirty-five or forty years ago, the Government imposed an extra tax for the purpose of putting down the Tai-ping rebellion, and the officials have continued to collect that tax ever since. Of course if the literati should move in the matter and report to Paoting-fu, the magistrate would be bounced at once; but they are not likely to do so. The tax is a small one, my own share not being more than five dollars or so."

China's whole public service is rotten with corruption. Offices with merely nominal salaries or none at all are usually bought by the payment of a heavy bribe and held for a term of three years, during which the incumbent seeks not only to recoup himself but to make as large an additional sum as possible. As the weakness of the Government and the absence of an outspoken public press leave them free from restraint, China is the very paradise of embezzlers. "Any man who has had the least occasion to deal with Chinese courts knows that 'every man has his price,' that not only every underling can be bought, but that 999 out of every 1,000 officials, high or low, will favour the man who offers the most money."[7] Dishonesty is not, as with the white race, simply the recourse in emergency of the unscrupulous man. It is the habitual practice, the rule of intercourse of all classes. The Chinese apparently have no conscience on the subject, but appear to deem it quite praise-worthy to deceive you if they can.

Gambling is openly, shamelessly indulged in by all classes. As for immorality, the Rev. Dr. J. Campbell Gibson of Swatow says that "while the Chinese are not a moral people, vice has never in China as in India, been made a branch of religion." But the Rev. Dr. C. H. Fenn, of Peking, declares "that every village and town and city—it would not be a very serious ex-aggeration to say every home,—fairly reeks with impurity." The Chinese are, indeed, less

7   Rev. Dr. C. H. Fenn, Peking.

openly immoral than the Japanese, while their venerated books abound with the praises of virtue. But medical missionaries could tell a dark story of the extent to which immorality eats into the very warp and woof of Chinese society. The five hundred monks in the Lama Temple in Peking are notorious not only for turbulence and robbery, but for vice. The temple is in a spacious park and includes many imposing buildings. The statue of Buddha is said to be the largest in China—a gilded figure about sixty feet high—colossal and rather awe-inspiring in "the dim religious light." But in one of the temple buildings, where the two monks who accompanied us said that daily prayers were chanted, I saw representations in brass and gilt that were as filthily obscene as anything that I saw in India. There is immorality in lands that are called Christian, but it is disavowed by Christianity, ostracized by decent people and under the ban of the civil law. But Buddhism puts immorality in its temples and the Government supports it. This particular temple has the yellow tiled roofs that are only allowed on buildings associated with the Imperial Court or that are under special Imperial protection. Mr. E. H. Parker, after twenty years' experience in China, writes,

"The Chinese are undoubtedly a libidinous people, with a decided inclination to be nasty about it…Rich mandarins are the most profligate class…Next come the wealthy merchants…The crapulous leisured classes of Peking openly flaunt the worst of vices.

Still, amongst all classes and ranks the moral sense is decidedly weak…Offenses which with us are regarded as almost capital—in any case as infamous crimes—do not count for as much as petty misdemeanours in China.[8]

More patent to the superficial observer is a cruelty which appears to be callously indifferent to suffering. This manifests itself not only in most barbarous punishments but in a thou-sand incidents of daily life. The day I entered China at Chefoo, I saw a dying man lying beside the road. Hundreds of Chinese were passing and repassing on the crowded thoroughfare. But none stopped to help or to pity and the sufferer passed through his last agony absolutely uncared for and lay with glazing eyes and stiffening form all unheeded by the careless throng. Twenty-four hours afterwards,

8   "China," pp. 272, 273

he was still lying there with his dead face upturned to the silent sky, while the world jostled by, buying, laughing, quarrelling, heedless of the tragedy of human life so near. And when in Ching-chou-fu, I stopped to see if I could not give some relief to a woman who was writhing in the street, I was hastily warned that if I touched her unasked, the populace might hold me responsible in the event of her death and perhaps demand heavy damages, if, indeed, it did not mob me on the spot. Undoubtedly the Chinese are often deterred from aiding a sufferer because they fear that if death occurs "bad luck" will follow them, a horde of real or fictitious relatives will clamour for damages, and perhaps a rapacious magistrate will take advantage of the opportunity to make a criminal charge which can be removed only by a heavy bribe. And so the sick and poor are often left to die uncared for in crowded streets, and drowning children are allowed to sink within a few yards of boats which might have rescued them. But everywhere in China, little attention is paid to suffering and many customs seem utterly heartless.

In spite, too, of the agnostic teachings of Confucius and their own practical temperament, the Chinese are a very superstitious people and live in constant terror of evil spirits. The grossest superstitions prevail among them, while beyond any other people known to us they are stagnant, spiritually dead, densely ignorant of those higher levels of thought and life to which Christianity has raised whole classes in Europe and America.

Some people who are ignorant of the real situation in China are being misled by an anonymous little book entitled "Letters From a Chinese Official." The author insists that Anglo-Saxon institutions are far inferior to the institutions of China. He declares that "our religion (Chinese) is more rational than yours, our morality higher and our institutions more perfect," and that there is less real happiness in Europe and America than in China. As for Christianity, he regards it as quite impracticable. He holds that Confucianism is feasible and that Christianity is not, and much more to the same effect. There is strong internal evidence that the author is not a Chinese at all, but a cynical European. At any rate, the book is an ex parte statement of the most glaring kind, omitting the good in Europe and America and the bad in China. One who has visited the Celestial Empire gasps when he reads that the Chinese houses are "cheerful and clean," that the Chinese live the life of the mind and the spirit to a far higher degree than the Christian peoples of the West, and that Chinese life has a dignity and peace and beauty which Europe cannot equal. "Such silence! Such sounds! Such perfume! Such colour!" the author rhapsodizes. Bishop Graves, of Shanghai, who has spent a quarter of a century in China and who is therefore presumably competent to speak, declares:

"Far be it from me to belittle the beauty of the Chinese landscape; but why did he not leave out that about the perfume? Why, you can smell China out at sea! However, it is just as easy to imagine the perfume as the rest of it, while you are writing... Exaggeration is the most conspicuous note of these 'Letters.' Any one who has not seen China can test whether this book is true to fact by comparing it with any narrative of sober travel, and if he happens to live in China, his own nose and eyes are a sufficient witness...The writer takes the worst of our morals, the weakest of our religion, the most debasing of our industrial conditions, the most pernicious of our vices, and against them he sets not the best that China can show, but an exaggerated picture which is false to fact. This is not argument but trickery, because it presumes on the fact that one's readers will know no better."

Indeed, the Rev. Dr. C. H. Fenn, who has resided in Peking for ten years, writes that he cannot believe that the author of "Letters from a Chinese Official" is a sincere man. He continues:

"I would be almost willing to assert that it is impossible for a man, brought up in China, then spending many years abroad, to return to China and write such a book in honesty and sincerity of heart. He could not possibly help knowing that nine-tenths of what he was writing about China was absolutely untrue, that her political, legal, social, domestic and personal life are rotten to the core, and that only in a few exceptional cases is any pretence even made of living according to the ethics of Confucius. It might be possible for an educated man, whose surroundings had always been of an exceptionally good character, and who had never gone outside of his own province or studied foreign books, to write with some enthusiasm of the beauties of Chinese life, but not for any one else."

Still, at a time when the Chinese are being vociferously abused, it is only fair that we should give them credit for the good qualities which they do possess. I ask with Dr. William Elliott Griffis: "In talking of our brother men, what shall be our general principle, detraction or fair play? Because lackadaisical writers picture the Christless nations as in the innocence of Eden, shall we, at the antipodes of fact and truth, proceed to blacken their characters? Shall we compare the worst in Canton, Benares or Zululand, with the best in London, Berlin or Philadelphia? Surely God cannot look with complacency or hear with delight much of the practical slander spoken among white folks and Anglo-Saxons of His children and our brothers."

There has been too much of a disposition to think of the Chinese as a mass, almost as we would regard immense herds of cattle or shoals of fish. Why not rather think of the Chinese as an individual, as a man of like passions with ourselves? Physically, mentally, and morally he differs from us only in degree, not in kind. He has essentially the same hopes and fears, the same joys and sorrows, the same susceptibility to pain and the same capacity for happiness. Are we not told that God "hath made of one blood all nations of men"? We complacently imagine that we are superior to the Chinese. But discussing the question as to what constitutes superiority and inferiority of race, Benjamin Kidd declares that "we shall have to set aside many of our old ideas on the subject. Neither in respect alone of colour, nor of descent, nor even of the possession of high intellectual capacity, can science give us any warrant for speaking of one race as superior to another." Real superiority is the result, not so much of anything inherent in one race as distinguished from another, as of the operation upon a race and within it of certain uplifting forces. Any superiority that we now possess is due to the action upon us of these forces. But they can be brought to bear upon the Chinese as well as upon us. We should avoid the popular mistake of looking at the Chinese "as if they were merely animals with a toilet, and never see the great soul in a man's face."[9] "There is nothing," says Stopford Brooke, "that needs so much patience as just judgment of a man. We ought to know his education, the circumstances of his life, the friends he has made or lost, his temperament, his daily work, the motives which filled the act, the health he had at the time—we ought to have the knowledge of God to judge him justly."

---

9   George Eliot.

We need in this study a truer idea of the worth and dignity of man as man, a realization that back of almond eyes and under a yellow skin are all the faculties and the possibilities of a human soul, to grasp the great thought that the Chinese is not only a man, but our brother man, made like ourselves in the image of God. Let us have the charity which sees beneath all external peculiarities our common humanity, which leads us to respect a man because he is a man; which, no matter what complexion he may have, no matter where he lives, no matter to what degradation he has fallen, will take him by the hand and endeavour to elevate him to a higher plane of life. For him we need an enthusiasm for humanity which shall not be a sentimental rhetoric, but a catholic, throbbing love, remembering that he is

"Heir of the same inheritance,
    Child of the self-same God,
He hath but stumbled in the path
    We have in weakness trod."

Ruskin reminds us that the filthy mud from the street of a manufacturing town is composed of clay, sand, soot and water; that the clay may be purified into the radiance of the sapphire; that the sand may be developed into the beauty of the opal; that the soot may be crystallized into the glory of the diamond and that the water may be changed into a star of snow. So man in Asia as well as in America may, by the transforming power of God's Spirit, be ennobled into the kingly dignity of divine sonship. We shall get along best with the Chinese if we remember that he is a human being like ourselves, responsive to kindness, appreciative of justice and capable of moral transformation under the influence of the Gospel. He differs from us not in the fundamental things that make for manhood, but only in the superficial things that are the result of environment. From this view-point, we can say with Shakespeare:—

"There is some sort of goodness in things evil,
Would men observingly distil it out."

Those who are wont to refer so contemptuously to the Chinese might profitably recall that when, in Dickens"'Christmas

Carol," the misanthropic Scrooge says of the poor and suffering: "If he be like to die, he had better do it and decrease the surplus population,"—the Ghost sternly replies:—

"Man, if man you be at heart, not adamant, forbear that wicked cant until you have discovered what the surplus is and where it is. Will you decide what men shall live, what men shall die? It may be that in the sight of heaven, you are more worthless and less fit to live than millions like this poor man's child. Ah, God! to hear the insect on the leaf pronouncing on the too much life among his hungry brothers in the dust!"

III
ATTITUDE TOWARDS FOREIGNERS—
CHARACTER AND ACHIEVEMENTS

TO understand China's attitude towards foreigners, the following considerations must be borne in mind:—

First, the conservative temperament of the Chinese. It is true but misleading, to say that they have "no word or written character for patriotism, but 150 ways of writing the characters for good luck and longlife." For while the Chinese may have little love for country, they have an intense devotion to their own customs. For nearly 5,000 years, while other empires have risen, flourished and fallen, they have lived apart, sufficient unto themselves, cherishing their own ideals, plodding along their well-worn paths, ignorant of or indifferent to the progress of the Western world, mechanically memorizing dead classics, and standing still comparatively amid the tremendous onrush of modern civilization. I say comparatively still, for if we carefully study Chinese history, we shall find that this vast nation has not been so inert as we have long supposed. The very revolutions and internal commotions of all kinds through which China has passed would have prevented mere inertia. But when we compare these movements and the changes that they have wrought with the kaleidoscopic transformations in Europe and America, China appears the most stationary of nations. She has moved less in centuries than western peoples have in decades. The restless Anglo-Saxon is alternately irritated and awed by this massive solidity, not to say stolidity. There is, after all, something impressive about it, the impressiveness of a mighty glacier which moves, indeed, but so slowly and majestically that the duration of an ordinary nation's life appears insignificant as compared with the almost timeless majesty of the Chinese Empire.

Second, the vastness of China. Her territory and population are so enormous that her people found sufficient scope for their energies within their own borders. They therefore felt independent of outsiders. The typical European nation is so limited in area and is so near to equally civilized and powerful peoples that it could not if it would live unto itself. The situation of most nations forces them into relations with others. But China had a third of the human race and a tenth of the habitable globe entirely to herself, with no neighbours who had anything that she really cared for. It was inevitable, therefore, that a naturally conservative people should become a self-centred and self-satisfied people.

Third, the character of adjacent nations. None of them were equal to the Chinese in civilization and learning, while in territory and population, they were relatively insignificant. Even Japan, by far the most powerful of them, has only a tenth of China's population, while her remarkable progress in intelligence and power is a matter of less than a couple generations. Until recently, indeed, Japan was as backward as China and was not ashamed to receive many of her ideas from her larger neighbour, as the number of Chinese characters in the Japanese language plainly show. As for China's other neighbours, who were they? Weak nations which abjectly sent tribute by commissioners who grovelled before the august Emperor of the Middle Kingdom, or barbarous tribes which the Chinese regarded about as Americans regard the aboriginal Indians. Gibson translates the following passage from a Chinese historian as illustrative at once of China's haughty contempt of outsiders and of her reasons for it:

"The former kings in measuring out the land put the Imperial territory in the centre. Inside was the Chinese Empire, and outside were the barbarous nations. The barbarians are covetous and greedy of gain. Their hair hangs down over their bodies, and their coats are buttoned on the left side. They have human faces, but the hearts of beasts. They are distinguished from the natives of the Empire both by their manners and their dress. They differ both in their customs and their food, and in language they are utterly unintelligible...On this account the ancient sage kings treated them like birds and beasts. They did not contract treaties, nor did they attack them. To form a treaty is simply to spend treasure and to be deceived; to attack them is simply to wear out the troops and provoke raids…Thus the outer are not to be brought inside. They must be held at a distance, avoiding familiarity…If they show a leaning towards right principles and present tributary offerings, they should be treated with a yielding etiquette; but bridling and repression must never be relaxed for conforming to circumstance. Such was the constant principle of the sage monarchs in ruling and controlling the barbarian tribes."

It is not surprising, therefore, that when foreigners from the distant West sought to force their way into China, the Chinese, knowing nothing of the countries from which they came, should have regarded them in accordance with their traditional belief and policy regarding the inferiority of all outsiders.

The resultant difficulty was intensified by the indifference, to use no harsher term, of the foreigner to the fact that the Chinese are a very ceremonious people, extremely punctilious in all social relations and disposed to regard a breach of etiquette as a cardinal sin. "Face" is a national institution which must be preserved at all hazards. No one can get along with the Chinese who does not respect it.

"It is an integral part of both Chinese theory and practice that realities are of much less importance than appearances. If the latter can be saved, the former may be altogether surrendered. This is the essence of that mysterious 'face' of which we are never done hearing in China. The line of Pope might be the Chinese national motto: 'Act well your part, there all the honour lies'; not, be it observed, doing well what is to be done, but consummate acting, contriving to convey the appearance of a thing or a fact, whatever the realities may be. This is Chinese high art; this is success. It is self-respect, and it involves and implies the respect of others. It is, in a word, 'face.' The preservation of 'face' frequently requires that one should behave in an arbitrary and violent manner merely to emphasize his protests against the course of current events. He or she must fly into a violent rage, he or she must use reviling and perhaps imprecatory language, else it will not be evident to the spectators of the drama, in which he is at the moment acting, that he is aware just what ought to be done by a person in his precise situation; and then he will have 'no way to descend from the stage,' or in other words, he will have lost 'face.'"[10]

Even in death this remains the ruling passion. Chinese coffins require much wood and are an expensive burden in this land where timber is scarce, for Confucius said that a coffin should be five inches thick. So the poorer Chinese thriftily meet this requirement by making the sides and ends hollow! Thus "face" is saved.

In these circumstances, it was very important that the relations of Europeans to China should be characterized not only by justice but by tact and at least decent respect for the feelings and customs of the people. The chief cause of China's hostility to foreigners undoubtedly lies in the notorious and often contemptuous disregard of these things by the majority of the white men who have entered China and by the Governments which have backed them.

There is much in the Chinese that is worthy of our respectful recognition. Multitudes are indeed, stolid and ignorant, but multitudes, too, have strong, intelligent features. Thousands of children have faces as bright and winning as those of American children. More strongly than ever do I feel that Europe and America have not done justice to the character of the Chinese. I do not refer to the bigoted and corrupt Manchu officials, or to the lawless barbarians who, like the "lewd fellows of the baser sort" in other lands, are ever ready to follow the leadership of a demagogue. But I refer to the Chinese people as a whole. Their view-point is so radically different from ours that we have often harshly misjudged them, when the real trouble has lain in our failure to understand them.

Let us be free enough from prejudice and passion to respect a people whose national existence has survived the mutations of a definitely known historic period of thirty-seven centuries and of an additional legendary period that runs back no man knows how far into the haze of a hoary antiquity; who are frugal, patient, industrious and respectful to parents, as we are not; whose astronomers made accurate recorded observations 200 years before Abraham left Ur; who used firearms at the beginning of the Christian era; who first grew tea, manufactured gunpowder, made pottery, glue and gelatine; who wore silk and lived in houses when our ancestors

---

10   Smith, "Rex Christus," pp. 107, 108.

wore the undressed skins of wild animals and slept in caves; who invented printing by movable types 500 years before that art was known in Europe; who discovered the principles of the mariner's compass without which the oceans could not be crossed, conceived the idea of artificial inland waterways and dug a canal 600 miles long; who made mountain roads which, in the opinion of Dr. S. Wells Williams, "when new probably equalled in engineering and construction anything of the kind ever built by Romans;" and who invented the arch to which our modern architecture is so greatly indebted.

In the Great Bell Temple two miles from Peking is one of the wonderful bells of the world. It is fourteen feet high, thirty-four feet in circumference at the rim, nine inches thick and weighs 120,000 pounds. It is literally covered inside and out with Chinese characters consisting of extracts from the sacred writings, and the Rev. Dr. John Wherry, who is an expert in the Chinese language, says that there is "not one imperfect character among them." The bell when struck by the big wooden clapper emits a deep musical note that can be heard for miles. Such a magnificent bell vividly illustrates the stage of civilization reached by the Chinese while Europe was comparatively barbarous, for the bell was cast as far back as 1406 in the reign of Yung-loh, and the present temple buildings were erected about it in 1578. The Germans began using paper in 1190, but Sven Hedin found Chinese paper 1,650 years old and there is evidence that paper was in common use by the Chinese 150 years before Christ. Until a few hundred years ago, European business was conducted on the basis of coin or barter. But long before that, the Chinese had banks and issued bills of exchange. There has recently been placed in the British Museum a bank-note issued by Hung-Wu, Emperor of China, in 1368.

The Chinese exalt learning and, alone among the nations of the earth, make scholarship a test of fitness for official position. True, that scholarship moves along narrow lines of Confucian classics, but surely such knowledge is a higher qualification for office than the brute strength which for centuries gave precedence among our ancestors. A Chinese writer explains as follows the gradations in relative worth as they are esteemed by his countrymen: "First the scholar: because mind is superior to wealth, and it is the intellect that distinguishes man above the lower orders of beings, and enables him to provide food and raiment and shelter for himself and for other creatures. Second, the farmer: because the mind cannot act without the body, and the body cannot exist without food, so that farming is essential to the existence of man, especially in civilized society. Third, the mechanic: because next to food, shelter is a necessity, and the man who builds a house comes next in honour to the man who provides food. Fourth, the tradesman: because, as society increases and its wants are multiplied, men to carry on exchange and barter become a necessity, and so the merchant comes into existence. His occupation—shaving both sides, the producer and consumer—tempts him to act dishonestly; hence his low grade. Fifth, the soldier stands last and lowest in the list, because his business is to destroy and not to build up society. He consumes what others produce, but produces nothing himself that can benefit mankind. He is, perhaps, a necessary evil."[11]

While the Government of China is a paternal despotism in form and while it is always weak and corrupt and often cruel and tyrannical in practice, nevertheless there is a larger measure of individual freedom than might be supposed. "There are no passports, no restraints on liberty, no frontiers, no caste prejudices, no food scruples, no sanitary measures, no laws except popular customs and criminal statutes. China is in many senses one vast republic, in which personal restraints have no existence."[12]

We must not form our opinion from the Chinese whom we see in the United States. True, most of them are kindly, patient and industrious, while some are highly intelligent. But, with comparatively few exceptions, they are from the lower classes of a single province of Kwan-tung—Cantonese coolies. The Chinese might as fairly form their opinion of Americans from our day-labourers. But there are able men in the Celestial Empire. Bishop Andrews returned from China to characterize the Chinese as "a people of brains." When Viceroy Li Hung Chang visited this country, all who met him unhesitatingly pronounced him a great man. The New York Tribune characterizes the late Liu Kun Yi, Viceroy of Nanking, as a man who "rendered inestimable services to China and to the whole world," "a man of action, who acted with a strong hand

11 Quoted by Beach, "Dawn on the Hills of T'ang," pp. 45, 46.
12 E. H Parker, "China."

and masterful leadership and at the same time with a justice and a generosity that made him at once feared, respected and loved."

After General Grant's tour around the world, he told Senator Stewart that the most astonishing thing which he had seen was that wherever the Chinese had come into competition with the Jew, the Chinese had driven out the Jew. We know the persistence of the Jew, that he has held his own against every other people. Despite the fact that he has no home and no Government, that he has been ridiculed and persecuted by all men, that everywhere he is an alien in race, country and religion, he has laboured on, patiently, resolutely, distancing every rival, surmounting every obstacle, compelling even his enemies to acknowledge his shrewdness and his determination till to-day in Russia, in Austria, in Germany, in England, the Jew is bitterly conceded to be master in the editorial chair, at the bar, in the universities, in the counting-house and in the banking office; while the proudest of monarchs will undertake no enterprise requiring large expenditure until he is assured of the support of the keen-eyed, swarthy-visaged men who control the sinews of war. Generations of exclusion from agriculture and the mechanical arts and of devotion to commerce, have developed and inbred in the Jew a marvellous facility for trade.

And yet this race, which has so abundantly demonstrated its ability to cope with the Greek, the Slav and the Teuton, finds itself outreached in cunning, outworn in persistence and over-matched in strength by an olive-complexioned, almond-eyed fellow with felt shoes, baggy trousers, loose tunic, round cap and swishing queue, who represents such swarming myriads that the mind is confused in the attempt to comprehend the enormous number. The canny Scotchman and the shrewd Yankee are alike discomfited by the Chinese. Those who do not believe it should ask the American and European traders who are being crowded out of Saigon, Shanghai, Bangkok, Singapore, Penang, Batavia and Manila. In many of the ports of Asia outside of China, the Chinese have shown themselves to be successful colonizers, able to meet competition, so that to-day they own the most valuable property and control the bulk of the trade. It is true that the Chinese are inordinately conceited; but shades of the Fourth of July orator, screams of the American eagle! it requires considerable self-possession in a Yankee to criticize any one else on the planet for conceit. The Chinese have not, at least, padded a census to make the world believe that they are greater than they really are. In June, 1903, the same New York newspaper that gave the horrible details of the burning of a negro by an American mob within thirty miles of Philadelphia announced that a Chinese, Chung Hui Wang, had taken the highest honours in the graduating class at Yale University. Another New York journal, in commenting on the fact that Chao Chu, son of the former Chinese minister, Wu Ting Fang, was graduated in 1904 at the Atlantic City High School as the valedictorian of a class of thirty-one, remarked:

"At every commencement there are honours enough to go around, and those won by the Celestial contestants will not be begrudged them. Yet it is not exactly flattering to smart American youth to realize that representatives of an effete civilization after a few years' acquaintance with western ways can meet our home talent on its own ground and carry off the prizes of scholarship."

A British consular official, who spent many years in China and who speaks the language, declares that in his experience of the Chinese their fidelity is extraordinary, their sense of responsibility in positions of trust very keen, and that they have a very high standard of gratitude and honour. "I cannot recall a case," he says, "where any Chinese friend has left me in the lurch or played me a dirty trick, and few of us can say the same of our own colleagues and countrymen." The Hon. Chester Holcombe, who quotes this, adds—"The writer, after years of experience and intimate acquaintance with all classes of Chinese from every part of the Empire, is convinced that the characterization of the race as thus given by those who at least are not over-friendly does it only scant justice."[13]

Many quote against the Chinese the familiar lines—

"—for ways that are dark
And for tricks that are vain,
The heathen Chinee is peculiar."

But whoever reads the whole poem will see the force of the London Spectator's opinion that it is a "satire of the American selfishness which is the main strength of the cry against the

---

13   The Outlook, February 13, 1904.

cheap labour of the Chinese," and that "it would not be easy for a moderately intelligent man to avoid seeing that Mr. Bret Harte wished to delineate the Chinese simply as beating the Yankee at his own evil game, and to delineate the Yankee as not at all disposed to take offense at the "cheap labour" of his Oriental rival, until he discovered that he could not cheat the cheap labourer half so completely as the cheap labourer could cheat him."

It is common for people to praise the Japanese and to sneer at the Chinese. All honour to the Japanese for their splendid achievements. With marvellous celerity they have adopted many modern ideas and inventions. They are worthy of the respect they receive. But those who have made a close study of both peoples unhesitatingly assert that the Chinese have more solid elements of permanence and power. The Japanese have the quickness, the enthusiasm, the intelligence of the French; but the Chinese unite to equal intelligence the plodding persistence of the Germans, and the old fable of the tortoise and the hare is as true of nations as it is of individuals. Unquestionably, the Chinese are the most virile race in Asia "Wherever a Chinese can get a foot of ground and a quart of water he will make something grow." Colquhoun quotes Richthofen as saying that "among the various races of mankind, the Chinese is the only one which in all climates, the hottest and the coldest, is capable of great and lasting activity." And he states as his own opinion: "She has all the elements to build up a great living force. One thing alone is wanted—the will, the directing power. That supplied, there are to be found in abundance in China the capacity to carry out, the brains to plan, the hands to work."

IV
A TYPICAL PROVINCE

SHANTUNG is not only one of the greatest, but it is in many respects one of the most interesting of all the provinces of China. Its length east and west is about 543 miles and in area it is nearly as large as the whole of New England. The name, Shantung, signifies "east of the mountains." Forests once existed, but tillable land has become so valuable that trees are now comparatively few save in the villages and temples and about the graves of the rich. But for the most part, Shantung resembles the great prairie regions of the western part of the United States, broken by occasional ranges of hills and low mountains. The soil is generally fertile, though in the southwestern part I found some stony regions where the soil is thin and poor. South of Chinan-fu one finds the loess, a light friable earth which yields so easily to wheel and hoof and wind and water that the stream of travel through successive generations has worn deep cuts in which the traveller may journey for hours and sometimes for days so far below the general level of the country that he can see nothing but the sides of the cut and in turn cannot be seen by others. The character of the soil and the power of the wind and rain have combined not only to excavate these long passages, but to cast up innumerable mounds and hills, often of such fantastic shapes that one is reminded of the quaint and curious formations in the Bad Lands of the Missouri, though the loess hillocks lack the brilliant colouring of the American formations.

Throughout the province as a whole, almost every possible square rod of ground is carefully cultivated by the industrious people, so that in the summer time the whole country appears to be continuous gardens and farms dotted with innumerable villages. Wheat appears to be the chief crop and, as in the Dakotas, the entire landscape seems to be one splendid field of waving, yellowing grain. But early in June the wheat disappears as if by magic, for the whole population apparently, men, women and children, turn out and harvest it with amazing quickness in spite of the fact that everything is done by hand. Men and donkeys carry the grain to smooth, hard ground spaces, where it is threshed by a heavy roller stone drawn by a donkey or an ox or by men, and several times I saw it drawn by women. Then it is winnowed by being pitched into the air for the wind to drive out the feathery chaff. The methods vividly illustrate the first Psalm and other Bible references—gleaning, muzzling "the ox when he treadeth out the corn," the threshing floor and "the chaff which the wind driveth away."

One might suppose that after the wheat harvest, stubble fields would be much in evidence. But they are not, for the millet promptly appears. It is hardly noticeable when the wheat is standing. But it grows rapidly, and as soon as the wheat is out of the way, it covers great areas with its refreshing green, looking in its earlier stages like young corn. It is of two varieties. One is a little higher than wheat, with hanging head and a small yellow grain. The other is the kao-liang, which grows to a height of about twelve feet. When small, it is thinned out to one stalk or sometimes two in a hill so that it can develop freely. This stalk is to the common people almost as serviceable as the bamboo to tropical dwellers. It is used for fences, ceilings, walls and many other purposes. The grain of the two varieties is the staple food, few but the richer classes eating rice which is not raised in the north and is high in price. A third species of millet, shu-shu, is used chiefly for distilling a whiskey that is largely used but almost always at home and at night so that little drunkenness is seen by the traveller.

Fuel is very scarce, trees being few and coal, though abundant, not being mined to any extent. So the people cook with stalks, straw, roots, etc., and in winter pile on additional layers of wadded cotton garments. Chinese houses are not heated as ours are, though the flues from the cooking fire, running under the brick kang, give some heat, too much at times.

Silk is produced in large quantities and mulberry trees are so common as to add greatly to the beauty of the country. As the cocoons cannot be left on the trees for fear of thieves, the leaves are picked off and taken into houses where the worms are kept.

Poppy fields, too, are numerous. The flowers are gloriously beautiful. I often saw men gathering the opium in the early morning. After the blossoms fall off, the pod is slit and the whitish juice, oozing out, is carefully scraped off. High hills rising to low mountains add beauty to the western part of Shantung, while the more numerous trees scattered over the fields as well as in the villages make extensive regions look like vast parks.

The people are among the finest types of the Chinese, tall, strong and, in many instances, of marked intellectual power. To the Chinese, Shantung is the most sacred of the provinces, for here were born the two mighty sages, Confucius and Mencius.

Politically, the Province is divided into ten prefectures, each under a prefectural magistrate, called a Chih-fu, and with a capital which has the termination "fu." I-chou-fu, for example, is a prefectural city. Each fu is subdivided into ten districts under a district magistrate or Chih-hsien, the capital, or county seat as we should call it, having the termination "hsien" or "hien" as for example Wei-hsien. There are 108 of these hsien cities. Between the fu and the hsien cities are a few chou cities as Chining-chou. They are practically small fus, Chining-chou having four hsiens under it. The magistrate is called a Chou-kwan and is responsible directly to a Tao-tai who is an official between the prefectural magistrate or Chih-fu and the Governor. There are three Tao-tais in the province. At the provincial capital are the treasurer or Fan-tai, the Nieh-tai or judge, the Hueh-tai or commissioner of education and the salt commissioner, Yen-yuen. These are all high officials. Over all is the Governor, virtually a monarch subject only to the nominal supervision of the Imperial Government at Peking. He is appointed and may at any time be removed by the Emperor, but during his tenure of office he has almost unlimited power.

My tour of China included two interesting months in this great province. As I approached Chefoo on the steamer from Korea, I was impressed by the beauty of the scene. The water was smooth and sparkling in the bright spring sunshine. The harbour is exceptionally lovely. The shore lines are irregular, terminating in a high promonotory on which are situated the buildings of the various consulates. To the right, as the traveller faces the city, is the business section with its wharves and well-constructed commercial buildings, while on the left is the wide curve of a fine beach on which front the foreign hotel and the handsome buildings of the China Inland Mission. Beyond the city, rises a noble hill on the slopes of which stand the buildings of the Presbyterian Mission. From the water, Chefoo is one of the most charming cities in all China.

Big, lusty Chinese in their wide, clumsy boats called sampans, swarmed in the harbour. Sculling alongside, the boatman caught the rail of the steamer with his boat-hook and with the agility of a monkey scrambled up the long pole, dropped it into the water and began to hustle for business. The babel of voices bidding for passengers was like the tumult of Niagara hack-drivers, but we were so fortunate as to be met by Dr. W. F. Faries and the Rev. W. O. Elterich of the Presbyterian Mission and under their skillful guidance, we were soon taken ashore.

A closer view of the Chinese city proved less attractive than the captivating one from the harbour. The population long ago over-ran the limits of the old city so that to-day most of the people are outside the walls. Within those ancient battlements, the streets are narrow and crooked, while the filth is indescribable. The visitor who wishes to see something of the work and to enjoy the hospitality of the noble company of Presbyterian missionaries on Temple Hill must either pass through that reeking mess or go around it. There is, after all, not much choice in the routes, for the Chinese population outside the walls has simply squatted there without much order, and the corkscrew streets are not only thronged with people and donkeys and mules, but malodorous with ditches through which all the nastiness of the crowded habitations trickles. Why pestilence does not carry off the whole population is a mystery to the visitor from the West, especially as he sees the pools out of which the people drink, their shores lined with washerwomen and the water dark and thick with the dirt of decades. Byron's words in "Childe Harold" are as true of Chefoo as of Lisbon:

"But whoso entereth within this town,
    That, sheening far, a celestial seems to be,
Disconsolate will wander up and down

'Mid many things unsightly to strange e'e;
For hut and palace show like filthily.
    The dingy denizens are reared in dirt,
No personage of high or mean degree
Doth care for cleanness of surtout, or shirt,
    Though shent with Egypt's plague, unkempt, unwashed, unhurt!"

The first open port of Shantung was Teng-chou-fu, a quaint old city on the far northeastern point of the Shantung promontory. It has been outstripped in importance by its later rival, Chefoo, and is now ignored by the through steamers and seldom visited by travellers. As the trip from Chefoo by land requires two long hard days over a mountain range and as time was precious, I decided to go by water. The regular coasting steamer was not running on account of danger from pirates, who had been unusually bold and murderous in attacking passing vessels. But I succeeded in hiring a small launch. It was a trip of fifty-five miles along the coast on the open sea, but the weather was good and so we risked it. Several of the missionaries took advantage of the occasion to visit friends in Tengchou-fu so that a pleasant little party was formed.

We had intended to start at 7:30 A. M., but some of our luggage and chair coolies, who had been engaged to take us from Temple Hill to the launch at 6:30, did not come, and we had to press into service some untrained "boys." Then, our chair coolies, who had been carefully instructed as to their destination and who had solemnly asserted that they knew just where to go, got separated from the others and calmly took us to the Union Church. We appreciated their apparent conviction that we needed to go to church, but we vainly tried to make them understand that we wanted to go somewhere else. The delay would have become exasperating if a small English boy who knew Chinese had not helped us out. Then the two coolies who were carrying our valises and the lunch-baskets went another way and sat down en route "to rest." They would doubtless be sitting there yet if, after waiting till our patience was exhausted, we had not sent men to find them. But that is Asia.

However, all arrived at last and at 8:20 A. M. we cast off. The day was glorious and as the sea was not rough enough to make any one ill, we had a delightful trip along the coast with its bare, brown hills so much resembling the scenery of California. We reached Teng-chou-fu at 3:15 and that the pirates were not imaginary was evident for as we entered the harbour, they made a dash and captured a junk less than a mile away. An alarm cannon was fired and soldiers were running to the beach as we landed.

While in Teng-chou-fu, we witnessed a pathetic ceremony. There had been no rain for several weeks. The kao-liang was withering and the farmers could not plant their beans on the ground from which the winter wheat had been cut. The people had become alarmed as the drought continued, and they were parading the streets bearing banners, wearing chaplets of withered leaves on their heads to remind the gods that the vegetation was dying, beating drums to attract the attention of the god, and ever and anon falling on their knees and praying—"O Great Dragon! send us rain." It was pitiful. This country is fertile but the population is so enormous that, in the absence of any manufacturing or mining, the people even in the most favoured seasons live from hand to mouth, and a drought means the starvation of multitudes.

V
A SHENDZA IN SHANTUNG

THE spring of 1901 was not the most propitious time for a tour of the province of Shantung. It was shortly after the suppression of the Boxer outbreak and the country was still in an unsettled condition. The veteran Dr. Hunter Corbett, who had resided in the province for a generation said, "We are living on a volcano and we do not know at what moment another eruption will occur." Students returning from the examinations at the capitol told the people that the Boxers were to rise again and kill all the foreigners and Chinese Christians. The missionaries did not believe the report, but they said that it might be believed by the people and cause a renewal of agitation as such rumours the year before had been an important factor in inciting the populace to violence. But the interior of this great province was one of the objective points of my tour and I could not miss it. Besides, if the missionaries could go, I could. Wives, however, were resolutely debarred. No woman had yet ventured into the interior and the authorities refused to approve their going. In case of trouble, a man can fight or run, but a woman is peculiarly helpless. Nor could we forget that the Chinese during the Boxer outbreak treated foreign women who fell into their hands with horrible atrocity. So the wives, rather against their will, remained in the ports.

Arrangements are apt to move slowly in this land of deliberation. The genial and efficient United States Consul at Chefoo, the Hon. John Fowler, joked me a little about my hurry to start, laughingly remarking that this was Asia and not New York, and that I must not expect things to be done on the touch of a button as at home. But finding that a German steamer was to leave the next day for Tsing-tau, the starting point for the interior, the energetic missionaries helped me to "hustle the East" to get off on it. The Chinese tailor gasped when I told him that I must have a khaki suit by six the following evening, but when he learned that I was to sail and therefore could not wait, he promised rather than lose the job. The next day the steamer agent notified me that the sailing hour had been changed to four o'clock. I sent word to the tailor with faint hope of ever seeing that suit, and when a later message gave three o'clock as the real time, I abandoned hope. But the enterprising Celestial made his fingers fly, finished the suit by 2:50 P. M., and took it to the house of my hostess. Finding that I had already gone to the steamer, he hurried off to the wharf, hired a sampan, sculled a mile and panting but triumphant placed the suit in my hands just as the steamer was getting under way. His charge for the suit, including all his trouble and the cost of the sampan, was $7 Mexican ($3.50).

Saturday found me in Tsing-tau, and Monday, I turned my face inland, accompanied by the Rev. J. H. Laughlin and Dr. Charles H. Lyon, and, as far as Wei-hsien, by the Rev. Frank Chalfant, all of the Presbyterian mission, besides Mr. William Shipway of the English Baptist mission, who was to accompany us as far as Ching-chou-fu. To-day, the traveller can journey to Chinan-fu, the capital, in a comfortable railway car, but I shall always be glad that my visit occurred in the old days when the native methods of transportation were the sole dependence, for at that time the new German railway was in operation only forty-six miles to the old city of Kiao-chou.

The modes of conveyance in the interior of China are five— the donkey, the sedan chair, the wheelbarrow, the cart and the shendza (mule litter), and naturally the first problem of the traveller is to decide which one he shall adopt.

The donkey is all right to one accustomed to horseback riding. But there is no protection from the sun and rain and foreign saddles are scarce. The traveller piles his bedding on the animal's back and climbs on top, sitting either astride or sideways. In either case, the feet dangle unsupported by stirrups. It is hard to make long trips in this way, to say nothing of the consideration that a man feels like an idiot in such circumstances. "The outside of a horse is indeed good for the inside of a man," but a mattress on top of a donkey is a different matter.

The chair is comfortable for short distances, but it is comparatively expensive and, as no change of position is possible, one soon becomes tired sitting in the fixed attitude. In pity to your coolies, you walk up-hill and you are exposed to inclement weather unless you hire a covered chair. This, however, is not only hot and stuffy, but it makes people think you an aristocrat, as only officials or the rich use such chairs in the country, though in cities they are a common means of conveyance. Besides, I had travelled in a chair in Korea and I wished to try something else in China.

The Chinese wheelbarrow is a clumsy affair with a narrow seat on each side of a central partition. When large and with an awning, it is not so uncomfortable, but it is not well adapted to a long journey as it is slow and toilsome. When the mud is deep, progress is almost impossible. Moreover, the labour of the barrow-men constantly excites the sympathy of the humane traveller and the dismal screech of the wheel revolving upon its unoiled axle is worse than the rasp of filing a saw. The Chinese depend upon the shrieks of the wheel to tell them how the axle is wearing, but the disconsolate foreigner finds that his nerves wear out much faster than the wooden axle. In Tsing-tau, that agonizing screech proved too much even for the stolid Germans and they posted an ordinance to the effect that all barrow axles must be greased. The Chinese demurred, but a few arrests taught them obedience, so that now the streets of the German metropolis no longer resound with the hysterical wails and moans so dear to the heart of the Celestial.

The Chinese cart is a curious affair. There are no roads in the interior of China, except the ruts that have been made by the passing of many feet and wheels for generations. In dry weather, they are thick with dust and in the wet season they are fathomless with mud. Almost everywhere they are distractingly crooked, and in many places they are plentifully bestrewn with boulders of varying sizes. Instead of spending money in making roads, the Chinese have applied their ingenuity to making an indestructible cart. They build it of heavy timbers, with massive wheels, thick spokes and ponderous hubs, and as no springs could survive the jolting of such a vehicle, the body of the cart is placed directly upon the huge axle. Then a couple of big mules are hitched up tandem and driven at breakneck speed. A runaway in an American farmer's wagon over a corduroy road but feebly suggests the miseries of travel in a Chinese cart. It may be good for a dyspeptic, but it is about the most uncomfortable conveyance that the ingenuity of man has yet devised. The unhappy passenger is hurled against the wooden top and sides and is so jolted and bumped that, as the small boy said in his composition, "his heart, lungs, liver, kidneys, stomach, bones and brains are all mixed up." I tried the cart for a while and gently but firmly intimated that if nothing better was available, I would walk. I am satisfied that nothing short of a modern battleship under full steam could make the slightest impression on the typical Chinese cart. In my humble opinion, a Chinese cart is like any other misfortune in life. When necessary, it should be taken uncomplainingly. But the person who takes it unnecessarily has not reached the years of discretion and should be assigned a guardian.

I therefore turned to the shendza. All things considered, it is the best conveyance for a long interior journey in China. It consists of a couple long poles with a rope basket work in the middle and a cover of matting. It is borne by two mules, and has the advantage of protecting the traveller from the sun and from light rains. An opening in the back gives him the benefit of any breeze while it is possible to get occasional relief by changing position, as he can either sit upright or lounge. Moreover, he can keep his bedding and a little food with him. He need not walk up hills in mercy to weary coolies and he can make the longer daily journeys which the superior endurance of mules permits. In ordinary conditions on level ground, my mules averaged about four miles an hour. The motion is a kind of sieve-and-pepper-box shaking that is not so bad, provided the mules behave themselves, which is not often. My rear mule had a meek and quiet spirit. He was a discouraged animal upon which the sorrows of life had told heavily and which had reached that age when he appeared to have no ambition in life except to stop and think or to lie down and rest. The lead mule, however, was a cantankerous beast that wanted to fight everything within reach and went into hysterics every time any other animal passed him. As this occurred a score of times a day, the uncertainties of the situation were interesting, especially when the rear mule paused or laid down without having previously notified the lead mule. At such times, the sudden stoppage of the power behind and the plunging of the power in front threatened the dislocation of the entire apparatus, and as there is no way for the traveller to get out except over the heels of a mule, life in a shendza is not always uneventful. But I soon got used to the motion and to the mules, and even learned to read and to doze in comparative comfort while the long-eared animals plodded and jerked on in their own way.

The most trying thing to the humane traveller is the soreness of the mules' backs. I insisted on having mules whose backs were sound, but was told by both missionaries and Chinese that they could not be had, especially in summer, as the swaying and jerking of the shendza and the sweat and dust under the heavy pack-saddle always make sores. It was all too true. I examined scores of mules and every one had raw and bleeding abrasions and, in some cases, suppurating ulcers. For a Chinese, our head muleteer was careful of his animals and washed them occasionally, but no practicable care apparently can prevent a shendza from making a sore back. The only solace I had was the evident indifference of the mules themselves. They had never known anything better, and seemed to take misery as a matter of course.

Our party, with the goods we had to carry, for my missionary friends were returning to their stations with the expectation of remaining, included three shendzas, two carts and a pack-mule for our provisions. But the "mule" turned out to be a donkey and unable to carry all we had planned for a larger animal. While wondering how we were to get our supplies carried, we learned that a construction train was about to start for the end of the track, which was said to be Kaomi, fifty-five li[14] beyond Kiao-chou. We got permission to ride on the flat car. In the hope that we might be able to secure a mule or another donkey in Kaomi, we got aboard, leaving our shendzas and carts to follow. After a lovely ride of an hour through wheat-fields interspersed with villages, our train stopped twelve li from Kaomi, an unfinished culvert making further progress impossible. As our caravan had gone by a different route and as no coolies could be hired where we were, the question was how to get our goods transported. Fortunately, a German Roman Catholic priest, who was also on the construction train and who had wheelbarrows

14   A li is about a third of a mile.

for his own goods, cordially told us to pile our luggage on top of his. We gratefully accepted this kind offer, and giving his coolies some extra cash for their labour, they good-naturedly accepted the additional burden, while we footed the twelve li to Kaomi.

But the progress of the barrows was slow and it was half-past eight when we reached Kaomi. In the darkness we could not find the inn which the magistrate had set aside for foreigners and the Chinese whom we met gave conflicting replies. But at that moment, two resident Roman Catholic priests, Austrians, appeared and one of them recognized Mr. Laughlin as the associate of Dr. Van Schoick, a Presbyterian medical missionary who had sympathetically treated a fellow priest during a long and dangerous illness several years before. He promptly invited us to go with him, declaring that Dr. Van Schoick had saved the life of his dearest friend. He was so cordially insistent that we accepted his invitation. Our shendzas, carts and pack-mule were we knew not where, and we were hungry after our long day. Warned by my experience in Korea that the traveller should never trust to the punctuality of natives and pack-animals, I had insisted on taking our bedding and a little food on the flat car. It was well that I did, for we did not see our shendzas that night as they arrived after the city gates had been shut so that they could not get in. But we had a little cocoa, tinned corn beef, condensed milk, butter and marmalade. Same German soldiers sent three loaves of coarse bread. Our priestly host added some Chinese bread, and so had a good supper and afterwards a sound sleep.

At half-past four the next morning, Mr. Laughlin remarked in a forty-horse power tone of voice that it was time to get up. By the time the reverberations had died away, we were so wide awake that further sleep was out of the question. Our cook was nowhere in sight, so we prepared our own breakfast from the remains of last night's meal.

Bidding a grateful farewell to our hospitable priests, we rode across an ancient lake bottom, low, flat, wheat-covered and hot enough to broil meat. At half-past ten o'clock, we reached Fau-chia-chiu, the boundary of the hinterland, where, near a temple just outside the wall, we found Governor Yuan Shih Kai's military escort awaiting us. It was after sundown when we reached Liu-chia-chuang, and we felt half inclined to spend the night there with some genial German military engineers, but our party had become separated during the day and as the others had taken a road that did not pass through Liu-chia-chuang, we pushed on to Hsi-an-tai, which we reached by a little after ten o'clock. By that time, it was so dark that it was impossible to go further and we found lodgment in a good-sized building which smelled to heaven. The odour was like that of a decomposing body. However, it was too late and we were too weary either to hunt up smells or to seek another lodging place. So after a hasty supper out of our tinned food, we put up our cots and went to bed, Mr. Chalfant making a few pleasant remarks about the bedbugs that always swarm in such a building, the centipedes that sometimes crawl into the ears or nostrils of sleepers and the scorpions that occasionally fall from the millet-stalk ceiling on to the bed or scuttle across the floor to bite the person who unwarily walks in his bare feet. Under the influence of such a soporific, I soon fell asleep. The next morning we rose early, and while the cook was preparing our coffee and eggs, we followed the trail of that awful odour to a corner of the building, where, under some millet stalks, we found a rude coffin which we had not noticed in the dim candlelight of the night before. A Chinese of whom we inquired said that it was empty. We could not in courtesy open a coffin before dozens of interested Chinese, but it was very plain to our olfactories that such an odour required a prompt funeral.

As usual, a great but silent crowd watched me as I wrote while the mules were being fed and at Hsien-chung, where we stopped at noon to repair a shendza, Mr. Chalfant translated a proclamation on a wall stating that an indemnity of 110,000 taels had to be paid for damage to the railway during the Boxer outbreak and that 14,773 taels had been assessed on Wei County. The people read it with scowling faces, but they said nothing to us, though they looked as if they wanted to.

At two o'clock, we entered the ruined Presbyterian compound, a mile southeast of the city of Wei-hsien. It was thrilling to hear on the scene of the riot Mr. Chalfant's account of the attack by about a thousand furious Boxers; to see the place just outside the gate where single-handed and with no weapon but a small revolver, he had heroically held the mob at bay for several hours until the swarming Boxers, awed by his splendid courage, divided, and while several hundred held his attention, the rest climbed over the wall at another place and fired the mission buildings. That the three missionaries escaped with their lives is a wonder. But Mr. Chalfant quickly ran to the house where Miss Hawes and Miss Boughton were awaiting him, hurried them down-stairs, and while the Boxers were smashing the furniture on the other side of a closed door, snatched up a ladder, assisted them over the compound wall at a point that was providentially unguarded and hid them in a field of grain until darkness enabled them to make their way exhausted but unhurt to a camp of German soldiers and engineers nine miles distant and to escape with them to Tsing-tau. It was a remarkable experience. If that door had not happened to be closed, and if a ladder had not been carelessly left by a servant beside the house, and if the attack itself had not occurred just before dark, undoubtedly all three would have been killed. On each of those three ifs, lives depended.

Mr. Fitch cordially welcomed us. Mr. Chalfant killed a centipede and various insects crawling on the walls near my cot and a little after nine I was asleep. The next day we took a walk through the city, impressed by its imposing wall and the throngs of people who followed us and watched every movement. Outside the wall, we saw a "baby house," a small stone building in which the dead children of the poor are thrown to be eaten by dogs! I wanted to examine it, but was warned not to do so, as the Chinese imagine that foreigners make their medicine out of children's eyes and brains, and our crowds of watching Chinese might quickly become an infuriated mob.

Immediately on our arrival, we had sent our cards to the district magistrate and in the afternoon he sent us an elaborate feast. As we were about to retire that evening, he called in a gorgeous chair with a retinue of twenty attendants. He stayed half an hour and was very cordial, and we had a pleasant interview. Wei-hsien is famous for its embroideries, and great quantities are made, the women workers receiving about fifty small cash a day (less than two cents). It was not necessary to go to the stores as in America. The shopkeepers brought a great number of pieces to our inn, covering the kang and every available table, chair and box with exquisite bits of handiwork. Lured by the sight I became reckless and bought four handsome pieces for 19,800 small cash ($6.06).

Resuming our journey on a warm, sunny day, we entered Chiang-loa at noon. It was market day, and the greatest crowd yet fairly blocked the streets. The soldiers had difficulty in clearing a way for us. But while much curiosity was expressed, there was no sign of hostility. Then we journeyed on through the interminable fields of ripening wheat. Soon, mountains, which we had dimly seen for several hours, grew more distinct and as we approached Ching-chou-fu towards evening, the scene was one of great beauty—the yellowing grain gently undulating in the soft breeze, the mountains not really more than 3,000 feet in height, but from our stand on the plain looking lofty, massive and delightfully refreshing to the eye after our hot and dusty journeying. The city has a population of about 25,000 and its numerous trees look so invitingly green that the traveller is eager to enter.

But in this case also, distance lent enchantment, for within, while there was not the filth of a Korean village, yet the narrow streets were far from clean. Not a blade of grass relieved the bare, dusty ground trampled by many feet, while the low, mud-plastered houses were not inviting. A Chinese seldom thinks of making repairs. He builds once, usually with rough stone plastered with mud or with sun-dried brick. The roof is thatched and the floor is the beaten earth, although in the better houses it is stone or brick. In time, the mud-plaster or, if the walls are of sun-dried brick, the wall itself begins to disintegrate. But it is let alone, as long as it does not make the house uninhabitable, while paint is unknown. So the general appearance of a Chinese town is squalid and tumbledown. Even the yamen of a district magistrate presents crumbling walls, unkempt courtyards, rickety buildings and paper-covered windows full of holes. The palaces of the rich are often expensive, but the Asiatic has little of our ideas of comfort and order.

The Rev. J. P. Bruce and Mr. R. C. Forsyth, of the English Baptist mission, the only members of the station who were present, gave us a hearty welcome. The green shrubbery, the bath-tub, the dinner of roast beef and the clean bedroom, were like a bit of hospitable old England set down in China. None of the buildings here were injured by the Boxers. But the marauders took whatever they could use, as dishes, utensils, glass, linen, clothes, silver and plated ware, jewelry, etc., the total loss being <Pd>4,000, including <Pd>1,000 for machinery. That machinery has an interesting history. One of the members of the mission, Mr. A. G. Jones, conceived the idea of relieving the poverty of the Chinese by introducing cotton weaving. Having some private means and being a mechanical genius, he spent two years and <Pd>1,000 in devising the necessary machinery, much of which he made himself. He had completed the plant and was trying to induce the Chinese to organize a company of Christians who would operate the factory, when the building was burned by the Boxers and the machinery reduced to a heap of twisted scrap-iron.

The women we met in these interior districts had only partially bound feet, though they were still far from the natural size. It was surprising to see how freely the women walked, especially as several that I saw were carrying babies. But it was rather a stumpy walk. Women of the higher class have smaller feet and never walk in the public streets.

We left Ching-chou-fu Monday morning, our genial hosts, including Mr. Shipway, who remained here, accompanying us a couple of miles. The trees were more numerous, and as the weather was cool, I greatly enjoyed the day. But the next day, we plodded under dripping skies and through sticky mud to Chang-tien, where a night of unusual discomfort in an inn literally alive with fleas and mosquitoes prepared us to enjoy a tiffin with a lonely English Baptist outpost, the genial Rev. William A. Wills, at Chou-tsun, which we reached at noon the following day, and then, thirty li further on, the gracious hospitality of the main station at Chou-ping. Only three men were present of the regular station force of seven families and two single women, but they gave us all the more abundant welcome in their isolation and loneliness. Of the 2,577 Chinese Christians of this station, 132 were murdered by the Boxers and seventy or more died from consequent exposure and injuries.

A vast, low lying plain begins forty li north of Chou-ping and extends northeastward as far as Tien-tsin. This plain is subject to destructive inundations from the Yellow River and the scenes of ruin and suffering are sometimes appalling. Our unattractive inn the next night was a two-story brick building with iron doors, stone floors, walls two and a-half feet thick and rooms dark, gloomy, ill-smelling as a dungeon and of course swarming with vermin, as savage bites promptly testified. My missionary companion said that it was probably an old pawnshop. Pawnbroking is esteemed an honourable, as well as lucrative, business in China, and the brokers are influential men and often have considerable property in their shops. The people are so poor that they sometimes pawn their winter clothes in summer and their summer ones in winter.

At noon the next day, we reached Chinan-fu, having made seventy li in six hours over muddy roads. Dr. James B. Neal of the Presbyterian mission was alone in the city and gave us hospitable welcome to his home and to the splendid missionary work of the station, though he rather suggestively stopped our coolies when they were about to carry our bedding into the house. He was wise, too, for that bedding had been used in too many native inns to be prudently admitted to a well-ordered household.

As we walked through the city, the narrow streets were literally jammed, for it was market day. Foreigners had been scarce since the Boxer outbreak a year before. Besides, many of the people were from the country where foreigners are seldom seen anyway. So we made as great a sensation as a circus in an American city. A multitude followed us, and wherever we stopped hundreds packed the narrow streets. Our soldiers cleared the way, but they had no difficulty, for though the people were inquisitive they were not hostile. Three magnificent springs burst forth in the heart of the city, one as large as the famous spring in Roanoke, Virginia, which supplies all that city with water. It was about a hundred feet across. The water might easily be piped all over Chinan-fu. But this is China, and so the people patiently walk to the springs for their daily supply.

VI
AT THE GRAVE OF CONFUCIUS

WE were now approaching the most sacred places of China. On a hot July afternoon of the second day from Chinan-fu, the capital of the province, we saw the noble proportions of Tai-shan, the holy mountain. The Chinese have five sacred mountains, but this is the most venerated of all. Its altitude is not great, only a little over 4,000 feet, but it rises so directly from the plain and its outlines are so majestic that it is really imposing. To the Chinese its height is awe-inspiring, for in all the eighteen provinces there is no loftier peak.

Stopping for the night at the ancient city of Tai-an-fu at the base of the mountain, we set out at six the next morning in chairs swung between poles borne by stalwart coolies. My curiosity was aroused when I found that they were Mohammedans and, as they cordially responded to my questionings, I found them very interesting. Centuries ago, their ancestors came to China as mercenaries, and taking Chinese wives settled in the country. But they have never intermarried since. They have adopted the dress and language of the Chinese, but otherwise they continue almost as distinct as the Jews in America. They instruct their children in the doctrines of Islam, though the Mohammedan rule that the Koran must not be translated has prevented all but a few literati from obtaining any knowledge of the book itself. They have done little proselyting, but natural increase, occasional reenforcements and the adoption of famine children have gradually swelled their ranks until they now number many millions in various parts of China. In some provinces they are very strong, particularly in Yun-nan and Kan-su where they are said to form a majority of the population. They are notorious for turbulence and are popularly known as "Mohammedan thieves." It must be admitted that they not infrequently justify their reputation for robbery, murder and counterfeiting. More than once they have fomented bloody revolutions, one of them, the great Panthay rebellion of 1885-1874, costing the lives of no less than two million Moslems before it was suppressed.

But those who bore me up the long slope of Tai-shan were as good-natured as they were muscular. There is no difficulty about ascending the mountain, for a stone-paved path about ten feet wide runs from base to summit. The maker of this road is unknown as the earliest records and monuments refer only to repairs. But he builded well and evidently with "an unlimited command of naked human strength," for the blocks of stone are heavy and the masonry of the walls and bridges is still massive.

As the slope becomes steeper, the path merges into long flights of solid stone steps. Near the summit, these steps become so precipitous that the traveller is apt to feel a little dizzy, especially in descending, for the chair coolies race down the steep stairway in a way that suggests alarming possibilities in the event of a misstep or a broken rope. But the men are sure-footed and mishaps seldom occur. The path is bordered by a low wall and lined with noble old trees. Ancient temples, quaint hamlets, numerous tea-houses and a few nunneries with vicious women are scattered along the route. A beautiful stream tumbles noisily down the mountainside close at hand, alternating swift rapids and deep, quiet pools, while as the traveller rises, he gains magnificent vistas of the adjacent mountains and the wide cultivated plain, yellow with ripening wheat, green with growing millet, and thickly dotted with the groves beneath which cluster the low houses of the villages.

Up this long, steep pathway to the Buddhist temples on the summit, multitudes of Chinese pilgrims toil each year, firmly believing that the journey will bring them merit. We reflected with a feeling of awe that

"The path by which we ascended has been trodden by the feet of men for more than four thousand years. One hundred and fifty generations have come and gone since the great Shun here offered up his yearly sacrifice to heaven. Fifteen hundred years before the bard of Greece composed his Epic, nearly one thousand years before Moses stood on Pisgah's mount and gazed over into the promised land, far back through the centuries when the world was young and humanity yet in its cradle, did the children of men ascend the vast shaggy sides of this same mountain, probably by this same path, and always to worship."[15]

After a night at Hsia-chang, we resumed our journey a little after daylight. The early morning air was delightfully cool and bracing, but the sun's rays became fierce as we entered the dry, sandy bed of the Wen River. By the time we reached the broad, shallow stream itself, I envied the two mules and the donkey that managed to fall into a hole, though I would have been happier if they had been thoughtful enough to discard my spare clothes and my food box before they tumbled into the muddy water. The whole day was unusually hot so that by the time we reached Ning-yang, we were ready for a night's rest which even fighting mules, vicious vermin, and quarrelling Chinese gamblers in the inn courtyard could not entirely destroy.

As we approached Chining-chou, the country became almost perfectly flat, a vast prairie. It was carefully cultivated everywhere, the kao-liang and poppy predominating. The soil was apparently rich, and the landscape was relieved from monotony by the green of the cultivated fields and the foliage of the village trees. Dominating all is the rather imposing walled city of Chining-chou. The high, strong wall, the handsome gates and towers, the trees bordering the little stream and the crowded streets looked quite metropolitan. With its imme-diate suburbs built Chinese fashion close to the wall, Chining-chou has 150,000 inhabitants. It is a business city with a considerable trade, the produce of a wide adjacent region being brought to it for shipment, as it is on the Grand Canal which gives easy and cheap facilities for exporting and importing freight. There is, moreover, no loss in exchange as the danger of shipping bullion silver makes the Chining business men eager to accept drafts for use in paying for the goods they buy in Shanghai. Consequently there is a better price for silver here than anywhere else in Shantung. The main street is narrow, shaded by matting laid on kao-liang stalks and lined with busy shops. Along the Grand Canal, there is a veritable

---

15   The Rev. Dr. Paul D. Bergen, pamphlet.

"Vanity Fair" filled with clothing booths and deafening with the cries of itinerant vendors.

But the loneliness of the missionary in Chining-chou is great, for he is far from congenial companionship. The tragedies of life are particularly heavy at such an isolated post. Mr. Laughlin showed me the house where his wife's body lay for a month after her death in May, 1899. Then, with his nine-year old daughter, he took the body in a house-boat down the Grand Canal to Chinkiang, a journey of sixteen days. What a heart-breaking journey it must have been as the clumsy boat crept slowly along the sluggish canal and the silent stars looked down on the lonely husband beside the coffin of his beloved wife. Yet he bravely returned to Chiningchou and while I travelled on, he remained with only Dr. Lyon for a companion. I was sorry to part with them for we had shared many long-to-be-remembered experiences, while at that time there was believed to be no small risk in remaining at such an isolated post. But Dr. Johnson and I had to go, and so early on the morning of June 17, we bade the brave fellows an affectionate good-bye and left them in that far interior city, standing at the East Gate till we were out of sight.

Fortunately, the day was fine for rain would have made the flat, black soil almost impassible. But as it was, we had a comfortable, dustless ride of sixty li to Yen-chou-fu, a city of unusually massive walls, whose 60,000 people are reputed to be the most fiercely anti-foreign in Shantung. Comparatively few foreigners had been seen in this region and many of them had been mobbed. The Roman Catholic priests, who are the only missionaries here, have repeatedly been attacked, while an English traveller was also savagely assaulted by these turbulent conservatives. But the Roman Catholics with characteristic determination fought it out, the German consul coming from Peking to support them, and at the time of my visit, they were building a splendid church, the money like that for the Chining-chou cathedral, coming from the indemnity for the murder of the two priests in 1897, which was in this diocese. Though great crowds stared silently at us, no disrespect was shown. On the contrary, we found that by order of the district magistrate an inn had been specially prepared for us, with a plentiful supply of rugs and cushions and screens, while a few minutes after our arrival, the magistrate sent with his compliments a feast of twenty-five dishes. Another stage of nine miles brought us at four o'clock to the famous holy city of China, Ku-fu, the home and the grave of Confucius.

Leaving our shendzas at an inn, we mounted the cavalry horses of our escort and hurried to the celebrated temple which stands on the site of Confucius' house. But to our keen disappointment, the massive gates were closed. The keeper, in response to our knocks, peered through a crevice, and explained that it was the great feast of the fifth day of the fifth month, that the Duke was offering sacrifices, and that no one, not even officials, could enter till the sacrifices were completed. "When will that be?" we queried. "They will continue all night and all day to-morrow," was the reply. We urged the shortness of our stay and solemnly promised to keep out of the Duke's way. The keeper's eyes watered as he imagined a present, but he replied that he did not dare let us in as his orders were strict and disobedience might cost him his position if not his life. So we sorrowfully turned away, and pushing through the dense throng which had swiftly assembled at the sight of a foreigner, we rode through the city and along the far-famed Spirit Road to the Most Holy Grove in which lies the body of Confucius. It is three li, about a mile, from the city gate. The road is shaded by ancient cedars and is called the Spirit Road because the spirit of Confucius is believed to walk back and forth upon it by night.

The famous cemetery is in three parts. The outer is said to be fifteen miles in circumference and is the burial-place of all who bear the honoured name of Confucius. Within, there is a smaller enclosure of about ten acres, which is the family burial place of the dukes who are lineal descendants of Confucius, mighty men who rank with the proudest governors of provinces. Within this second enclosure, is the Most Holy Cemetery itself, a plot of about two acres, shaded like the others by fine old cedars and cypresses. Here are only three graves, marked by huge mounds under which lie the dust of Confucius, his son and his grandson. That of the Sage, we estimated to be twenty-five feet high and 250 feet in circumference. In front of it is a stone monument about fifteen feet high, four feet wide and sixteen inches thick. Lying prone before that is another stone of nearly the same size supported by a heavy stone pedestal. There is no name, but on the upright monument are Chinese characters which Dr. Charles Johnson, my travelling companion, translated: "The Acme of Perfection and Learning-Promoting King," or more freely—"The Most Illustrious Sage and Princely Teacher."

Uncut grass and weeds grew rankly upon the mounds and all over the cemetery, giving everything an unkempt appearance. One species is said to grow nowhere else in China and to have such magical power in interpreting truth that if a leaf is laid upon an abstruse passage of Confucius, the meaning will immediately become clear. There are several small buildings in the enclosure, but dust and decay reign in all, for there is no merit in repairing a building that some one else has erected. As with his house, the Chinese will spend money freely to build a temple, but after that he does nothing. So even in the most sacred places, arches and walls and columns are usually crumbling, grounds are dirty and pavement stones out of place.

A feeling of awe came over me as I remembered that, with the possible exception of Buddha, the man whose dust lay before me had probably influenced more human beings than any other man whom the world has seen. Even Christ Himself has thus far not been known to so many people as Confucius, nor has any nation in which Christ is known so thoroughly accepted His teachings as China has accepted those of Confucius. Dr. Legge indeed declares that "after long study of his character and opinions, I am unable to regard him as a great man," while Dr. Gibson "seeks in vain in his recorded life and words for the secret of his power," and can only conjecture in explanation that "he is for all time the typical Chinaman; but his greatness lies in his displaying the type on a grand scale, not in creating it." But it is difficult even for the non-Chinese mind to look at such a man with unbiassed eyes. Surely we need not begrudge the meed of greatness to one who has moulded so many hundreds of millions of human beings for 2,400 years and who is more influential at the end of that period than at its beginning. Grant that "he is for all time the typical Chinaman." Could a small man have incarnated "for all time" the spirit of one-third of the human race? All over China the evidences of Confucius' power can be seen. Temples rise on every hand. Ancestral tablets adorn every house. The writings of the sage are diligently studied by the whole population. When, centuries ago, a jealous Emperor ruthlessly burned the Confucian books, patient scholars reproduced them, and to prevent a recurrence of such iconoclastic fury, the Great Confucian Temple and the Hall of Classics in Peking were erected and the books were inscribed on long rows of stone monuments so that they could never be destroyed again. As a token of the present attitude of the Imperial family, the Emperor once in a decade proceeds in solemn state to this temple and enthroned there expounds a passage of the sacred writings. For more than two millenniums, the boys of the most numerous people in the world have committed to memory the Confucian primer which declares that "affection between father and son, concord between husband and wife, kindness on the part of the elder brother and deference on the part of the younger, order between seniors and juniors, sincerity between friends and associates, respect on the part of the ruler and loyalty on that of the minister—these are the ten righteous courses equally binding on all men;" that "the five regular constituents of our moral nature are benevolence, righteousness, propriety, knowledge, and truth;" and that "the five blessings are long life wealth, tranquillity, desire for virtue and a natural death."

Surely these are noble principles. That their influence has been beneficial in many respects, it would be folly to deny. They have lifted the Chinese above the level of many other Asiatic nations by creating a more stable social order, by inculcating respect for parents and rulers, and by so honouring the mother that woman has a higher position in China than in most other non-Christian lands.

And yet Confucianism has been and is the most formidable obstacle to the regeneration of China. While it teaches some great truths, it ignores others that are vital. It has lifted the Chinese above the level of barbarism only to fix them almost immovably upon a plane considerably lower than Christianity. It has developed such a smug satisfaction with existing conditions that millions are wellnigh impervious to the influences of the modern world. It has debased respect for parents into a blind worship of ancestors so that a dead father, who may have been an ignorant and vicious man, takes the place of the living and righteous God. It has fostered not only premature marriages but concubinage in the anxiety to have sons who will care for parents in age and minister to them after death. It makes the child virtually a slave to the caprice or passion of the parent. It leads to a reverence for the past that makes change a disrespect to the dead, so that all progress is made exceedingly difficult and society becomes fossilized. "Whatever is is right" and "custom" is sacred. Man is led so to centralize his thought on his own family that he becomes selfish and provincial in spirit and conduct, with no outlook beyond his own narrow sphere. Expenditures which the poor can ill-afford are remorselessly exacted for the maintenance of ancestral worship so that the living are often impoverished for the sake of the dead. $151,752,000 annually, ancestral worship is said to cost—a heavy drain upon a people the majority of whom spend their lives in the most abject poverty, while the development of true patriotism and a strong and well-governed State has been effectively prevented by making the individual solicitous only for his own family and callously indifferent to the welfare of his country. Confucianism therefore is China's weakness as well as China's strength, the foe of all progress, the stagnation of all life.

Confucianism, too, halts on the threshold of life's profoundest problems. It has only dead maxims for the hour of deepest need. It gives no vision of a future beyond the grave. It is virtually an agnostic code of morals with some racial variations. Wu Ting Fang, formerly Chinese Minister to the United States, frankly declares that "Confucianism is not a religion in the practical sense of the word," and that "Confucius would be called an agnostic in these days." To "the Venerable Teacher" himself, philosophy opened no door of hope. Asked about this one day by a troubled inquirer, he dismissed the question with the characteristic aphorism— "Imperfectly acquainted with life, how can we know death?" And there the myriad millions of Confucianists have dully stood ever since, their faces towards the dead past, the future a darkness out of which no voice comes.

But just because their illustrious guide took them to the verge of the dark unknown and left them there, other teachers came in to occupy the region left so invitingly open. Less rational than Confucius, their success showed anew that the human mind cannot rest in a spiritual vacuum and that if faith does not enter, superstition will. Taoism and Buddhism proceeded to people the air and the future with strange and awful shapes. Popular Chinese belief as to the future is gruesomely illustrated in the Temple of Horrors in Canton with its formidable collection of wooden figures illustrating the various modes of punishment—sawing, decapitation, boiling in oil, covering with a hot bell, etc. At funerals, bits of perforated paper are freely scattered about in the hope that the inquisitive spirits will stop to examine them and thus give the body a chance to pass. In any Chinese cemetery, one may see little tables in front of the graves covered with tea, sweetmeats and sheets of gilt and silver paper, so that if a spirit is hungry, thirsty or in need of funds, it can get drink, food or money from the gold or silver mines (paper).

In the Temple for Sickness, in Canton, where multitudes of sufferers pray to the gods for healing, we saw an old woman kneeling before a statue of Buddha, holding aloft two blocks of wood and then throwing them to the floor. If the flat side of one and the oval side of the other were uppermost, the omen was good, but if the same sides were up, it was bad. Others shook a box of numbered sticks till one popped out and then a paper bearing the corresponding number gave the issue of the disease. The stones of the court were worn by many feet and the pathos of the place was pitiful.

Theoretically, "Confucianism is a system of morals, Taoism a deification of nature and Buddhism a system of metaphysics. But in practice all three have undergone many modifications.

With every age the character of Taoism has changed. The philosophy of its founder is now only an antiquarian curiosity. Modern Taoism is of such a motley character as almost to defy any attempt to educe a well-ordered system from its chaos."[16] As for Buddhism, its founder would not recognize it, if he could visit China to-day. The lines:—

"Ten Buddhist nuns, and nine are bad;
The odd one left is doubtless mad—"

are suggestive of the depth to which the religion of Guatama has fallen.

Indeed, it would be a mistake to suppose that the Chinese people are divided into three religious bodies as, for example,

16   Smith, "Rex Christus," pp. 62, 72.

Americans are divided into Protestants, Roman Catholics and Jews. Each individual Chinese is at the same time a Confucian, a Buddhist and a Taoist, observing the ceremonies of all three faiths as circumstances may require, a Confucian when he worships his ancestors, a Buddhist when he implores the aid of the Goddess of Mercy, and a Taoist when he seeks to propitiate the omnipresent fung-shuy (spirits of wind and water), and he has no more thought of inconsistency than an American who is at the same time a Methodist, a Republican and a Mason. Dr. S. H. Chester says that when he was in Shanghai, he saw a Taoist priest conducting Confucian worship in a Buddhist temple. Even if inconsistency were proved to the Chinese, he would not be in the least disturbed for he cares nothing for such considerations. "Hence it is that the Chinese religion of to-day has become an inextricable blending of the three systems."[17] "The ancient simplicity of the state religion has been so far corrupted as to combine in one ritual gods, ghosts, flags and cannon. It has become at once essentially polytheistic and pantheistic."[18]

The result is that the average Chinese lives a life of terror under the sway of imaginary demons. He erects a rectangular pillar in front of his door so that the dreaded spirits cannot enter his house without making an impossible turn. He gives his tiled roof an upward slant at each of the eaves so that any spirit attempting to descend will be shunted off into space. Nor is this superstition confined to the lower classes. The haughty, foreign-travelled Li Hung Chang abjectly grovelled on the bank of the Yellow River to propitiate an alleged demon that was believed to be the cause of a disastrous flood, and as late as June 4, 1903, the North-China Daily News published the following imperial decree:

"Owing to the continued drought, in spite of our prayers for rain, we hereby command Chen Pih, Governor of Peking, to proceed to the Dragon temple at Kanshan-hsien, Chih-li Province, and bring from thence to Peking an iron tablet possessing rain-producing virtues, which we will place up for adoration and thereby bring forth the much-desired rain."

---

17   Gibson, "Mission Methods and Mission Policy in South China."

18   Williams, "Middle Kingdom."

And so the followers of the most "rational" of teachers are among the most superstitious people in the world. In attempting to clear the mind of error, the great agnostic simply left it "empty, swept and garnished for seven other spirits worse than the first."

As in the deepening twilight we thoughtfully left the last resting-place of the mighty dead, a platoon of thirty Chinese soldiers approached, drew their swords, dropped upon one knee and shouted. The movement was so unexpected and the shout so startlingly strident that my horse shied in terror and I had visions of immediate massacre. But having learned that politeness is current coin the world over, as soon as I could control my prancing horse, I raised my hat and bowed. Whereupon the soldiers rose, wheeled into line and marched ahead of us to our inn in the city. Dr. Johnson explained that the words shouted in unison were: "May the Great Man have Peace," and that the platoon was an escort of honour from the yamen of the district magistrate!

On the way, we stopped to visit the temple of Yen, the favorite disciple whose early death left Confucius disconsolate. The grounds are spacious. There is a remarkably fine tree, tall, graceful and with silvery white bark. A huge stone turtle was reverently kissed by one of our escort, who fondly believed that he who kissed the turtle's mouth would never be ill. But as usual in China, the temple itself, though originally it must have been beautiful, is now crumbling in decay.

It was late when we returned, and as we were about to retire, wearied with the toils of the day, the district magistrate called with an imposing retinue and cordially inquired whether we had seen all that we wished to see. When we replied that we had been unable to enter the great temple, he graciously said that he would have pleasure in informing the Duke, who would be sure to arrange for our visit. The result was a message at two o'clock in the morning to the effect that we might visit the temple at daylight in the interval between the cessation of the sacrifices of the night and their resumption at seven o'clock in the morning. Accordingly we rose at three o'clock, and after a hurried breakfast by candle-light, we proceeded to the temple. About a hundred Chinese were awaiting us, among them two men in official dress. We did not deem it courteous to ask who or what they were, but we supposed them to be from the magistrate's yamen, and as they were evidently familiar with the temple, we gladly complied with their cordial invitation to follow them.

I wish I had power to describe adequately all we saw in that vast enclosure of about thirty acres, with its stately trees, its paved avenues, its massive monuments, and, above all, its imposing temple and scores of related buildings. One was the Lieh Kew Kwei Chang Tien, the Temple of the Wall of the Many Countries. Here are 120 tablets, each about sixteen by twenty-two inches, and in the centre three larger ones measuring two feet in width by four and a-half feet in height. In front of these is a stone three and a-half feet by four and a-half, and bearing the inscription: "Tribute from the Ten Thousand Countries of the World." The Chinese solemnly believe that in these tablets all the nations of the earth have acknowledged the preeminence of Confucius.

Then we visited three gloomy buildings where the animals for sacrifice are killed—one for cattle, one for sheep and one for pigs. Beyond them, we entered temples to the wife of Confucius, to his parents and to the "Five Generations of Ancestors," though the last-mentioned contains tablets to nine generations instead of five. On every side are scores of monuments, erected by or in honour of famous kings, some of them by the monarchs of dynasties which flourished before the Christian era.

Most notable of all is the great temple of the sage himself, standing well back on a spacious stone-paved terrace, around which runs a handsome marble balustrade. The eye is at once arrested by the twenty-eight noble marble pillars, ten in front, ten in the rear and four at each end. The ten in front are round and elaborately carved, as magnificent a series of columns as I ever saw. The others are smooth, octagonal pillars, but traced with various designs in black.

Within, there are twelve other columns about four feet in diameter and twenty-five feet high, each cut from a single tree and beautifully polished. Naturally, the central object of interest is a figure of Confucius of heroic size but impossible features. In front is the tablet with costly lacquered ornaments and pedestals, and an altar on which were a bullock and two pigs, each carefully scraped and dressed and lying with heads towards the statue and tablet. In several other temples, notably in the one to the Five Generations of Ancestors, other animals were lying, some evidently offered the day before and others awaiting the worship of the day now beginning. Altogether I counted nineteen sacrificial animals—one bullock, eight sheep and ten pigs. The great temple is of noble proportions, with an overhanging roof of enormous size but constructed on such graceful lines as to be exquisitely beautiful. But within dust reigns, while without as usual the grass and weeds grow unchecked.

Last of all we visited the library, though the name is a misnomer, for there are no books in it and our courteous guides said there never had been. We ascended the narrow stairs leading from the vast, empty, dusty room on the lower floor through an equally empty second story to the third and topmost story, which is the home of hundreds of doves. Going out on the narrow balustrade under the eaves in the gray dawn of the morning, I looked upon the gorgeous gilded roof of the temple near by and then down upon the many ancient buildings, the darkly solemn pines, the massive monuments resting on ponderous stone turtles, and the group of Chinese standing among the shadows and with faces turned curiously upward. Suddenly a dove flew over my head and then the sun rose slowly and majestically above the sombre tree-tops, throwing splendid floods of light upon us who stood aloft. But the Chinese below were in the sombre shades of a night that for them had not yet fully ended. I would fain believe that the physical was a parable of the spiritual. All the maxims of the Acme of Perfection and Learning-Promoting King have not brought the Chinese out of moral twilight. After all these centuries of ceaseless toil, they still remain amid the mists and shadows. But their faces are beginning to turn towards the light of a day whose sun already touches the mountain-tops. Some even now are in that "marvellous light," and it cannot be long before shining hosts of God shall pour down the mountain-sides, chasing on noiseless feet and across wide plains the swiftly retreating night "until the day dawn and the shadows flee away."

At the outer gate, we bade good-bye to the dignified officials who had so hospitably conducted us through this venerable and historic place and who had taken such kindly pains to explain its ancient relics and customs. Who were they? we secretly wondered. Imagine our feelings when the lieutenant in command of our escort afterwards informed us that they were the guardian of the temple and the Duke himself!

Leaving the city of the mighty dead, we journeyed through a lovely region guarded by distant mountains. At the walled city of Sisui, sixty li distant, soldiers met us and apparently the whole population lined the streets as we rode to our inn, where the yamen secretary was awaiting us with a feast. This inn, too, had been specially cleaned, and there were cushions, red cloths for the seats, and a screen for the door. In the afternoon, the country became rougher. But while the soil was thinner, the scenery was finer, an undulating region traversed by a shining river and bounded by mountains which gradually drew nearer. One hundred and ten li from Ku-fu, we stopped for the night at Pien-kiao, a small city with an unusually poor inn but a magnificent spring. It gushed up over an area twenty-five feet square and with such volume that the stream ran away like a mill-race. The Emperor Kien Lung built a retaining wall about the spring and a temple and summer-house adjoining. The wall is as solid as ever, but only a few crumbling pillars and fragments remain of the temple and pavilion. The Emperor affirmed that he was told in a vision that if he would build a stone boat, the waters of the spring would float it to Nanking whither he wished to go. So he built the boat of heavy cut stone, with a twelve-foot beam and a length of fifty-five feet. It is still there with the prow five feet above the ground, but the rest of the boat has sunk almost to the level of the earth about it. Is the old Emperor's idea any more absurd to us than our iron boats would have been to him?

The sun struggled long with heavy mists the following morning and the air was so cool that I had to wrap myself in a blanket in the shendza. By eight, the sun gained the victory and we had another breezy, perfect June day. But the road was stony and trying beyond anything we had yet seen. The villages were evidently poorer, as might be expected on such a rocky soil. The people stared silently and did not so often return my smiles. Whether they were sullen or simply boorish and unaccustomed to foreigners I could only conjecture. Few white men had been seen there.

A hard day's journey of 140 li through a rocky region brought us to Fei-hsien. Rain was falling the next morning and the Chinese muleteers do not like to travel in rain. But the prospect was for a steady pour and as we were in a wretched inn and only ninety li from Ichou-fu, we wanted to go on. A present of 600 small cash for each muleteer (twenty cents) overcame all scruples. Just as I had comfortably ensconced myself in my shendza with an oilcloth on top and a rubber blanket in front, I saw a centipede on my leg, but I managed to slay him before he bit me. By nine, the rain ceased and though the clouds still threatened, we had a cool and comfortable ride through hundreds of fields of peanuts, indigo and millet to I-tang, where we stopped for tiffin at a squalid inn kept by a tall, dilapidated looking Chinese, who rejoiced in the name of Confucius. He was really a descendant of the sage and was very proud of the fact that his bones were in due time to rest in the sacred cemetery at Ku-fu.

By 5:40 P. M. we reached Ichou-fu, where the solitary Rev. W. W. Faris was glad to see another white man. A stay of several days was marked by many pleasant incidents. There was much of interest for a visitor to see. The mission work at Ichou-fu, Presbyterian, includes two hospitals, one for men and one for women, a chapel and separate day schools for boys and girls. The church has about a hundred members and in the outstations there are ten other organized churches besides ten unorganized congregations. All these churches and congregations provide their own chapels and pay their own running expenses. Here also the officials were most courteous. The Prefect, who promptly called with a retinue of fifty soldiers and attendants, was a masterful looking man who conversed with intelligence on a wide variety of topics. The day before our departure, we gave a feast to the leading men of the city in return for their many courtesies. Every invitation was accepted and thirty-five guests were present. They remained till late and were apparently highly pleased.

Late in the evening, a youth who had painfully walked 180 li, came to Dr. Johnson's dispensary and presented the following note of introduction:

> "Our office a servant who getting a yellow sick, which suffered a few year and cured for nothing. he trusted me to beg you to save his sick and I now ordered him to going before you to beg you remedy facely. With many thanks to you,
>
> > "Yours sincerely,
> > "V. T. GEE."

Having done all that was possible in so short a time to "save his sick," we resumed our journey, thirty Chinese Christians accompanying us to the River I, a li from the city. The atmosphere was gloriously clear and on the second day out, crossing some high ridges, we had superb views of wide cultivated valleys, and of Ku-chou, a famous city that is said to contain more literary graduates than any other city of its size in the province.

Then followed a more level country with interminable fields of kao-liang and many orchards of walnuts, pears and cherries, while low mountains rose in the background. Men and horses were tired after our long and hard journey, and the mules' backs were becoming very sore. But the end drew near and the fifth day from Ichow-fu we reached Yueh-kou, the border of the German hinterland. The German line is near Kiaochou, but the rule is that Chinese soldiers must not come beyond this point, 100 li from the line, and that German soldiers shall not cross it going the other way except on the line of the railroad. Here therefore our escort had to leave us, as Chinese and Germans have agreed that any armed men crossing the line may be fired on, and even if there should be no casualty, both the German and Chinese authorities might justly have protested if Americans violated the compact. I suggested going on without an escort to our proposed night stop thirty li further. But my more experienced companions thought it dangerous to spend the night alone at an inn within this belt, as the villagers near the line were as bitter against foreigners as any in the province, the German brusqueness and ruthlessness having greatly exasperated them.

So we spent the night at Yueh-kou. No one interfered with us the next day and by getting an early start, we covered ninety long li to Kiao-chou by noon. After five weeks in a mule litter, it seemed wonderful to make 138 li in three hours in a railway car. By 6:50 P. M., we reached Tsing-tau, having, the missionaries said, succeeded in "hustling the East to a remarkable degree." My note-book reads—"A bath, clean clothes, a hot supper and a good night's sleep removed the last vestige of weariness."

VII

SOME EXPERIENCES OF A TRAVELLER—
FEASTS, INNS AND SOLDIERS

THE hardships of interior travelling were less than I had supposed. It is true that there were many experiences which, if enumerated, would make a formidable list. But each as it arose appeared insignificant. As a whole, the trip was as enjoyable as any vacation tour. The weather was as a rule fine. The sun was often hot in the middle of the day, but cool breezes usually tempered the heat of the afternoon, while the nights required the protection of blankets. There was some rain at times, but not enough to impede seriously our progress. It was altogether the most perfect May and June weather I have ever seen. Nor was it exceptional, according to Dr. Charles Johnson who has spent many years in North China. But of course I saw Shantung at its most favourable period. July and August are wet and hot, while the winters are clear and cold.

I found a trunk an unmitigated nuisance. Though it was made to order for a pack-mule, no pack-mules could be hired in that harvest season, and the trunk was too heavy for one side of a donkey, even after transferring all practicable articles to the shendza. So it had to be put in a cart, and as a cart cannot keep up with a shendza, I was often separated from my trunk for days at a time. Besides, a couple valises would have held all necessary clothing anyway. I took a light folding cot and a bag held a thin mattress, small pillow, sheets and two light blankets, so that I had a very comfortable bed under the always necessary mosquito net.

We also took a supply of tinned food to which we could usually add by purchase en route chickens and eggs, while occasionally in the proper season, we could secure string-beans, onions, cucumbers, apricots, peanuts, walnuts and radishes. So we fared well. The native food cannot be wisely depended upon by a foreigner. He cannot maintain his strength, as the poorer Chinese do, on a diet of rice and unleavened bread, while the food of the well-to-do classes, when it can be had, is apt to be so greasy and peculiar as to incite his digestive apparatus to revolt. Indeed, a Chinese feast is one of his most serious experiences. Most heartily, indeed, did I appreciate the kindly motives of the magistrates who invited me to these feasts, for their purpose was as generously hospitable as the purpose of any American who invites a visitor to dinner. But the Chinese bill-of-fare includes dishes that are rather trying to a Christian palate, and good form requires the guest to taste at least each dish, for if he fails to do so, he makes his host "lose face"—a serious breach of etiquette in China. For example, here is the menu of a typical Chinese feast to which I was invited, the dishes being served in the order given, sweets coming first and soup towards the last in this land of topsy-turveydom:

1. Small cakes (five kinds), sliced pears, candied peanuts, raw water-chestnuts, cooked water-chestnuts, hard-boiled ducks' eggs (cut into small pieces), candied walnuts, honied walnuts, shredded chicken, apricot seeds, sliced pickled plums, sliced dried smoked ham (cut into tiny pieces), shredded sea moss, watermelon seeds, shrimps, bamboo sprouts, jellied haws. All the above dishes were cold. Then followed hot:

2. Shrimps served in the shell with vinegar, sea-slugs with shredded chicken, bits of sweetened pork and shredded dough—the pork and sea-slugs being cooked and served in fragrant oil.

3. Bamboo sprouts, stewed chicken kidneys.

4. Spring chicken cooked crisp in oil.

5. Stewed sea-slugs with ginger root and bean curd, stewed fungus with reed roots and ginger tops (all hot).

6. Tarts with candied jelly, sugar dumplings with dates.
7. Hot pudding made of "the eight precious vegetables," consisting of dates, watermelon seeds, chopped walnuts, chopped chestnuts, preserved oranges, lotus seeds, and two kinds of rice, all mixed and served in syrup—a delicious dish.
8. Shelled shrimps with roots of reeds and bits of hard-boiled eggs, all in one bowl with fragrant oil, biscuits coated with sweet seeds.
9. Glutinous rice in little layers with browned sugar between, minced pork dumplings, steamed biscuits.
10. Omelette with sea-slugs and bamboo sprouts, all in oil, bits of chicken stewed in oil, pork with small dumplings of flour and starch.
11. Stewed pigs' kidneys, shrimps stewed in oil, date pie.
12. Vermicelli and egg soup.
13. Stewed pork balls, reed roots, bits of hard-boiled yolks of eggs, all in oil.
14. Birds' nest soup.

The appetite being pretty well sated by this time, the following delicacies were served to taper off with:

15. Chicken boiled in oil, pork swimming in a great bowl of its own fat, stewed fish stomachs, egg soup.
16. Steamed biscuit.

Tea was served from the beginning and throughout the feast. It was made on the table by pouring hot water into a small pot half full of tea leaves, the pot being refilled as needed. The tea was served without cream or sugar, and was mild and delicious. Rice whiskey in tiny cups is usually served at feasts, though it was often omitted from the feasts given to us. The Chinese assert that the alcohol is necessary "to cut the grease." There is certainly enough grease to cut.

The guests sit at small round tables, each accommodating about four. There are, of course, no plates or knives or forks though small china spoons are used for the soups. All the food is cut into small pieces before being brought to the table, so that no further cutting is supposed to be necessary. Each article of food is brought on in a single dish, which is placed in the centre of the table, and then each guest helps himself out of the common dish with his chop-sticks, the same chop-sticks being used during the entire meal. It is considered a mark of distinguished courtesy for the host to fish around in the dish with his own chop-sticks for a choice morsel and place it in front of the guest. With profound emotion, at almost every feast that I attended in China, I saw my considerate hosts take the chop-sticks which had made many trips to their own mouths, stir around in the central dish for a particularly fine titbit and deposit it on the table before me. And of course, not to be outdone in politeness, I ate these dainty morsels with smiles of gratified pride. As each of the Chinese at the table deemed himself my host, and as the Chinese are extremely polite and attentive to their guests, the table soon became wet and greasy from the pieces of pork, slugs and chicken placed upon it as well as from the drippings from the chop-sticks in their constant trips from the serving bowls.

However, two small brass bowls, fitting together, are placed beside each guest, who is expected to sip a little water from the upper one, rinse his mouth with it and expectorate it into the lower one. The emotion of the foreign visitor is intensified when he learns that it is counted polite to make all the noise possible by smacking the lips as a sign that the food is delicious, sucking the tea or soup noisily from the spoon to show that it is hot, and belching to show that it is enjoyed. Often, a dignified official would let his tea stand until it was cold, but when he took it up, he would suck it with a loud noise as if it were scalding hot, as he was too polite to act as if it were cold.

But the American or European, who inwardly groans at a Chinese repast and who felicitates himself on the alleged superior methods of his own race, may well consider how his own customs impress a Celestial. A Chinese gentleman who was making a tour of Europe and America wrote to a relative in China as follows:

"You cannot civilize these foreign devils. They are beyond redemption. They will live for weeks and months without touching a mouthful of rice, but they eat the flesh of bullocks and sheep in enormous quantities. That is why they smell so badly; they smell like sheep themselves. Every day they take a bath to rid themselves of their disagreeable odours but they do not succeed. Nor do they eat their meat cooked in small pieces. It is carried into the room in large chunks, often half raw, and they cut and slash and tear it apart. They eat with knives and prongs. It makes a civilized being perfectly nervous. One fancies himself in the presence of sword-swallowers. They even sit down at the same table with women, and the latter are served first, reversing the order of nature."

So I humbly adapted myself as best I could to Chinese customs and learned to like many of the natives' dishes, though to the last, there were some that I merely nibbled to "save the face" of mine host. Some of the dishes were really excellent and as a rule all were well-cooked, although the oil in which much of the food was steeped made it rather greasy. My digestive apparatus is pretty good, but it would take a copper-lined stomach to partake without disaster of a typical Chinese feast. But for that matter so it would to eat a traditional New England dinner of boiled salt pork, corned beef, cabbage, turnips, onions and potatoes, followed by a desert of mince pie and plum pudding and all washed down by copious draughts of hard cider.

Chinese inns do not impoverish even the economical traveller. Our bill for our tiffin stop was usually 100 small cash, a little more than three cents, for our entire party of about a score of men and animals. For the night, the common charge was 700 cash, twenty-three cents. Travellers are expected to provide their own food and bedding and to pay a small extra sum for the rice and fodder used by their servants and mules, but even then the cost appears ridiculously small to a foreigner. Still, the most thoroughly seasoned traveller can hardly consider a Chinese inn a comfortable residence. It is simply a rough, one-story building enclosing an open courtyard. The rooms are destitute of furniture except occasionally a rude table. The floor is the beaten earth, foul with the use of scores and perhaps hundreds of years. The windows are covered with oiled paper which admits only a dim light and no air at all. The walls are begrimed with smoke and covered with cobwebs. Across the end of the room is the inevitable kang—a brick platform under which the cooking fire is built and on which the traveller squats by day and sleeps by night. The unhappy white man who has not been prudent enough to bring a cot with him feels as if he were sleeping on a hot stove with "the lid off."

The inns between Ichou-fu and Chining-chou were the poorest I saw, and if a man has stopped in one of them, he has been fairly initiated into the discomforts of travelling in China. But wherever one goes, the heat and smoke and bad air, together with the vermin which literally swarms on the kang and floor and walls, combine to make a night in a Chinese inn an experience that is not easily forgotten. However, the foreign traveller soon learns, perforce, to be less fastidious than at home and I found myself hungry enough to eat heartily and tired enough to sleep soundly in spite of the dirt and bugs. But the heat and bad air as the summer advanced were not so easily mastered, and so I began to sleep in the open courtyard, finding chattering Chinese and squealing mules less objectionable than the foul-smelling, vermin-infested inns, since outside I had at least plenty of cool, fresh air.

There is no privacy in a Chinese inn. The doors, when there are any, are innocent of locks and keys, while the Chinese guests as well as the innkeeper's family and the people of the neighbourhood have an inquisitiveness that is not in the least tempered by bashfulness. But nothing was ever stolen, though some of our supplies must have been attractive to many of the poverty stricken men who crowded about us. On one occasion, an inn-employee, who was sent to exchange a bank-note for cash, did not return. There was much excited jabbering, but Mr. Laughlin firmly though kindly held the innkeeper responsible and that worthy admitted that he knew who had taken the money and refunded it. So all was peace. The innkeeper was probably in collusion with the thief. This was our only trouble of the kind, though we slept night after night in the public inns with all our goods lying about wholly unprotected. Occasionally, especially in the larger towns, there was a night watchman. But he was a noisy nuisance. To convince his employers that he was awake, he frequently clapped together two pieces of wood. All night long that strident clack, clack, clack, resounded every few seconds. It is an odd custom, for of course it advertises to thieves the location of the watchman. But there is much in China that is odd to an American.

On a tour in Asia, the foreigner who does not wish to be ill will exercise reasonable care. It looks smart to take insufficient sleep, snatch a hurried meal out of a tin can, drink unboiled water and walk or ride in the sun without a pith hat or an umbrella. Some foreigners who ought to know better are careless about these things and good-naturedly chaff one who is more particular. But while one should not be unnecessarily fussy, yet if he is courageous enough to be sensible, he will not only preserve his health, but be physically benefited by his tour, while the heedless man will probably be floored by dysentery or even if he escapes that scourge will reach his destination so worn out that he must take days or perhaps weeks to recuperate. I was not ill a day, made what Dr. Bergen called "the record tour of Shantung," and came out in splendid health and spirits just because I had nerve enough to insist on taking reasonable time for eating and sleeping, boiling my drinking water, and buying the fresh vegetables and fruit with which the country abounded. From this view-point, Dr. Charles F. Johnson, who escorted me from Chining-chou to Tsing-tau, was a model. With no loss of time, with but trifling additional expense and with comparatively little extra trouble, he had an appetizing table, while water bottles and fruit tins were always cooled in buckets of well water so that they were grateful to a dusty, thirsty throat. It is not difficult to make oneself fairly comfortable in travelling even when nearly all modern conveniences are wanting and it pays to take the necessary trouble.

Throughout the tour, we were watched in a way that was suggestive. When United States Consul Fowler first told me that Governor Yuan Shih Kai would send a military escort with me, I said that I was not proud, that I did not care to go through Shantung with the pomp and panoply of war, that I was on a peaceful, conciliatory errand, and preferred to travel with only my missionary companions. But he replied that while the province was then quiet, no one could tell what an hour might bring forth, that in the tension that existed even a local and sporadic attack on a foreigner might be a signal for a new outbreak, that the Governor was trying to keep the people in hand, and that as he was held responsible for consequences he must be allowed to have his own men in charge of a foreign party that purposed to journey so far into the interior. So, of course, I yielded.

When I lifted up my eyes and looked on the escort at Kiao-chou, I felt that my fears of pomp and panoply had been groundless, for the "escort" consisted of two disreputable-looking coolies who had apparently been picked up on the street and who were armed with antiquated flint-locks that were more dangerous to their bearers than to an enemy. I am sure that these "guards" would have been the first to run at the slightest sign of danger. We did not see them again till we reached Kaomi, where we gave them a present and sent them back, glad to be rid of them. We afterwards learned that they were only the retainers of the local Kiao-chou yamen to see us to the border of the hinterland, which Governor Yuan's troops were not permitted to cross.

But the men who met us at the border were soldiers of another type—powerful looking cavalrymen on excellent horses. Remembering the stories we had heard regarding the murder of foreigners by Chinese troops who had been sent ostensibly to guard them, we were relieved to find that there were only three of them, and as there were three of us, we felt safe, for we believed that in an emergency we could whip them. When on leaving Wei-hsien the number increased to five and then to six, we became dubious. But we concluded that as we were active, stalwart men, we might in a pinch manage twice our number of Chinese soldiers or, if worst came to worst, as we were unencumbered by women, children or luggage, we could sprint, on the old maxim,

"He that fights and runs away
Will live to fight another day."

But when a little later, the force grew to eleven and then to fifteen, we were hopelessly out-classed, especially as they were well-mounted and armed not only with swords but with modern magazine rifles.

The result, however, proved that our fears were groundless, for the men were good soldiers, intelligent, respectful, well-drilled, and thoroughly disciplined. They treated us with strict military etiquette, standing at attention and saluting in the most approved military fashion whenever they spoke to us or we to them. I was not accustomed to travelling in such state. Our three shendzas meant six mules and three muleteers, one for each shendza. Our cook and "boy" each had a donkey, and a pack-mule was necessary for our food supplies. So including the men and horses of the escort, we usually had nineteen men and twenty animals and a part of the time we had even a larger number. We therefore made quite a procession, and attracted considerable attention. I suspect, however, that some of those shrewd Chinese were not deceived as to my humble station at home for one man asked the missionary who accompanied me whether I travelled with an escort in America!

The lieutenant commanding our escort said that he received forty-two taels a month,[19] the sergeants eleven taels, and the privates nine taels. The men buy their own food, but their clothing, horses, provender, etc., are furnished by the Government. This is big pay for China. The lieutenant further said that Governor Yuan Shih Kai had thirty regiments of a nominal strength of 500 each and an actual strength of 250, making a total of 7,500, and that the soldiers had been drilled by German officers at Tien-tsin. There are no foreign officers now connected with the force, but there are two foreign educated Chinese who receive 300 taels a month each. He further said that all the men with us had killed Boxers and that he was confident that they could rout 1,000 of them. An illustration of the reputation of these troops occurred during my visit in Paoting-fu a little later. A messenger breathlessly reported that the Allied Villagers, who had banded themselves together to resist the collection of indemnity, had captured a city only ninety li southward and that they intended to march on Paoting-fu itself. Three thousand of Yuan Shih Kai's troops had been ordered to go to Peking to prepare for the return of the Emperor and Empress Dowager, but the French general at Paoting-fu had forbade them coming beyond a point a hundred li south of Paoting-fu, so that they were then encamped there awaiting further orders. The Prefect hastily wired Viceroy Li Hung Chang in Peking asking him to order these troops to retake the recaptured city, as the Imperial troops were "needed here," a euphemism for saying that they were useless. Li Hung Chang gave the desired order and the seasoned troops of Yuan Shih Kai made short work of the Allied Villagers.

19   A tael equals sixty-five cents at the present rate of exchange.

At any rate, those who escorted me through Shantung were certainly good soldiers. They had splendid horses and took good care of them, while several evenings they gave us as fine exhibitions of sword drill as I ever saw. I was interested to find that seven of them belonged to a total abstinence society, though none of them were Christians. I became really attached to them. They were very patient, although my journey compelled them to make a long and hard march for which they received no extra pay. On the last evening of the trip, I gave them a feast in the most approved Chinese style. I made a little farewell address and gave the officer in charge the following letter which seemed to please them greatly:—

"June 27th, 1901.

"To His Excellency,
    "General Yuan Shih Kai,

    "Governor of the Province of Shantung, China,
"SIR:

"In completing my tour of the Province of Shantung, I have pleasure in expressing my high appreciation, and that of the missionaries of the Presbyterian Church who accompanied me, of the excellent conduct of the soldiers who formed our escort under the command of (Lieutenant) Wang Pa Chung. Both he and his troopers were courteous and faithful, attentive to every duty and meriting our admiration for the perfection of their discipline.

"We regret the death of one of their horses, but we are satisfied that the soldier was in no way to blame. The animal died in the inn courtyard early in the morning.

"I have had pleasure in giving the officer and his men a feast. In addition I offered them a present, but the Wang Pa Chung declined to accept it.

"Thanking you for your courtesy in detailing such good soldiers for our escort,

    "I have, sir, the honour to be
        "Your obedient servant,
(Signed) "ARTHUR J. BROWN."

I was impressed by the refusal to accept the present, which was a considerable sum to Chinese. But the men were evidently under strict orders. The lieutenant was polite and grateful, but he said that he "could not accept a gift if it were ten thousand taels."

During the whole tour, these soldiers watched us with a fidelity that was almost embarrassing at times. Not for a moment did they lose sight of us except when we were in the mission compounds. If we took a walk about a village, they followed us. Eating, sleeping or travelling, we were always watched. Several times we tried to escape such espionage, or to induce the soldiers to turn back. We did not feel our need of them, nor did I desire my peaceful mission to be associated with military display. Besides, if hostility had been manifested, a dozen Chinese soldiers would have been of little avail among those swarming millions. But our efforts and protests were vain and we had no alternative but to submit with the best grace possible.

Nor was this all, for many of the magistrates whose districts we crossed en route added other attentions. Indeed, they appeared to be almost nervously anxious that no mishap should befall us. I had sent no announcement of my coming to any one except my missionary friends, nor had I asked for any favour or protection save the usual passport through the United States Consul. But the first Tao-tai I met politely inquired about my route, and, as I afterwards learned, sent word to the next magistrate. He in turn forwarded the word to the one beyond, and so on throughout the whole trip. As we approached a city, uniformed attendants from the chief magistrate's yamen usually met us and escorted us, sometimes with much display of banners and trumpets and armed guards, to an inn which had been prepared for our reception by having a little of its dirt swept into the corners and a few of its bugs killed. Then would come a feast of many courses of Chinese delicacies. A call from the magistrate himself often followed, and he would chat amicably while great crowds stood silently about.

There was something half pathetic about the attentions we received. Our journey was like a triumphal procession. For example, twenty li from Chang Ku a messenger on horseback met us. He had evidently been on the watch, for after kneeling he galloped back with the news of our approach. Soon a dozen soldiers in scarlet uniforms appeared, saluted, wheeled and marched before us to an inn where we found rugs on the floor and kangs, a cloth on the table and two elevated seats covered with scarlet robes. Attendants from the yamen with their red tasselled helmets were numerous and attentive. Basins of water were brought and presently the magistrate sent an elaborate feast. As we finished the repast, the magistrate himself called. He was very affable and made quite a long call. In like manner the district magistrate of Fei-hsien sent his secretary, personal flags and twenty soldiers twenty li to meet us. They knelt as we approached and shouted in unison—"We wish the great man peace!" So as usual we entered the town with pomp and circumstance, our own escort added to the local one making a brave show.

And these were typical experiences. We could not prevent them and to resent them would have made the official "lose face" and so embittered him. At Pien-kiao, where a hundred of Governor Yuan Shih Kai's troops were stationed, the whole garrison turned out, meeting us a couple of miles from the city and escorting us to our inn with blares of trumpets which Dr. Johnson said were only sounded for high officials. We were awakened at three o'clock the next morning by the bellowing of calves and the braying of mules in the inn courtyard, and as we had our longest day's journey ahead of us, we rose, breakfasted at four by candle-light and were on the road at a quarter of five. But in spite of the early hour, the whole garrison again turned out and lined the road at "present arms" as we passed.

Think of the mayor of an American city of fifty or a hundred thousand habitants hastening to call in state on three unknown travellers, who were simply stopping for luncheon at a hotel, and sending a couple dozen policemen to escort them in and out of town! The Shantung Chinese are a strong, proud, independent people, and it must have cost them something to be so effusive to foreigners. There was doubtless in it some real regard for Americans and American missionaries. But policy was probably also a factor. The officials felt that any further attack on foreigners would be a pretext for further foreign aggression, an excuse for Germany to advance from Kiao-chou, and they were anxious not to give occasion for it. Each official was apparently determined to make it plain that he was doing his duty in trying to protect these foreigners so that if they got hurt it would not be his fault. Perhaps, too, he was not averse to showing the populace that foreigners had to be guarded. I was half ashamed to travel in that way. But I could not help myself. Sometimes I felt that the guard was not so much for us as for the Chinese, assuring nervous officials that foreigners should have no further excuse for aggression and warning the evil-disposed that they must not commit acts which might get the officials into trouble.

Whatever the reasons were, they were plainly impersonal. No one of us had any official status nor were we as individuals of any consequence whatever to Chinese officials. We were simply white men and as such we were regarded as representatives of a race which had made its power felt. Perhaps the soldiers and the orders of Governor Yuan Shih Kai had much to do with the quietness of the people, but some way I felt perfectly safe. Whether any attack would have been made if I had been allowed to journey quietly with my one or two missionary companions, I am not competent to judge. Foreigners who had lived many years in China told me before starting that my life would not be safe beyond rifle shot. They have told me since that the profuse attentions that we received were mere pretence, that the very officials who welcomed us as honoured guests probably cursed our race as soon as our backs were turned, and that if the people had not understood from the presence of troops and from the magistrates' marked personal attentions that we were not to be molested, we might have met with violence in a dozen places. The opinions of such experienced men were not to be lightly set aside.

All I can say is that on these suppositions the Chinese are masters of the art of dissimulation, for in all our journeyings through the very heart of the region where the Boxers originated, and where the anti-foreign hatred was said to be bitterest, we saw not a sign of unfriendliness. The typical official received us with the courtesy of a "gentleman of the old school." The vast throngs that quickly assembled at every stopping place, while silent, were respectful. We tried to behave decently ourselves, to speak kindly to every man, to pay fair prices for what we bought; in short, to act just as we would have acted in America. And every man to whom we smiled, smiled in return. Wherever we asked a civil question we got a civil answer. Coolies would stop their barrows, farmers leave their fields to direct us aright. In all our travelling in the interior, amid a population so dense that we constantly marvelled, we never heard a rude word or saw a hostile sign. I naturally find it difficult to believe that those pleasant, obliging people would have killed us if they had not been restrained by their magistrates, and that the officials who exerted themselves to show us all possible honour would have gladly murdered us if they had dared.

And yet less than a year before, the Chinese had angrily destroyed the property and venomously sought the lives of foreigners who were as peaceably disposed as we were, ruthlessly hunting men and women who had never done them wrong, and who had devoted their lives to teaching the young and healing the sick and preaching the gospel of love and good will. Why they did this we shall have occasion to observe in a later chapter.

PART II

THE COMMERCIAL FORCE AND THE ECONOMIC REVOLUTION

VIII
WORLD CONDITIONS THAT ARE
AFFECTING CHINA[20]

SEVERAL outside forces have pressed steadily and heavily upon the exclusiveness and conservatism of the Chinese, and though they have not yet succeeded in changing the essential character of the nation, they have set in motion vast movements which have already convulsed great sections of the Empire and which are destined to affect stupendous transformations. The first of these forces is foreign commerce.

To understand the operation of this force, we must consider that its impact has been enormously increased by the extension of facilities for intercommunication. The extent to which these have revolutionized the world is one of the most extraordinary features of our extraordinary age. It is startlingly significant of the change that has taken place that Russia and Japan, nations 7,000 miles apart by land and a still greater distance by water, are able in the opening years of the twentieth century to wage war in a region which one army can reach in four weeks and the other in four days, and that all the rest of the world can receive daily information as to the progress of the conflict. A half century ago, Russia could no more have sent a large army to Manchuria than to the moon, while down to the opening of her ports by Commodore Perry in 1854, the few wooden vessels that made the long journey to Japan found an

---

20   Part of this chapter appeared as an article in the American Monthly Review of Reviews, October, 1904.

unprogressive and bitterly anti-foreign heathen nation with an edict issued in 1638 still on its statute books declaring—"So long as the sun shall continue to warm the earth, let no Christian be so bold as to come to Japan; and let all know that the King of Spain himself, or the Christian's God, or the great God of all, if He dare violate this command, shall pay for it with his head."

Nor were other far-eastern peoples any more hospitable. China, save for a few port cities, was as impenetrable as when in 1552 the dying Xavier had cried—"O Rock, Rock, when wilt thou open!" Siam excluded all foreigners until the century's first quarter had passed, and Laos saw no white man till 1868. A handful of British traders were so greedily determined to keep all India as a private commercial preserve that, forgetting their own indebtedness to Christianity, they sneered at the proposal to send missionaries to India as "the maddest, most expensive, most unwarranted project ever proposed by a lunatic enthusiast," while as late as 1857, a director of the East India Company declared that "he would rather see a band of devils in India than a band of missionaries." Korea was rightly called "the hermit nation" until 1882; and as for Africa, it was not till 1873 that the world learned of that part of it in which the heroic Livingstone died on his knees, not till 1877 that Stanley staggered into a West Coast settlement after a desperate journey of 999 days from Zanzibar through Central Africa, not till 1884 that the Berlin Conference formed the International Association of the Congo guaranteeing that which has not yet been realized "liberty of conscience" and "the free and public exercise of every creed."

Even in America within the memory of men still living, the lumbering, white-topped "prairie schooner" was the only conveyance for the tedious overland journey to California. Hardy frontiersmen were fighting Indians in the Mississippi Valley, and the bold Whitman was "half a year" in bearing a message from Oregon to Washington.

The Hon. John W. Foster tells us in his "Century of American Diplomacy" that "General Lane, the first territorial governor of Oregon, left his home in Indiana, August 27, 1848, and desiring to reach his destination as soon as possible, travelling overland to San Francisco and thence by ship, reached his post on the first of March following—the journey occupying six months. At the time our treaty of peace and independence was signed in 1783, two stage-coaches were sufficient for all the passengers and nearly all the freight between New York and Boston." It is only seventy years since the Rev. John Lowrie, with his bride and Mr. and Mrs. Reed, rode horseback from Pittsburg through flooded rivers and over the Allegheny Mountains to Philadelphia, whence it took them four and a-half months to reach Calcutta.

Nor was this all, for scores of the conveniences and even necessities of our modern life were unknown at the beginning of the nineteenth century. To get some idea of the vastness of the revolution in the conditions of living, we have but to remind ourselves that "in the year 1800 no steamer ploughed the waters; no locomotive traversed an inch of soil; no photographic plate had ever been kissed by sunlight; no telephone had ever talked from town to town; steam had never driven mighty mills and electric currents had never been harnessed into telegraph and trolley wires."[21] "In all the land there was no power loom, no power press, no large manufactory in textiles, wood or iron, no canal. The possibilities of electricity in light, heat and power were unknown and unsuspected. The cotton gin had just begun its revolutionary work. Intercommunication was difficult, the postal service slow and costly, literature scanty and mostly of inferior quality."[22]

How marvellously the application of steam as a motive power has united once widely separated regions. So swiftly have the changes come and so quickly have we adapted ourselves to them that it is difficult to realize the magnitude of the transformation that has been achieved. We can ride from Pittsburg to Philadelphia in eight hours and to Calcutta in twenty-two days. The journey across our own continent is no longer marked by the ox-cart and the campfire and the bones of perished expeditions. It is simply a pleasant trip of less than a week, and in an emergency in August, 1903, Henry P. Lowe travelled from New York to Los Angeles, 3,241 miles, in seventy-three hours and twenty-one minutes. Populous states covered with a network of railway and telegraph lines invite the nations of the world to join them in celebrating at St. Louis the "Purchase" of a region which a hundred years ago was as foreign to the American people as the Philippines now are. The

21   The Rev. Dr. Theodore Cuyler.
22   Address of the Bishops of the M. E. Church, 1900.

Rev. Dr. Calvin Mateer, who in 1863 was six months in reaching Chefoo, China, on a voyage from whose hardships his wife never fully recovered, returned in a comfortable journey of one month in 1902. To-day, for all practical purposes, China is nearer New York than California once was.

No waters are too remote for the modern steamer. Its smoke trails across every sea and far up every navigable stream. Ten mail steamers regularly run on the Siberian Yenisei, while the Obi, flowing from the snows of the Little Altai Mountains, bears 302 steam vessels on various parts of its 2,000-mile journey to the Obi Gulf on the Arctic Ocean. Stanley could now go from Glasgow to Stanley Falls in forty-three days. Already there are forty-six steamers on the Upper Congo. From Cape Town, a railway 2,000 miles long runs via Bulawayo to Beira on the Portuguese coast, while branch lines reach several formerly inaccessible mining and agricultural regions. June 22, 1904, almost the whole population of Cape Town cheered the departure of the first through train for Victoria Falls, where the British Association for the Advancement of Science has been invited to meet in 1905. Uganda is reached by rail. Five hundred and eighty miles of track unite Mombasa and Victoria Nyanza. Sleeping and dining cars safely run the 575 miles from Cairo to Khartoum where only five years ago Lord Kitchener fought the savage hordes of the Mahdi. The Englishman's dream of a railroad from Cairo to the Cape is more than half realized, for 2,800 miles are already completed. In 1903, Japan had 4,237 miles of well managed railways which in 1902 carried 111,211,208 passengers 14,409,752 tons of freight. India is gridironed by 25,373 miles of steel rails which in 1901 carried 195,000,000 passengers. A railroad parallels the Burmese Irrawaddy to Bhamo and Mandalay. In Siam you can ride by rail from Bangkok northward to Korat and westward to Petchaburee. The Trans-Siberian Railway now connects St. Petersburg and Peking. In Korea, the line from Chemulpho to Seoul connects with lines under construction both southward and northward, so that ere long one can journey by rail from Fusan on the Korean Strait to Wiju on the Yalu River. As the former is but ten hours by sea from Japan and as the latter is to form a junction with the Trans-Siberian Railway, a land journey in a sleeping car will soon be practicable from London and Paris to the capitals of China and Korea, and, save for the ferry across the Korean Strait, to any part of the Mikado's kingdom. The locomotive runs noisily from Jaffa to venerable Jerusalem and from Beirut over the passes of Lebanon to Damascus, the oldest city in the world. A projected line will run from there to the Mohammedan Mecca, so that soon the Moslem pilgrims will abandon the camel for the passenger coach. Most wonderful of all is the Anatolian Railway which is to run through the heart of Asia Minor, traversing the Karamanian plateau, the Taurus Mountains and the Cilician valleys to Haran where Abraham tarried, and Nineveh where Jonah preached, and Babylon where Nebuchadnezzar made an image of gold, and Bagdad where Haroun-al-Raschid ruled, to Koweit on the Persian Gulf.

In a single month forty-five Philadelphia engines have been ordered for India. The American locomotive is to-day speeding across the steppes of Siberia, through the valleys of Japan, across the uplands of Burmah and around the mountainsides of South America. "Yankee bridge-builders have cast up a highway in the desert where the chariot of Cambyses was swallowed up by the sands. The steel of Pennsylvania spans the Atbara, makes a road to Meroe," and crosses the rivers of Peru. Trains on the two imperial highways of Africa—the one from Cairo to the Cape and the other from the upper Nile to the Red Sea—are to be hauled by American engines over American bridges, while the "forty centuries" which Napoleon Bonaparte said looked down from the pyramids see not the soldiers of France, but the manufacturing agents of Europe and America. Whether or not we are to have a political imperialism, we already have an industrial imperialism.

Walter J. Ballard declares[23] that the aggregate capital invested in railways at the end of 1902 was $36,850,000,000 and that the total mileage was 532,500 distributed as follows:—

	Miles
United States	202,471
Europe	80,708
Asia	41,814
South America	28,654
North America (Except U. S.)	24,032
Australia	15,649
Africa	4,187

23   New York Sun, July 13, 1903.

Jules Verne's story, "Around the World in Eighty Days" was deemed fantastic in 1873. But in 1903, James Willis Sayre of Seattle, Washington, travelled completely around the world in fifty-four days and nine hours, while the Russian Minister of Railroads issues the following schedule of possibilities when the Trans-Siberian Railroad has completed its plans:—

```
From St. Petersburg to Vladivostok ....................10     days
 "     Vladivostok to San Francisco ....................10      "
 "     San Francisco to New York .......................4<1/2>"
 "     New York to Bremen................................7      "
 "     Bremen to St. Petersburg ..........................1<1/2>"
                                                       ---------
      Total..............................................33 days
```

As for the risks incident to such a tour, it is significant that for my own journey around the world, a conservative insurance company, for a consideration of only fifty dollars, guaranteed for a year to indemnify me in case of incapacitating accident to the extent of fifty dollars a week and in case of death to pay my heirs $10,000. And the company made money on the arrangement, for I met with neither illness nor accident. With a very few unimportant exceptions, there are now no hermit nations, for the remotest lands are within quick and easy reach.

And now electricity has ushered in an era more wondrous still. Trolley cars run through the streets of Seoul and Bangkok. The Empress Dowager of China wires her decrees to the Provincial Governors. Telegraph lines belt the globe, enabling even the provincial journal to print the news of the entire world during the preceding twenty-four hours. We know to-day what occurred yesterday in Tokyo and Beirut, Shanghai and Batanga. The total length of all telegraph lines in the world is 4,908,921 miles,—the nerves of our modern civilization. And it is remarkable not only that Europe has 1,764,790 miles, America 2,516,548 miles and Australia 277,419 miles, but that Africa has 99,409 miles and Asia 310,685 miles, Japan alone having, in 1903, 84,000 miles beside 108,000 miles of telephone wires.

I found the telegraph in Siam and Korea, in China and the Philippines, in Burma, India, Arabia, Egypt and Palestine. Camping one night in far Northern Laos after a toilsome ride on elephants, I realized that I was 12,500 miles from home, at as remote a point almost as it would be possible for man to reach. All about was the wilderness, relieved only by the few houses of a small village. But walking into that tiny hamlet, I found at the police station a telephone connecting with the telegraph office at Chieng-mai, so that, though I was on the other side of the planet, I could have sent a telegram to my New York office in a few minutes. Nor was this an exceptional experience, for the telegraph is all over Laos, as indeed it is over many other Asiatic lands.

From the recesses of Africa comes the report that the Congo telegraph line, which will ultimately stretch across the entire belt of Central Africa, already runs 800 miles up the Congo River from the ocean to Kwamouth, the junction of the Kassai and Congo Rivers. A Belgian paper states that "a telegram dispatched from Kwamouth on January 15th was delivered at Boma half an hour later. For the future, the Kassai is thus placed in direct and rapid communication with the seat of Government, and Europe is also brought close to the centre of Africa. Only a few years ago, news took at least two months to reach Boma from the Kassai, and the reply would not be received under another two months, and this only if the parties were available and the steamer ready to start."

More significant still are the submarine cables which aggregate 1,751 in number and over 200,000 miles in length and which annually transmit more than 6,000,000 messages, annihilating the time and distance which formerly separated nations. When King William IV of England died in 1837, the news was thirty-five days in reaching America. But when Queen Victoria passed away January 22, 1901, at 6:30 P. M., the afternoon papers describing the event were being sold in the streets of New York at 3:30 P. M. of the same day! As I rose to address a union meeting of the English speaking residents of Canton, China, on that fateful September day of 1901, a message was handed me which read, "President McKinley is dead." So that by means of the submarine cable, that little company of Englishmen and Americans in far-off China bowed in grief and prayer simultaneously with multitudes in the home land.

Not only Europe and America, but Siberia and Australia, New Zealand and New Caledonia, Korea and the Kameruns, Laos and Persia are within the sweep of this modern system of intercommunication. The latest as well as one of the most important links in this world system is the Commercial Pacific Cable between Manila and San Francisco.

President Roosevelt gave a significant illustration of the perfection of this system when, on the completion of the Commercial Pacific Cable July 4, 1903, he flashed a message around the earth in twelve minutes, while a second message sent by Clarence H. Mackay, President of the Pacific Cable Company, made the circuit of the earth in nine minutes.

What additional possibilities are involved in the wireless system of telegraphy we can only conjecture, but it is already apparent that this system has passed the experimental stage and that it is destined to achieve still more amazing results. A startling illustration of its possibilities was given by the Japanese fleet March 22, 1904. A cruiser lay off Port Arthur and by wireless messages enabled battleships, riding safely eight miles away, to bombard fortifications which they could not see and which could not see them.

Commerce has taken swift and massive advantages of these facilities for intercommunication. Its ships whiten every sea. The products of European and American manufacture are flooding the earth. The United States Treasury Bureau of Statistics (1903) estimates that the value of the manufactured articles which enter into the international commerce of the world is four billions of dollars and that of this vast total, the United States furnishes 400,000,000, its foreign trade having increased over 100 per cent. since 1895. While the bulk of the foreign trade of the United States is with Europe, American business men are gradually awaking to the greatness of their opportunity in Asia. A characteristic example of their aggressiveness was given when President James J. Hill, of the Great Northern Railroad, testified before a Government Commission, October 20, 1902:—

"We arranged with a line of steamers to connect with our road so that we could get the Oriental outlet. I remember when the Japanese were going to buy rails, I asked them where they were going to buy, and they said in England or Belgium. I asked them to wait until I telegraphed. I wired and made the rates, so that we made the price $1.50 a ton lower and sold for America 40,000 tons of rails. Then I got them to try a little of the American cotton, telling them if it was not satisfactory I would pay for the cotton, and the result was satisfactory."

In these ways, the interrelation of nations is becoming closer and closer, their separation from the world's life more and more difficult. Dr. Josiah Strong well observes:—

"Until the nineteenth century, there was but little contact between different peoples throughout the world. They were separated, not only by distances hard to overcome, but by differences of speech, of faith, of mental habit and mode of life, of custom and costume, of government and law, and isolation tended steadily to emphasize the divergence which already existed. Thus increasing differences of environment perpetuated and intensified the differences of civilization which they had created. In other words, until the nineteenth century, the stream of tendency down all the ages was towards diversity. Then came the change, the results of which are, in their magnitude and importance, beyond calculation. Steam annihilated nine-tenths of space, and electricity has cancelled the remainder. Isolation is, therefore, becoming impossible, for the world is now a neighbourhood. This means that differences of environment will, from this time on, become constantly less. The swift ships of commerce are mighty shuttles which are weaving the nations together into one great web of life."

IX
THE ECONOMIC REVOLUTION IN ASIA[24]

THE result of the operation of this commercial force is an economic revolution of vast proportions. When ever I went in Asia, I found wider interest in this subject than in the aggressions of European nations. The reason is obvious. The common people in Asia care little for politics, but the price of food and raiment touches every man, woman and child at a sensitive point. Almost everywhere, the old days of cheap living are passing away. Steamers, railways, telegraphs, newspapers, labour-saving machinery, and the introduction of western ideas are slowly but surely revolutionizing the Orient. Shantung wheat, which formerly had no market beyond a radius of a few dozen miles from the wheat-field, can now be shipped by railroad and steamship to any part of the world, and every Chinese buyer has to pay more for it in consequence. In like manner new facilities for export have doubled, trebled and, in some places, quadrupled the price of rice in China, Siam and Japan. The Consul-General of the United States at Shanghai reports that the prices of seventeen staple articles of export have increased sixteen per cent. in twenty years while in Japan the increase in the same articles for the same period was thirty-one per cent.[25]

The depreciation in the value of silver has still further complicated the situation. The common Chinese tael, which

---

24 Part of this chapter appeared as an article in the Century Magazine, March, 1904.

25 "Commercial China," p. 2902.

formerly bought from 1,500 to 1,800 cash (the current coin of China), now buys only 950 cash. The Shanghai tael brings 897 cash, and the Mexican dollar only 665. This of course, means that the common people, who use only cash, have to pay a larger number of them for the necessaries of life. The same difficulty is being felt to a greater or less extent in many other countries of Asia, while in China, an already serious advance in prices is being heightened by the heavy import taxes which have been levied to meet the indemnity imposed by the Western Powers on account of the Boxer outbreak.

The prices of labour and materials have sharply advanced in consequence of the enormous demands incident to the construction of railways, with their stations, shops and round-houses, the vast engineering schemes of the Germans at Tsing-tau, the British at Wei-hai Wei and the Russians at Port Arthur, the extensive scale on which the Legations have rebuilt in Peking, the reconstruction of virtually the entire business portions of both Peking and Tien-tsin, as well as the coincident rebuilding of the mission stations of all denominations, Protestant and Catholic. It will be readily understood what all this activity means in a land where there are as yet but limited supplies of the kind of skilled labourers required for foreign buildings, and where the requisite materials must be imported from Europe and America by firms who "are not in China for their health."

It is futile to hope that the competition will be materially less next year, or the year after, or the year after that. Commerce and politics are planning works in China which will not be completed for many years. Railway officials told me of projected lines which will require decades for construction. China has entered upon an era of commercial development. The Western world has come to stay, and while there may be temporary reactions, as there have been at home, prices are not likely to return to their former level. There are vast interior regions which will not be affected for an indefinite period, but for the coast provinces, primitive conditions are passing forever.

The knowledge of modern inventions and of other foods and articles has created new wants. The Chinese peasant is no longer content to burn bean oil; he wants kerosene. In scores of humble Laos homes and markets I saw American lamps costing twenty rupees apiece, and a magistrate proudly showed me a collection of nineteen of these shining articles. Forty thousand dollars worth of these lamps were sold in Siam last year. The narrow streets of Canton are brilliant with German chandeliers and myriads of private houses throughout the Empire are lighted by foreign lamps. The desire of the Asiatic to possess foreign lamps is only equalled by his passion for foreign clocks. I counted twenty-seven in the private apartments of the Emperor of China and my wife counted nineteen in a single room of the Empress Dowager's palace, while cheaper ones tick to the delighted wonder of myriads of humbler people. The ambitious Syrian scorns the mud roof of his ancestors and will only be satisfied with bright red tiles imported from France. In almost every Asiatic city I visited, I found shops crowded with articles of foreign manufacture. "Made in Germany" is as familiar a phrase in Siam as in America. Many children in China are arrayed only in the atmosphere, but when I was in Taian-fu, in the far interior of Shantung, hundreds of parents were in consternation because the magistrate had just placarded the walls with an edict announcing that hereafter boys and girls must wear clothes and that they would be arrested if found on the streets naked. At a banquet given to the foreign ministers by the Emperor and the Empress Dowager in the famous Summer Palace twelve miles from Peking, the distinguished guests cut York ham with Sheffield knives and drank French wines out of German glasses. Everywhere articles of foreign manufacture are in demand, and shrewd Chinese merchants are stocking their shops with increasing quantities of European and American goods. The new Chinese Presbyterian Church at Wei-hsien typifies the elements that are entering Asia for it contains Chinese brick, Oregon fir beams, German steel binding-plates and rods, Belgian glass, Manchurian pine pews, and British cement.

India is eagerly buying American rifles, tools, boots and shoes, while vast regions which depend upon irrigation are becoming interested in American well-boring outfits. Persia is demanding increasing quantities of American padlocks, sewing-machines and agricultural implements. German, English and American machinery is equipping great cotton factories in Japan. I saw Russian and American oil tins in the remotest villages of Korea. Strolling along the river bank one evening in Paknampo, Siam, I heard a familiar whirring sound and entering found a bare-legged Siamese busily at work on a sewing-machine of American make. Nearly five hundred of them are sold in Siam every year, and I found them in most of the cities that I visited in other Asiatic countries. When I left Lampoon on an elephant, six hundred miles north of Bangkok, a Laos gentleman rode beside me for several miles on an American bicycle. There are thousands of them in Siam. His Majesty himself frequently rides one and His Royal Highness, Prince Damrong, is president of a bicycle club of four hundred members. The king's palace is lighted by electricity and the Government buildings are equipped with telephones, and as the nobles and merchants see the brilliancy of the former and the convenience of the latter, they want them, too. In many parts of Asia people, who but a decade or two ago were satisfied with the crudest appliances of primitive life, are now learning to use steam and electrical machinery, to like Oregon flour, Chicago beef, Pittsburg pickles and London jam, and to see the utility of foreign wire, nails, cutlery, drugs, paints and chemicals.

Many other illustrations of a changed condition might be cited. Knowledge increases wants and the Oriental is acquiring knowledge. He demands a hundred things to-day that his grandfather never heard of, and when he goes to the shops to buy his daily food, he finds that the new market for it which the foreigner has opened has increased the price.

Americans are the very last people who can consistently criticise this tendency in Asia. It is the foreigner who has created it, and the American is the most prodigal of all foreigners. I never realized until I visited other lands how extravagant is the scale of American life, not only among the rich, but the so-called poor. My morning walk to my New York office takes me along Christopher Street, and I have often seen in the garbage cans of tenement houses pieces of bread and meat and half-eaten vegetables and fruit that would give the average Asiatic the feast of a lifetime. In Europe, Americans are notorious as spendthrifts. In the Philippine Islands, they have thrown about their money in a way which has inaugurated an era of reckless lavishness comparable only to the California days of "forty-nine." In the port cities of China, the porters asked me extortionate prices because I was an American. Two or three coolies would seize a suit case or change it from man to man every few minutes, on the pretense that it was heavy. In Tien-tsin, you hire a jinrikisha and presently you find a second man pushing behind, though the road is smooth as a floor. In a few minutes a third appears to push on the other side, and once a fourth took hold between the second and third. All of course demand pay, and it is difficult to shake them off. They do not understand your protests, or they pretend not to, and you have to be emphatic to get rid of them. At Tong-ku, my sampan men calmly insisted on two dollars for a service that was worth but forty cents. Everywhere, I found that it was wiser to make all purchases and bargains through trusty native Christians, or to ascertain in advance what a given service was really worth, pay it and walk off, deaf to all protestations and complaints, even though as in Seoul, Korea, the men plaintively sat around for hours. In Cairo, a certain hotel charged me on the supposition that because I was an American, I was a millionaire or a fool—perhaps both. True, we have hack-drivers and hotel-keepers in America who are equally rapacious, and a New Yorker in particular need not go away from home to be overcharged. But it is just because we have become so accustomed to this careless profusion at home that we exhibit it abroad.

But it is useless to protest against the increased cost of living in Asia. It is as much beyond individual control as the tides. The causes which are producing it are not even national but cosmopolitan.

Nor should we ignore the fact that this movement is, in some respects at least, beneficial. It means a higher and broader scale of life and such a life always costs more than a low and narrow one. This economic revolution in Asia is a concomitant of a Christian civilization which brings not only higher prices but wider intellectual and spiritual horizons, a general enlarging and uplifting of the whole range of life. There are indeed some vicious influences accompanying this movement, as brighter lights usually have deeper shadows.

But surely it is for good and not for evil that the farmers of Hunan can now ship their peanuts to England and with the proceeds vary the eternal monotony of a rice-diet; that the girls of Siam are being taught by missionary example that modesty requires the purchase of a garment for street wear which will cover at least the breasts; that the Korean should learn that it is better to have a larger house so that the girls of the family need not sleep in the same room as the boys; and that all China should discover the advantages of roads over rutty, corkscrew paths, of sanitation over heaps of putrid garbage and of wooden floors over filth-encrusted ground. Christianity inevitably involves some of these things, and to some extent the awakening of Asia to the need of them is a part of the beneficent influence of a gospel which always and everywhere renders men dissatisfied with a narrow, squalid existence. To make a man decent morally is to beget in him a desire to be decent physically.

The native Christians, especially the pastors and teachers, are the very ones who first feel this movement towards a higher physical life. Nor should we repress it in them, for it means an environment more favourable to morals and to the stability of Christian character as well as a healthful example to the community in which they live. To say, therefore, that the average annual income of a Hindu is rupees twenty-seven (nine dollars) is not to adduce a reason for holding the pastors and evangelists of India down to that scale. They should, indeed, live near enough to the plane of their countrymen to keep in sympathetic touch with them. But they should not be expected or allowed to huddle in the dark, unventilated hovels of the masses of the people, or, by confining themselves to one scanty meal a day, have that gaunt, half-famished look which makes my heart ache every time I think of the walking skeletons I saw in India. I am not ashamed but proud of the fact that it costs the average Christian more to live in Asia than it costs the average heathen, that the houses of the Laos Christians are better than the single-roomed sheds about them, that the graduates of our Siam mission schools for girls wear shirt waists instead of sunshine, that the members of any one of our Korean churches spend more money on soap than a whole village of their heathen neighbours whose bodies are caked with the accumulations of years of neglect, that the sessions of our Syrian churches are Christian gentlemen in appearance as well as in fact, and that the houses of our Chinese Christians do not mix pigs, chickens and babies in one lousy, malodorous company.

But these altered conditions have not yet brought the ability to meet them. The cost of living has increased faster than the resources of the people. Only France and Russia are primarily political in their foreign policy. England, Germany and the United States are avowedly commercial. They talk incessantly about "the open door." Their supreme object in Asia is to "extend their markets." They are producing more than they can use themselves, and they seek an opportunity to dispose of their surplus products. They are less concerned to bring the products of Asia into their own territories. Indeed, Germany and particularly the United States have built a tariff wall about themselves, expressly to protect home industries from outside competition, and not a few American manufacturers have recently been on the verge of panic on account of Japanese competition. Europe and America are trying to force their own manufactures on to Asia and to take in return only what they please.

In time, this will probably right itself, in part at least. While the farmers of the Mississippi Valley find living much more expensive than it was two generations ago, they also find that they get more for their wheat and that they eat better food and wear better clothes and build better houses than their grandfathers. The era of railroads ended the days of cheap living, but it ended as well days when the farmer had to confine himself to a diet of corn-bread and salt pork, when his home was destitute of comforts and his children had little schooling and no books. So the American working man of today has to pay more for the necessaries of life than the working man of Europe, but he is nevertheless the best paid, the best fed, the best clothed and the best housed working man in the world, a far better and more intelligent citizen because of these very conditions.

The same changes will doubtless take place in Asia. That great continent is capable of producing enormous quantities of food, minerals and both raw and manufactured articles which the rest of the world will sooner or later want. Already this foreign demand is bringing comparative wealth to the rug dealers of Syria, the silk embroiderers of China and the cloisonne' and porcelain makers of Japan. But only an infinitesimal part of the total population has thus far profited largely by this wider market. Where one man amasses wealth in this way, 100,000 men find that aggressive foreign traders exploit their wares by flooding the shops with tempting articles which they can ill-afford to buy. The difficulty is rapidly becoming acute. My inquiries in Japan led me to the conclusion that while the cost of the staple articles of living has increased nearly 100 per cent. in the last twenty years, the financial ability of the average Japanese has not increased thirty per cent. In China, Siam, India, the Philippine Islands, and Syria I found substantially similar anxieties though the proportions naturally varied. "True, there has been commerce since the early ages, but caravans could afford to carry only precious goods, like fine fabrics, spices and gems. These luxuries did not reach the multitude, and could not materially change environment. But modern commerce scatters over all the world the products of every climate, in ever increasing quantities."

So the economic revolution in Asia is characterized, as such revolutions usually are in Europe and America, by wide-spread unrest and, in some places, by violence. The oldest of continents is the latest to undergo the throes of the stupendous transformation from which the newest is slowly beginning to emerge. The transition period in Asia will be longer and perhaps more trying, as the numbers involved are vaster and more conservative; but the ultimate result cannot fail to be beneficial both to Asia and to the whole world.

It is therefore too late to discuss the question whether the character and religions of these nations should be disturbed. They have already been disturbed by the inrush of new ideas and by the ways as well as by the products of the white man. Like their ancient temples, the religions of Asia are cracking from pinnacle to foundation. The natives themselves realize that the old days are passing forever. India is in a ferment. Japan has leaped to world prominence. The power of the Mahdi has been broken and the Soudan has been opened to civilization. The King of Siam has made Sunday a legal holiday and is frightening his conservative subjects by his revolutionary changes, while Korea is changing with kaleidoscopic rapidity.

Whereas the opening years of the sixteenth century saw the struggle for civilization, of the seventeenth century for religious liberty, of the eighteenth century for constitutional government, of the nineteenth century for political freedom, the opening years of the twentieth century witness what Lowell would have called:—

"One death-grapple in the darkness 'twixt
Old systems and the word."

X

FOREIGN TRADE AND FOREIGN VICES

THE influences that are thus surging into the Middle Kingdom are tremendous. The beginnings of China's foreign trade date back to the third century, though it was not until comparatively recent years that it grew to large proportions. To-day the leading seaports of China have many great business houses handling vast quantities of European and American goods. The most persistent effort is made to extend commerce with the Chinese. That the effort is successful is shown by the fact that the foreign trade of China increased from 217,183,960 taels in 1888 to 583,547,291 taels in 1904. This shows the enormous gain of 168 per cent., though this is slightly modified by the fact that the report for 1904 includes goods to the value of 402,639 taels carried by Chinese vessels which, though plying between native and foreign ports, were not formerly reported through the customs. According to official reports,[26] the foreign trade of China has been growing rapidly during recent years, the only falling off having been in the Boxer outbreak year 1900. In 1891, the imports into China were, in round numbers, 134,000,000 taels and the exports were 101,000,000, a total of 235,000,000, and an excess of imports of 33 per cent. In 1904 the imports had advanced to 344,060,608 taels and the exports to 239,486,683 taels, a total of 583,547,291 taels, an increase of 148 per cent. and an excess of imports of 44 per cent. In 1899 the total foreign trade of China had reached 460,000,000 taels. The next year it dropped

---

26 "Returns of Trade for 1904," published by the Maritime Customs Department of China.

to 370,000,000 taels, but in 1901 it sprang to 438,000,000 taels, and has advanced nearly 150,000,000 taels within the past three years.[27]

The share of the United States is larger than one might infer from the reports, as no inconsiderable part of our trade goes to China by way of England and Hongkong and is often credited to the British total instead of to ours. American trade has, moreover, rapidly increased since 1900. We now sell more cotton goods to China than to all other countries combined, the exports having increased from $5,195,845 in 1898 to $27,000,000 in 1905.[28] In the year 1904, 63,529,623 gallons of kerosene oil valued at $7,202,110 were shipped from the United States to China. The development of the flour trade has been extraordinary, the sales having risen from $89,305 in 1898 to $5,360,139 in 1904.

In Hongkong, I found American flour controlling the market. I learned on inquiry that years before, a firm in Portland, Oregon, had sent an agent to introduce its flour. The rice-eating Chinese did not want it, but the agent stayed, gave away samples, explained its use and pushed his goods so energetically and persistently that after years of labour and the expenditure of tens of thousands of dollars a market was created. Now that firm sells in such enormous quantities that its numerous mills must run day and night to supply the demand, and the annual profits run into six figures. That city of Portland alone exported to Asia, chiefly China, in 1903:—

849,360 barrels flour	$2,974,620
522,887 bushels wheat	413,901
46,847,975 feet lumber	647,355
Miscellaneous merchandise	352,879

Total	$4,414,651

While cotton goods, kerosene oil and flour are our chief exports to China, there is a growing demand for many other American products. The utility of the American locomotive has become so apparent that in 1899, engines costing $732,212 were

---

27 "Returns of Trade for 1904," published by the Maritime Customs Department of China.

28 Year ending June, 1905.

sent to China and additional orders are received every few months. With the enormous forests bordering the Pacific Ocean in the states of Oregon and Washington, and with the development of cheap water transportation, there is a rapidly widening market in China for American lumber. Eastern Asia is too densely peopled to have large forests, and those she has are not within easy reach. Native lumber, therefore, is scarce and often small and crooked. That in common use comes from Manchuria and Korea. I was impressed in Tsing-tau to find that the Germans are using Oregon lumber and to be told that it is considered the best, and in the long run, the cheapest. Oregon pine costs more than the Korean and Manchurian, but it is superior in size and quality. The transportation charges to the interior, however, are a heavy addition. Manchurian pine can be delivered at such an interior city as Wei-hsien, via the junk port of Yang-chia-ko and thence by land, for twenty dollars, gold, per thousand square feet, which is considerably less than the Tsing-tau retail price for Asiatic lumber. Oregon lumber costs in Shanghai, thirty-two dollars gold, per thousand, but an importer estimated that it could be delivered at Tsingtau for twenty-five dollars gold per thousand in large quantities.

The exports of the United States to China, according to the reports of Consul-General Goodnow of Shanghai, increased from $11,081,146 in 1900 to $18,175,484 in 1901 and $22,698,282 in 1902, while for 1904 they reached the total of about $24,000,000, a gain of nearly 125 per cent. since 1900 and of several hundred per cent. as compared with 1894.

Meantime, the United States imported from China goods to the value of $30,872,244 in 1904, which is an increase of $14,255,956 over the imports for 1901. Silk and tea are the principal items in this trade, the figures for the former being $10,220,543 and for the latter $7,294,570, though of goatskins we took $2,556,541, wool $2,325,445, and matting $1,615,838. The United States is now the third nation in trade relations with China. This is the more remarkable when we consider the statement of the late Mr. Everett Frazar of the American Asiatic Association that in January, 1901, there were only four American business firms in all China. When our business men establish their own houses in China instead of dealing as now through European and Chinese firms, it is not unreasonable to expect that the United States will outstrip its larger rivals Great Britain and France, though, as I have already intimated, it is one thing to ship foreign goods to China and quite another thing to control them after their arrival, for the Chinese are disposed to manage that trade themselves and they know how to do it.

Unfortunately the stream of foreign trade with China has been contaminated by many of the vices which disgrace our civilization. The pioneer traders were, as a rule, pirates and adventurers, who cheated and abused the Chinese most flagrantly. Gorst says that "rapine, murder and a constant appeal to force chiefly characterized the commencement of Europe's commercial intercourse with China." There are many men of high character engaged in business in the great cities of China. I would not speak any disparaging word of those who are worthy of all respect. But it is all too evident that "many Americans and Europeans doing business in Asia are living the life of the prodigal son who has not yet come to himself." Profane, intemperate, immoral, not living among the Chinese, but segregating themselves in foreign communities in the treaty ports, not speaking the Chinese language, frequently beating and cursing those who are in their employ, regarding the Chinese with hatred and contempt,—it is no wonder that they are hated in return and that their conduct has done much to justify the Chinese distrust of the foreigner. The foreign settlements in the port cities of China are notorious for their profligacy. Intemperance and immorality, gambling and Sabbath desecration run riot. When after his return from a long journey in Asia, the Rev. Dr. George Pentecost was asked—"What are the darkest spots in the missionary outlook?" he replied:—

"In lands of spiritual darkness, it is difficult to speak of 'darkest spots.' I should say, however, that if there is a darkness more dark than other darkness, it is that which is cast into heathen darkness by the ungodliness of the American and European communities that have invaded the East for the sake of trade and empire. The corruption of Western godliness is the worst evil in the East. Of course there are noble exceptions among western commercial men and their families, but as a rule the European and American resident in the East is a constant contradiction to all and everything which the missionary stands for."

Most of the criticisms of missionaries which find their way into the daily papers emanate from such men. The missionaries do not gamble or drink whiskey, nor will their wives and daughters attend or reciprocate entertainments at which wine, cards and dancing are the chief features. So, of course, the missionaries are "canting hypocrites," and are believed to be doing no good, because the foreigner who has never visited a Chinese Christian Church, school or hospital in his life, does not see the evidences of missionary work in his immediate neighbourhood. The editor of the Japan Daily Mail justly says:—[29]

"We do not suggest that these newspapers which denounce the missionaries so vehemently desire to be unjust or have any suspicion that they are unjust. But we do assert that they have manifestly taken on the colour of that section of every far eastern community whose units, for some strange reason, entertain an inveterate prejudice against the missionary and his works. Were it possible for these persons to give an intelligent explanation of the dislike with which the missionary inspires them, their opinions would command more respect. But they have never succeeded in making any logical presentment of their case, and no choice offers except to regard them as the victims of an antipathy which has no basis in reason or reflection, That a man should be anti-Christian and should de-vote his pen to propagating his views is strictly within his right, and we must not be understood as suggesting that the smallest reproach attaches to such a person. But on the other hand, it is within the right of the missionary to protest against being arraigned before judges habitually hostile to him, and it is within the right of the public to scrutinize the pronouncements of such judges with much suspicion."

Charles Darwin did not hesitate to put the matter more bluntly still. He will surely not be deemed a prejudiced witness, but he plainly said of the traders and travellers who attack missionaries:—

"It is useless to argue against such reasoners. I believe that, disappointed in not finding the field of licentiousness quite so open as formerly, they will not give credit to a morality which they do not wish to practice, or to a religion which they undervalue or despise."

These facts are a suggestive commentary on the popular notion that civilization should precede Christianity. The Rev. Dr. James Stewart, the veteran missionary of South Africa, says that it is an "unpleasant and startling statement, unfortunately true, that contact with European nations seems always to have resulted in further deterioration of the African races...Trade and commerce have been on the West Coast of Africa for more than three centuries. What have they made of that region? Some of its tribes are more hopeless, more sunken morally and socially, and rapidly becoming more commercially valueless, than any tribes that may be found throughout the whole of the continent. Mere commercial influence by its example or its teaching during all that time has had little effect on the cruelty and reckless shedding of blood and the human sacrifices of the besotted paganism which still exists near that coast." Of his experience in New Guinea, James Chalmers declared:—"I have had twenty-one years' experience among natives. I have lived with the Christian native, and I have lived, and dined, and slept with cannibals. But I have never yet met with a single man or woman, or with a single people, that civilization without Christianity has civilized."

Substantially similar statements might be made regarding other lands.

"The more we open the world to what we call civilization, and the more education we give it of the kind we call scientific, the greater are the dangers to modern society, unless in some way we contrive to make all the world better. Brigands armed with repeating rifles and supplied with smokeless gunpowder are brigands still, but ten times more dangerous than before. The vaste hordes of human beings in Asia and Africa, so long as they are left in seclusion, are dangerous to their immediate neighbours; but, when they have railroads, steamboats, tariffs, and machine guns, while they retain their savage ideals and barbarous customs, they become dangerous to all the rest of the world."[30]

A Christless civilization is always and everywhere a curse rather than a blessing. From the Garden of Eden down, the fall of man has resulted from "the increase of knowledge and of power unaccompanied by reverence...No evolution is stable which neglects the moral factor or seeks to shake itself free from the eternal duties of obedience and of faith...The Song of Lamech echoes from a remote antiquity the savage truth that 'the first results of civilization are to equip hatred and render revenge more deadly,...a savage exultation in

30   Christian Register, December 3, 1903.

the fresh power of vengeance which all the novel instruments have placed in their inventor's hands."[31]

What is civilization without the gospel? The essential elements of our civilization are the fruits of Christianity, and the tree cannot be transplanted without its roots. Can a railroad or a plow convert a man? They can add to his material comfort; they can enlarge the opportunities of the gospel, but are they the gospel itself? What does civilization without Christianity mean? It means the lust of the European and American soldiers which is rotting the native Hawaiians, the European and American liquor which is debauching the Africans, the opium which is enervating the Chinese, 6,000 tons a year coming from India at a profit of $32,000,000 to the English Government.[32]

How can such a civilization prepare the way for Christianity? As a matter of fact, the Chinese already have a civilization, and if our civilization is considered apart from its distinctively Christian elements, it is not so much superior to the Chinese as we are apt to imagine. The differences are chiefly matters of taste and education. The truth is that always and everywhere,—

"civilization, so far from obliterating iniquity, imports into the world iniquities of its own. It changes to some degree the aspects of iniquity, but does not make them less. Further than that its effect is rather regularly to dress iniquity in a less repulsive and more attractive form, and in that way makes it more difficult to get rid of than before. There is no sin so insinuating as refined and elegant sin, and of that civilization is the expert patron and champion. The sin that is the devil's chief stock in trade is not what is going on in Hester Street, but on the polite avenues…Evangelization conducts to civilization, but civilization has no necessary bearing on evangelization; that is to say, there is in civilization no energy inherently calculated to yield gospel facts. By carrying schools and arts, trade and manufacture, among people that are now savages you may be able to refine the quality of their deviltry, but that is not even the first step towards making angels, or even saints of them."[33]

---

31   The Rev. Dr. George Adam Smith, D. D., "Yale Lectures," pp. 95-97.

32   The Rev. Dr. Henry van Dyke, Sermon.

33   The Rev. Dr. Charles H. Parkhurst, Sermon.

Lowell is said to have administered the following stinging rebuke to the skeptical critics who sneered about missionaries and declared the adequacy of civilization without them:—

"When the microscopic search of skepticism, which has hunted the heavens and sounded the seas to disprove the existence of a Creator, has turned its attention to human society and has found a place on this planet ten miles square where a decent man can live in decency, comfort and security, supporting and educating his children unspoiled and unpolluted; a place where age is reverenced, manhood respected, womanhood honoured, and human life held in due regard; when skeptics can find such a place ten miles square on this globe where the gospel of Christ has not gone and cleared the way, and laid the foundation and made decency and security possible, it will then be in order for the skeptical literati to move thither and there ventilate their views."

But we may add Darwin's conjecture that "should a voyager chance to be at the point of shipwreck on some unknown coast, he will devoutly pray that the lesson of the missionary may have extended thus far." Bishop Thoburn says that no nation without Christianity has ever advanced a step, and that while in Washington there are 6,000 models of plows invented by Americans, India is using the same plow as in the days of David and Solomon. But wherever Christ's gospel goes, true civilization appears. "A better soul will soon make better circumstances; but better circumstances will not necessarily make a better soul."[34]

> "We must be here to work,
> And men who work can only work for men,
> And not to work in vain must comprehend
> Humanity, and so work humanly,
> And raise men's bodies still by raising souls."

---

34   The Rev. Dr. James H. Snowden.

XI
THE BUILDING OF RAILWAYS[35]

THE extension of trade has naturally been accompanied not only by the increase of foreign steamship lines to the numerous port cities of China, but by the development of almost innumerable coastwise and river vessels. Many of these are owned and operated by the Chinese themselves, but as steamers came with the foreigners and as they drive out the native junks and bring beggary to their owners, the masses of the Chinese cannot be expected to feel kindly towards such competition, however desirable the steamer may appear to be from the view-point of a more disinterested observer. But this interference with native customs has been far less revolutionary than that of the railways.

The pressure of foreign commerce upon China has naturally resulted in demands for concessions to build railways, in order that the country might be opened up for traffic and the products of the interior be more easily and quickly brought to the coast. The first railroad in China was built by British promoters in 1876. It ran from Shanghai to Woosung, only fourteen miles. Great was the excitement of the populace, and no sooner was it completed than the Government bought it, tore up the road-bed, and dumped the engines into the river. That ended railway-building till 1881, when, largely through the influence of Wu Ting-fang, late Chinese Minister to the United States, the Chinese themselves, under

---

35 Part of this chapter appeared as an article in the American Monthly Review of Reviews, February, 1904.

the guidance of an English engineer, built a little line from the Kai-ping coal mines to Taku, at the mouth of the Pei-ho River and the ocean gate way to the capital. Seeing the benefit of this road, the Chinese raised further funds, borrowed more from the English, and gradually extended it 144 miles to Shan-hai Kwan on the north, while they ran another line to Tien-tsin, twenty-seven miles from Tong-ku, and thence onward seventy-nine miles direct to Peking. This system forms the Imperial Railway and belongs to the Chinese Government, though bonds are held by the English, who loaned money for construction, and though English and American engineers built and superintended the system. The local staff, however, is Chinese.

No more concessions were granted to foreigners till 1895, but then they were given so rapidly that, in 1899 when the Boxer Society first began to attract attention, there were, including the Imperial Railway, not only 566 miles in operation, but 6,000 miles were projected, and engineers were surveying rights of way through whole provinces. Much of the completed work was undone during the destructive madness of the Boxer uprising, but reconstruction began as soon as the tumult was quelled. According to the Archiv fur Eisenbahnwesen of Germany, the total length of the railways in use in 1903 in China was 1,236 kilometers or about 742 miles.

Several foreign nations have taken an aggressive part in this movement. In the north, Russia, not satisfied with a terminus at cold Vladivostok where ice closes the harbour nearly half the year, steadily demanded concessions which would enable her Trans-Siberian Railway to reach an ice-free winter port, and thus give her a commanding position in the Pacific and a channel through which the trade of northern Asia might reach and enrich Russia's vast possessions in Siberia and Europe. So Russian diplomacy rested not till it had secured the right to extend the Trans-Siberian Railway southward from Sungari through Manchuria to Tachi-chao near Mukden. From there one branch runs southward to Port Arthur and Dalny and another southwestward to Shan-hai Kwan, where the great Wall of China touches the sea. As connection is made at that point with the Imperial Railway to Taku, Tien-tsin and Peking, Moscow 5,746 miles away, is brought within seventeen days of Peking. Thus, Russian influence had an almost unrestricted entrance to China on the North, while a third branch from Mukden to Wiju, on the Korean frontier, will connect with a projected line running from that point southward to Seoul, the capital of Korea. A St. Petersburg dispatch, dated November 26, 1903, states that a survey has just been completed from Kiakhta, Siberia, to Peking by way of Gugon, a distance of about a thousand miles. This road, if built, will give the Russians a short cut direct to the capital.

In the populous province of Shantung, a German railroad, opened April 8, 1901, runs from Tsing-tau on Kiao-chou Bay into the heart of the populous Shantung Province via Weihsien. The line already reaches the capital, Chinan-fu, while ulterior plans include a line from Tsing-tau via Ichou-fu to Chinan-fu, so that German lines will ere long completely encircle this mighty Province. At Chinan-fu, this road will meet another great trunk line, partly German and partly English, which is being pushed southward from Tien-tsin to Chin-kiang. An English sydicate, known as the British-Chinese Corporation, is to control a route from Shanghai via Soochow and Chin-kiang to Nanking and Soochow via Hangchow to Ningpo, while the Anglo-Chinese Railway Syndicate of London is said to be planning a railway from Canton to Cheng-tu-fu, the provincial capital of Sze-chuen. Meanwhile, the original line from Shanghai to Wu-sung has been reconstructed by the English.

One of the most valuable concessions in China has been obtained by the Anglo-Italian Syndicate in the Provinces of Shan-si and Shen-si for it gives the right to construct railways and to operate coal mines in a region where some of the most extensive anthracite deposits in the world are located. A beginning has already been made, and when the lines are completed, the industrial revolution in China will be mightily advanced.

An alleged Belgian syndicate, to which was formed with then wholly disinterested assistance of the French and Russian legations, obtained in 1896 a concession to construct the Lu Han Railway from Peking 750 miles southward to Hankow, the commercial metropolis on the middle Yang-tze River. It is significant, however, that while the Belgian syndicate was temporarily embarrassed, the Russo-Chinese Bank of Peking aided the Chinese Director-General of Railways to begin the section running from Peking to Paoting-fu. The road is open to Shunte-fu, 300 miles south of Peking and to Hsu-chou, 434 kilometers north of Hankow. The Russo-Chinese Bank is building a branch line from Ching-ting via Tai-yuen-fu to

Singan-fu in Shen-si, where it will be well started on the beaten caravan route between north China and Russian Central Asia. On November 13, 1903, the Belgian International Eastern Company signed a contract to construct a railway from Kai-feng-fu, the capital of the Province of Honan, 110 miles west to Honan-fu.

I found the line running south from Peking well-built with solid road-bed, massive stone culverts, iron bridges, and heavy steel rails. The first and second class coaches are not attractive in appearance, and though the fare for the former is double that of the latter, the chief discernible difference is that in the first class compartment, which is usually in one end of a second-class car, the seats are curved and the passengers fewer in number, while in the second-class the seats are straight boards and are apt to be crowded with Chinese coolies. Neither class is upholstered and neither would be considered comfortable in America, but after the weeks I had spent in a mule-litter, anything on rails seemed luxurious. Our train was a mixed one,—the first-class compartments containing a few French officers, the second-class filled with Chinese coolies and French soldiers, while a half-dozen flat cars were loaded with horses and mules. A large Roger's locomotive from Paterson, New Jersey, drew our long train smoothly and easily, though the schedule was so slow and the stops so long that we were seven hours and a half in making a run of a hundred miles.

Railway-building in South China, outside of French territory, began with a line from Canton to Hankow which was projected in 1895 by Senator Calvin S. Brice, William Barclay Parsons being the engineer. The usual governmental difficulties were encountered, but in 1902 an imperial decree gave the concession to the American-China Development Company. American capital was to finance the road, though with some European aid. The company had the power, under its concession, to issue fifty-year five per cent. gold bonds to the amount of $42,500,000, the interest being guaranteed by the Chinese Government. The main line will be 700 miles long, and branches will increase the total mileage to 900. On November 15, 1903, a section ten miles long from Canton to Fat-shan was formally opened for traffic in the presence of the Hon. Francis May, colonial secretary and registrar-general of the Hongkong Government, a large number of Europeans and Americans, and immense crowds of Chinese who manifested their excitement by an almost incessant rattle of fire-crackers. By October, 1904, trains were running regularly to Sam-shui, about twenty-five miles beyond Fat-shan. This is a branch line. The main line will run on the other side of the West River. In 1905, the government decided to complete the line itself and cancelled the concession, paying the company as indemnity $6,750,000. A line from Kowloon to Canton has been planned for some time and it is likely to be hastened by the announcement in the South China Morning Post, May 12, 1904, that an American-Chinese syndicate had obtained a concession, granted to the authorities of Macao by China through a special Portuguese Minister, to construct a railway from Macao to Canton. The syndicate hopes to secure American capital and the British merchants of Hongkong are a little nervous as they think of the possibility of an independent outlet for the Canton-Hankow Railway at Macao.

It will thus be seen that if these vast schemes can be realized there will not only be numerous lines running from the coast into the interior, but a great trunk line from Canton through the very heart of the Empire to Peking, where other roads can be taken not only to Manchuria and Korea but to any part of Europe.

In the farther south, the French are equally busy. By the Franco-Chinese Convention of June 20, 1895, a French company secured the right to construct a railroad from Lao-kai to Yun-nan-fu. The French had a road from Hai-fong in Tong-king to Sang-chou at the Chinese frontier, and in 1896 they obtained from China a concession to extend it to Nanning-fu, on the West River. This privilege has since been enlarged so that the line will be continued to the treaty port of Pak-hoi on the Gulf of Tong-king. The French fondly dream of the time when they can extend their Yun-nan Railway northward till it taps and makes tributary to French Indo-China the vast and fertile valley of the upper Yang-tze River. Meanwhile, the English talk of a line from Kowloon, opposite Hongkong, to Canton, and of connecting their Burma Railroad, which already runs from Rangoon to Kun-long ferry, with the Yang-tze valley, so that the enormous trade of southern interior China may not flow into a French port, as the French so ardently desire, but into an English city.

It would be impossible to describe adequately the far-reaching effect upon China and the Chinese of this extension of modern railways. We have had an illustration of its meaning in America, where the transcontinental railroads resulted in the amazing development of our western plains and of the Pacific Coast. The effect of such a development in China can hardly be overestimated, for China has more than ten times the population of the trans-Mississippi region while its territory is vaster and equally rich in natural resources. As I travelled through the land, it seemed to me that almost the whole northern part of the Empire was composed of illimitable fields of wheat and millet, and that in the south the millions of paddy plots formed a rice-field of continental proportions. Hidden away in China's mountains and underlying her boundless plateaus are immense deposits of coal and iron; while above any other country on the globe, China has the labour for the development of agriculture and manufacture. Think of the influence not only upon the Chinese but the whole world, when railroads not only carry the corn of Hunan to the famine sufferers in Shantung, but when they bring the coal, iron and other products of Chinese soil and industry within reach of steamship lines running to Europe and America. To make all these resources available to the rest of the world, and in turn to introduce among the 426,000,000 of the Chinese the products and inventions of Europe and America, is to bring about an economic transformation of stupendous proportions.

Imagine, too, what changes are involved in the substitution of the locomotive for the coolie as a motive power, the freight car for the wheelbarrow in the shipment of produce, and the passenger coach for the cart and the mule-litter in the transportation of people. Railways will inevitably inaugurate in China a new era, and when a new era is inaugurated for one-third of the human race the other two-thirds are certain to be affected in many ways.

That the transformation is attended by outbreaks of violence is natural enough. Even such a people as the English and the Scotch were at first inimical to railroads, and it is notorious that the great Stephenson had to meet not only ridicule but strenuous opposition. Everybody knows, too, that in the United States stage companies and stage drivers did all they could to prevent the building of railroads, and that learned gentlemen made eloquent speeches which proved to the entire satisfaction of their authors that railways would disarrange all the conditions of society and business and bring untold evils in their train. If the alert and progressive Anglo-

Saxon took this initial position, is it surprising that it should be taken with far greater intensity by Orientals who for uncounted centuries have plodded along in perfect contentment, and who now find that the whole order of living to which they and their fathers have become adapted is being shaken to its foundation by the iron horse of the foreigner? Millions of coolies earn a living by carrying merchandise in baskets or wheeling it in barrows at five cents a day. A single railroad train does the work of a thousand coolies, and thus deprives them of their means of support. Myriads of farmers grew the beans and peanuts out of which illuminating oil was made. But since American kerosene was introduced in 1864, its use has become well-nigh universal, and the families who depended upon the bean-oil and peanut-oil market are starving. Cotton clothing is generally worn in China, except by the better classes, and China formerly made her own cotton cloth. Now American manufacturers can sell cotton in China cheaper than the Chinese can make it themselves.

All this is, of course, inevitable. It is indeed for the best interests of the people of China themselves, but it enables us to understand why so many of the Chinese resent the introduction of foreign goods. That much of this business is passing into the hands of the Chinese themselves does not help the matter, for the people know that the goods are foreign, and that the foreigners are responsible for their introduction.

Nor are racial prejudices and vested interests the only foes which the railway has to encounter in China. As we have seen, the Chinese, while not very religious, are very superstitious. They people the earth and air with spirits, who, in their judgment, have baleful power over man. Before these spirits they tremble in terror, and no inconsiderable part of their time and labour is devoted to outwitting them, for the Chinese do not worship the spirits, except to propitiate and deceive them. They believe that the spirits cannot turn a corner, but must move in a straight line. Accordingly, in China you do not often find one window opposite another window, lest the spirits may pass through. You will seldom find a straight road from one village to another village, but only a distractingly circuitous path, while the roads are not only crooked, but so atrociously bad that it is difficult for the foreign traveller to keep his temper. The Chinese do not count their own inconvenience if they can only baffle their demoniac foes. It is the custom of the Chinese to bury their dead wherever a geomancer indicates a "lucky" place. So particular are they about this that the bodies of the wealthy are often kept for a considerable period while a suitable place of interment is being found. In Canton there is a spacious enclosure where the coffins sometimes lie for years, each in a room more or less elaborate according to the taste or ability of the family. The place once chosen immediately becomes sacred. In a land which has been so densely populated for thousands of years, graves are therefore not only innumerable but omnipresent. In my travels in China, I was hardly ever out of sight of these conical mounds of the dead, and as a rule I could count hundreds of them from my shendza.

Every visitor to Canton and Chefoo will recall the hilly regions just outside of the old city walls that are literally covered with graves, those of the richer classes being marked by small stone or brick amphitheatres. Yet these are cemeteries not because they have been set apart for that purpose, but because graves have gradually filled all available spaces.

The Chinese reverence their dead and venerate the spots in which they lie. From a Chinese view-point it is an awful thing to desecrate them. Not only property and those sacred feelings with which all peoples regard their dead are involved but also the vital religious question of ancestral worship. Accordingly Chinese law protects all graves by heavy sanctions, imposing the death penalty by strangling on the malefactor who opens a grave without the permission of the owner, and by decapitation if in doing so the coffin is opened or broken so as to expose the body to view. Imagine then their feelings when they see haughty foreigners run a railroad straight as an arrow from city to city, opening a highway over which the dreaded spirits may run, and ruthlessly tearing through the tombs hallowed by the most sacred associations.

No degree of care can avoid the irritations caused by railway construction. In building the line from Tsing-tau to Kiao-chou, a distance of forty-six miles, the Germans, as far as practicable, ran around the places most thickly covered with graves. But in spite of this, no less than 3,000 graves had to be removed. It was impossible to settle with the individual owners, as it was difficult in many cases to ascertain who they were, most of the graves being unmarked, and some of the families concerned having died out or moved away. Moreover, the Oriental has no idea of time, and dearly loves to haggle, especially with a foreigner whom he feels no compunction in swindling. So the railway company made its negotiations with the local magistrates, showing them the routes, indicating the graves that were in the way, and paying them an average of $3 (Mexican) for removing each grave, they to find and settle with the owners. This was believed to be fair, for $3 is a large sum where the coin in common circulation is the copper "cash," so small in value that 1,600 of them equal a gold dollar, and where a few dozen cash will buy a day's food for an adult. But while some of the Chinese were glad to accept this arrangement, others were not. They wanted more, or they had special affection for the dead, or that particular spot had been carefully selected because it was favoured by the spirits. Besides, the magistrates doubtless kept a part of the price as their share. Chinese officials are underpaid, are expected to "squeeze" commissions, and no funds can pass through their hands without a percentage of loss. Then, as the Asiatic is very deliberate, the company was obliged to specify a date by which all designated graves must be removed. As many of the bodies were not taken up within that time, the company had to remove them.

In these circumstances, we should not be surprised that some of the most furiously anti-foreign feeling in China was in the villages along the line of that railroad. Why should the hated foreigner force his line through their country when the people did not want it? Of course, it would save time, but, as an official naively said, "We are not in a hurry." So the villagers watched the construction with ill-concealed anger, and to-day that railroad, as well as most other railroads in North China, can only be kept open by detachments of foreign soldiers at all the important stations. I saw them at almost every stop,—German soldiers from Tsing-tau to Kiao-chou, British from Tong-ku to Peking, French from Peking to Paoting-fu, etc.

Nevertheless, railways in China are usually profitable. It is true that the opposition to the building of a railroad is apt to be bitter, that mobs are occasionally destructive, and that locomotives and other rolling stock rapidly deteriorate under native handling unless closely watched by foreign superintendents. But, on the other hand, the Government is usually forced to pay indemnities for losses resulting from violence. The road, too, once built, is in time appreciated by the thrifty Chinese, who swallow their prejudices and patronize it in such enormous numbers, and ship by it such quantities of their produce, that the business speedily becomes remunerative, while the population and the resources of the country are so great as to afford almost unlimited opportunity for the development of traffic.

As a rule, on all the roads, the first-class compartments, when there are any, have comparatively few passengers, chiefly officials and foreigners. The second-class cars are well filled with respectable-looking people, who are apparently small merchants, students, minor officials, etc. The third-class cars, which are usually more numerous, are packed with chattering peasants. The first-class fares are about the same as ordinary rates in the United States. The second-class are about half the first-class rates, and the third-class are often less than the equivalent of a cent a mile. This is a wise adjustment in a land where the average man is so thrifty and so poor that he would not and could not pay a price which would be deemed moderate in America, and where his scale of living makes him content with the rudest accommodations. Very little baggage is carried free, twenty pounds only on the German lines, so that excess baggage charges amount to more than in America.

The freight cars, during my visit, were, for the most part, loaded with the materials and supplies necessitated by the work of railway-construction and by the extensive rebuilding of the native and foreign property which had been destroyed by the Boxers. But in normal conditions the railways carry inland a large number of foreign manufactured articles, and in turn bring to the ports the wheat, rice, peanuts, ore, coal, pelts, silk, wool, cotton, matting, paper, straw-braid, earthenware, sugar, tea, tobacco, fireworks, fruit, vegetables, and other products of the interior. Short hauls are the rule, thus far, both for passengers and freight. This is partly because the long-distance lines within the Empire are not yet completed, and partly because the typical Chinese of the lower classes in the interior provinces has never been a score of miles away from his native village in his life, and has been so accustomed to regard a wheelbarrow trip of a dozen miles as a long journey that he is a little cautious, at first, in lengthening his radius of movement. But he soon learns, especially as the struggle for existence in an overcrowded country begets a desire to take advantage of an opportunity to better his condition elsewhere. Once fairly started, he is apt to go far, as the numbers of Chinese in Siam, the Philippines, and America clearly show. The literary and official classes are less apt to go abroad, but they are more accustomed to moving about within the limits of the Empire, as they must go to the central cities for their examinations, and as offices are held for such short terms that magistrates are frequently shifted from province to province. When this vast population of naturally industrious and commercial people becomes accustomed to railways and gets to moving freely upon them, stupendous things are likely to happen, both for China and for the world.

And so the foreign syndicates relentlessly continue the work of railway-construction. Trade cannot be checked. It advances by an inherent energy which it is futile to ignore. And it ought to advance for the result will inevitably be to the advantage of China. A locomotive brings intellectual and physical benefits, the appliances which mitigate the poverty and barrenness of existence and increase the ability to provide for the necessities and the comforts of life. In one of our great locomotive works in America I once saw twelve engines in construction for China, and my imagination kindled as I thought what a locomotive means amid that stagnant swarm of humanity, how impossible it is that any village through which it has once run should continue to be what it was before, how its whistle puts to flight a whole brood of hoary superstitions and summons a long-slumbering people to new life. We need regret only that these benefits are so often accompanied by the evils which disgrace our civilization.

PART III

THE POLITICAL FORCE AND THE NATIONAL PROTEST

XII
THE AGGRESSIONS OF
EUROPEAN POWERS

THE political force was set in motion partly by the ambitions of European powers to extend their influence in Asia, and partly by the necessity for protecting the commercial interests referred to in the preceding chapters. The conservatism and exclusiveness of the Chinese, the disturbance of economic conditions caused by the introduction of foreign goods, and the greed and brutality of foreign traders combined to arouse a fierce opposition to the lodgment of the foreigner. The early trading ships were usually armed, and exasperated by the haughtiness and duplicity of the Chinese officials and their greedy disposition to mulct the white trader, they did not hesitate to use force in effecting their purpose.

But the nations of Europe, becoming more and more convinced of the magnitude of the Chinese market, pressed resolutely on; and with the hope of creating a better understanding and of opening the ports to trade, they sent envoys to China. The arrival of these envoys precipitated a new controversy, for the Chinese Government from time immemorial considered itself the supreme government of the world, and, not being accustomed to receive the agents of other nations except as inferiors, was not disposed to accord the white man any different treatment. The result was a series of collisions followed by territorial aggressions that were numerous enough to infuriate a more peaceably disposed people than the Chinese.

The Portuguese were the first to come, a ship of those venturesome traders appearing near Canton in 1516. Its reception was kindly, but when the next year brought eight armed vessels and an envoy, the friendliness of the Chinese changed to suspicion which ripened into hostility when the Portuguese became overbearing and threatening. Violence met with violence. It is said that armed parties of Portuguese went into villages and carried off Chinese women. Feuds multiplied and became more bloody. At Ningpo, the Chinese made awful reprisal by destroying thirty-five Portuguese ships and killing 800 of their crews. The execution of one or more of the members of a delegation to Peking brought matters to a crisis, and in 1534, the Portuguese transferred their factories to Macao, which they have ever since held, though it was not till 1887 that their position there was officially recognized. Portuguese power has waned and Macao to-day is an unimportant place politically, but it is significant that this early foreign settlement in China has been and still is such a moral plague spot that the Chinese may be pardoned if their first impressions of the white man were unfavourable.

The Spaniards were the next Europeans with whom the Chinese came into contact. In this case, however, the contact was due not so much to the coming of the Spaniards to China as to their occupation in 1543 of the Philippine Islands, with which the Chinese had long traded and where they had already settled in considerable numbers. Mutual jealousies resulted and Castilian arrogance and brutality ere long engendered such bitterness that massacre after massacre of the Chinese occurred, that of 1603 almost exterminating the Chinese population of Manila.

The growing demand for coffee, which Europeans had first received in 1580 from Arabia, brought Dutch ships into Asiatic waters in 1598. After hostile experiences with the Portuguese at Macao, they seized the Pescadores Islands in 1622. But the opposition of the Chinese led the Dutch to withdraw to Formosa, where their stormy relations with natives, Chinese from the mainland and Japanese finally resulted in their expulsion in 1662. Since then the Dutch have contented themselves with a few trading factories chiefly at Canton and with their possessions in Malaysia, so that they have been less aggressive in China than several other European nations.

A more formidable power appeared on the scene in 1635, when four ships[36] of the English East India Company sailed up the Pearl River. The temper of the newcomers was quickly shown when the Chinese, incited by the jealous Portuguese, sought to prevent their lodgment, for the English, so the record quaintly runs, "did on a sudden display their bloody ensigns, and…each ship began to play furiously upon the forts with their broadsides…put on board all their ordnance, fired the council-house, and demolished all they could." Then they sailed on to Canton, and when their peremptory demand for trading privileges was met with evasion and excuses, they "pillaged and burned many vessels and villages…spreading destruction with fire and sword." Describing this incident, Sir George Staunton, Secretary of the first British embassy to China, naively remarked—"The unfortunate circumstances under which the English first got footing in China must have operated to their disadvantage and rendered their situation for some time peculiarly unpleasant."[37] But as early as 1684, they had established themselves in Canton.

June 15, 1834, a British Commission headed by Lord Napier arrived at Macao, and the 25th of the same month proceeded to Canton empowered by an act of Parliament to negotiate with the Chinese regarding trade "to and from the dominions of the Emperor of China, and for the purpose of protecting and promoting such trade."[38] The government of Canton, however, refused to receive Lord Napier's letter for the character-istic reason that it did not purport to be a petition from an inferior to a superior. In explaining the matter to the Hong merchants with a view to their bringing the explanation to the attention of Lord Napier, the haughty Governor reminded them that foreigners were allowed in China only as trading agents, and that no functionary of any political rank could be allowed to enter the Empire unless special permission were given by the Imperial Government in response to a respectful petition. He added:—

---

36 Parker, "China," p. 9, places the number of ships at five and the date as 1637.

37 Foster, "American Diplomacy in the Orient," p. 5.

38 Foster, p. 57.

"To sum up the whole matter, the nation has its laws. Even England has its laws. How much more the Celestial Empire! How flaming bright are its great laws and ordinances. More terrible than the awful thunderbolts! Under this whole bright heaven, none dares to disobey them. Under its shelter are the four seas. Subject to its soothing care are ten thousand kingdoms. The said barbarian eye (Lord Napier), having come over a sea of several myriads of miles in extent to examine and have superintendence of affairs, must be a man thoroughly acquainted with the principles of high dignity."[39]

As might be expected, the equally haughty British representative indignantly protested; but without avail. He was asked to return to Macao, and was informed that the Governor could not have any further communication with him except through the Hong merchants, and in the form of a respectful petition. The Governor indignantly declared:—

"There has never been such a thing as outside barbarians sending a letter...It is contrary to everything of dignity and decorum. The thing is most decidedly impossible...The barbarians of this nation (Great Britain) coming to or leaving Canton have beyond their trade not any public business; and the commissioned officers of the Celestial Empire never take cognizance of the trivial affairs of trade...The some hundreds of thousands of commercial duties yearly coming from the said nation concern not the Celestial Empire to the extent of a hair or a feather's down. The possession or absence of them is utterly unworthy of one careful thought."[40]

Whereupon the proud Briton published and distributed a review of the case, as he saw it, which closed as follows:—

"Governor Loo has the assurance to state in the edict of the 2d instant that 'the King (my master) has hitherto been reverently obedient.' I must now request you to declare to them (the Hong merchants) that His Majesty, the King of England, is a great and powerful monarch, that he rules over an extent of territory in the four quarters of the world more comprehensive in space and infinitely more so in power than the whole empire of China; that he commands armies of bold and fierce soldiers, who have conquered wherever they went; and that he is possessed of great

39   Foster, p. 59.
40   Ibid, p. 60.

ships, where no native of China has ever yet dared to show his face. Let the Governor then judge if such a monarch will be 'reverently obedient' to any one."[41]

The result of the increasing irritation was a decree by the Governor of Canton peremptorily forbidding all further trade with the English, and in retaliation the landing of a British force, the sailing of British war-ships up the river and a battle at the Bogue Forts which guarded the entrance of Canton. A truce was finally arranged and Lord Napier's commission left for Macao, August 21st, where he died September 11th of an illness which his physician declared was directly due to the nervous strain and the many humiliations which he had suffered in his intercourse with the Chinese authorities. The Governor meantime complacently reported to Peking that he had driven off the barbarians!

The strain was intensified by the determination of the British to bring opium into China. The Chinese authorities protested and in 1839 the Chinese destroyed 22,299 chests of opium valued at $9,000,000, from motives about as laudable as those which led our revolutionary sires to empty English tea into Boston Harbor. England responded by making war, the result of which was to force the drug upon an unwilling people, so that the vice which is to-day doing more to ruin the Chinese than all other vices combined is directly traceable to the conduct of a Christian nation, though the England of to-day is presumably ashamed of this crime of the England of two generations ago.

It would, however, be inaccurate to represent Chinese objection to British opium as the sole cause of the "Opium War" of 1840, for the indignities to which foreign traders and foreign diplomats were continually subjected in their efforts to establish commercial and political relations with the Chinese were rapidly drifting the two nations into war. Still, it was peculiarly unfortunate and it put foreigners grievously in the wrong before the Chinese that the overt act which developed the long-gathering bitterness into open rupture was the righteous if irregular seizure by the Chinese of a poison that the English from motives of unscrupulous greed were determined to force upon an unwilling people. The probability that war would have broken out in time even if there had been no dispute about opium

41   Foster, pp. 61, 62.

does not mitigate the fact that from the beginning, foreign intercourse with China was so identified with an iniquitous traffic that the Chinese had ample cause to distrust and dislike the white man.

This hostility was intensified when the war resulted in the defeat of the Chinese and the treaty of Nanking in 1842 with its repudiation of all their demands, the compulsory cession of the island of Hongkong, the opening of not only Canton but Amoy, Foochow, Shanghai, and Ningpo as treaty ports, the location of a British Consul in each port, and, most necessary but most humiliating of all, the recognition of the extra-territorial rights of all foreigners so that no matter what their crime, they could not be tried by Chinese courts but only by their own consuls. This treaty contributed so much to the opening of China that Dr. S. Wells Williams characterized it as "one of the turning points in the history of mankind, involving the welfare of all nations in its wide-reaching consequences." It was therefore a lasting benefit to China and to the world. But the Chinese did not then and do not yet appreciate the benefit, especially as they saw clearly enough that the motive of the conqueror was his own aggrandizement.

Unhappily, too, the next war between England and China, though fundamentally due to the same conditions as the "Opium War," was again precipitated by a quarrel over opium, the lorcha Arrow loaded with the obnoxious drug and flying the British flag being seized by the Chinese. Once more they suffered sore defeat and humiliating terms of peace in the treaty of 1858. The effort of the Peking Government to close the Pei-ho River against an armed force caused a third war in 1860 in which the British and French captured Peking, and by their excesses and cruelties still further added to the already long list of reasons why the Chinese should hate their European foes.

Nor did foreign aggression stop with this war. In 1861, England, in order to protect her interests at Hongkong, wrested from China the adjacent peninsula of Kowloon. In 1886, she took Upper Burma, which China regarded as one of her dependencies. In 1898, finding that Hongkong was still within the range of modern cannon in Chinese waters seven miles away, England calmly took 400 square miles of additional territory, including Mirs and Deep Bays.

The visitor does not wonder that the British coveted Hongkong, for it is one of the best harbours in the world. Certainly no other is more impressive. Noble hills, almost mountains, for many are over 1,000 feet and the highest is 3,200, rise on every side. Crafts of all kinds, from sampans and slipper-boats to ocean liners and war-ships, crowd the waters, for this is the third greatest port in the world, being exceeded in the amount of its tonnage only by Liverpool and New York. The city is very attractive from the water as it lies at the foot and on the slopes of the famous Peak. The Chinese are said to number, as in Shanghai, over 300,000, while the foreign population is only 5,000. But to the superficial observer the proportions appear reversed as the foreign buildings are so spa-cious and handsome that they almost fill the foreground. The business section of the city is hot and steaming, but an inclined tramway makes the Peak accessible and many of the British merchants have built handsome villas on that cooler, breezier summit, 1,800 feet above the sea. The view is superb, a majestic panorama of mountains, harbour, shipping, islands, ocean and city. By its possession and fortification of this island of Hongkong, England to-day so completely controls the gateway to South China that the Chinese cannot get access to Canton, the largest city in the Empire, without running the gauntlet of British guns and mines which could easily sink any ships that the Peking Government could send against it, and the whole of the vast and populous basin of the Pearl or West River is at the mercy of the British whenever they care to take it. When we add to these invaluable holdings, the rights that England has acquired in the Yang-tze Valley and at Wei-hai Wei in Shantung, we do not wonder that Mr. E. H. Parker, formerly British Consul at Kiung-Chou, rather naively remarks:—

"In view of all this, no one will say, however much in matters of detail we may have erred in judgment, that Great Britain has failed to secure for herself, on the whole, a considerable number of miscellaneous commercial and political advantages from the facheuse situation arising out of an attitude on the part of the Chinese so hostile to progress."[42]

France, as far back as 1787, obtained the Peninsula of Tourane and the Island of Pulu Condore by "treaty" with the King of Cochin-China. The French soon began to regard Annam as within their sphere of influence. In 1858, they seized Saigon and from it as a base extended French power throughout Cochin-China

---

42　"China," pp. 95, 96.

and Cambodia, the treaty of 1862 giving an enforced legal sanction to these extensive claims. Not content with this, France steadily pushed her conquests northward, compelling one concession after another until in 1882, she coolly decided to annex Tong-king. The Chinese objected, but the war ended in a treaty, signed June 9, 1885, which gave France the coveted region. These vast regions, which China had for centuries regarded as tributary provinces, are now virtually French territory and are openly governed as such.

The beginnings of Russia's designs upon China are lost in the haze of mediaeval antiquity. Russian imperial guards are frequently mentioned at the Mongol Court of Peking in the thirteenth century.[43] In 1652, the Russians definitely began their struggle with the Manchus for the Valley of the Amur, a struggle which in spite of temporary defeats and innumerable disputes Russia steadily and relentlessly continued until she obtained the Lower Amur in 1855, the Ussuri district in 1860 and finally, by the Cassini Convention of September, 1896, the right to extend the Siberian Railway from Nerchinsk through Manchuria. How Russia pressed her aggressions in this region we shall have occasion to note in a later chapter.

43   Parker, "China," p. 96.

XIII
THE UNITED STATES AND CHINA

THE relations of the United States with China have, as a rule, been more sympathetic than those of European nations. Americans have not sought territorial advantage in China and on more than one occasion, our Government has exerted its influence in favour of peace and justice for the sorely beset Celestials.

The flag of the United States first appeared in Chinese waters on a trading ship in 1785. From the beginning, Americans had less trouble with the Chinese than Europeans had experienced, partly because they had recently been at war with the English whom the Chinese hated and feared, and partly because they were less violently aggressive in dealing with the Chinese. By the treaties of July and October, 1844, the United States peacefully reaped the advantages which England had obtained at the cost of war. November 17, 1856, two American ships were fired upon by the Bogue Forts, but in spite of the hostilities which resulted, the representatives of the United States appeared to find more favour with the Chinese than those of any other power in the negotiations at Tien-tsin in 1858, and their treaty was signed a week before those of the French and the British. Article X provided that the "United States shall have the right to appoint consuls and other commercial agents, to reside at such places in the dominions of China as shall be agreed to be opened"; and Article XXX that,

"should at any time the Ta-Tsing Empire grant to any nation or the merchants or citizens of any nation any right, privileges or favour connected with either navigation, commerce, political or other intercourse which is not conferred by this treaty, such right, privilege and favour shall at once freely inure to the benefit of the United States, its public officers, merchants and citizens."

In the settlement of damages, the Chinese agreed to pay to the United States half a million taels, then worth $735,288. When the adjustments with individual claimants left a balance of $453,400 in the treasury, Congress, to the unbounded and grateful surprise of the Chinese, gave it back to them. Mr. Burlingame, the celebrated United States Minister to China, became the most popular foreign minister in Peking within a short time after his arrival in 1862, and so highly did the Chinese Government appreciate his efforts in its behalf that during the American Civil War it promptly complied with his request to issue an edict forbidding all Confederate ships of war from entering Chinese ports. Mr. Foster declares that "such an order enforced by the governments of Europe would have saved the American commercial marine from destruction and shortened the Civil War."[44]

The treaty of Washington in 1868 gave great satisfaction to the Chinese Government as it contained pacific and, appreciative references to China, an express disclaimer of any designs upon the Empire and a willingness to admit Chinese to the United States. The treaty of 1880, however, considerably modified this willingness and the treaty of 1894 rather sharply restricted further immigration. But in the commercial treaty of 1880, the United States, at the request of the Chinese Government, agreed to a clause peremptorily forbidding any citizen of the United States from engaging in the opium traffic with the Chinese or in any Chinese port.

Our national policy was admirably expressed in the note sent by the Hon. Frederick F. Low, United States Minister at Peking, to the Tsung-li Yamen, March 20, 1871:—

"To assure peace in the future, the people must be better informed of the purposes of foreigners. They must be taught that merchants are engaged in trade which cannot but be beneficial to both native and foreigner, and that missionaries seek only the welfare of the people, and are engaged in no political plots or intrigues against the Government. Whenever cases occur in which the missionaries overstep the bounds of decorum, or interfere in

---

44   Foster, "American Diplomacy in the Orient," p. 259.

matters with which they have no proper concern, let each case be reported promptly to the Minister of the country to which it belongs. Such isolated instances should not produce prejudice or engender hatred against those who observe their obligations, nor should sweeping complaints be made against all on this account. Those from the United States sincerely desire the reformation of those whom they teach, and to do this they urge the examination of the Holy Scriptures, wherein the great doctrines of the present and a future state, and also the resurrection of the soul, are set forth, with the obligation of repentance, belief in the Saviour, and the duties of man to himself and others. It is owing, in a great degree, to the prevalence of a belief in the truth of the Scnptures that Western nations have attained their power and prosperity. To enlighten the people is a duty which the officials owe to the people, to foreigners, and themselves; for if, in consequence of ignorance, the people grow discontented, and insurrection and riots occur, and the lives and property of foreigners are destroyed or imperilled, the Government cannot escape its responsibility for these unlawful acts."

Referring to this note, the Hon. J. C. B. Davis, acting Secretary of State, wrote to Mr. Low, October 19, 1871:—

"The President regards it (your note to the Tsung-li Yamen) as wise and judicious…Your prompt and able answer to these propositions leaves little to be said by the Department…We stand upon our treaty rights; we ask no more, we expect no less. If other nations demand more, if they advance pretensions inconsistent with the dignity of China as an independent Power, we are no parties to such acts. Our influence, so far as it may be legitimately and peacefully exerted, will be used to prevent such demands or pretensions, should there be serious reason to apprehend that they will be put forth. We feel that the Government of the Emperor is actuated by friendly feelings towards the United States."

But while the Government of the United States has been thus considerate and just in its dealings with the Chinese in China, it has, singularly enough, been most inconsiderate and unjust in its treatment of Chinese in its own territory, and its policy in this respect has done not a little to exasperate the Chinese. The Chinese began to come to America in 1848, when two men and one woman arrived in San Francisco on the brig Eagle. The discovery of gold soon brought multitudes, the year 1852 alone seeing 2,026 arrivals. There are now about 45,000 Chinese in California and 14,000 in Oregon and Washington. New York has about 6,300 Chinese, Philadelphia 1,150, Boston 1,250, and many other cities have little groups, while individual Chinese are scattered all over the country, though the total for the United States, excluding Alaska and Hawaii, is only 89,863.

The attitude of the people of the Pacific coast towards the the Chinese is an interesting study. At first, they welcomed their Oriental visitors. In January, 1853, the Hon. H. H. Haight, afterwards Governor of California, offered at a representative meeting of San Francisco citizens this resolution—"Resolved that we regard with pleasure the presence of greater numbers of these people (Chinese) among us as affording the best opportunity of doing them good and through them of exerting our influence in their native land." And this resolution was unanimously adopted. Moreover in a new country, where there was much manual labour to be done in developing resources and constructing railways, and where there were comparatively few white labourers, the Chinese speedily proved to be a valuable factor. They were frugal, patient, willing, industrious and cheap, and so the corporations in particular encouraged them to come.

But as the number of immigrants increased, first dislike, then irritation and finally alarm developed, particularly among the working classes who found their means of livelihood threatened by the competition of cheaper labour. The newspapers began to give sensational accounts of the "yellow deluge" that might "swamp our institutions" and to enlarge upon the danger that white labourers would not come to California on account of the presence of Chinese. The "sand lot orator" appeared with his frenized harangues and the political demagogue sought favour with the multitudes by pandering to their passions. Race prejudice, moreover, must always be taken into account, especially when two races attempt to live together. The terms Jew and Gentile, Greek and barbarian, Roman and enemy are suggestive of the distrust with which one race usually regards another. Christianity has done much to moderate it, but it still exists, and let the resident of the North and East who remembers the recent race riots in Illinois and Ohio and New York think charitably of his brethren who are confronted by the Chinese problem in California. So May 6, 1882, Congress passed the Restriction Act, which, as amended July 5, 1884, and reenacted in 1903, is now in force.

There are thousands of high-minded Christian people who are unselfishly and lovingly toiling for the temporal and spiritual welfare of this Asiatic population in America. They rightly feel that the people of the United States have a special duty towards these Orientals, that the purifying power of Christianity can remove the dangers incident to their presence in our communities, and that if we treat them aright they will, on their return to China, mightily influence their countrymen. But the kindly efforts of these Christian people are unfortunately insufficient to offset the general policy of the American people as a whole, especially as that policy is embodied in a stern law that is most harshly enforced.

Americans are apt to think of themselves as China's best friends and the facts stated show that there is some ground for the claim. But before we exalt ourselves overmuch, we might profitably read the correspondence between the Chinese Ministers at Washington and our Secretaries of State regarding the outrages upon Chinese in the United States. Many Chinese have suffered from mob violence in San Francisco and Tacoma and other Pacific Coast cities almost as sorely as Americans have suffered in China. Some years ago, they were wantonly butchered in Rock Springs, Wyoming, and it was as difficult for the Chinese to get indemnity out of our Government as it was for the Powers to get indemnity out of China for the Boxer outrages.

President Cleveland, in a message to Congress in 1885, felt obliged to make an allusion to this that was doubtless as humiliating to him as it was to decent Americans everywhere. The Chinese Minister to the United States, in his presentation of the case to Secretary of State Bayard, "massed the evidence going to show that the massacre of the subjects of a friendly Power, residing in this country, was as unprovoked as it was brutal; that the Governor and Prosecuting Attorney of the Territory openly declared that no man could be punished for the crime, though the murderers attempted no concealment; and that all the pretended judicial proceedings were a burlesque." All this Mr. Bayard was forced to admit. Indeed he did not hesitate to characterize the proceedings as "the wretched travesty of the forms of justice," nor did he conceal his "indignation at the bloody outrages and shocking wrongs inflicted upon a body of your countrymen," and his mortification that "such a blot should have been cast upon the record of our Government." There was sarcastic significance in the cartoon of the Chicago Inter-Ocean representing a Chinese reading a daily paper one of whose columns was headed "Massacre of Americans in China," while the other column bore the heading, "Massacre of Chinese in America." Uncle Sam stands at his elbow and ejaculates, "Horrible, isn't it?" To which the Celestial blandly inquires, "Which?"

In the North American Review for March, 1904, Mr. Wong Kai Kah, an educated Chinese gentleman, plainly but courteously discusses this subject under the caption of "A Menace to America's Oriental Trade." He justly complains that though the exclusion law expressly exempts Chinese merchants, students and travellers, yet as a matter of fact a Chinese gentleman is treated on his arrival as if he were a criminal and is "detained in the pen on the steamship wharf or imprisoned like a felon until the customs officials are satisfied."

The Hon. Chester Holcombe, formerly Secretary of the American Legation at Peking and a member of the Chinese Immigration Commission of 1880, cites some illlustrations of the harshness and unreasonableness of the exclusion law.[45] A Chinese merchant of San Francisco visited his native land and brought back a bride, only to find that she was forbidden to land on American soil. Another Chinese merchant and wife, of unquestioned standing in San Francisco, made a trip to China, and while there a child was born. On returning to their home in America, the sapient officials could interpose no objection to the readmission of the parents, but peremptorily refused to admit the three-months old baby, as, never having been in this country, it had no right to enter it! Neither of these preposterous decisions could be charged to the stupidity or malice of the local officials, for both were appealed to the Secretary of the Treasury in Washington and were officially sustained by him as in accordance with the law, though in the latter case, the Secretary, then the Hon. Daniel Manning, in approving the action, had the courageous good sense to write: "Burn all this correspondence, let the poor little baby go ashore, and don't make a fool of yourself."

---

45   Article in The Outlook, April 23, 1904.

Still more irritating and insulting, if that were possible, was the treatment of the Chinese exhibitors at the Louisiana Purchase Exposition at St. Louis in 1904. Our Government formally invited China to participate, sending a special commission to Peking to urge acceptance. China accepted in good faith, and then the Treasury Department in Washington drew up a series of regulations requiring "that each exhibitor, upon arrival at any seaport in this country, should be photographed three times for purposes of identification, and should file a bond in the penal sum of $5,000, the conditions of which were that he would proceed directly and by the shortest route to St. Louis, would not leave the Exposition grounds at any time after his arrival there, and would depart for China by the first steamer sailing after the close of the Exposition. Thus a sort of Chinese rogues' gallery was to be established at each port, and the Fair grounds were to be made a prison pen for those who had come here as invited guests of the nation, whose presence and aid were needed to make the display a success. It is only just to add that, upon a most vigorous protest made against these courteous(?) regulations by the Chinese Government and a threat to cancel their acceptance or our invitation, the rules were withdrawn and others more decent substituted. But the fact that they were prepared and seriously presented to China shows to what an extent of injustice and discourtesy our mistaken attitude and action in regard to Chinese immigration has carried us."

No right-minded American can read without poignant shame, Luella Miner's recent account[46] of the experiences of Fay Chi Ho and Kung Hsiang Hsi, two Chinese students who, after showing magnificent devotion to American missionaries during the horrors of the Boxer massacres, sought to enter the United States. They were young men of education and Christian character who wished to complete their education at Oberlin College, but they were treated by the United States officials at San Francisco and other cities with a suspicion and brutality that were "more worthy of Turkey than of free Christian America." Arriving at the Golden Gate, September 12, 1901, it was not until January 10, 1903, that they succeeded in reaching Oberlin, and those sixteen months were filled with indignities from which all the efforts of influential friends

46   "Two Heroes of Cathay," p. 223 sq.

and of the Chinese Minister to the United States were unable to protect them. Whatever reasons there may be for excluding coolie labourers, there can be none for excluding the bright young men who come here to study. "An open door for our merchants, our railway projectors, our missionaries, we cry, and at the same time we slam the door in the faces of Chinese merchants and travellers and students—the best classes who seek our shores."

The fear that the Chinese would inundate the United States if they were permitted to come under the same conditions as Europeans is not justified by the numbers that came before the exclusion laws became so stringent, the total Chinese population of the United States up to 1880, when there was no obstacle to their coming except the general immigration law, being only 105,465—the merest handful among our scores of millions of people. The objections that they are addicted to gambling and immorality, that they come only for temporary mercenary purposes and that they do not become members of the body politic but segregate themselves in special communities, might be urged with equal justice by the Chinese against the foreign communities in the port cities of China. Segregating themselves, indeed! How can the Chinese help themselves, when they are not allowed to become naturalized and are treated with a dislike and contempt which force them back upon one another?

As for the charge that they teach the opium habit to white boys and girls, it may be safely affirmed that all the Americans who have acquired that dread habit from the Chinese are not equal to a tenth of the number of Chinese women and girls who have been given foul diseases by white men in China. Mr. Holcombe declares:—

"Our unfair treatment of China in this business will some day return to plague us. Entirely aside from the cavalier and insulting manner with which we have dealt with China, and the inevitably injurious effect upon our relations and interests there, it must be said that our action has been undignified, unworthy of any great nation, a sad criticism upon our sense of power and ability to rule our affairs with wisdom and moderation, and unbecoming our high position among the leading governments of the world…We have treated Chinese immigrants—never more than a handful when compared with our population—as though we were in a frenzy of fear of them. We have forsaken our wits in this question, abandoned all self-control, and belittled our manhood by treating each incoming Chinaman as though he were the embodiment of some huge and hideous power which, once landed upon our shores, could not be dealt with or kept within bounds. Yet in point of fact he is far more easily kept in bounds and held obedient to law than some immigrants from Europe…It must be admitted as beyond question that the coming of the Chinese to these shores should be held under constant supervision and strict limitations. And so should immigration from all other countries. The time has come when we ought to pick and choose with far greater care than is exercised, and to exclude large numbers who are now admitted…It is this discrimination alone which is unjust to China, which she naturally resents, and which does us serious harm in our relations with her people."

Commenting on the regulations promulgated by the Secretary of Commerce and Labour, July 27, 1903, regarding the admission of Chinese, the Hon. David J. Brewer, Associate Justice of the Supreme Court of the United States, declared:—

"Can anything be more harsh and arbitrary? Coming into a port of the United States, as these petitioners did into the port of Malone, placed as they were in a house of detention, shut off from communication with friends and counsel, examined before an inspector with no one to advise or counsel, only such witnesses present as the inspector may designate, and upon an adverse decision compelled to give notice of appeal within two days, within three days the transcript forwarded to the Commissioner-General, and nothing to be considered by him except the testimony obtained in this star chamber proceeding. This is called due process of law to protect the rights of an American citizen, and sufficient to prevent inquiry in the courts…

"Must an American citizen, seeking to return to this his native land, be compelled to bring with him two witnesses to prove the place of his birth or else be denied his right to return, and all opportunity of establishing his citizenship in the courts of his country? No such rule is enforced against an American citizen of Anglo-Saxon descent, and if this be, as claimed, a government of laws and not of men, I do not think it should be enforced against American citizens of Chinese descent…

"Finally, let me say that the time has been when many young men from China came to our educational institutions to pursue their studies when her commerce sought our shores and her people came to build our railroads, and when China looked upon this country as her best friend. If all this be reversed and the most populous nation on earth becomes the great antagonist of this Republic, the careful student of history will recall the words of Scripture, 'they have sown the wind, and they shall reap the whirlwind,' and for cause of such antagonism need look no further than the treatment accorded during the last twenty years by this country to the people of that nation."[47]

It is not surprising that while Chinese students are turning in large numbers to other lands, there are only 146 in the United States. It is a serious matter and it may have a far reaching effect upon the future of China and of mankind when the coming men of the Far East, desiring to place themselves in touch with modern conditions, are compelled to avoid the one Christian nation in all the world which boasts the most enlightened institutions and the highest development of liberty.

Meanwhile, Mr. E. H. Parker rather sarcastically remarks:—

"The United States have always been somewhat prone to pose as the good and disinterested friend of China, who does not sell opium or exercise any undue political influence. These claims to the exceptional status of all honest broker have been a little shaken by the sharp treatment of Chinese in the United States, Honolulu and Manila."[48]

The Chinese Government long expostulated against the barbarity and injustice of the exclusion laws and finally, finding expostulations of no avail, the scholars and merchants of China organized in 1905 a boycott against American trade. This quickly brought public feeling in the United States to its senses. President Roosevelt sternly ordered all local officials to be humane and sensible in their enforcement of the law under pain of instant dismissal, and the press began to demand a new treaty. It is gratifying to know

---

47   Dissenting opinion in the case of the United States, Petitioner vs. Sing Tuck or King Do and thirty-one others, April 25, 1904.

48   "China," p. 105.

that in the future Chinese immigrants are likely to be more justly treated, but it is not pleasant to reflect that the American people apparently cared little about the iniquity of their anti-Chinese laws until Chinese resentment touched their pockets.

XIV
DIPLOMATIC RELATIONS—TREATIES

IN view of some of the facts presented in the two preceding chapters, it is not surprising that the efforts of foreign powers to establish diplomatic relations with the Chinese Government were rather tempestuous. A full account of the negotiations would require a separate volume. For two generations, nation after nation sought to protect its growing interests in China and to secure recognition from the Chinese Government, only to be met by opposition that was sometimes courteous and sometimes sullen, but always inflexible until it was broken down by force. Each envoy on presenting his letters was politely told in substance that the Chinese official concerned was extremely busy, that to his deep regret it would not be possible to grant an immediate conference, but that as soon as possible he would have pleasure in selecting a "felicitous day" on which they could hold a "pleasant interview";[49] and when the envoys, worn out by the never-ending procrastination, finally gave up in disgust and announced their intention of returning home, the typical Chinese official blandly replied, as the notorious Yeh did to United States Minister Marshall in January, 1854,—"I avail myself of the occasion to present my compliments, and trust that, of late, your blessings have been increasingly tranquil."[50]

Scores of European and American diplomatic agents had substantially the same experience. United States Minister Reed, in

49   Foster, "American Diplomacy in the Orient," p. 205,
50   Foster, p. 213.

1858, truly said that the replies of the Chinese to the memorials and letters of the foreign envoys were characterized by "the same unmeaning profession, the same dexterous sophistry; and, what is more material, the same passive resistance; the same stolid refusal to yield any point of substance."[51]

Nor can it be denied that the Chinese had some ground for holding foreign nations at arms' length as long as they could, for with a few exceptions, prominent among whom were some American ministers, notably Mr. Burlingame, the foreign envoys were far from being tactful and conciliatory in their methods of approach to a proud and ancient people. Mr. Foster reminds us that in the negotiations which terminated in the treaty of 1858,

"The British were pushing demands not insisted upon by the other Powers, and they could only be obtained by coercive measures. The reports in the Blue Books and the London newspapers show that Mr. Lay, who personally conducted the negotiations for Lord Elgin, when he found the Chinese commissioners obdurate, was accustomed to raise his voice, charge them with having 'violated their pledged word,' and threaten them with Lord Elgin's displeasure and the march of the British troops to Peking. And when this failed to bring them to terms, a strong detachment of the British army was marched through Tien-tsin to strike terror into its officials and inhabitants. Lord Elgin in his diary records the climax of these demonstrations: 'I have not written for some days, but they have been busy ones. We went on fighting and bullying, and getting the poor commissioners to concede one point after another, till Friday the 25th.' The next day the treaty was signed, and he closes the record as follows: 'Though I have been forced to act almost brutally, I am China's friend in all this.' There can be no doubt that notwithstanding the seeming paradox, Lord Elgin was thoroughly sincere in this declaration, and that his entire conduct was influenced by a high sense of duty and by what he regarded as the best interests of China."[52]

But can we wonder that the Chinese were irritated and humiliated by the method adopted?

That treaty of 1858 gave some notable advantages to foreigners, for it conceded the rights of foreign nations to send

51   Foster, p. 236.
52   "American Diplomacy in the Orient," pp. 241, 242.

diplomatic representatives to Peking, the rights of foreigners to travel, trade, buy, sell and reside in an increasing number of places, and on the persistent initiative of the French envoy, powerfully supported by the famous Dr. S. Wells Williams, Christianity was especially recognized, and the protection, not only of missionaries but all Chinese converts to Christianity, was specifically guaranteed. Of course, by the convenient "most favoured nation clause" any concession obtained by one country, was immediately claimed by all other countries.

It was this treaty which included the famous Toleration Clause regarding Christian missions as follows:

"The principles of the Christian religion, as professed by the Protestant and Roman Catholic Churches, are recognized as teaching men to do good, and to do to others as they would have others do to them. Hereafter those who quietly profess and teach these doctrines shall not be harassed or persecuted on account of their faith. Any person, whether citizen of the United States or Chinese convert, who, according to these tenets, shall peaceably teach and practice the principles of Christianity shall in no case be interfered with or molested."

The charge has been made that the toleration clauses were smuggled into the treaties without the knowledge of the Chinese, so that the claims to recognition and protection which were subsequently based upon it rest upon an unfair foundation. It is indeed possible, as Dr. S. Wells Williams, the author, frankly admits[53] "that if the Chinese had at all comprehended what was involved in these four toleration articles, they would never have signed one of them." But perhaps the same thing might be said of most treaties that have been signed in Asia. The fact remains, however, that the articles referred to were not placed in them without the knowledge of the Chinese. Dr. Williams explicitly states that he and the Rev. Dr. W. A. P. Martin, called upon the Chinese Commissioners and that

"some of the articles of our draft were passed without objection, those relating to toleration (of Christianity in China) and the payment of claims were copied off to show the Commissioner,

<hr>

53   "The Life and Letters of Samuel Wells Williams, LL. D.," p. 271.

those permitting and regulating visits to Peking were rejected, and others were amended, the colloquy being conducted with considerable animation and constant good humour on his part."[54]

In a letter written many years afterwards and dated New Haven, September 12, 1878, Dr. Williams states that the first draft of the Toleration Clauses was rejected by the Chinese Commissioners, as he believes at the instigation of the French Legation, because the clause recognized Protestant missions. Dr. Williams then states that as soon as he could, he drew up another form of the same article and laid it before the Chinese Imperial Commissioners. He writes:—

"It was quite the same article as before, but they accepted it without any further discussion or alteration; however, the word 'whoever' in my English version was altered by Mr. Reed to 'any person, whether citizen of the United States, or Chinese convert, who'—because he wished every part of the treaty to refer to United States citizens, and cared not very much whether it had a toleration article or not. I did care, and was thankful to God that it was inserted. It is the only treaty in existence which contains the royal law."

In Dr. Williams' Journal for June 18, 1858, the following record appears:

"I went to sleep last night with the impression that after such a reply from the Minister it would be vain to urge a new draft, but after a restless sleep I awoke to the idea of trying once more, this time saying nothing about foreign missionaries. The article was sketched as soon as I could write it and sent off by a messenger before breakfast; it was a last chance, and every hope went with it for success. At half-past nine an answer came. Permission for Christians meeting for worship and the distribution of books was erased, while the words open ports were inserted in such a connection that it was rendered illegal for any one, native or otherwise, to profess Christianity anywhere else. The design was merely to restrict missionaries to the ports, but the effect would be detrimental in the highest degree to natives. I decided at once to go to see the Viscount and try to settle the question with him personally. Chairs were called, whose bearers seemed to Martin and

54 "The Life and Letters of Samuel Wells Williams, LL. D.," p. 261.

me an eternity in coming, but at last we reached the house where Captain Du Pont and his marines so unexpectedly turned up last Saturday. Our amendment was handed to Chang, who began to cavil at it, but he was promptly told that he must take it to the Commissioners for approval as it stood, since this was the form we were decided on. Our labour and anxiety were all repaid, and ended by his return in a few minutes announcing Kweilang's assent to the article as it now stands in the treaty."

In order to settle this point beyond all possible doubt, I recently wrote to the Rev. Dr. W. A. P. Martin, now in China, asking him to give me his recollection of the incident. He replied as follows:—

"The charge that the toleration article was 'smuggled into the treaty of 1858' is so far from the truth that those who make it can be shown to be either superficial or uncandid. If it means that 'the Chinese did not know what they were agreeing to, I answer that they could have no excuse for ignorance. An edict granting toleration had been issued as early as 1845. This had been followed by more than ten years of missionary work at the newly opened ports—quite sufficient to make them acquainted with the character of Protestant missions. Of Roman Catholic missions prior to the edict, they had centuries of experience. Moreover, during our negotiations at Tien-tsin, they had ample time for a fresh study of the subject, the draft of our treaty being under daily discussion for more than a week before it was signed. Nor was our draft the first to bring up the question of toleration. The Russian Treaty signed on June 13th (five days in advance of ours) contained one explicit provision for the toleration of Christianity under the form of the Greek Church; but it made no reference to Protestant or Roman Catholic. Not only was the American Treaty the first to give these a legal status, it gives the Chinese a sample of Christian teaching in the Golden Rule, which Dr. Williams inserted in the article expressly to show them what they were agreeing to. Never were negotiations more open and above board. In their earlier stages I gave a copy of my book on the Evidences of Christianity to Jushon, one of the deputies, who was so much pleased with it, that he became my friend and greeted me warmly on my removal to Peking. That the Chinese Ministers had any conception of the new force they were admitting into their country, I do not assert; but I hold strongly that this spiritual force is the only thing that can raise the Chinese people out of their present state of semi-barbarism.

"W. A. P. MARTIN.

"Wuchang, China, February 18, 1904."

It was not until 1861, that legations were established in Peking. But while this gave foreign nations a solid foothold at the capital, it did not by any means give them the recognition that they demanded, for their intercourse with the court was still hedged about with innumerable exactions and indignities. The Hon. Thomas Francis Wade, British Minister at Peking, in a long note to the Chinese Minister Wen Hsiang, dated June 18, 1871, discussing the troubles that had arisen between the Chinese and foreigners, justly said:

"It is quite impossible that China should ever attain to a just appreciation of what foreign Powers expect of her, or that she should insure from foreign Powers what she conceives due to her, until she have honestly accepted the conditions of official intercourse which are the sole guarantees against international differences. The chief of these is an interchange of representatives. I do not say that it is a panacea for all evil; but it is incontestable that without it wars would be of far more frequent recurrence, and till China is represented in the West, I see no hope of our ever having done with the incessant recriminations and bickerings between the Yamen and foreign legations, by which the lives of diplomatic agents in Peking are made weary. If China is wronged, she must make herself heard; and, on the other hand, if she would abstain from giving offense, she must learn what is passing in the world beyond her."

The Chinese Government was slow in coming to this view, but western nations steadily persisted. One by one new concessions were wrung from the reluctant Chinese. Mr. E. H. Parker[55] has tabulated as follows the treaties of foreign powers with China from 1689 to 1898:—

{Pages 171 to 173 are these tables...They are formatted landscape-wise on the pages and should be typed in a viewable format or added as an image file.}

---

55   "China," pp. 113-115.

XV
RENEWED AGGRESSIONS

NOT content with innumerable aggressions and extorted treaty concessions, Western nations boldly discussed the dismemberment of China as certain to come, and authors and journalists disputed as to which country should possess the richest parts of the Empire whose impotence to defend itself was taken for granted. Chinese ministers in Europe and America reported these discussions to their superiors in Peking. The English papers in China republished some of the articles and added many effective ones of their own, so that speedily all the better-informed Chinese came to know that foreigners regarded China as "the carcass of the East."

Nor was all this talk empty boasting. China saw that France was absorbing Siam and had designs on Syria; that Britain was already lord of India and Egypt and the Straits Settlements; that Germany was pressing her claims in Asiatic Turkey; that Russia had absorbed Siberia and was striving to obtain control of Palestine, Persia and Korea; and that Italy was trying to take Abyssinia. Moreover the Chinese perceived that of the numerous islands of the world, France had the Loyalty, Society, Marquesas, New Hebrides and New Caledonia groups, and claimed the Taumotu or Low Archipelago; that Great Britain had the Fiji, Cook, Gilbert, Ellice, Phoenix, Tokelan and New Zealand groups, with northern Borneo, Tasmania, and the whole of continental Australia, besides a large assortment of miscellaneous islands scattered over the world wherever they would do the most good; that Germany possessed the Marshall group and Northeast New Guinea, and divided with England the

Solomons; that Spain had the Ladrones, the 652 islands of the Carolines, the 1,725 more or less of the Philippines, beside some enormously valuable holdings in the West Indies; that the Dutch absolutely ruled Java, Sumatra, the greater part of Borneo, all of Celebes and the hundreds of islands eastward to New Guinea, half of which was under the Dutch flag; that the new world power on the American continent took the Hawaiian Islands and in two swift campaigns drove Spain out of the West Indies and the Philippines, not to return them to their inhabitants but to keep them herself; and that in the Samoan and Friendly Islands, resident foreigners owned about everything worth having and left to the native chiefs only what the foreigners did not want or could not agree upon. As for mighty Africa, the Berlin Conference of 1884 was the signal for a game of grab on so colossal a scale that to-day out of Africa's 11,980,000 square miles, France owns 3,074,000, Great Britain 2,818,000, Turkey 1,672,000, Belgium 900,000, Portugal 834,000, Germany 864,000, Italy 596,000, and Spain 263,000,—a total of 10,980,000, or ten-elevenths of the whole continent, and doubtless the Powers will take the remaining eleventh whenever they feel like it. Well does the Rev. Dr. James Stewart call this "the most stupendous and unparalleled partition of the earth's surface ever known in the world's history…The vast area was partitioned, annexed, appropriated, or converted into 'spheres of influence,' or 'spheres of interest'; whatever may be the exact words we may use, the result is the same. Coast lands and hinterlands all went in this great appropriation, and mild is the term for the deed."[56]

"Gobbling the globe," this process has been forcefully if inelegantly termed. No wonder that the white race has been bitterly described as "the most arrogant and rapacious, the most exclusive and intolerant race in history."

We can understand, therefore, the alarm of the Chinese as they saw the greedy foreigners descend upon their own shores in such ways as to justify the fear that what remained of the Celestial Empire, too, would be speedily reduced to vassalage. Germany, which was among the last of the European powers to obtain a foothold in China, but which had been growing more and more uneasy as she saw the acquisitions of her rivals, suddenly found her

56   "Dawn in the Dark Continent," pp. 17, 18.

opportunity in the murder of two German Roman Catholic priests in the province of Shantung, December 1897, and on the 14th of that month Admiral Diedrich landed marines at Kiao-chou Bay. At that time nothing but a few straggling, poverty-stricken Chinese villages were to be seen at the foot of the barren hills bordering the bay. But the keen eye of Germany had detected the possibilities of the place and early in the following year, under the forms of an enforced ninety-nine year lease, Germany took this splendid harbour and the territory bordering it, and at Tsing-tau began to push her interests so aggressively that the whole province of Shantung was thrown into the most intense excitement and alarm.

Knowing how recently the city had been founded, I looked upon it with wonder. It was only three years and a half since the Germans had taken possession, but no boom city in the United States ever made more rapid progress in so short a period. Not a Chinese house could be seen, except a village in the distance. But along the shores rose a city of modern buildings with banks, department stores, public buildings, comfortable residences, a large church and imposing marine barracks. Landing, I found broad streets, some of them already well paved and others being paved by removing the dirt to a depth of twelve inches and then filling the excavation solid with broken rock. The gutters were wide and of stone, the sewers deep and, in some cases, cut through the solid rock.

The city was under naval control, the German Governor being a naval officer. Several war-ships were lying in the harbour. A large force of marines was on shore, and the hills commanding the city and harbour were bristling with cannon. The Germans were spending money without stint. No less than 11,000,000 marks were being expended that year for streets, sewers, water and electric light works, barracks, fortifications, wharves, a handsome hotel and public buildings, while the Government had appropriated 50,000,000 Mex. (5,000,000 a year for ten years) for deepening and enlarging the inner harbour. But in addition to these Government expenditures, many enterprising business men were undertaking large enterprises on their own account. It was apparent to the most casual observer that Germany had entered Shantung to stay and that she considered the whole vast province of Shantung as her sphere of influence. The railway, already referred to in a former chapter, was being constructed into the interior with solid road-bed, steel ties and substantial stone stations. German mining engineers were prospecting for minerals and everything indicated large plans for a permanent occupation.

The site of Tsing-tau is beautiful and exceptionally healthful. While the ports of Teng-chou and Chefoo are also in Shantung, the first is now of little importance, for it is on the northeastern part of the promontory with a mountain range behind it so that it is difficult of access from the interior. Chefoo, which was not opened as a port until later, rapidly superseded Teng-chou in importance and continues to grow with great rapidity. But it is plain that the Germans intend to make Tsing-tau, only twenty hours distant by steamer, the chief port of Shantung, and as they have the railroad, they will doubtless succeed.

From hundreds of outlying villages, the Chinese are flocking into Tsing-tau, attracted by the remunerative employment which the Germans offer, for of course, tens of thousands of labourers are necessary to carry out the extensive improvements that are planned. The thrifty Chinese are quite willing to take the foreigner's money, however much they may dislike him. Since the white man is here, we might as well get what we can out of him, the Celestials philosophically argue. And so the Germans, who had ruthlessly destroyed the old, unsani-tary Chinese villages which they had found on their arrival, laid out model Chinese villages on the outskirts of the city. The new Chinese city is about two and a half miles from the foreign city and is connected with it by a splendid macadamized road for which the Germans filled ravines, cut through the solid rock of the hillsides and made retaining walls and culverts of solid masonry. Some of the old stone houses were allowed to remain, but many of the poorer houses were demolished, streets were straightened and the whole city placed under strict sanitary supervision. The Chinese as they came in were told where and how their houses must be erected on the regularly laid out streets. The houses are numbered and many of the stores have signs in both German and Chinese. At the time of my visit, the Chinese city had a population of 8,000, the streets were crowded, and marketing, picture and theatrical exhibitions and all the forms of life, so common in Chinese cities, were to be seen on every side. Since then, the population has greatly increased, while another

Chinese city has been laid out on the open ground on the other side of the foreign city. There is every indication that Tsing-tau is to become one of the great port cities of China, and the opportunities for trade, the coming of steamships and the construction of the railway are making it an attractive place to multitudes of ambitious Chinese.

The German Government owns all the land in and about Tsing-tau, and will not sell save on condition that approved buildings are erected within three years. The single tax plan has been adopted, that is, there is no tax on buildings but there is a six per cent. tax on all land that is sold. This shuts out the land speculator who has injured so many American cities. No man can buy cheap land and let it lie idle while it rises in value as the result of his neighbour's improvements and the growth of the community. The German Government will do its own speculating and reap for itself the increment of its costly and elaborate improvements. It is making a noble city. Streets, sewers, buildings, docks, sea walls, harbour-dredging, tree planting—all point to great and far-reaching plans, while under pretext of guarding the railroad, troops are being gradually pushed into the interior. The Kaomi garrison, in the hinterland eighteen miles beyond the Kiao-chou city line and sixty-four from Tsing-tau, consisted of 100 men when I was there in the spring of 1901. A few months later it was 1,000. Plainly the Germans are moving in.

The ease and dispatch with which Germany succeeded in obtaining an enormously valuable strategic point in the rich province of Shangtung aroused the cupidity of rival nations, and they threw off all pretense to decency in their scramble for further territories. Russian statesmen had long ago seen that the Pacific Ocean was to be the arena of world events of colossal significance to the race. We have noted in a former chapter how she had already extended her territory till she touched the Pacific Ocean on the far north and how, partly that she might develop it, but primarily that she might have a highway through it to the great ocean which lies beyond, she had begun the construction of the Trans-Siberian Railway, the late Czar, Alexander III, guaranteeing out of his own private funds 350,000,000 rubles towards the necessary expense. The most southern port of Russia on the Pacific Ocean was Vladivostok, which was therefore made the terminus of the line and rapidly and strongly fortified. But Russia was not content with a harbour which is closed by ice six months in the year. She therefore began to press her way southward through Manchuria. In November, 1894, Japan had wrested from China the peninsula terminating in Port Arthur, and the treaty of Shimonoseki, at the close of the war, had given Japan the Liao-tung peninsula, opened four Manchurian ports to foreign trade, and conceded to Japan valuable commercial rights in Manchuria, rights which gave the Japanese virtual ascendancy. Ostensibly in the interests of China, but really of her own ambition, Russia gravely said that it would never do to permit Japan to remain in Manchuria, virtuously declaring that "the integrity of China must be preserved at all costs." She persuaded France and Germany to join her in notifying the Japanese Government that "it would not be permitted to retain permanent possession of any portion of the mainland of Asia." Japan, feeling at that time unprepared to fight three European powers, was forced to relinquish the prize of victory. The solicitude of Russia for the integrity of helpless China was quite touching, but it did not prevent her from making one encroachment after another upon the coveted territory until March 8, 1898, to the rage and chagrin of Japan, she peremptorily demanded for herself and March 27th of the same year obtained Port Arthur including Ta-lien-wan and 800 square miles of adjoining territory. She speciously declared that "her occupation of Port Arthur was merely temporary and only to secure a harbour for wintering the Russian fleet." But grim significance was given to her action by the prompt appearance at Port Arthur of 20,000 Russian soldiers and 90,000 coolies who were set to work developing a great modern fortification almost under the eyes of the Chinese capital.

As it was expedient, however, to have a commercial city on the peninsula as well as a fortification, as the harbour of Port Arthur was not large enough for both naval and commercial purposes, and as the Russians did not wish anyway to make their fortified base accessible to the rest of the world, they decided to build a city forty-five miles north of Port Arthur and call it Dalny, which quite appropriately means "far away." Most cities grow, but this was too slow a method for the purpose of the Slav, and therefore, a metropolis was forthwith made to order as a result of an edict issued by the Czar, July 30, 1899.

The harbour of Dalny is an exceptionally fine one with over thirty feet of water at low tide so that the largest vessels can lie alongside the docks and transfer their cargoes directly to trains for Europe. Great piers were constructed; enormous warehouses and elevators erected; gas, electric light, water and street-car plants installed; wide and well-sewered streets laid out; and a thoroughly modern and handsome city planned in four sections, the first of which was administrative, the second mercantile, the third residence, and the fourth Chinese. The Russians were sparing neither labour nor expense in the construction of this ambitious city which, by January, 1904, already had a population of over 50,000, and represented a reported expenditure of about $150,000,000. April 9, 1902, Russia solemnly promised to evacuate Manchuria October 8, 1903. But when that day came, she remained, as every one knew that she would, under the unblushing pretext that Manchuria was not yet sufficiently pacified to justify her withdrawal from a region where her interests were so great. As Manchuria was at the time as quiet as some of Russia's European provinces, the reason alleged reminds one of the Arab's reply to a man who wished to borrow his rope—"I need it myself to tie up some sand with." "But," expostulated the would-be borrower, "that is a poor excuse for you cannot tie up sand with a rope." "I know that," was the calm rejoinder, "but any excuse will serve when I don't want to do a thing." So to the concern of China, the envy of Europe and the wrath of Japan, Manchuria practically became a Russian province until Japan, unable to restrain her exasperation longer and feeling that Russia's plans were a menace to her own safety, had developed her army and navy and begun the war which not only arrested the advance of the Slav but expelled him from most of the territory he had seized.

Not to be outdone by Germany and Russia, other nations made haste to seize what they could find. April 2, 1898, England secured the lease of Lin-kung, with all the islands and a strip ten miles wide on the mainland, thus giving the British a strong post at Wei-hai Wei. April 22d, France peremptorily demanded, and May 2d obtained, the bay of Kwangchou-wan, while Japan found her share in a concession for Foochow, Woosung, Fan-ning, Yo-chou and Chung-wan-tao. By 1899, in all China's 3,000 miles of coast line, there was not a harbour in which she could mobilize her own ships without the consent of the hated foreigner.

A clever Chinese artist in Hongkong grimly drew a cartoon of the situation of his country as he and his countrymen saw it. The Russian Bear, coming down from the north, his feet planted in Manchuria and northern Korea, sees the British Bulldog seated in southern China, while "The Sun Elf" (Japan), sitting upon its Island Kingdom, proclaims that "John Bull and I will watch the Bear." The German Sausage around Kiau-chou makes no sign of life, but the French Frog, jumping about in Tonquin and Annam and branded "Fashoda and Colonial Expansion," tries to stretch a friendly hand to the Bear over the Bulldog's head. Then, to offset this proffered assistance to the Bear, the Chinese artist, with characteristic cunning, brings in the New World power. He places the American Eagle over the Philippines, its beak extended towards the Bulldog, and writes upon it the phrase, "Blood is thicker than water."[57]

As far as Americans have any sympathy at all with European schemes for conquest in China, they naturally look with more favour on England and Germany than on France and Russia. The reason is apparent. England establishes honest and beneficent government wherever she goes and makes its advantages freely accessible to the citizens of other nations, so that an American is not only as safe but as unrestricted in all his legitimate activities as he would be in his own land. Germany, too, while not so hospitable as England, is nevertheless a Teutonic, Protestant power under whose ascendancy in Shantung our missionaries find ample freedom. But France and Russia are more narrowly and jealously national in their aims. Their possessions are openly regarded as assets to be managed for their own interests rather than for those of the na-tives or of the world. The colonial attitude of the former towards all Protestant missionary work is dictated by the Roman Catholic Church and is therefore hostile to Protestants, while the Russian Greek Church tolerates no other form of religion that it can repress. A recent traveller reports that Russia has put every possible obstruction in the way of reopening the mission stations that were abandoned during the Boxer outbreak. She has already put Manchuria under the Greek archimandrite of Peking, and has sought to limit all

---

57 Reproduced in the Newark, N. J., Evening News, January 9, 1904

Christian teaching to the members of the Orthodox Greek Church. It is significant that Russia is strenuously opposing, under a variety of pretexts, the "open door" which Secretary Hay obtained from China in Manchuria, while there is ground for suspecting that Russian influence in Constantinople is preventing, or at least delaying as long as possible, that legal recognition of American rights in Turkey which the Sultan has already granted to several other nations. As for Russian ascendancy in Manchuria, everybody knows that it is inimical to the interests of other countries and that there will be little freedom of trade if Russia can prevent it.

XVI
GROWING IRRITATION OF THE CHINESE—THE REFORM PARTY

THE effect of the operation of these commercial and political forces upon a conservative and exclusive people was of course to exasperate to a high degree. A proud people were wounded in their most sensitive place by the ruthless and arrogant way in which foreigners broke down their cherished wall of separation from the rest of the world and trampled upon their highly-prized customs and institutions.

It must be admitted that the history of the dealings of the Christian powers with China is not altogether pleasant reading. The provocation was indeed great, but the retaliation was heavy. And all the time foreign nations refused to grant to the Chinese the privileges which they forced them to grant to others. We sometimes imagine that the Golden Rule is peculiar to Christianity. It is indeed in its highest form, but its spirit was recognized by Confucius five centuries before Christ. His expression of it was negative, but it gave the Chinese some idea of the principle. They were not, therefore, pleasantly impressed when they found the alleged Christian nations violating that principle. Even Christian America has not been an exception. We have Chinese exclusion laws, but we will not allow China to exclude Americans. We sail our gunboats up her rivers, but we would not allow China to sail gunboats into ours. If a Chinese commits a crime in America, he is amenable to American law as interpreted by an American court. But if an American commits a crime in China, he can be tried only by his consul; not a Chinese court in the Empire has jurisdiction over him, and the people naturally infer from this that we have no confidence in their sense of justice or in their administration of it.

This law of extra-territoriality is one of the chief sources of irritation against foreigners, for it not only implies contempt, but it makes foreigners a privileged class. Said Minister Wen Hsiang in 1868:—"Take away your extra-territorial clause, and merchant and missionary may settle anywhere and everywhere. But retain it, and we must do our best to confine you and our trouble to the treaty ports." But unfortunately this is a cause of resentment that Western nations cannot prudently remove in the near future. While we can understand the resentment of the Chinese magistrates as they see their methods discredited by the foreigner, it would not do to subject Europeans and Americans to Chinese legal procedure. The language of Mr. Wade, the British Minister, to Minister Wen Hsiang in June, 1, is still applicable:—

"Experience has shown that, in many cases, the latter (law of China) will condemn a prisoner to death, where the law of England would be satisfied by a penalty far less severe, if indeed, it were possible to punish the man at all. It is to be deplored that misunderstandings should arise from a difference in our codes; but I see no remedy for this until China shall see fit to revise the process of investigation now common in her courts. So long as evidence is wrung from witnesses by torture, it is scarcely possible for the authorities of a foreign power to associate themselves with those of China in the trial of a criminal case; and unless the authorities of both nationalities are present, there will always be a suspicion of unfairness on one side or the other. This difficulty surmounted, there would be none in the way of providing a code of laws to affect mixed cases; none, certainly, on the part of England; none, in my belief, either, on the part of any other Power."[58]

Meantime, as the Hon. Frederick F. Low, United States Minister at Peking, wrote to the State Department at Wash-

---

58   Correspondence Respecting the Circular of the Chinese Government of February 9, 1871, Relating to Missionaries. Presented to both Houses of Parliament by command of Her Majesty, 1872.

ington, March 20, 1871:—"The dictates of humanity will not permit the renunciation of the right for all foreigners that they shall be governed and punished by their own laws."

But the Chinese do not see the question in that light. Their methods of legal procedure are sanctioned in their eyes by immemorial custom and they fail to understand why forms that, in their judgment, are good enough for Chinese are not also good enough for despised foreigners. When we take into consideration the further fact that the typical white man, the world over, acts as if he were a lord of creation, and treats Asiatics with more or less condescension as if they were his inferiors, we can understand the very natural resentment of the Chinese, who have just as much pride of race as we have, and who indeed consider themselves the most highly civilized people in the world. The fact that foreign nations are able to thrash them does not convince them that those nations are superior, any more than a gentleman's physical defeat by a pugilist would satisfy him that the pugilist is a better man. It is not without significance that the white man is generally designated in China as "the foreign devil."

The natural resentment of the Chinese in such circumstances was intensified by the conduct of the foreign soldiery. Army life is not a school of virtue anywhere, particularly in Asia where a comparatively defenseless people open wide opportunities for evil practices and where Asiatic methods of opposition infuriate men. In almost every place where the soldiers of Europe landed, they pillaged and burned and raped and slaughtered like incarnate fiends. Chefoo to-day is an illustration of the effect. It is a city where foreigners have resided for forty years, where there are consuls of all nations and extensive business relations with other ports, where foreign steamers regularly touch and where war-ships frequently lie. There were five formidable cruisers there during my visit. Surely the Chinese of Chefoo should understand the situation. But during the troubles of 1860, French troops were quartered there and their conduct was so atrociously brutal and lustful that Chefoo has ever since been bitterly anti-foreign. The Presbyterian missionaries have repeatedly tried to do Christian work in the old walled city, but have never succeeded in gaining a foothold, and all their local missionary work is confined to the numerous population which has come from other parts of the province and settled around Chefoo proper. Nothing but battleships in the harbour kept that old city from attacking foreigners during the Boxer outbreak. Even to-day the cry "kill, kill" is sometimes raised as a foreigner walks through the streets, and inflammatory placards are often posted on the walls.

With the record of foreign aggressions in China before us, can we wonder that the Chinese became restive? The New York Sun truly says: "It was while Chinese territory was thus virtually being given away that the people became uneasy and riots were started; the people felt that their land had been despoiled." The Hon. Chester Holcombe truly remarks:—

"Those who desire to know more particularly what the Chinese think about it, how they regard the proposed dismemberment of the Empire and the extinction of their national life, are referred to the Boxer movement as furnishing a practical exposition of their views. It contained the concentrated wrath and hate of sixty years' slow growth. And it had the hearty sympathy of many, many millions of Chinese, who took no active part in it. For, beyond a doubt, it represented to them a patriotic effort to save their country from foreign aggression and ultimate destruction…The European Powers have only themselves to thank for the bitter hatred of the Chinese and the crash in which it culminated. Governmental policies outrageous and beyond excuse, scandalous diplomacy, and unprovoked attacks upon the rights and possessions of China, have been at the root of all the trouble."[59]

And shall we pretend innocent surprise that the irritation of the Chinese rapidly grew? Suppose that after the murder of the Chinese in Rock Springs, Wyoming, a Chinese fleet had been able to seize New York and Boston Harbours, and suppose our Government had been weak enough to acquiesce. Would the American people have made any protest? Would the lives of Chinese have been safe on our streets? And was it an entirely base impulse that led the men of China violently to oppose the forcible seizure of their country by aliens? The Empress Dowager declared in her now famous edict:—

"The various Powers cast upon us looks of tiger-like voracity, hustling each other in their endeavours to be first to seize upon our

---

59   Article in The Outlook, February 13, 1904,

innermost territories. They think that China, having neither money nor troops, would never venture to go to war with them. They fail to understand, however, that there are certain things which this Empire can never consent to, and that, if hard pressed, we have no alternative but to rely upon the justice of our cause, the knowledge of which in our breasts strengthens our resolves and steels us to present a united front against our aggressors."

That would probably be called patriotic if it had emanated from the ruler of any other people.

When with Russia in Manchuria, Germany in Shantung, England in the valleys of the Yang-tze and the Pearl, France in Tonquin and Japan in Formosa, the whole Empire appeared to be in imminent danger of absorption, the United States again showed itself the friend of China by trying to stem the tide. Our great Secretary of State, John Hay, sent to the European capitals that famous note of September, 1899, which none of them wanted to answer but which none of them dared to refuse, inviting them to join the United States in assuring the apprehensive Chinese that the Governments of Europe and America had no designs upon China's territorial integrity, but simply desired an "open door" for commerce, and that any claims by one nation of "sphere of influence" would "in no way interfere with any treaty port or any vested interest" within that sphere, but that all nations should continue to enjoy equality of treatment. In response, the Russian Government, December 30, 1899, through Count Mouravieff, suavely declared:—

"The Imperial Government has already demonstrated its firm intention to follow the policy of the 'open door.'…As to the ports now opened or hereafter to be opened to foreign commerce by the Chinese Government,…the Imperial Government has no intention whatever of claiming any privileges for its own subjects to the exclusion of other foreigners."

The other Powers also assented. But it was all in vain. Matters had already gone too far, and, beside, the Chinese knew well enough that the Powers were not to be trusted beyond the limits of self-interest.

Some of the Chinese, it is true, had the intelligence to see that changes were inevitable, and the result was the development of a Reform Party among the Chinese themselves. It was not large, but it included some influential men, though, unfortunately, their zeal was not always tempered by discretion. The war with Japan powerfully aided them. True, many of the Chinese do not yet know that there was such a war, for news travels slowly in a land whose railway and telegraph lines, newspapers and post-offices are yet few, and whose average inhabitant has never been twenty miles from the village in which he was born. But some who did know realized that Japan had won by the aid of Western methods. An eagerness to acquire those methods resulted. Missionaries were besieged by Chinese who wished to learn English. Modern books were given a wide circulation. Several of the influential advisers of the Emperor became students of Occidental science and political economy. In five years, 1893-1898, the book sales of one society—that for the Diffusion of Christian and General Knowledge Among the Chinese—leaped from $817 to $18,457, while every mission press was run to its utmost capacity to supply the new demands.

A powerful exponent of the new ideas appeared in the great Viceroy, Chang Chih-tung. He wrote a book, entitled "China's Only Hope," exposing the causes of China's weakness and advocating radical reforms. The book was printed by the Tsung-li Yamen, and by royal command copies were sent to the high officials of the Empire. Big yellow posters advertised it from the walls of leading cities, and in a short time a million copies were sold. It is hardly an exaggeration to say that "this book made more history in a shorter time than any other modern piece of literature, that it astonished a kingdom, convulsed an Empire and brought on a war."

The Reform Party urged the young Emperor to use the imperial power for the advancement of his people. He yielded to the pressure and became an eager and diligent student of the Western learning and methods. In the opening months of the year 1898, he bought no less than 129 foreign books, including a Bible and several scientific works, besides maps, globes, and wind and current charts. Nor did he stop with this, but with the ardour of a new convert issued the now famous reform edicts, which, if they could have been carried into effect, would have revolutionized China and started her on the high road to national greatness. These memorable decrees have been summarized as follows:

1. Establishing a university at Peking.

2. Sending imperial clansmen to study European and American Governments.
3. Encouraging art, science and modern agriculture
4. Expressing the willingness of the Emperor to hear the objections of the conservatives to progress and reform.
5. Abolishing the literary essay as a prominent part of the Government examinations
6. Censuring those who attempted to delay the establishment of the Peking Imperial University.
7. Directing that the construction of the Lu Han railway be carried on with more vigour.
8. Advising the adoption of Western arms and drill for all the Tartar troops.
9. Ordering the establishment of agricultural schools in the provinces to teach improved methods of agriculture.
10. Ordering the introduction of patent and copyright laws.
11. Ordering the Board of War and the Foreign Office to report on the reform of the military examinations.
12. Offering special rewards to inventors and authors.
13. Ordering officials to encourage trade and assist merchants.
14. Ordering the foundation of school boards in every city in the Empire.
15. Establishing a Bureau of Mines and Railroads.
16. Encouraging journalists to write on all political subjects.
17. Establishing naval academies and training ships.
18. Summoning the ministers and provincial authorities to assist the Emperor in his work of reform.
19. Directing that schools be founded in connection with all the Chinese legations in foreign countries for the benefit of the children of Chinese in those countries.
20. Establishing commercial bureaus in Shanghai for the encouragement of trade.
21. Abolishing six useless Boards in Peking.
22. Granting the right to memorialize the Throne by sealed memorials.

23. Dismissing two presidents and four vice-presidents of the Board of Rites for disobeying the Emperor's orders that memorials should be presented to him unopened.
24. Abolishing the governorships of Hupeh, Kwang-tung and Yun-nan as a useless expense to the country.
25. Establishing schools for instruction in the preparation of tea and silk.
20, Abolishing the slow courier posts in favour of the Imperial Customs' Post.
27 Approving a system of budgets as in Western countries.

But, alas, it is disastrous to try to "hustle the East." The Chinese are phlegmatic and will endure much, but this was a little too much. Myriads of scholars and officials, who saw their hopes and positions jeopardized by the new tests, protested with all the virulence of the silversmiths of Ephesus, and all the conservatism of China rallied to their support.

Meantime, the Yellow River, aptly named "China's Sorrow," again overflowed its banks, devastating a region 100 miles long and varying from twenty-five to fifty miles wide. Three hundred villages were swept away and 1,000,000 people made homeless. Famine and pestilence speedily followed, so that the whole catastrophe assumed appalling proportions. Even American communities are apt to become reckless and riotous in time of calamity, and in China this tendency of human nature was intensified by a superstition which led the people to believe that the disaster was due to the baleful influence of the foreigners, or that it was a punishment for their failure to resist them, while in the farther north a drought led to equally superstitious fury against "the foreign devils."

The virile and resolute Empress-Dowager headed the reaction against the headlong progressiveness of the young Emperor. September 22, 1898, the world was startled by an Imperial Decree which read in part as follows:—

"Her Imperial Majesty the Empress-Dowager, Tze Hsi, since the first years of the reign of the late Emperor Tung Chih down to our present reign, has twice ably filled the regency of the Empire, and never did her Majesty fail in happily bringing to a successful issue even the most difficult problems of government. In all things we have ever placed the interests of our Empire before those of others, and, looking back at her Majesty's successful handiwork, we are now led to beseech, for a third time, for this assistance from her Imperial majesty, so that we may benefit from her wise and kindly advice in all matters of State. Having now obtained her Majesty's gracious consent, we truly consider this to be a great boon both to ourselves as well as to the people of our Empire. Hence we now command that from henceforth, commencing with this morning, the affairs of state shall be transacted in the ordinary Throne Hall, and that to-morrow (23rd) we shall, at the head of the Princes and Nobles and Ministers of our Court, attend in full dress in the Ching-cheng Throne Hall, to pay ceremonial obeisance to her Imperial Majesty the Empress-Dowager. Let the Board of Rites draw up for our perusal the ceremonies to be observed on the above occasion."[60]

The youthful son of Toanwong was appointed heir to the throne and the ambitious father immediately proceeded to use his enhanced prestige to set the Empire in a blaze.

---

60   Pott, "The Outbreak in China," pp. 56, 57.

XVII
THE BOXER UPRISING

THE now famous Boxers were members of two of the secret societies which have long flourished in China. To the Chinese they are known as League of United Patriots, Great Sword Society, Righteous Harmony Fists' Association and kindred names. Originally, they were hostile to the foreign Manchu dynasty. When Germany made the murder of two Roman Catholic missionaries a pretext for pushing her political ambitions, the Boxers naturally arrayed themselves against them. As the champions of the national spirit against the foreigners, the membership rapidly increased. Supernatural power was claimed. Temples were converted into meeting-places, and soon excited men were drilling in every village.

The real ruler of China at this time, as all the world knows, was the Empress Dowager, who has been characterized as "the only man in China." At any rate, she is a woman of extraordinary force of character. She was astute enough to encourage the Boxers, and thus turn one of the most troublesome foes of the Manchu throne against the common enemy, the foreigner. Under her influence, the depredations of the Boxers, which were at first confined to the Shantung Province, spread with the swiftness of a prairie fire, until in the spring of 1900 the most important provinces of the Empire were ablaze and the legations in Peking were closely besieged. In the heat of the conflict and under the agonizing strain of anxiety for imperilled loved ones, many hard things were said and written about the officials who allied themselves with the Boxers. But Sir Robert Hart, who personally knew them and who suffered as much as any one from their fury, candidly wrote after the siege: "These men were eminent in their own country for their learning and services, were animated by patriotism, were enraged by foreign dictation, and had the courage of their convictions. We must do them the justice of allowing that they were actuated by high motives and love of country," though he adds, "that does not always or necessarily mean political ability or highest wisdom."

And so the irrepressible conflict broke out. It had to come, a conflict between conservatism and progress, between race prejudice and brotherhood, between superstition and Christianity, the tremendous conflict of ages which every nation has had to fight, and which in China was not different in kind, but only on a more colossal scale because there it involved half the human race at once. Of course it was impossible for so vast a nation permanently to segregate itself. The river of progress cannot be permanently stayed. It will gather force behind an obstacle until it is able to sweep it away. The Boxer uprising was the breaking up of this fossilized conservatism. It was such a tumultuous upheaval as the crusades caused in breaking up the stagnation of mediaeval Europe. As France opposed the new ideas, which in England were quietly accepted, only to have them surge over her in the frightful flood of the revolution, so China entered with the violence always inseparable from resistance the transition which Japan welcomed with a more open mind.

Though missionaries were not the real cause of the Boxer uprising, its horrors fell most heavily upon them. This was partly because many of them were living at exposed points in the interior while most other foreigners were assembled in the treaty ports where they were better protected; partly because the movement developed such hysterical frenzy that it attacked with blind, unreasoning fury every available foreigner, and partly because in most places the actual killing and pillaging were not done by the people who best knew the missionaries but by mobs from the slums, ruffians from other villages, or, as in Paoting-fu and Shan-si, in obedience to the direct orders of bigoted officials.

And so it came to pass that the innocent suffered more than the guilty. Dr. A. H. Smith[61] concluded after careful inquiry that "the devastating Boxer cyclone cost the lives of 135 adult Protestant missionaries and fifty-three children and of thirty-five Roman Catholic Fathers and nine Sisters. The Protestants were in connection with ten different missions, one being unconnected. They were murdered in four provinces and in Mongolia, and belonged to Great Britain, the United States and Sweden. No such outbreak against Christianity has been seen in modern times. The destruction of property was on the same continental scale. Generally speaking, all mission stations north of the Yellow River, with all their dwelling-houses, chapels, hospitals, dispensaries, schools, and buildings of every description were totally destroyed, though there were occasional exceptions, of which the village where these pages are written was one. The central and southern portions of the Empire were only partially affected by the anti-foreign madness, not because they were under different conditions, but mainly through the strong repressive measures of four men, Liu Kun Yi and Chang Chih-tung, Governors-General of the four great provinces in the Yang-tse Valley; Yuan Shih Kai in Shantung, and a Manchu, Tuan Fang, in Shen-si. The jurisdiction of this quartette made an impassable barrier across which the movement was unable to project itself in force, but much mischief in an isolated way was wrought in nearly every part of China not rigorously controlled."

So many volumes have been written about the Boxer Uprising that it is not necessary to double the size of this book in order to recount the details. For the full narrative, the reader is referred to the books mentioned below.[62] But I cannot for-bear some

---

61 "Rex Christus," p. 210.
62 "China in Convulsion," Arthur H. Smith; "The Outbreak in China," F. L. Hawks Pott; "The World Crisis in China, 1900," Allen S. Will; "Siege Days," A. H. Mateer; "The Siege of Peking," Wm. A. P. Martin; "The Providence of God in the Siege of Peking," C. H. Fenn; "The Tragedy of Paoting-fu," Isaac C. Ketler; "The China Martyrs of 1900," Robert C. Forsythe; "China," James H. Wilson, "China's Book of Martyrs," Luella Miner; "Two Heroes of Cathay," Luella Miner; "Through Fire and Sword in Shan-si," E. H. Edwards;

description of the scenes of massacre that I personally visited. I was unable to go to the remoter province of Shan-si where so many devoted men and women laid down their lives and where many who escaped death endured indescribable hardships. But in the province of Shantung, where the Boxer Uprising originated, I was witness to the ruin that was wrought in many places, though the iron hand of the great Governor, Yuan Shih Kai, prevented much bloodshed. Then I turned to the northern province of Chih-li where official hands, instead of restraining, actually guided and goaded the maddened rioters.

After a delightful voyage of eighteen hours from Chefoo over a smooth sea, we anchored outside the bar, nine miles from shore, the tide not permitting our steamer to cross with its heavy load. A tug took us off and entering the Pei-ho River, we passed the famous Taku forts to the railway wharf at Tong-ku. It was significant to find foreign flags flying over the Taku forts and also over the mud-walled villages near by. Scores of merchant steamers, transports and war vessels were lying off Taku as well as hundreds of junks. The river was full of smaller craft among which were several Japanese and American gunboats. The railroad station presented a motley appearance. A regiment of Japanese had just arrived and while we were waiting, three train-loads of British Sikhs and several cars of Austrian marines and British "Tommy Atkins" came in. The platform was thronged with officers and soldiers of various nationalities, including a few Russians.

Nothing could be more dreary than the mud flats that the traveller to the imperial city first sees. The greater part of the way from Taku to Peking, the soil is poor and little cultivated. But as we advanced, kao-liang fields were more frequent, though the growth was far behind that in Shantung at the same season. Small trees were numerous during the latter half of the trip. The soil being too thin for good crops, the people grow more fuel and fruit.

Evidences of the great catastrophe were seen long before reaching the capital. Burned villages and battered buildings lined the route. At Tien-tsin several of the foreign buildings had shell

---

"Chinese Heroes," I. T. Headland; "Martyred Missionaries of the C. I. M.," Broomhall; "The Crisis in China," G. B. Smith and others.

holes. One corrugated iron building near the railway station was pierced like a sieve and thousands of native houses were in ruins. The city wall had been razed to the ground and a highway made where it had stood—an unspeakable humiliation to the proud commercial metropolis. The Japanese soldiers teased the citizens by telling them that "a city without a wall is like a woman without clothes," and the people keenly felt the shame implied in the taunt.

In Peking, the very fact that the railroad train on which we travelled rushed noisily through a ragged chasm in the wall of the Chinese city, and stopped at the entrance of the Temple of Heaven, was suggestive of the consequences of war. The city, as a whole, was not as badly injured as I had expected to find it, but the ravages of war were evident enough. Wrecked shops, crumbled houses, shot-torn walls were on every side, while the most sacred places to a Chinese and a Manchu had been profaned. At other times the Purple Forbidden City, the Winter and Summer Palaces, the Temple of Heaven and kindred imperial enclosures are inaccessible to the foreigner. But a pass from the military authorities opened to us every door. We walked freely through the extensive grounds and into all the famous buildings—including the throne rooms which the highest Chinese official can approach only upon his knees and with his face abjectly on the stone pavement—and the private apartments of the Emperor and the Empress Dowager. I was impressed by the vastness of the Palace buildings and grounds, the carvings of stone and wood, and the number of articles of foreign manufacture. But thousands of Americans in moderate circumstances have more spacious and comfortable bedrooms than those of the Emperor and Empress Dowager of China. All the living apartments looked cheerless. The floors were of artificial stone or brick in squares of about 20 x 20 inches and of course everything was covered with dust. The far-famed Temple of Heaven is the most artistic building in China, a dream of beauty, colour and grace. For a generation before the siege of Peking, no foreigner except General Grant had entered that sacred enclosure, and the Chinese raised a furore because Li Hung Chang admitted even the distinguished American. As I freely walked about the place, photographed the Temple and stood on the circular altar that is supposed to be the centre of the earth and where the Emperor worships alone at the winter solstice, British Sikhs lounged under the trees, army mules munched the luxuriant grass and quartermasters' wagons stood in long rows near the sacred spot where a Chinese would prostrate himself in reverence and fear.

We rode past innumerable ruined buildings and through motley throngs of Manchus, Chinese, German, French, Italian, British and Japanese soldiers to the Presbyterian compound at Duck Lane, which, though narrow, is not so unimportant a street as its name implies. But where devoted missionaries had so long lived and toiled, we saw only shapeless heaps of broken bricks and a few tottering fragments of walls. At the Second Street compound there was even greater ruin, if that were possible. Silently we stood beside the great hole which had once been the hospital cistern and from which the Japanese soldiers, after the siege, had taken the bodies of a hundred murdered Chinese. Not all had been Christians, for in that carnival of blood, many who were merely suspected of being friendly to foreigners were killed, while foes took advantage of the tumult to pay off old scores of hate.

The first reports that had come to New York were that four-fifths of the Chinese Christians and three-fourths of the boys and girls in the boarding-schools had been killed or had died under the awful hardships of that fatal summer. But as the months passed, first one and then another and another were found. Husbands searched for wives, parents for children, brothers for sisters, until a considerable number of the missing ones had been found, though the number of the lost was still great.

About two hundred of these surviving Christians and their families were living together in native buildings adjoining the residence in which we were entertained. Their history was one of agony and bereavement. Including those who fell at Paoting-fu, 191 of their fellow Christians had received the crown of martyrdom, so that almost every survivor had lost father or mother, brother or sister or friend. The Chinese are supposed to be a phlegmatic people and not given to emotion. But never have I met a congregation more swiftly responsive than this one in Peking as I bore to them kindly messages from many friends in other lands.

The Roman Catholic Cathedral was immortalized by Bishop Favier's defense during the memorable siege. The mission buildings occupy a spacious and strongly-walled compound in the Manchu city. Hundreds of bullet and shell holes in the roofs and walls were suggestive evidences of the fury of the Boxer attack, while great pits marked the spots where mines had been exploded.

I called on the famous Bishop. He was, for he has since died, a burly, heavily-bearded Frenchman of about sixty-five apparently. He received us most cordially and readily talked of the siege. He said that of the eighty Europeans and 3,400 Christians with him in the siege, 2,700 were women and children. Four hundred were buried, of whom forty were killed by bullets, twenty-five by one explosion, eighty-one by another and one by another. Of the rest, some died of disease but the greater part of starvation. Twenty-one children were buried at one time in one grave. Beside these 400 who were killed or who died, many more were blown to pieces in explosions so that nothing could be found to bury. Fifty-one children disappeared in this way and not a fragment remained.

The first month of the siege, the food allowance was half a pound a day. The first half of the second month, it was reduced to four ounces, but for the second half only two ounces could be served and the people had to eat roots, bark and the leaves of trees and shrubs. Eighteen mules were eaten during the siege. The Bishop said that in the diocese outside of Peking, 6,000 Chinese Catholics, including three native priests, were killed by the Boxers. Only four European priests were killed, one in Peking and three outside. "Not one foreign priest left the diocese during the troubles," a statement that is equally true of the Presbyterian missionaries and, so far as I know, of those of other churches.

Clouds lowered as we left Peking, July 6th, on the Peking and Hankow Railway for Paoting-fu, that city of sacred and painful interest to every American Christian. Soon rain began to fall, and it steadily continued while we rode over the vast level plain, through unending fields of kao-liang, interspersed with plots of beans, peanuts, melons and cucumbers, and mud and brick-walled villages whose squalid wretchedness was hidden by the abundant foliage of the trees, which are the only beauty of Chinese cities. At almost every railway station, roofless buildings, crumbling walls and broken water tanks bore painful witness to the rage of the Boxers. At Liang-hsiang-hsien the first foreign property was destroyed, and all along the line outrages were perpetrated on the inoffensive native Christians. Nowhere else in China was the hatred of the foreigner more violent, for here hereditary pride and bigoted conservatism, unusually intense even for China, were reinforced by Boxer chiefs from the neighbouring province of Shantung, and were particularly irritated by the aggressiveness of Roman Catholic priests and by the construction of the railroad. It is only 110 miles from Peking to Paoting-fu. But the schedule was slow and the stops long, so that we were six hours in making the journey. Arriving at the large, well-built brick station, we bumped and splashed in a Chinese cart through narrow, muddy streets to the residence of a wealthy Chinese family that had deemed a hasty departure expedient when the French and British forces entered the city, and whose house had been assigned by the magistrate as temporary quarters for the Presbyterian missionaries.

Protestant mission work at Paoting-fu was begun only about thirty years ago by the American Board. The station was never a large one, the total nominal force of missionaries up to the Boxer outbreak being two ordained married men, Ewing and Pitkin, one physician, Dr. Noble, and two single women, the Misses Morrill and Gould. In the whole station field including the out-stations, there were not more than 300 Christians and those were south of a line drawn through the centre of the city of Paoting-fu. There were two boarding-schools, one for boys and one for girls, both small, and a general hospital.

The China Inland Mission had no mission work at Paoting-fu, but as the city is at the head of navigation of the Paoting-fu River from Tien-tsin and was also at that time the terminus of the Peking and Hankow Railway, the Mission made it a point of trans-shipment and of formation of cart and shendza trains for its extensive work in the Shan-si and Shen-si provinces, and kept a forwarding agent there, Mr. Benjamin Bagnall.

The Presbyterian station was not opened till 1893, and the force at the time of the outbreak consisted of three ordained men, the Revs. J. Walter Lowrie, J. A. Miller, and F. E. Simcox, two medical men, George Yardley Taylor and C. V. R. Hodge, and one single woman, Dr. Maud A. Mackay. All of the men except Lowrie and Taylor were married, and the former had his mother, Mrs. Amelia P. Lowrie, with him. With the exception of a dispensary and street chapel in rented quarters in the city, the station plant was at the compound where, on a level tract 660 feet in length by 210 feet in width, there were four residences and a hospital and chapel combined, with, of course, the usual smaller outbuildings. The only educational work, beside one out-station day-school, was a small boarding-school for girls recently started and occupying a little building originally intended for a stable.

This was the situation up to the fateful month of June, 1900. Rumours of impending trouble were numerous, but missionaries in China become accustomed to threatening placards and slanderous reports. Though it was evident that the opposition was becoming more bitter, the missionaries did not feel that they would be justified in abandoning their work. Several, however, were temporarily absent for other reasons. Of the Congregational missionaries, Dr. and Mrs. Noble and Mrs. Pitkin were on furlough in America and Mr. and Mrs. Ewing were spending a few weeks at the seaside resort, Pei-tai-ho, so that Mr. Pitkin, Miss Morrill and Miss Gould were the only ones left at the station. Of the Presbyterian missionaries Mr. and Mrs. Miller were also at Pei-tai-ho, Mrs. Lowrie had sailed for America the 26th of May, and Mr. Lowrie, who had accompanied her to Shanghai, was at Tien-tsin on his way back to Paoting-fu. The missionaries remaining at the station were thus five,—Dr. Taylor, Mr. and Mrs. Simcox and their three children, and Dr. and Mrs. Hodge. The China Inland forwarding agent, Mr. Bagnall, with his wife and little girl, was in his house south of the city wall near the American Board compound, and with him was the Rev. William Cooper, who was on his way to Shanghai after a visit to the Shan-si Mission and whose family was then at Chefoo.

It is impossible to ascertain all the details of the massacre. None of the foreigners live to tell the painful story. No other foreigners reached Paoting-fu until the arrival of the military expedition in October, three and a half months later. The Chinese who had participated in the massacre were then in hiding. Spectators were afraid to talk lest they, too, might be held guilty. Most of the Chinese Christians who had been with the missionaries were killed, while others were so panic-stricken that they could remember only the particular scenes with which they were directly connected. Moreover, in those three and a half months such battles and national commotions had occurred, including the capture of Peking and the flight of the Emperor, that the people of Paoting-fu had half forgotten the murder of a few missionaries in June.

In these circumstances, full information will probably never be obtained, though additional facts may yet turn up from time to time. But from all that can be learned, and from the piecing together of the scattered fragments of information carefully collected by Mr. Lowrie, who accompanied the expedition, it appears that Thursday, June 28th, several Chinese young men who had been studying medicine under Dr. Taylor came to him at the city dispensary, warned him of the impending danger and urged him to leave. When he refused they besought him to yield, and though several of them were not Christians, so strong was their attachment to their teacher that they shed tears.

Dr. Taylor placed the dispensary and its contents, together with the adjacent street chapel, in charge of the district magistrate and returned to the mission compound outside the city. That very afternoon startling proof was given that foreboding was not ill-founded, for the Rev. Meng Chi Hsien, the native pastor of the Congregational Church, was seized while in the city, his hands cut off, and the next morning he was beheaded.

The missionaries then decided to leave, drew their silver from the local bank and hired carts. But an official assured them that there would be no further trouble, and they concluded to remain. It is doubtful whether they could have escaped anyway, for the very next afternoon, Saturday, June 30th, a mob left the west gate of the city, and marching northward parallel to the railroad, turned eastward through a small village near the mission compound, which has always been the resort of bad characters, and attacked the mission between five and six o'clock.

The first report that all the missionaries were together in the house of Mr. Simcox is now believed to have been erroneous. The Hodges were there, but Dr. Taylor was in his own room in the second story of Mr. Lowrie's house. Seizing a magazine rifle belonging to Mr. Lowrie, he showed it to the mob and warned them not to come nearer. But the Boxers pressed furiously on, in the superstitious belief that the foreigner's bullet could not harm them. Then, being alone, and with the traditions of a Quaker ancestry strong within him, he chose rather to die himself than to inflict death upon the people he had come to save. The Boxers set fire to the house, and the beloved physician, throwing the rifle to the floor, disappeared amid the flame and smoke. But the body was not consumed, for a Chinese living in a neighbouring village said afterwards that he saw it lying in the ruins of the house several days later, and that he gave it decent burial in a field near by. But there are hundreds of unmarked mounds in that region, and when the foreign expedition arrived in October, he was unable to indicate the particular one which he had made for Dr. Taylor's remains. Mr. Lowrie made diligent search and opened a number of graves, but found nothing that could be identified.

In the Simcox house, however, the two men were charged with the defense of women and children, and to protect them if possible from unspeakable outrage, when they realized that persuasion was vain, they felt justified as a last desperate resort in using force. The testimony of natives is to the effect that at least two Boxers were killed in the attack, one of them the Boxer chief, Chu Tu Tze, who that very day had received the rank of the gilt button from the Provincial Judge as a recognition of his anti-foreign zeal and an encouragement to continue it. He was shot through the head while vociferously urging the assault from the top of a large grave mound near the compound wall.

The story that little Paul and Francis Simcox, frightened by the heat and smoke, ran out of the house and were despatched by the crowd and their bodies thrown into a well now appears to be unfounded. All died together, Mr. and Mrs. Simcox and their three children, and Dr. and Mrs. Hodge; Mr. Simcox being last seen walking up and down holding the hand of one of his children.

It is at least some comfort that they were spared the outrages and mutilations inflicted on so many of the martyrs of that awful summer, for unless some were struck by bullets, death came by suffocation in burning houses—swiftly and mercifully. No Boxer hand touched them, living or dead, but within less than an hour from the beginning of the attack, the end came, and the flames did their work so completely that, save in the case of Dr. Taylor, nothing remained upon which fiendish hate could wreak itself. Husbands and wives died as they could have wished to die—together, and at the post of duty.

The next morning the Boxers, jubilant over their success of the night before, trooped out to the American Board compound in the south suburb. The two ladies took refuge in the chapel, while Mr. Pitkin remained outside to do what he could to keep back the mob. But he was speedily shot and then decapitated. His body, together with the bodies of several of the members of the Meng family, was thrown into a hastily-dug pit just outside the wall of the compound, but his head was borne in triumph to the Provincial Judge, who was the prime mover in the outbreak. He caused it to be fixed on the inside of the city wall, not far from the southeast corner and nearly opposite the temple in which the remaining missionaries were imprisoned. There, the Chinese say, it remained for two or three weeks, a ghastly evidence of the callous cruelty of a people many of whom must have known Mr. Pitkin and the good work done at the mission compound not far distant. When sorrowing friends arrived in October, the head could not be found, but it has since been recovered and buried with the bodies of the other martyrs.

The fate of the young women, Miss Morrill and Miss Gould, thus deprived of their only protector, was not long deferred. After the fall of Mr. Pitkin, they were seized, stripped of all their clothing except one upper and one lower garment, and led by the howling crowd along a path leading diagonally from the entrance of the compound to the road just east of it. Miss Gould did not die of fright as she was taken from the chapel, as was at first reported, but at the point where the path enters the road, a few hundred yards from the chapel, she fainted. Her ankles were then tied together, and another cord lashed her wrists in front of her body. A pole was thrust between legs and arms, and she was carried the rest of the way, while Miss Morrill walked, characteristically giving to a beggar the little money at her waist, talking to the people, and with extraordinary self-possession endeavouring to convince her persecutors of their folly. And so the procession of bloodthirsty men, exulting in the possession of two defenseless women one of them unconscious, wended its way northward to the river bank, westward to the stone bridge, over it and to a temple within the city, not far from the southeast corner of the wall.

Meantime, Mr. Cooper, Mr. and Mrs. Bagnall and their little daughter had begun the day in Mr. Bagnall's house, which was a short distance east of the American Board compound, and on the same road. Seeing the flames of the hospital, which was the first building fired by the Boxers, they fled eastward along the road to a Chinese military camp, about a quarter of a mile distant, whose commanding officer had been on friendly terms with Mr. Bagnall. But in the hour of need he arrested them, ruthlessly despoiled them of their valuables, and sent them under a guard to the arch conspirator, the Provincial Judge. It is pitiful to hear of the innocent child cling-ing in terror to her mother's dress. But there was no pity in the heart of the brutal judge, and the little party was sent to the temple where the Misses Morrill and Gould were already imprisoned.

All this was in the morning. A pretended trial was held, and about four in the afternoon of the same day, all were taken to a spot outside the southeast corner of the city wall, and there, before the graves of two Boxers, they were beheaded and their bodies thrown into a pit.

Months passed before any effort was made by the foreign armies in Peking to reach Paoting-fu. Shortly after the occupation of the capital, I wrote to the Secretary of State in Washington reminding him again of the American citizens who at last accounts were at Paoting-fu, and urging that the United States commander in Peking be instructed to send an expedition there, not to punish for I did not deem it my duty to discuss that phase of the question, but to ascertain whether any Americans were yet living and to make an investigation as to what had happened.

Secretary Hay promptly cabled Minister Conger, who soon wired back that all the Americans at Paoting-fu had been killed. The United States forces took no part in the punitive expeditions sent out by the European commanders, partly, no doubt, because our Government preferred to act on the theory that it would be wiser to give the Chinese Government an opportunity to punish the guilty, and partly because the Administration did not desire the United States to be identified with the expeditions which were reputed to equal the Boxers in the merciless barbarity of burning, pillaging, ravishing and killing.

Still, it is not pleasing to reflect that though there was an ample American force in Peking only 110 miles away, we were indebted to a British general for the opportunity to acquire any accurate information as to the fate of eleven Americans. An expedition of inquiry, at least, might have been sent. But as it was, it was not till October that three columns of Europeans (still no Americans) left for Paoting-fu. One column was French, under General Baillard.

The second was British and German under Generals Campbell and Von Ketteler, both of these columns starting from Tien-tsin. The third column left Peking and was composed of British and Italians led by General Gaselee. The plan was for the three columns to unite as they approached the city. But General Baillard made forced marches and reached Paoting-fu October 15th, so that when General Gaselee arrived on the 17th, he found, to his surprise and chagrin, that the French had already taken bloodless possession of the city. The British and German columns from Tien-tsin did not arrive till the 20th and 21st. With them came the Rev. J. Walter Lowrie, who had obtained permission to accompany it as an interpreter for the British.

The allied Generals immediately made stern inquisitions into the outrages that had been committed, which, of course, included those upon Roman Catholics as well as upon Protestants. Mr. Lowrie, as the only man who could speak Chinese, and the only one, too, who personally knew the Chinese, at once came into prominence. To the people, he appeared to have the power of life and death. All examinations had to be conducted through him. All accusations and evidence had to be sifted by him. The guilty tried to shift the blame upon the innocent, and enemies sought to pay off old scores of hatred upon their foes by charging them with complicity in the massacres. It would have accorded with Chinese custom if Mr. Lowrie had availed himself to the utmost of his opportunity to punish the antagonists of the missionaries, especially as his dearest friends had been remorselessly murdered and all of his personal property destroyed. It was not in human nature to be lenient in such circumstances, and the Chinese fully expected awful vengeance.

Great was their amazement when they saw the man whom they had so grievously wronged acting not only with modera-tion and strict justice, but in a kind and forgiving spirit. Every scrap of testimony was carefully analyzed in order that no innocent man might suffer. Instead of securing the execution of hundreds of smaller officials and common people, as is customary in China in such circumstances, Mr. Lowrie counselled the Generals to try Ting Jung, who at the time of the massacre was Provincial Judge but who had since been promoted to the post of Provincial Treasurer and acting Viceroy; Kwei Heng the commander of the Manchu garrison, and Weng Chan Kwei the colonel in command of the Chinese Imperial forces who had seized the escaping Bagnall party and sent them back to their doom. The evidence plainly showed that these high officials were the direct and responsible instigators of the uprising, that they had ordered every movement, and that the crowd of smaller officials, Boxers and common people had simply obeyed their orders. The three dignitaries were found guilty and condemned to death.

Was ever retributive justice more signally illustrated than in the place in which they were imprisoned pending Count von Waldersee's approval of the sentence? The military authorities selected the place, not with reference to its former uses, of which indeed they were ignorant, but simply because it was convenient, empty and clean. But it was the Presbyterian chapel and dispensary in which Mr. Lowrie had so often preached the gospel of peace and good will and the martyred Dr. Taylor had so often healed the sick in the name of Christ.

Not long afterwards, the three officials were led to a level, open space, just east of a little clump of trees not far from the southwest corner of the city wall, and as near as practicable to the place where the missionaries had been beheaded, and there, in the presence of all the foreign soldiers, they were themselves beheaded.

Nor was this all, for Chinese officials are never natives of the cities they govern, but are sent to them from other provinces. Moreover, they usually remain in one place only a few years. The people fear and obey them as long as they are officials, but often care little what becomes of them afterwards. They had not befriended them during their trial and they did not attend their execution. The Generals therefore felt that some punishment must be inflicted upon the city. A Chinese city is proud of the stately and ponderous towers which ornament the gates and corners of its massive wall and protect the inhabitants from foes, human and demoniac. All of these, but two comparatively small ones, were blown up by order of the foreign generals. The temples which the Boxers had used for their meetings, including the one in which the American Board and China Inland missionaries had been imprisoned, were also destroyed, while the splendid official temple of the city, dedicated to its patron deity, was utterly wrecked by dynamite.

Not till March 23d could memorial services be held. Then a party of missionaries and friends came down from Peking. The surviving Christians assembled. The new city officials erected a temporary pavilion on the site of the Presbyterian compound, writing over the entrance arch: "They held the truth unto death." Within, potted flowers and decorated banners adorned the tables and walls. The scene was solemnly impressive. Mr. Lowrie, Dr. Wherry and Mr. Killie and others made appropriate addresses to an audience in which there were, besides themselves, fifteen missionaries representing four denominations, German and French army officers, Chinese officials and Chinese Christians. A German military band furnished appropriate music and two Roman Catholic priests of the city sent flowers and kind letters. The following day a similar service was held on the site of the American Board compound.

We sadly visited all these places. It was about the hour of the attack that we approached the Presbyterian compound. Of the once pleasant homes and mission buildings, not even ruins were left. A few hundred yards away, the site could not have been distinguished from the rest of the open fields if my companions had not pointed out marks mournfully intelligible to them but hardy recognizable by a stranger. The very foundations had been dug up by Chinese hunting for silver, and every scrap of material had been carried away. Even the trees and bushes had been removed by the roots and used for firewood. In front of the site of the Simcox house are a few unmarked mounds. All but one contain the fragments of the bodies of the Chinese helpers and Christians, and that one, the largest, holds the few pieces of bones which were all that could be found in the ruins of the house in which the missionaries perished. A few more may yet be found. We ourselves discovered five small pieces which Dr. Charles Lewis afterwards identified as human bones. But their charred and broken condition showed how completely the merciful fire had done its work of keeping the sacred remains from the hands of those who would have shamefully misused them. The American Board and China Inland Mission compounds were also in ruins, a chaos of desolation. But as the martyred missionaries and native Christians were beheaded and not burned, their bodies have been recovered and interred in a long row of twenty-three graves.

The negotiations of foreign Powers with the Chinese regarding the payment of indemnity were, as might be expected, protracted and full of difficulties. Some of the Powers favoured extreme demands which, if acceded to, would have ruined the Empire or resulted in its immediate partition, even if they did not cause a new and more bitter outbreak of hostilities. Other Powers, notably the United States, favoured moderate terms, holding that China should not be asked to pay sums that were clearly beyond her ability. After almost interminable disputes, the total sum to be paid by China was, by the final protocol signed September 7, 1901, fixed at 450,000,000 taels to be paid in thirty-nine annual installments with interest at four per cent. on the deferred payments and to be distributed as follows:

Country	taels
Germany	90,070,515
Austria-Hungary	4,003,920
Belgium	8,484,345
Spain	135,315
United States	32,939,055[63]
France	70,878,240
Portugal	92,250
Great Britain	50,712,795
Italy	26,617,005
Japan	34,793,100
Netherlands	82,100
Russia	230,371,120
International (Sweden and Norway, $62,820)	212,490

	450,000,000

The treaty was not calculated to make the Chinese think more kindly of their conquerors. Besides the payment of the heavy indemnity, the Powers exacted apologies to Germany for the murder of its minister and to Japan for the assassination of the chancellor of its legation, the erection of monuments in foreign cemeteries

---

63   The equivalent of $24,168,357.

and the making of new commercial treaties. The Chinese were cut to the quick by being told, among other things, that they must not import firearms for two years; that no official examinations would be held for five years in the cities where foreigners had been attacked; that an important part of the imperial capital would be added to the already spacious grounds of the foreign legations and that the whole would be fortified and garrisoned by foreign guards; that the Taku forts which defended the entrance to Peking would be razed and the railway from the sea to the capital occupied by foreign troops; that members of anti-foreign societies were to be executed; that magistrates even though they were viceroys were to be summarily dismissed and disgraced if they did not prevent anti-foreign outbreaks and sternly punish their ring-leaders; that court ceremonies in relation to foreign ministers must be conformed to Western ideas; that the Tsung-li Yamen (Foreign Office) must be abolished and a new ministry of foreign affairs erected, the Wai-wu Pu, which must be regarded as the highest of the departments instead of the lowest. China's cup of humiliation was indeed full.

PART IV

THE MISSIONARY FORCE AND THE CHINESE CHURCH

XVIII
BEGINNINGS OF THE MISSIONARY ENTERPRISE—THE TAI-PING REBELLION AND THE LATER DEVELOPMENT

THE first definite knowledge of the true God appears to have come to China with some Jews who are said to have entered the Empire in the third century. Conjecture has long been busy with the circumstances of that ancient migration. That the colony became fairly numerous may be inferred from the fact that in 1329 and again in 1354, the Jews are mentioned in the Chinese records of the Mongol dynasty, while early in the seventeenth century Father Ricci claimed to have discovered a synagogue built in 1183. In 1866, the Rev. Dr. W. A. P. Martin, then President of the Tung-wen College at Peking, visited Kai-fung-fu, the centre of this Jewish colony, and on a monument he found an inscription which included the following passage:—

"With respect to the religion of Israel, we find that our first ancestor was Adam. The founder of the religion was Abraham; then came Moses who established the law, and handed down the sacred writings. During the dynasty of Han (B. C. 200-A, D. 226) this religion entered China. In the second year of Hiao-tsung, of the Sung dynasty (A. D. 1164), a synagogue was erected in Kai-fung fu. Those who attempt to represent God by images or pictures do but vainly occupy themselves with empty forms. Those who honour and obey the sacred writings know the origin of all things.

Eternal reason and the sacred writings mutually sustain each other in testifying whence men derived their being. All those who profess this religion aim at the practice of goodness and avoid the commission of vice."[64]

Dr. Martin writes that he inquired in the market-place:—

"Are there among you any of the family of Israel?" "I am one," responded a young man, whose face corroborated his assertion; and then another and another stepped forth until I saw before me representatives of six out of the seven families into which the colony is divided. They confessed with shame and grief that their holy and beautiful house had been demolished by their own hands. It had for a long time, they said, been in a ruinous condition; they had no money to make repairs; they had, moreover, lost all knowledge of the sacred tongue; the traditions of the fathers were no longer handed down and their ritual worship had ceased to be observed. In this state of things they had yielded to the pressure of necessity and disposed of the timbers and stones of that venerable edifice to obtain relief for their bodily wants…Their number they estimated, though not very exactly, at from three to four hundred…No bond of union remains, and they are in danger of being speedily absorbed by Mohammedanism or heathenism."[65]

There is something pathetic about that forlorn remnant of the Hebrew race. "A rock rent from the side of Mount Zion by some great national catastrophe and projected into the central plain of China, it has stood there while the centuries rolled by, sublime in its antiquity and solitude."[66]

In his Life of Morrison, Townsend reminds us that the Christian Church early realized that it could not ignore so vast a nation, while its very exclusiveness attracted bold spirits. As far back as the first decade of the sixth century (505 A. D.), Nestorian monks appear to have begun a mission in China. Romance and tragedy are suggested by the few known facts regarding that early movement. Partly impelled by conviction, partly driven by persecution, those faithful souls travelled beyond the bounds of the Roman Empire, and rested not till they had made the formidable journey across

---

64 Martin, "A Cycle of Cathay," p. 275.

65 Martin, "A Cycle of Cathay," pp. 275, 276, 277.

66 Martin, p. 278.

burning deserts and savage mountains to the land of Sinim. That some measure of success attended their effort is probable. Indeed there are hints in the ancient records of numerous churches and of the favour of the great Emperor Tai Tsung in 635. But however zealous the Nestorians may have been for a time, it is evident that they were finally submerged in the sea of Chinese superstition. A quaint monument, discovered in 1625 at Hsi-an-fu, the capital of Shen-si, on which is inscribed an outline of the Nestorian effort from the year 630 to 781, is the only trace that remains of what must have been an interesting and perhaps a thrilling missionary enterprise.

The Roman Catholic effort began in 1293, when John de Corvino succeeded in reaching Peking. Though he was elevated to an Archbishopric and reinforced by several priests, this effort, too, proved a failure and was abandoned.

Two and a-half centuries of silence followed, and then in 1552, the heroic Francis Xavier set his face towards China, only to be prostrated by fever on the Island of Sancian. As he despairingly realized that he would never be able to set his foot on that still impenetrable land, he moaned: "Oh, Rock, Rock, when wilt thou open!" and passed away.

But in 1581, another Jesuit, the learned and astute Matteo Ricci, entered Canton in the guise of a Buddhist priest. He managed to remain, and twenty years later he went to Peking in the dress of a literary gentleman. In him Roman Catholicism gained a permanent foothold in China, and although it was often fiercely persecuted and at times reduced to feebleness, it never became wholly extinct. Gradually it extended its influence until in 1672 the priests reported 300,000 baptized Chinese, including children. In the nineteenth century, the growth of the Roman Church was rapid. It is now strongly entrenched in all the provinces, and in most of the leading cities its power is great. There are twenty-seven bishops and about six hundred foreign priests. The number of communicants is variously estimated, but in 1897 the Vicar Apostolic of Che-kiang, though admitting that he could not secure accurate statistics, estimated the Roman Catholic population at 750,000.

It is not to the credit of Protestantism that it was centuries behind the Roman Church in the attempt to Christianize China. It was not till 1807, that the first Protestant missionary arrived.

January 31st, of that year, Robert Morrison, then a youth of twenty-five, sailed alone from London under appointment of the London Missionary Society (Congregational). As the hostile East India Company would not allow a missionary on any of its ships, Morrison had to go to New York in order to secure passage on an American vessel. As he paid his fare in the New York ship owner's office, the merchant said with a sneer: "And so, Mr. Morrison, you really expect that you will make an impression on the idolatry of the great Chinese Empire?" "No, sir," was the ringing reply, "I expect God will."

The ship Trident left New York about May 15th and did not reach Canton till September 8th. For two years Morrison had to live and study in Canton and the Portuguese settlement of Macao with the utmost secrecy, dreading constantly that he might be forced to leave. For a time, he never walked the streets by daylight for fear of attracting attention, but exercised by night. His own countrymen were hostile to his purpose and his Chinese language teachers were impatient and insolent. It was not till February 20, 1809, the date of his marriage to Miss Morton, that his employment as translator by the East India Company gave him a secure residence. Still, however, he could not do open missionary work, but was obliged to present Christianity behind locked doors to the few Chinese whom he dared to approach. In these circumstances, he naturally gave his energies largely to language study and translation, and in 1810 he had the joy of issuing a thousand copies of a Chinese version of the Book of Acts.

Seven weary, discouraging years passed before Morrison baptized his first convert, July 16, 1814, and even then he had to administer the sacrament at a lonely spot where unfriendly eyes could not look. At his death in 1834, there were only three Chinese Christians in the whole Empire. Successors carried on the effort, but the door was not yet open, and the work was done against many obstacles and chiefly in secret till the treaty of Nanking, in 1842, opened the five ports of Amoy, Canton, Foochow, Ningpo and Shanghai. Missionaries who had been waiting and watching in the neighbouring islands promptly entered these cities. Eagerly they looked to the great populations in the interior, but they were practically confined to the ports named till 1858, when the treaty of Tien-tsin opened other cities and officially conceded the rights of missionary residence and labour.

The work now spread more rapidly, not only because it was conducted in more centres and by a larger force of missionaries, but because it was carried into the interior regions by Chinese who had heard the gospel in the ports.

The Tai-ping Rebellion soon gave startling illustration of the perversion of the new force. Begun in 1850 by an alleged Christian convert who claimed to have a special revelation from heaven as a younger brother of Christ, it spread with amazing rapidity until in 1853 it had overrun almost all that part of China south of the Yang-tze-kiang, had occupied Nanking and Shanghai, and had made such rapid progress northward that it threatened the capital itself. It was the most stupendous revolution in history, shaking to its foundations a vast and ancient empire, involving the destruction of an almost inconceivable amount of property and, it is said, of the lives of twenty millions of human beings.

If this great rebellion had been wisely guided, it would undoubtedly have changed the history of China and perhaps, by this time, of the greater part of Asia, for it proposed to overthrow idolatry, to unseat the Manchu dynasty, and to found an empire on the principles of the Christian religion. So nearly indeed did it attain success that if it had not been opposed by European nations, it would probably have attained its object. But the weight of their influence was thrown in favour of the Government. The American Frederick T. Ward and the English Charles George Gordon organized and led the "Ever Victorious Army" of Chinese troops against the revolutionists. Most significant of all, the leaders of the rebellion itself, freed from the restraint which foreigners might perhaps have exerted, quickly discarded whatever Christian principles they had started with and rapidly demoralized the movement at its centre by giving themselves up to an arrogance, vice, and cruelty which were worse than those of the government they sought to overturn. Mr. McLane, then United States Minister, truly reported to Washington:—

"Whatever may have been the hopes of the enlightened and civilized nations of the earth, in regard to this movement, it is now apparent that they neither profess nor apprehend Christianity, and whatever may be the true judgment to form of their political power, it can no longer be doubted that intercourse cannot be established or maintained on terms of equality."

The recapture of Nanking in 1864 marked the final turning of the tide, and in an incredibly short time the whole insurrection collapsed. The rebellion, vast as it was, is now after all but an episode in the history of the great Empire. But the fact that any man on such a platform could so quickly develop an insurrection of such appalling proportions significantly suggests the possibilities of change in China when new movements are rightly directed.

Freed from this gigantic travesty of its true character, the growth of Christianity in China became more rapid. The following table is eloquent:

1807	0 communicants
1814	1 "
1834	3 "
1842	6 "
1853	350 "
1857	1,000 "
1865	2,000 "
1876	13,515 "
1886	28,000 communicants
1889	37,287 "
1893	55,093 "
1887	80,682 "
1903	112,808 "

The number of Protestant missionaries is 2,950, of whom 1,233 are men, 868 are wives and 849 are single women. Of the whole number, 1,483 are from Great Britain, 1,117 from America and 350 from continental Europe. Other interesting statistics are 5,000,000 adherents, 2,500 stations and out-stations, 6,388 Chinese pastors and helpers, 1,819 day-schools and 170 higher institutions of learning, twenty-three mission presses with an annual Output Of 107,149,738 pages, thirty-two periodicals, 124 hospitals and dispensaries treating in a single year 1,700,452 patients; while the asylums for the orphaned and blind and deaf number thirty-two.

It will thus be seen that Christian missions in China are being conducted upon a large scale. It would be difficult to overestimate the silent and yet mighty energy represented by such work, steadily continued through a long series of years, and representing the life labours of thousands of devoted men and women and an annual expenditure of hundreds of thousands of dollars.

True, the number of Christians is small in comparison with the population of the Empire, but the gospel has been aptly compared to a seed. It is indeed small, but seeds generally are. Lodged in a crevice of a rock, a seed will thrust its thread-like roots into fissures so tiny that they are hardly noticeable. Yet in time they will rend the rock asunder and firmly hold a stately tree. Now the seed of the gospel has been fairly lodged in the Chinese Empire. It is a seed of indestructible vitality and irresistible transforming power. It has taken root, and it is destined to produce mighty changes. It was not without reason that Christianity was spoken of as a force that "turned the world upside down," though it only does this where the world was wrong side up. It is significant that the word translated "power" in Romans 1:16, "The gospel is the power of God," is in the Greek the word that we have anglicized in common speech as "dynamite." We might, therefore, literally translate Paul's statement: "The gospel is the dynamite of God." That dynamite has been placed under the crust of China's conservatism, and the extraordinary transformations that are taking place in China are, in part at least, the results of its tremendous explosive force.

The scope of this book does not permit an extended account of the missionary movement in China. It has been given in many volumes that are easily accessible."[67] Nearly all of the Protestant

67 The reader is referred to "The Middle Kingdom," Williams; "Christian Progress in China," Foster (1889); "Story of the China Inland Mission," Guinness; "China and Formosa," Johnston (1897); Record of the General Conference of the Protestant Missionaries of China held in Shanghai, 1890; Report of the Ecumenical Missionary Conference held in New York, 1900; "Mission Problems and Mission Methods in South China," Gibson; "Mission Methods in Manchuria," Ross; "Women of the Middle Kingdom," McNabb; "Among the Mongols," Gilmour; "East of the Barrier," Graham; "In the Far East," Guinness; "The Cross and the Dragon," Henry; "From Far Formosa," Mackay; "Dawn on the Hills of T'ang," Beach; "China and the Chinese," Nevius; "Our Life in China,"

churches, European and American, are represented and their missionaries are teaching the young, healing the sick, translating the Word of God, creating a wholesome literature, and preaching everywhere and with a fidelity beyond all praise the truths of the Christian religion. Self-sacrificing devotion and patient persistence in well-doing are written on every page of the history of missions in China, while emergencies have developed deeds of magnificent heroism. Men and women have repeatedly endured persecution of the most virulent kind rather than forsake their converts, and a number "of whom the world was not worthy" have laid down their lives for conscience' sake. There are few places in all the world that are more depressing to a white man than a Chinese city. The dreary monotony and squalor of its life are simply indescribable. Chefoo is usually considered one of the most attractive cities in China, and the missionaries who reside there are regarded as fortunate above their brethren. But even a brief stay will convince the most sceptical that nothing but the strongest considerations of duty could induce one who has freedom of choice to remain any longer than is absolutely necessary. Yet for forty-two years, missionaries have lived and toiled amid these unattractive surroundings, their houses on Temple Hill in the midst of the innumerable graves which occupy almost every possible space not actually covered by the mission buildings and grounds. But steadily the missionaries have toiled on, with faith and courage and love, and they are slowly but surely effecting marked changes. One by one, the Chinese are being led to loftier views of life and while the old city still continues to live in the ancient way, hundreds of Chinese families, amid the numerous population outside of the walls and in the outlying villages, have begun to conform themselves to the new and higher conditions of life represented by the Christian missionaries.

Several schools, a handsome church, a hospital, the only institution for deaf mutes in China and a wide-reaching itinerating

---

Mrs. Nevius; "Life of John Livingston Nevius," Nevius; "Rex Christus," Smith; "John Kenneth Mackenzie," Bryson; "Princely Men in the Heavenly Kingdom," Beach; "James Gilmour of Mongolia," Lovett; "Griffith John," Robson; "Robert Morrison," Townsend; "With the Tibetans in Tent and Temple," Rijnhart.

work, are features of the mission enterprise in Chefoo. The visitor will be particularly interested in Dr. Hunter Corbett's street chapel and museum. The building is situated opposite the Chinese theatre and is well adapted to its purpose. Dr. Corbett and a helper stand at the door and invite passers-by, while a blind boy plays on a baby organ and sings. The chapel, which holds about sixty or seventy, is soon filled. Dr. Corbett preaches to the people for half an hour and then ad-mits them to the museum which occupies several rooms in the rear. It is a wonderful place to the Chinese who never weary of watching the stuffed tiger, the model railway and the scores of interesting objects and specimens that Dr. Corbett has collected from various lands. Then the people leave by a door opening on the back street, another service being held with them in the last room. Several audiences a day are thus handled. It is hard work, for the men as a rule are from many outlying villages, unaccustomed to listening and knowing nothing of Christianity. But Dr. Corbett speaks with such animation and eloquence that not an eye is taken from him. Few are converted in the chapel, but friendships are gained, doors of opportunity opened, tracts distributed, men led to think, and on country tours Dr. Corbett invariably meets people who have been to the museum and who cordially welcome him to their homes. He declares that after thirty years' experience, he thoroughly believes in such work when followed up by faithful itineration. Seventy-two thousand attended the chapel and museum in the year 1900 in spite of the Boxer troubles. The chapel is open every day, except that the museum is closed on Sundays, and the attendance is now larger than ever.

After dinner, we strolled down to Dr. Nevius' famous orchard. It is a beautiful spot. Here the great missionary found his recreation after his arduous labours. Yet even in his hours of rest, he was eminently practical. Seeing that the Chinese had very little good fruit and believing that he might show them how to secure it, he brought from America seeds and cuttings, carefully cultivated them and, when they were grown, freely distributed the new seeds and cuttings to the Chinese, explaining to them the methods of cultivation. Today, as the result of his forethought and generosity, several foreign fruits have become common throughout North China. But the orchard is deteriorating as the Chinese will not prune the trees. They are so greedy for returns that they do not like to diminish the number of apples or plums in the interest of quality.

At sunset, I made a pilgrimage with Mrs. Nevius to the cemetery, where, after forty years of herculean toil, the mighty missionary sleeps. We sat for a long time beside the grave, and the aged widow, speaking of her own end, which she appeared to feel could not be far distant, said that she wished to be buried beside her husband and that for this reason she did not want to go to the United States, preferring to remain in Chefoo until her summons came.

The scene was very beautiful as the sun set and the moon rose above the quiet sea. Standing beside the grave of the honoured dead and under the solemn pines, the traveller gains a new sense of the beneficence and dignity of the missionary force that is operating through such consecrated lives of the living and the dead.

XIX
MISSIONARIES AND NATIVE LAWSUITS

IN considering the effects of the operation of this missionary force, we are at once confronted by the complaint of many Chinese that missionaries interfere on behalf of their converts in lawsuits. This complaint has been taken up and circulated by foreign critics until it has become one of the most formidable of the objections to missionary work. The difficulty will be understood when we remember that, though the Chinese are not a warlike people, they are litigious to an extraordinary degree. The struggle for existence in such a densely populated country often results in real or fancied entanglements of rights. So the Chinese are forever disputing about something, and the magistrates and village headmen are beset by clamorous hordes who demand a settlement of their alleged grievances. Naturally the Chinese Christians do not at once outgrow this national disposition. Whether they do or not, their profession of Christianity makes them an easy mark for the greedy and envious. Jealousy and dislike of the native who abandons the faith of his fathers and espouses "the foreigner's religion" frequently hale him into court on trumped-up charges and the notorious prejudice and corruption of the average magistrate often result in grievous persecution. The terrified Christian naturally implores the missionary to save him. It is hard to resist such an appeal. But the defendant is not always so innocent as he appears to be, and whether innocent or guilty, the interference of the foreigner irritates both magistrate and prosecutor, while it not infrequently arouses the resentment of the whole community by giving the idea that the Christians are a privileged class who are not amenable to the ordinary laws of the land. When, as sometimes happens, the Christians themselves get that idea and presume upon it, the difficulty becomes acute. Speaking of the Chinese talent for indirection, the Rev. Dr. Arthur H. Smith says:—

"It is this which makes it so difficult for the most conscientious and discreet missionary to be quite sure that he is in possession of all the needed data in any given case. The difficulty in getting at the bottom facts frequently is that there are no facts available, and, as the pilots say, 'no bottom.' Every Protestant missionary is anxious to have his flock of Christians such as fear God and work righteousness, but in the effort to compass this end he not infrequently finds that when endeavouring to investigate the 'facts' in any case he is chasing a school of cuttlefish through seas of ink."[68]

An illustration of this occurred during my visit in Ichou-fu. A magistrate who needed some wheelbarrows sent out his men to impress them. The rule in such cases is that only empty barrows can be seized. But the yamen underlings found the father of a mission helper with loaded barrows at an inn, stole his goods and forced him to pay them a sum of money for the privilege of keeping his barrows. The helper complained and Dr. C. F. Johnson yielded only so far as to write a guarded letter to the magistrate simply stating his confidence that if the magistrate found that injustice had been done, he would remedy it. But that letter brought the missionary into the case and he found himself forced to see it through or "lose face" with the Chinese Christians and especially the helper who was the son of the man robbed. He soon discovered, moreover, that the wronged man was telling contradictory stories about the value of goods stolen and the amount of money he had to pay to save his barrows. The situation speedily became embarrassing and the sorely-tried missionary, though he had acted from the best of motives and in the most conservative way, vowed that he would never interfere again in such disputes, as irritation and harm were almost certain to result.

I asked Sir Robert Hart whether in his opinion a missionary should seek to obtain justice for a persecuted man or should remain silent? He replied:—

68   "Rex Christus," pp. 103, 107.

"Intervention in matters litigated ought to be absolutely eschewed. Let the missionary content himself with making his disciples good men and good citizens, and let him leave it to the duly authorized officials to interpret and apply the law and administer their affairs in their own way. Individual Christianity has as many shades and degrees as men's faces. There are converts and converts, but even the most godly of them may give his neighbour just reason to take offense, and the most saintly among them may get involved in the meshes of the law. In such cases let the missionary stand aloof. There is, too, such a thing as hypocrisy, much better let the schemer get his deserts than hurt the church's character by following sentiment into interference. You ask what is to be done when there is persecution to be dealt with? First of all, I would advise the individual or the community to live it down, and, as a last resort, report the fact with appropriate detail and proof to the Legation in Peking for the assistance and advice of the minister. 'Watch thou in all things, endure afflictions, do the work of an evangelist, make full proof of thy ministry.'"

It is customary for the friends of Protestant missionaries to answer the critic's charge of interference in native lawsuits by stating that it does not justly lie against them, but only against the Roman Catholics, the rule of the Protestant missionaries being to avoid such interference save in rare and extreme cases. Mr. Alexander Michie, however, declares that Protestant missionaries are not entitled to such exemption, and that, while they may not interfere so frequently as the Catholics, they nevertheless interfere often enough to bring them under the same condemnation.[69]

There are undoubtedly cases of imprudence, but after diligent inquiry, I am persuaded that the Protestant missionaries as a class are keenly alive to the risks of interference in native lawsuits and that they are increasingly careful in this respect. They feel with the Rev. J. C. Garritt of Hangchow that "the most important form which prejudice has taken of late is the belief that foreigners aid or at least countenance their converts in the carrying of lawsuits through the yamens, or in the business of private settlement of disputes, and that if we can only practically demonstrate to the

---

69   Address in Shanghai, 1901.

public that we are not in that business, we shall have overcome one very serious obstacle to our work."

"The policy of the Chinese Government during the past few years has been to avoid trouble by letting the foreigner have his own way whenever possible. More than once the Chinese official has said in substance to non-Christian litigants: 'You are right and your Christian accusers are wrong; but if I decide in your favour the foreigner will appeal the case to the Governor or to the Peking foreign office and I shall suffer.' Such things are charged, justly or unjustly, to the account of both Protestant and Romanist."[70]

A broad induction as to the facts has been made by the Rev. Dr. Paul D. Bergen, President of Shantung Protestant University. He wrote to a large number of missionaries representing all Protestant denominations as to their practice and convictions regarding this subject. Seventy-three answered and Dr. Bergen tabulated their replies. As to the results of the concrete cases of intervention cited, fifty-three are reported to have been beneficial, twenty-six are characterized as doubtful, four as mixed and sixty-seven as bad. This leaves the remaining cases "suspended in the air," and Dr. Bergen conjectures that "perhaps the missionary felt in such a confused mental state at their conclusion, that he was quite unable to work out the complicated equation of their results."

"But surely the result that only fifty-three cases are reported to have been of unmistakable benefit, while sixty-seven are set down as resulting in evil, ought to give us thought. In short, in the yamen intercession in behalf of prosecuted Christians, it is the deliberate opinion of seventy-three missionaries that, as a matter of personal experience, sixty-seven cases have wrought only evil, while only fifty-three have been productive of good. The balance is on the wrong side. We must decide, in view of these replies, that there exists in general rather a pessimistic opinion as to the advantages of applying to the yamen in behalf of Christians."

Summing up briefly the results of this inquiry, we note the following points, which will embody the views of a very large majority of the Protestant missionaries of experience in the Empire:—

"First,—That it is highly desirable to keep church troubles out of the yamen, but that there are times when we cannot do

---

70   The Rev. Dr. L. J. Davies, Tsing-tau.

so without violating our sense of justice and our sense of duty towards an injured brother.

"Second,—Official assistance is to be sought in such troubles only when all other means of relief have been tried in vain. Always seek to settle these difficulties out of court.

"Third,—When official assistance is requested, our bearing should be friendly and courteous in the spirit, at least in the first instance, of asking a favour of the official, rather than demanding a right…We should be extremely careful about trying to bring pressure to bear on an official.

"Fourth,—In the presence of the native Christian, and especially of those chiefly concerned, as well as in our own closets, we should cherish a deep sense of our absolute dependence on heavenly rather than on earthly protection, and remind the Christians that, as Dr. Taylor has so tersely put it, their duty is 'to do good, suffer for it and take it patiently.'

"Fifth,—Only in grave cases should matters be pushed to the point of controversy or formal appeal.

"Sixth,—Christians and evangelists should be solemnly warned against betraying an arrogant spirit upon the successful termination of any trouble.

"Seventh,—Previous to the carrying of a case before the official, let the missionary be sure of his facts. Each case should be patiently, thoroughly and firmly examined. Receive individual testimony with judicious reserve. Be not easily blinded by appeals to the emotions. Be especially ready to receive any one from the opposition, and give his words due weight. Do not be too exclusively influenced by the judgment of any one man, however trusted.

"Eighth,—In the course of negotiation beware of insisting on monetary compensation for the injured Christian. In greatly aggravated cases this may occasionally be unavoidable. But should it be made a condition of settlement, see to it that the damages are under, rather than over, what might have been demanded. It is almost sure to cause subsequent trouble, both within and without, if a Christian receives money under such circumstances.

"Ninth,—When unhappily involved in a persecution case with the official, we should remember that we are not lawyers, and therefore make no stand on legal technicalities, nor allow ourselves to take a threatening attitude, although we may be subjected to provocation; we should be patient, dignified and strong in the truth, making it clear to the official that this is all that we seek in order that the ends of justice may be satisfied.

"Tenth,—It would be well on every fitting occasion to exhort those under our care to avoid frequenting yamens or cultivating intimacy with their inhabitants, unless, indeed, we feel assured that their motive is the same as that animating our Lord when He mingled with publicans and sinners."

A widely representative conference of Protestant missionaries issued in 1903 the following manifesto and sent copies in Chinese to all officials throughout the Empire:

"Chinese Christians, though church-members, remain in every respect Chinese citizens, and are subject to the properly constituted Chinese authorities. The sacred Scriptures and the doctrines of the church teach obedience to all lawful authority and exhort to good citizenship; and these doctrines are preached in all Protestant churches. The relation of a missionary to his converts is thus that of a teacher to his disciples, and he does not desire to arrogate to himself the position or power of a magistrate.

"Unfortunately, it sometimes happens that unworthy men, by making insincere professions, enter the church and seek to use this connection to interfere with the ordinary course of law in China. We all agree that such conduct is entirely reprehensible, and we desire it to be known that we give no support to this unwarrantable practice

"On this account we desire to state that for the information of all that: (a) The Protestant Church does not wish to interfere in law cases. All cases between Christians and non-Christians must be settled in the courts in the ordinary way. Officials are called upon to administer fearlessly and impartially justice to all within their jurisdiction. (b) Native Christians are strictly forbidden to use the name of the church or its officers in the hope of strengthening their positions when they appear before magistrates. The native pastors and preachers are appointed for teaching and exhortation, and are chosen because of their worthy character to carry on this work. To prevent abuses in the future, all officials are respectfully requested to report to the missionary every case in which letters or cards using the name of the church or any of its officers are brought into court. Then proper inquiry will be made and the truth become clear."

The policy of the British Government on this subject was clearly expressed by Earl Granville in his note of August 21, 1871, to the British Minister at Peking:

"The policy and practice of the Government of Great Britain have been unmistakable. They have uniformly declared, and now repeat, that they do not claim to afford any species of protection to Chinese Christians which may be construed as withdrawing them from their native allegiance, nor do they desire to secure to British missionaries any privileges or immunities beyond those granted by treaty to other British subjects. The Bishop of Victoria was requested to intimate this to the Protestant missionary societies in the letter addressed to him by Mr. Hammond by the Earl of Clarendon's direction on the 13th of November, 1869, and to point out that they would 'do well to warn converts that although the Chinese Government may be bound by treaty not to persecute, on account of their conversion, Chinese subjects who may embrace Christianity, there is no provision in the treaty by which a claim can be made on behalf of converts for exemption from the obligations of their natural allegiance, and from the jurisdiction of the local authorities. Under the creed of their adoption, as under that of their birth, Chinese converts to Christianity still owe obedience to the law of China, and if they assume to set themselves above those laws, in reliance upon foreign protection, they must take the consequence of their own indiscretion, for no British authority, at all events, can interfere to save them.'"

The policy of the United States Government was stated with equal clearness in a note of the Hon. Frederick F. Low, United States Minister at Peking, to the Tsung-li Yamen, dated March 20, 1871:

"The Government of the United States, while it claims to exercise, under and by virtue of the stipulations of treaty, the exclusive right of judging of the wrongful acts of its citizens resident in China, and of punishing them when found guilty according to its own laws, does not assume to claim or exercise any authority or control over the natives of China. This rule applies equally to merchants and missionaries, and, so far as I know, all foreign Governments having treaties with China adhere strictly to this rule. In case, however, missionaries see that native Christians are being persecuted by the local officials on account of their religious opinions, in violation of the letter and spirit of the twenty-ninth article of the treaty between the United States and China, it would be proper, and entirely in accordance with the principles of humanity and the teachings of their religion, to make respectful representation of the facts in such cases to the local authorities direct, or through their diplomatic representative to the foreign office; for it cannot be presumed that the Imperial Government would sanction any violation of treaty engagement, or that the local officials would allow persecutions for opinion's sake, when once the facts are made known to them. In doing this the missionaries should conform to Chinese custom and etiquette, so far as it can be done without assuming an attitude that would be humiliating and degrading to themselves."

The question is one of the most difficult and delicate of all the questions with which the missionary must deal. On the one hand, every impulse of justice and humanity prompts him to befriend a good man who is being persecuted for righteousness' sake. But on the other hand, sore experience has taught him the necessity of caution. The pressure upon him is so frequent and trying that it becomes the bete noire of his life. The outsider may wisely hesitate before he adds to that pressure. The citations that have been given show that the missionaries themselves understand the question quite as well as any one else and that they are competent to deal with it.

XX
MISSIONARIES AND THEIR
OWN GOVERNMENTS

THE relation of the missionary to the consular and diplomatic representatives of his own government is another topic of perennial criticism. Some European Governments have persistently and notoriously sought to advance their national interest through their missionaries. France and Russia have been particularly active in this way, the former claiming large rights by virtue of its position as "the protector of Catholic missions." The result is that the average Chinese official regards all missionaries as political agents who are to be watched and feared. Dr. L. J. Davies, a Presbyterian missionary, says that he has been repeatedly asked his rank as "an American official," whether he "reported in person" to his "emperor" on his return to his native land, how much salary his government allowed him, and many other questions the import of which was manifest.

The typical consul and minister, moreover, find that no small part of their business relates to matters that are brought to their attention by missionaries. Sometimes they manifest impatience on this account. One consul profanely complained to me that three-fourths of his business related to the missionary question. He forgot, however, that nine-tenths of the nationals under his jurisdiction were missionaries, so that in proportion to their numbers, the missionaries gave him less trouble than the non-missionary Americans. In answer to an inquiry by the Rev. Dr. Paul D. Bergen, of the Presbyterian Mission, seventy-three missionaries, of from five to thirty years' experience, and representing most of the Protestant boards, reported a total of only fifty-two applications through consul or minister. The Hon. John Barrett, formerly Minister of the United States to Siam, writes: "Let us be fair in judging the missionaries. Let the complaining merchant, traveller or clubman take the beam from his own eye before he demands that the mote be taken from the missionary's eye. In my diplomatic experience in Siam, 150 missionaries gave me less trouble in five years than fifteen merchants gave me in five months."

Doubtless some diplomats would be glad to have the missionaries expatriate themselves. In the United States Senate the Hon. John Sherman is reported to have said that "if our citizens go to a far-distant country, semi-civilized and bitterly opposed to their movements, we cannot follow them there and protect them. They ought to come home." Is, then, the missionary's business less legitimate than the trader's? Is a man entitled to the protection of his country if he goes to the Orient to sell whiskey and rifles, but does he forfeit that protection if he goes there to preach the gospel of temperance and peace?

Critics may be reminded that missionaries are American citizens; that when gamblers and drunkards and adventurers and distillery agents in China claim the rights of citizenship, the missionary does not forfeit his rights by a residence in China for the purpose of teaching the young, healing the sick, distributing the Bible and preaching the gospel of Christ, particularly when treaties expressly guarantee him protection in the exercise of these very privileges. It is odd to find some people insisting that a dissolute trader should be allowed to go wherever he pleases and raising a tremendous hubbub if a hair of his head is injured, while at the same time they appear to deem it an unwarranted thing for a decent man to go to China on a mission of peace and good-will.

While the individual missionary is, of course, free to renounce his claim to the protection of home citizenship, such renunciation is neither necessary nor expedient. There is not the slightest probability that our Government will require it, and if it should, the public sentiment of the United States would not tolerate such an order for a week. No self-respecting nation can expatriate its citizens who go abroad to do good. The policy of the United States was indicated in the note of the Hon. J. C. B. Davis, acting Secretary of State, to the United States Minister at Peking, October 19, 1871.

"The rights of citizens of the United States in China are well defined by treaty. So long as they attend peaceably to their affairs they are to be placed on a common footing of amity and good-will with subjects of China, and are to receive and enjoy for themselves, and everything appertaining to them, protection and defense from all insults and injuries. They have the right to reside at any of the ports open to foreign commerce, to rent houses and places of business, or to build such upon sites which they have the right to hire. They have secured to them the right to build churches and cemeteries, and they may teach or worship in those churches without being harassed, persecuted, interfered with, or molested. These are some of the rights which are expressly and in terms granted to the United States, for their citizens, by the Treaty of 1858. If I rightly apprehend the spirit of the note of the Foreign Office, and of the regulations which accompany it, there is, to state it in the least objectionable form, an apprehension in the yamen that it may become necessary to curtail some of these rights, in consequence of the alleged conduct of French missionaries. This idea cannot be entertained for one moment by the United States."

This position was given new emphasis by the note sent by Secretary of State John Hay to the Hon. Horace Porter, United States Ambassador to France, in response to a communication from the American Chamber of Commerce in Paris in 1903. In this note Mr. Hay said:

"The Government holds that every citizen sojourning or travelling abroad in pursuit of his lawful affairs is entitled to a passport, and the duration of such sojourn the department does not arrogate to itself the right to limit or prescribe."

The governments of continental Europe have repeatedly shown themselves quick to resent an infringement upon the treaty rights of their subjects who are in China as missionaries. The Hon. Thomas Francis Wade, British Minister at Peking, wrote to Minister Wen Hsiang in June, 1871:—"The British Government draws no distinction between the missionaries and any other of its non-official subjects." This sentiment was emphatically reiterated by Earl Granville in a note from the foreign office in London to Mr. Wade dated August 21, 1871:

"Her Majesty's Government cannot allow the claim that the missionaries residing in China must conform to the laws and customs of China to pass unchallenged. It is the duty of a missionary, as of every other British subject, to avoid giving offense as far as possible to the Chinese authorities or people, but he does not forfeit the rights to which he is entitled under the treaty as a British subject because of his missionary character."

But while this is the only possible policy for a government, it is surely reasonable to expect that the persons concerned will exercise moderation and prudence in their demands. The China Island Mission does not permit its missionaries to appeal to their Government officials without special permission from headquarters. Many missionaries of other societies would probably resent such a limitation of their liberty as citizens. But as the act of the individual often involves others, it might be well to make the approval of the station necessary, and, wherever practicable, of the mission. Nine-tenths of the missionaries do not and will not unnecessarily write or telegraph for the intervention of minister or consul. But the tenth man may be benefited by the counsel of his colleagues who know or who may be easily acquainted with the facts. The American Presbyterian Board in a formal action has expressed the wise judgment that "appeals to the secular arm should always and everywhere be as few as possible." It is not in the civil or military power of a country to give the missionary success. In the crude condition of heathen society, the temptation is sometimes strong to appeal for aid to "the secular arm" of the home government. Occasions may possibly arise in which it will be necessary to insist upon rights. Nevertheless, as a rule, it will be well to remember that "the weapons of our warfare are not carnal but mighty through God," and that "the servant of the Lord must not strive, but be gentle unto all men." The argument of the sword is Mohammedan, not Christian. The veteran Rev. J. Hudson Taylor holds that in the long run appeals to home governments do nothing but harm. He says he has known of many riots that have never been reported and of much suffering endured in silence which have "fallen out rather to the furtherance of the gospel," and that "if we leave God to vindicate our cause, the issue is sure to prove marvellous in spirituality."

The critics have vociferously charged that after the suppression of the Boxer uprising, the missionaries greatly embarrassed their governments by demanding bloody vengeance upon the Chinese. It may indeed be true that among the thousands of Roman Catholic and Protestant missionaries in China, some temporarily lost their self-control and gave way to anger under the awful provocation of ruined work, burned homes, outraged women and butchered Chinese Christians. How many at home would or could have remained calm in such circumstances? But it is grossly unjust to treat such excited utterances as representative of the great body of missionary opinion. The missionaries went to China and they propose to stay there because they love and believe in the Chinese, and it is very far from their thought to demand undue punishment for those who oppose them. They sensibly expected a certain amount of opposition from tradition, heathenism, superstition and corruption, and they are not disposed to call for unmanly or unchristian measures when that trouble falls upon them which fell in even greater measure on the Master Himself.

It is true that some of the missionaries felt that the ringleaders of the Boxers, including those in high official position who more or less secretly incited them to violence, should be punished. But they were not thinking of revenge, so much as of the welfare of China, the restoration to power of the best element among the Chinese, and the reasonable security of Chinese Christians and of foreigners who have treaty rights. Many missionaries feel that there is no hope for China save in the predominance of the Reform Party, and that if the reactionaries are to remain in control, the outlook is dark indeed, not so much for the foreigner as for China itself. The men who were guilty of the atrocities perpetrated in the summer of 1900 violated every law, human and divine, and some of the missionaries demanded their punishment only in the same spirit as the ministers and Christian people of the United States who with united voice demanded the punishment of the four young men in Paterson, New Jersey, who had been systematically outraging young girls.

Nevertheless, as to the whole subject of the policy which should be adopted by our Government in China, I believe that it would be wise for both the missionaries and the mission boards to be cautious in proffering advice, and to leave the responsibility for action with the lawfully constituted civil authorities upon whom the people have placed it. Governments have better facilities for acquiring accurate information as to political questions than missionaries have. They can see the bearings of movements more clearly than those who are not in political life and can discern elements in the situation that are not so apparent to others. Moreover, they must bear the blame or praise for consequences. They can ask for missionary opinion if they want it. Generations of protest against priestly domination, chiefly by Protestant ministers themselves, have developed in both Europe and America a disposition to resent clerical interference in political questions. This is particularly true of matters in Asia, where the political situation is so delicate. The opinions publicly expressed by the missionaries as to the policy, which, in their judgment, should be adopted by our Government and by the European Powers have included not only many articles of individual missionaries in newspapers and magazines, but formal communications of bodies or committees of missionaries. Conspicuous examples are the protests of missionaries assembled in Chefoo and Shanghai in 1900 against the decision of the American Government to withdraw its troops from Peking, to recognize the Empress Dowager and to omit certain officials from the list of those who were to be executed or banished, and, in particular, the letter addressed by "the undersigned British and American missionaries representative of societies and organizations that have wide interests in China to their Excellencies the Plenipotentiaries of Great Britain and the United States accredited to the Chinese Government."

These actions were taken by men whose character, ability and knowledge of the Chinese entitle them to great weight, and who were personally affected in the security of their lives and property and in the interests of their life-work by the policy adopted by their respective Governments. All were citizens who did not abdicate their citizenship by becoming missionaries, and whose status and rights in China, as such, have been specifically recognized by treaty. All, moreover, expressed their views with clearness, dignity and force. From the viewpoint of right and privilege, and, indeed, political duty as citizens, they were abundantly justified in expressing their opinions.

On the other hand, there are many friends of missions who doubt whether formal declarations of judgment "as missionaries," on political and military questions, were accorded much influence by diplomats; whether they did not increase the popular criticism of missionaries to an extent which more than counterbalanced any good that they accomplished; whether they did not identify the missionary cause with "the consul and gunboat" policy which Lord Salisbury charged upon it; and whether they did not prejudice their own future influence over the Chinese and strengthen the impression that the mis-sionaries are "political emissaries." In reply to my inquiry as to his opinion, Sir Robert Hart expressed himself as follows:—

"As for punitive measures, etc., I have really no personal knowledge of the action taken by American missionaries, and hearsay is not a good foundation for opinion. It is said that vindictive feeling rather than tender mercy has been noticed. But even if so, it cannot be wondered at, so cruel were the Chinese assailants when they had the upper hand. The occasion has been altogether anomalous, and it is only at the parting of the ways the difference of view comes in. That what was done merited almost wholesale punishment is a view most will agree in—eyes turned to the past—but when discussion tries to argue out what will be best for the future, some will vote for striking terror, and others for trusting more to the more slowly working but longer lasting effect of mercy. I do not believe any missionary has brought anybody to punishment who did not richly deserve it. But some people seem to feel it would have been wiser for ministers of the gospel to have left to 'governors' the 'punishment of evil-doers.' For my part, I cannot blame them, for without their assistance much that is known would not have been known, and, although numbers of possibly innocent, inoffensive and non-hostile people may have been overwhelmed in this last year's avalanche of disaster, there are still at large a lot of men whose punishment would probably have been a good thing for the future. One can only hope that their good luck in escaping may lead them to take a new departure, and with their heads in the right direction."[71]

Wisely or unwisely—the former, I venture to think—the interdenominational conference of American mission boards having work in China, held in 1900, declined to make representations to our Government on questions of policy during the Boxer uprising. They necessarily had much correspondence with Washington

---

71   Letter to the author with permission to print, July, 1901.

regarding the safety of missionaries during the siege, but when I inquired of Secretary of State Hay as to the accuracy of the later newspaper charges that mission boards were urging the Government to retaliatory measures, he promptly replied: "No communications of this nature have been received from the great mission boards or from their authorized representatives."

But let us hear the missionaries themselves on this subject. An interdenominational committee, headed by the Rev. Dr. Calvin W. Mateer, prepared a reply to this criticism, which has been circulated throughout China and has received the assent of so large a number of missionaries of all churches and nationalities that it may be taken as representing the views of fully nine-tenths of the whole body of Protestant missionaries in the Empire. This letter should be given the widest possible currency, as expressing the views of men who are the peers of any equal number of Christian workers in the world. It is dated May 24, 1901, and, after discussing the question of the responsibility for the Boxer uprising, the letter continues:

"With reference to the second point—that we have manifested an unchristian spirit in suggesting the punishment of those who were guilty of the massacre of foreigners and native Christians— we understand that the criticism applies chiefly to the message sent by the public meeting held in Shanghai in September last.

"1. It should, in the first place, be borne in mind that the resolutions passed at that meeting were called for by the proposal of the Allies to evacuate Peking immediately after the relief of the Legations. It was felt, not only by missionaries but by the whole of the foreign residents in China, that such a course would be fraught with the greatest disaster, inasmuch as it would give sanction to further lawlessness.

"2. Further it must be remembered that, while suggesting that a satisfactory settlement 'should include the adequate punishment of all who were guilty of the recent murders of foreigners and native Christians,' it was left to the Powers to decide what that 'adequate punishment' should be. Moreover, when taking such measures as were necessary, they were urged to 'make every effort to avoid all needless and indiscriminate slaughter of Chinese and destruction of their property.'

"3. By a strange misunderstanding we find that this suggestion has been interpreted as though it were animated by an unchristian spirit of revenge. With the loss of scores of friends and colleagues still fresh upon us, and with stories of cruel massacres reaching us day by day, it would not have been surprising had we been betrayed into intemperate expressions; but we entirely repudiate the idea which has been read into our words. If governments are the ministers of God's righteousness, then surely it is the duty of every Christian Government not only to uphold the right but to put down the wrong, and equally the duty of all Christian subjects to support them in so doing. For China, as for Western nations, anarchy is the only alternative to law. Both justice and mercy require the judicial punishment of the wrong-doers in the recent outrages. For the good of the people themselves, for the upholding of that standard of righteousness which they acknowledge and respect, for the strengthening and encouragement of those officials whose sympathies have been throughout on the side of law and order, and for the protection of our own helpless women and children and the equally helpless sons and daughters of the Church, we think that such violations of treaty obligations, and such heartless and unprovoked massacres as have been carried out by official authority or sanction, should not be allowed to pass unpunished. It is not of our personal wrongs that we think, but of the maintenance of law and order, and of the future safety of all foreigners residing in the interior of China, who, it must be remembered, are not under the jurisdiction of Chinese law, but, according to the treaties, are immediately responsible to, and under the protection of, their respective Governments."

The reply rather pathetically concludes:

"It is unhappily the lot of missionaries to be misunderstood and spoken against, and we are aware that in any explanation we now offer we add to the risk of further misunderstanding; but we cast ourselves on the forbearance of our friends, and beg them to refrain from hasty and ill-formed judgments. If, on our part, there have been extreme statements, if individual missionaries have used intemperate words or have made demands out of harmony with the spirit of our Divine Lord, is it too much to ask that the anguish and peril through which so many of our number have gone during the last six months should be remembered, and that the whole body should not be made responsible for the hasty utterances of the few?"

A perplexing phase of the relation of missionaries to their own governments develops in times of disturbance. Should missionaries remain at their stations when their minister or consul think that they ought to withdraw to the port where they can be more easily protected? Should they make journeys that the consul deems imprudent or return to an abandoned station before he regards the trouble as ended? This question became acute in connection with the Boxer outbreak when mis-sionaries sometimes differed with ministers or consuls as to whether they should go or stay. On the one hand it may be urged that missionaries are under strong obligations to attach great weight to the judgment of their minister or consul. If they receive the benefits and protection of citizenship, and if by their acts they may involve their governments, they should recognize the right of the authorized representatives of those governments to counsel them. The presumption should be in favour of obedience to that counsel, and it should not be disregarded without clear and strong reasons.

But the fact cannot be ignored that, whatever may be the personal sympathies of individual ministers or consuls, diplomacy as such considers only the secondary results of missions, and not the primary ones. Government officials, speaking on missionary work, almost invariably dwell on its material and civilizing rather than its spiritual aspects. They do not, as officials, feel that the salvation of men from sin and the command of Christ to evangelize all nations are within their sphere. Moreover, diplomacy is proverbially and necessarily cautious. Its business is to avoid risks, and, of course, to advise others to avoid them. The political situation, too, was undeniably uncertain and delicate. The future was big with possibility of peril. In such circumstances, we should expect diplomacy to be anxious and to look at the whole question from the prudential viewpoint.

But the missionary, like the soldier, must take some risks. From Paul down, missionaries have not hesitated to face them. Christ did not condition His great command upon the approval of Caesar. It was not safe for Morrison to enter China, and for many years missionaries in the interior were in grave jeopardy. But devoted men and women accepted the risk in the past, and they will accept it in the future. They must exercise common sense. And yet this enterprise is unworldly as well as worldly, and when the soldier boldly faces every physical peril, when the trader unflinchingly jeopardizes life and limb in the pursuit of gold—I found a German mining engineer and his wife living alone in a remote village soon after the Boxer excitement—should the missionary be held back?

If, however, after full and careful deliberation, missionaries feel that it is their duty to disregard the advice of their minister or consul, they should consult their respective boards and if the boards sustain them, all concerned should accept responsibility for the risks involved.

But if missionaries do not permit governments to control their movements, they should not be too exacting in their demands on them when trouble comes. The Rev. Dr. Henry M. Field once said:—

"A foreign missionary is one who goes to a strange country to preach the gospel of our salvation. That is his errand and his defense. The civil authorities are not presumed to be on his side. If he offends the sensibilities of the people to whom he preaches, he is supposed to face the consequences. If he cannot win men by the Word and his own love for their souls, he cannot call on the civil or military powers to convert them. Nor is the missionary a merchant, in the sense that he must have ready recourse to the courts for a recouping of losses or the recovery of damages. Commercial treaties cannot cover all our missionary enterprises. Confusion of ideas here has confounded a good many fine plans and zealous men. It is a tremendous begging of the whole question to insist on the nation's protection of the men who are to subvert the national faith. Property rights and preaching rights get closely entwined, and it is difficult to untangle them at times, but the distinction is definite and the difference often fundamental. By confusing them we weaken the claims of both. And when our Christian preachers get behind a mere property right in order to defend their right to preach a new religion, they dishonour themselves and defame the faith they profess. To get behind diplomatic guaranties in order to evangelize the nations is to mistake the sword for the Spirit, to rely on the arm of flesh and put aside the help of the Almighty."

That is, in my judgment, stating the case rather strongly. Doubtless Dr. Field did not mean that governments would be justified in discriminating against missionaries and he would probably have been one of the first to protest if they had done so.

He was addressing missionaries, reminding them that they could do in liberty what the governments could not do in law, and exhorting against any disposition to depend unduly upon the sword of the secular arm. At any rate, he was a devoted friend of missions and as such his words are deserving of thoughtful consideration.

XXI
RESPONSIBILITY OF MISSIONARIES FOR THE BOXER UPRISING

CRITICS vociferously assert that the missionaries were chiefly responsible for the Boxer uprising and for most of the prejudice of the Chinese against foreigners. As to the general accuracy of this charge, the reader has doubtless formed some impression from what has been said in the preceding chapters regarding the objects and methods of foreign trade and foreign politics. Still, it is but fair to remember that there are 3,854 missionaries in China, representing almost every European and American nationality and no less than nine Roman Catholic and sixty-seven Protestant boards.[72] As might be expected, the standard of appointment varies. A few boards, while insisting upon high spiritual qualifications, do not insist upon equal qualifications of some other kinds, while in all societies an occasional missionary proves to be visionary and ill-balanced. But in the great majority of the boards, the standard of appointment is very high, and while occasional mistakes are made, yet as a rule the missionaries represent the best type of Protestant Christianity. They are, as a class, men and women of education, refinement and ability—in every respect the equals and as a rule the superiors of the best class of non-missionary Europeans and Americans in China.

Now it is manifest that criticisms which may be true of some missionaries may not be true of the missionary body as a whole.

---

72   The Chinese Recorder.

As a matter of fact, the average critic has in mind either the Roman Catholic priests or the members of some independent society. This is notably true of Michie. Many of the charges are not true even of them, but of the charges that I have seen that have any foundation at all, nine-tenths do not apply to the missionaries of church boards. It is always fair, therefore, to ask a critic, "To which class of missionaries do you refer?"

The clearest line of distinction is between the Protestants and the Roman Catholics. The latter number 904. They have been in China the longest. They have the largest following,[73] and their methods are radically different from those of the Protestant missionaries. It is not denied that some of the priests are high-minded, intelligent men and that some of the Protestants lack wisdom. But comparing the two classes broadly, no one who is at all conversant with the facts will regard the Protestants as inferior. I do not wish to be unjust to the Roman Catholic missionaries in China. Many good things might be said regarding the work which some of them are doing. I personally called at several Roman Catholic stations in various parts of the Empire and I have vivid recollections of the kindness with which I was received, while more than once I was impressed by the unmistakable evidences of devotion and self-sacrifice. It was pleasant to hear many Protestant missionaries declare that they had never heard a suspicion as to the moral character of the priests. I did not hear any in all north China. The lives of the Roman Catholic missionaries are hard and narrow and they have no relief in the companionships of wife and children, in furloughs or in medical attendance, for they have no medical missionaries, while not infrequently the priest lives alone in a village. Dead to the world, with no families and no expectation of returning to their native land, trained from boyhood to a monastic life, drilled to unquestioning obedience and to few personal needs, their ambition is not to get anything for themselves but to strengthen the Church for which the individual priest unhesitatingly sacrifices himself, content if by his complete submergence of his own interests he has helped to make her great. With such men, Rome is a mighty power in Asia. But the sincere, devoted man may be even more dangerous if his zeal is wrongly

---

73   720,540 Roman Catholics—compare p. 223 for Protestants.

directed, and the question under discussion now is not the personal character of individuals, but the general policy of the Church. As to the character and effects of this policy I found a remarkable unanimity of opinion in China, and I could easily produce from my note-books the names of scores of credible witnesses to the substantial accuracy of my position.

Whatever may be said in favour of the Roman Catholics, it is unquestionable that their methods are far more irritating to the Chinese than the methods of the Protestants. Led by able and energetic bishops, the priests acquire all possible business property, demand large rentals, build imposing religious plants, and baptize or enroll as catechumens all sorts of people. It is notorious that the Roman Catholic priests quite generally adopt the policy of interference on behalf of their converts. Through the Minister of France at Peking they obtained an Imperial Edict, dated March 15, 1899, granting them official status, so that the local priest is on a footing of equality with the local magistrate, and has the right of full access to him at any time. Whether or not intended by the Roman Catholic Church, the impression is almost universal in China among natives and foreigners alike that, if a Chinese becomes a Catholic, the Church will stand by him through thick and thin, in time and in eternity. There are, indeed, exceptions. Dr. Johnson, of Ichou-fu, told me of a Roman Catholic Christian who, during the Boxer troubles, stealthily moved his goods into Ichou-fu, burned his house, and then put in a claim for indemnity. The heathen neighbours, when asked to pay, informed the priest. He summoned the man, who confusedly said that if he had not burned the house, the Boxers would have done so, and he thought he had better do it at a convenient time as it was sure to be burned anyway. The priest promptly decided that he must suffer the loss himself. So the priests do not always stand by their converts whether right or wrong.

No one, however, who is familiar with the general course of the Roman Catholic Church in China, will deny that, as a rule, the priests boldly champion the cause of their converts. This is one secret of Rome's great and rapidly growing power in China, and unquestionably, too, it is one of the chief causes of Chinese hostility to missions. After many years of observation, Dr. J. Campbell Gibson writes:—

"In the missions of the Church of Rome, they (treaty rights) are systematically, and I am afraid one must say unscrupulously, used for the gathering in of large numbers of nominal converts, whose only claim to the Christian name is their registration in lists kept by native catechists, in which they are entered on payment of a small fee, without regard to their possession of any degree of Christian knowledge or character. In the event of their being involved in any dispute or lawsuit, the native catechists or priests, and even the foreign Roman Catholic missionaries, take up their cause and press it upon the native magistrates. Not infrequently a still worse course is pursued. Intimation is sent round the villages in which there are large numbers of so-called Catholic converts and these assemble under arms to support by force the feuds of their co-religionists. The consequence is that the Catholic missions in southern China, and I believe in the north also, are bitterly hated by the Chinese people and by their magistrates. By terrorizing both magistrates and people, they have secured in many places a large amount of apparent popularity; but they are sowing the seeds of a harvest of hatred and bitterness which may be reaped in deplorable forms in years to come."[74]

In my own interviews with Chinese officials, it was my custom to lead the conversation towards the motives of those who had attacked foreigners during the Boxer uprising, and without exception the officials mentioned, among other causes, the interference of Roman Catholic priests with the administration of the law in cases affecting their converts. In several places in the interior, this was the only reason assigned.

Said an intelligent Chinese official in Shantung: "The whole trouble is not with the Protestants but with the Catholics. Protestant Christians do not go to law so often, and when they do, the Protestant missionary does not, as a rule, interfere unless he is sure they are right. But the Catholic Christians are constantly involved in lawsuits, and the priests invariably stand by them right or wrong. The priests seem to think that their converts cannot be wrong. The result is that many Chinese join the Roman Catholic Church to get the help of the priests in the innumerable lawsuits that the Chinese are always waging. And it is not surprising in such circumstances that Catholic Christians are a bad lot." When

---

74   "Mission Problems and Mission Methods in South China," pp. 309, 310.

I asked the magistrate of Paoting-fu why the people had killed such kindly and helpful neighbours as the Congregational and Presbyterian missionaries, he replied:—"The people were angered by the interference of the Roman Catholics in their lawsuits. They felt that they could not obtain justice against them, and in their frenzy they did not distinguish between Catholics and Protestants." The Roman Catholic Mission in the prefecture of Paoting-fu, it should be remembered, is about two centuries old, and the Catholic population is about 12,000, so that the few hundreds of converts who have been gathered in the recent work of the Protestants are very small in comparison, while the splendid cathedral of the Roman Church, the spectacular character of its services and the official status and aggressiveness of its priests intensify the disproportion. The term Christian, therefore, to the average man of Paoting-fu naturally means a Roman Catholic rather than a Protestant.

Perhaps we should make some allowance for Oriental forms of statement to one who was known to be a Protestant. The politeness of an Oriental host to a guest is not always limited by veracity, and it is possible that to Roman Catholics the officials may blame the Protestants. But such unanimity of testimony among so many independent and widely separated officials must surely count for something, especially when the grounds for it are so notorious. Undoubtedly, there are many sincere Christians among the Roman Catholic Chinese, but judging from the almost universal testimony that I heard in China, the Roman Church is a veritable cave of Adullam for unscrupulous and revengeful Chinese.

The evidence does not rest upon the testimony of Protestants alone. If any one will take the trouble to look up the diplomatic correspondence on this subject, he will find ample and convincing testimony. February 9, 1871, the Tsung-li Yamen addressed to the Foreign Legations at Peking a memorandum together with eight propositions, the whole embodying the complaints and objections of the Chinese Government to missionaries and their work in China, and suggesting certain regulations for the future. This memorandum included the following paragraph:—

"The missionary question affects the whole question of pacific relations with foreign powers—the whole question of their trade. As the Minister addressed cannot but be well aware, wherever missionaries of the Romish profession appear, ill-feeling begins between them and the people, and for years past, in one case or another, points of all kinds on which they are at issue have been presenting themselves. In earlier times when the Romish missionaries first came to China, styled, as they were, 'Si Ju,' the Scholars of the West, their converts no doubt for the most part were persons of good character; but since the change of ratifications in 1860, the converts have in general not been of a moral class. The result has been that the religion that professes to exhort men to virtue has come to be lightly thought of; it is in consequence, unpopular, and its unpopularity is greatly increased by the conduct of the converts who, relying on the influence of the missionaries, oppress and take advantage of the common people (the non-Christians): and yet more by the conduct of the missionaries themselves, who, when collisions between Christians and the people occur, and the authorities are engaged in dealing with them, take part with the Christians, and uphold them in their opposition to the authorities. This undiscriminating enlistment of proselytes has gone so far that rebels and criminals of China, pettifoggers and mischief-makers, and such like, take refuge in the profession of Christianity, and covered by this position, create disorder. This has deeply dissatisfied the people, and their dissatisfaction long felt grows into animosity, and their animosity into deadly hostility. The populations of different localities are not aware that Protestantism and Romanism are distinct. They include both under the latter denomination. They do not know that there is any distinction between the nations of the West. They include them all under one denomination of foreigners, and thus any serious collision that occurs equally compromises all foreigners in China. Even in the provinces not concerned, doubt and misgiving are certain to be largely generated."

The memorandum and its attached propositions are interesting reading as showing the impression which the Chinese Government had of Roman Catholic missionary work. The third proposition included the following statement:—

"They (Roman Catholic converts) even go so far as to coerce the authorities and cheat and oppress the people. And the foreign missionaries, without inquiring into facts, conceal in every case the Christian evil-doer, and refuse to surrender him to the authorities for punishment. It has even occurred that malefactors who have been guilty of the gravest crimes have thrown themselves into the profession of Christianity, and have been at once accepted and screened (from justice). In every province do the foreign missionaries interfere at the offices of the local authorities in lawsuits in which native Christians are concerned. For example in a case that occurred in Sze-chuen in which some native Christian women defrauded certain persons (non-Christians) of the rent owing to them, and actually had these persons wounded and killed, the French Bishop took on himself to write in official form (to the authorities) pleading in their favour. None of these women were sentenced to forfeit life for life taken, and the resentment of the people of Sze-chuen in consequence remains unabated."

Mr. Wade, the British Minister at Peking, in reporting this memorandum and its appended propositions to Earl Granville, June 8, 1871, said:

"The promiscuous enlistment of evil men as well as good by the Romish missionaries, and their advocacy of the claims advanced by these ill-conditioned converts, has made Romanism most unpopular; and the people at large do not distinguish between Romanist and Protestant, nor between foreigner and foreigner; not that Government has made no effort to instruct the people, but China is a large Empire…Three-fourths of the Romish missionaries in China, in all, between 400 and 500 persons, are French; and Romanism in the mouths of non-Christian Chinese is as popularly termed the religion of the French as the religion of the Lord of Heaven."

June 27th of that year, Earl Granville wrote to Lord Lyons that he had said to the French Charge d'Affaires:—

"I told M. Gavard that I could not pretend to think that the conduct of the French missionaries, stimulated by the highest and most laudable object, had been prudent in the interest of Christianity itself, and that the support which had been given by the representatives of France to their pretensions was dangerous to the future relations of Europe with China."

The Hon. Frederick F. Low, United States Minister at Peking, in communicating that memorandum and the attached propositions to the State Department in Washington, March 20, 1871, said:—

"A careful reading of the Memorandum clearly proves that the great, if not only, cause of complaint against the missionaries comes from the action of the Roman Catholic priests and the native

Christians of that faith…Had they (the Chinese Goverment) stated their complaints in brief, without circumlocution, and stripped of all useless verbiage, they would have charged that the Roman Catholic missionaries, when residing away from the open ports, claim to occupy a semi-official position, which places them on an equality with the provincial officer; that they deny the authority of the Chinese officials over native Christians, which practically removes this class from the jurisdiction of their own rulers; that their action in this regard shields the native Christians from the penalties of the law, and thus holds out inducements for the lawless to join the Catholic Church, which is largely taken advantage of; that orphan asylums are filled with children, by the use of improper means, against the will of the people; and when parents, guardians, and friends visit these institutions for the purpose of reclaiming children, their requests for examination and restitution are denied, and lastly, that the French Government, while it does not claim for its missionaries any rights of this nature by virtue of treaty, its agents and representatives wink at these unlawful acts, and secretly uphold the missionaries…I do not believe, and, therefore I cannot affirm, that all the complaints made against Catholic missionaries are founded in truth, reason, or justice; at the same time, I believe that there is foundation for some of their charges. My opinions, as expressed in former despatches touching this matter, are confirmed by further investigation…"

On the same date, Minister Low wrote to the Tsung-li Yamen:—

"It is a noticeable fact, that among all the cases cited there does not appear to be one in which Protestant missionaries are charged with violating treaty, law or custom. So far as I can ascertain, your complaints are chiefly against the action and attitude of the missionaries of the Roman Catholic faith; and, as these are under the exclusive protection and control of the Government of France, I might with great propriety decline to discuss a matter with which the Government of the United States has no direct interest or concern, for the reason that none of its citizens are charged with violating treaty or local law, and thus causing trouble."

This tendency of the Chinese to confuse Roman Catholics and Protestants is further illustrated by the note addressed by Minister Wen Hsiang to Sir R. Alcock:—

"Extreme indeed would be the danger if, popular indignation having been once aroused by this opposition to the authorities, the hatred of the whole population of China were excited like that of the people of Tientsin against foreigners, and orders, though issued by the Government, could not be for all that put in force... Although the creeds of the various foreign countries differ in their origin and development from each other, the natives of China are unable to see the distinction between them. In their eyes all (teachers of religion) are 'missionaries from the West,' and directly they hear a lying story (about any of these missionaries), without making further and minute inquiry (into its truth), they rise in a body to molest him."

As for Protestant missionaries, it would be useless to assert that every one of the 2,950 has always been blameless in this matter. Moreover, it must be borne in mind that there is a sense in which the gospel is a revolutionary force. Christ Himself said that He came not to send peace on earth but a sword, and to set a man at variance against his father. There is usually more or less of a protest in a heathen land when a man turns from the old faith to the new one. The refusal to contribute to the temple sacrifices and to worship the ancestral tablets is sure to be followed by a furious outcry. The convert is apt to be assailed as a traitor to the national custom and as having entered into league with the foreigner.

To the Chinese, moreover, all white men are "Christians" and "foreign devils," and all alike stand for the effort to foreignize and despoil China. Except where personal acquaintance has taught certain communities that there is a difference between white men, the evil acts of one foreigner or of one aggressive foreign Government are charged against all the members of the race, just as in the pioneer days in the American colonies, a settler whose wife had been killed by an Indian took his revenge by indiscriminately shooting all the other Indians he could find. Any hatred that the Chinese may have against Christianity is due, not so much to its religious teachings, as to its identification with the foreign nations whose religion Christianity is supposed to be and whose aggressions the Chinese have so much reason to fear and to hate.

For this reason, the introduction of Buddhism and Mohammedanism is not parallel, and to base an argument against Christianity on the alleged fact that the other faiths easily succeeded in domesticating themselves in China is to confuse facts. Neither Buddhism nor Mohammedanism entered China as an aggressive propaganda by foreigners. The Chinese themselves brought in Buddhism, and it spread chiefly because it grafted into itself many Chinese superstitions and did not oppose Chinese vices, but rather assimilated them. Why should the people have opposed a religion which interfered with nothing that they valued and reenforced their darling prejudices? As for Islam, we have already seen[75] that it is the faith of early immigrants and their descendants, that its followers do not propagate it, that they live in separate communities, are disliked by the Chinese and are often at open war with them. Christianity, on the contrary, comes to China with foreigners who have no intention of settling down as permanent members of Chinese society, who are classed as representatives of nations which are regarded as more or less hostile and unjust, and who preach their religion as a vital spiritual faith which opposes all wrong, uproots all superstition and aims at the moral reconstruction of every man. Of course, therefore, Christianity must expect a reception different in some respects from that which was given to Buddhism and Mohammedanism.

It is the shallowest of all objections to missions that Mr. Francis Nichols urged in the North American Review when he insisted that "the missionary is not engaged to be a reformer," but that "his mission is to preach the gospel—nothing more."

"Is the gospel then simply a patent arrangement by which idolaters can get to heaven, without disturbing their idolatry or the vices associated with it? was not Christ a reformer? and Paul also, and his successors, who, by their preaching, gave the idols of Rome to the moles and the bats, and robbed the Coliseum of its gladiatorial shows? It is the glory of Christianity that on questions of truth and righteousness it makes no compromise. Its mission is to save the world by reforming it...Who that understands the genius of Christianity can fail to see that China Christianized must be very different from China as it now is?"[76]

After making all due allowance for these things, however, the fact still remains that opposition of this sort in China is usually local and sporadic. It affects a greater or less number of individuals and

---

75   Chapter VI.

76   The Rev. Dr. Calvin Mateer, Teng chou.

families and occasionally a community, but it does not move a whole population to the frenzy of a national uprising. The anti-foreign hatred of the Boxers was fierce in thousands of cities and villages where there were no missionaries or Chinese Christians at all. In the sphere of religion proper, the Chinese are not an intolerant people. They are almost wholly devoid of sec-tarian spirit. The coming of another religion would not of itself excite serious opposition, for having become accustomed to the presence and intermingling of several religions, it would not antecedently occur to the Chinese that a fourth faith would involve the abandonment of the others. They would be more apt to infer that the new could be accepted in harmony with the old in the established way. So the worst foe that the Christian missionary has to encounter is not hostility but indifference.

As a rule, the Chinese have not strenuously objected to the Protestant missionaries as missionaries. It is the policy of the mission boards to avoid all unnecessary interference with native customs. So far from coveting official equality with Chinese magistrates, an overwhelming majority of the Protestant missionaries throughout the Empire expressly declined to avail themselves of the offer of the Chinese Government to give them the same privileges and official status that was accorded to the Roman Catholic priests and bishops in the Imperial decree of March 15, 1899.

"The very thing which missionaries seek to avoid is denationalizing their converts. So far as mission schools at the ports are concerned, it is not the missionary who is chiefly responsible for what foreignizing is done. The Chinese who patronize these schools want their children to learn foreign accomplishments. Such schools, however, form but a very small part of the extensive educational work done by American missionaries in China."[77]

Many of the missionaries, especially in the interior stations, don Chinese clothing, shave their heads and wear a queue. Everywhere the missionaries learn the Chinese language, try to get into sympathy with the people, teach the young, heal the sick, comfort the dying, distribute relief in time of famine, preach the gospel of peace and good-will, and, in the opinion of unprejudiced judges, are upright, sensible and useful workers. Not only men but women travel far into the interior, the former frequently alone and

---

77   The Rev. Dr. Calvin H. Mateer.

unarmed. They go into the homes of the people, preach in village streets, sleep unprotected in Chinese houses, and receive much personal kindness from all classes.

The experience of the Presbyterian mission at Chining-chou is an illustration of what has occurred in scores of communities. When Dr. Stephen A. Hunter and the Rev. William Lane tried to open a station in 1890, they were mobbed and driven out, barely escaping with their lives. But in June, 1892, the Rev. J. A. Laughlin arrived and was permitted to buy property and, in September, to bring his family and begin permanent residence. There are hereditary bands of robbers in the neighbourhood, and more than once they attacked the mission compound. But gradually the peaceful purpose and the beneficent life of the missionaries became known and active opposition ceased. When the Boxer outbreak occurred, there were about 150 baptized adults, besides a considerable number of children and adherents. During the troubles, only two of the Christians recanted, the rest holding together and continuing regular services. The mission property was undisturbed during the whole period. It is true, the officials were friendly; but even Governor Yuan Shih Kai's influence could not prevent some loss in his own capital. In Chining-chou not a thing was touched, a striking testimony to the friendliness of the people towards the missionaries whom they had learned to love. As I approached the city with the returning missionaries, a group of thirty met us with beaming faces. For nearly a year, they had been without a missionary and their joy at seeing Mr. Laughlin was unmistakable. As we passed through the city to the mission-compound in the southeast suburb, people in almost every door and window smiled and bowed a welcome. Nor was this cordiality confined to the Christians; many of all classes being outspoken in their manifestations of respect and affection.

Nor is it true that the Chinese sense of propriety is so out-raged, as some critics would have us believe, by the coming of single-women missionaries. It is true that in a land where all women are supposed to marry at an early age and where their freedom of movement is rigidly circumscribed, the position of the unmarried woman, however discreet she may be, is sometimes embarrassingly misunderstood until the community becomes better acquainted with her mission and character. But the opposition of the Chinese on this account has been grossly exaggerated by those whose prior hostility to all missionary work predisposed them to make as much capital as possible out of the small gossip on this subject. Even if the misunderstanding were as general and as bitter as some allege, it would not follow that single women should be withdrawn, for such misunderstanding grows out of a false and vicious conception of the female sex and its relation to man and society, and it is just that conception which Christianity should and does correct. For that matter, the position of the single man is also misunderstood, while no other person in all China is more fiercely hated by the Chinese than the white traders in the treaty ports who are the chief source of the criticisms upon missionaries. The experience of every mission board operating in China has shown that a Chinese town soon learns that the single-woman missionary is a pure-minded, large-hearted and unselfish worker, who from the loftiest of motives devotes herself to the teaching of women and children and to self-sacrificing ministries to the sick and suffering. No other foreigners are more beloved by the people than the single-women missionaries.

It is simply foolish to say that the missionary is responsible for the prompt appearance of the consul and the gunboat. The true missionary goes forth without either consul or gunboat. He devotes his life to ameliorating the sad conditions which prevail in heathen communities. His reliance is not upon man, but upon God. But as soon as his work begins to tell, the trader appears to buy and sell in the new market. The statesman casts covetous eyes on the newly opened territory. Christianity civilizes, and civilization increases wants, stimulates trade and breaks down barriers. The conditions of modern civilization are developed. Then the consul is sent, not because the missionary asks for him, but because his government chooses to send him. Sooner or later some local trouble occurs, and the Government takes advantage of the opportunity to further its territorial or commercial ambitions. "Missionaries responsible, indeed!" writes Dr. H. H. Jessup. "The diplomats of Europe know better. Had there been no grabbing of seaports and hinterlands, no forcing modern improvements and European goods down the throats of the Chinese, the missionaries would have been let alone now as in the past."

It is the foreign idea that the Chinese dislikes, the interference with his cherished customs and traditions. A railroad alarms and angers him more than half a hundred missionaries. A plowshare cuts through more of his superstitions than a mission school. He does not want the methods of our western civilization, and he resents the attempt to push them upon him. If no other force had been at work than the foreign missionary, the anti-foreign agitation would never have started. It is significant that those who protest that we ought not to force our religion upon the Chinese do not appear to think that there is anything objectionable in forcing our trade upon them. The animosity of the Chinese has been primarily excited, not by the missionary, but by the trader and the politician, and the missionary suffers chiefly because he comes from the country of the trader and the politician and is identified with them as a member of the hated race of foreigners.

On this whole subject, I have been at some pains to collect the testimony of men whose positions are a guarantee not only of knowledge but of impartiality.

The Hon. George F. Seward, formerly United States Minister to Chipa, declares:—

"The people at large make too much of missionary work as an occasion for trouble. There are missionaries who are iconoclasts, but this is not their spirit. In great measure, they are men of education and judgment. They depend upon spiritual weapons and good works. For every enemy a missionary makes, he makes fifty friends. The one enemy may arouse an ignorant rabble to attack him. While I was in China, I always congratulated myself on the fact that the missionaries were there. There were good men and able men among the merchants and officials, but it was the missionary who exhibited the foreigner in benevolent work as having other aims than those which may justly be called selfish. The good done by missionaries in the way of education, of medical relief and of other charities cannot be overstated. If in China there were none other than missionary influences, the upbuilding of that great people would go forward securely…I am not a church member, but I have the profoundest admiration for the missionary as I have known him in China. He is a power for good and for peace, not for evil."

President James B. Angell, also formerly United States Minister to China, replies as follows to the question, "Are the Chinese averse to the introduction of the Christian religion":—

"No, not in that broad sense. They do not seem to fear for the permanency of their own religion. It is not that they object to missionaries and the Christian religion as much as it is that the missionaries are foreigners. A more serious cause of the uprising is the wide-spread suspicion among the natives, since the Japanese war, that the foreigners are going to partition China. It is not strange that all these conditions cause friction and excitement. The Chinese want to be left to themselves and the one word 'foreigners' sums up the great cause of the present trouble."

The Hon. Charles Denby, after thirteen years' experience as United States Minister to China, wrote:—

"I unqualifiedly, and in the strongest language that tongue can utter, give to these men and women who are living and dying in China and the Far East my full and unadulterated commendation... No one can controvert the fact that the Chinese are enormously benefited by the labours of the missionaries. Foreign hospitals are a great boon to the sick. In the matter of education, the movement is immense. There are schools and colleges all over China taught by the missionaries. There are also many foreign asylums in various cities which take care of thousands of waifs. The missionaries translate into Chinese many scientific and philosophical works. There are various anti-opium hospitals where the victims of this vice are cured. There are industrial schools and workshops. There are many native Christian churches. The converts seem to be as devout as people of any other race. As far as my knowledge extends, I can and do say that the missionaries in China are self-sacrificing; that their lives are pure; that they are devoted to their work; that their influence is beneficial to the natives; that the arts and sciences and civilization are greatly spread by their efforts; that many useful western books are translated by them into Chinese; that they are the leaders in all charitable work, giving largely themselves and personally disbursing the funds with which they are intrusted; that they do make converts, and such converts are mentally benefited by conversion." And after the Boxer outbreak he added:—"I do not believe that the uprising in China was due to hatred of the missionaries or of the Christian religion. The Chinese are a philosophic people, and rarely act without reasoning upon the causes and results of their actions. They have seen their land disappearing and becoming the property of foreigners, and it was this that awakened hatred of foreigners and not the actions of the missionaries or the doctrines that they teach."

The present United States Minister, the Hon. Edwin H. Conger, has repeatedly borne similar testimony, publicly assuring the missionaries of his "personal respect and profound gratitude for their noble conduct."

The Hon. John W. Foster, ex-Secretary of State and counsel for the Chinese Government in the settlement with Japan, writes:—

"The opinion formed by me after careful inquiry and observation is that the mass of the population of China, particularly the common people, are not specially hostile to the missionaries and their work. Occasional riots have occurred, but they are almost invariably traced to the literati or prospective office-holders and the ruling classes. These are often bigoted and conceited to the highest degree, and regard the teachings of the missionaries as tending to overthrow the existing order of Government and society, which they look upon as a perfect system, and sanctified by great antiquity…The Chinese, as a class, are not fanatics in religion and if other causes had not operated to awaken a national hostility to foreigners, the missionaries would have been left free to combat Buddhism and Taoism, and carry on their work of establishing schools and hospitals."

Wu Ting-fang, Chinese Minister to Washington during the Boxer uprising, while frankly stating that "missionaries are placed in a very delicate situation," and that "we must not be blind to the fact that some, in their excessive zeal, have been indiscreet," nevertheless as frankly added:—

"It has been commonly supposed that missionaries are the sole cause of anti-foreign feeling in China. This charge is unfair. Missionaries have done a great deal of good in China. They have translated useful works into the Chinese language, published scientific and educational journals and established schools in the country. Medical missionaries especially have been remarkably successful in their philanthropic work."

The Hon. Benjamin Harrison, late President of the United States, replied to my inquiry in the terse remark:—"If what Lord Salisbury says were true, the reflection would not be upon the missionaries, but upon the premiers."

General James H. Wilson, of the United States Army, the second in command of the American forces in Peking, adds his testimony:—

"Our missionaries, after the earlier Jesuits, were almost the first in that wide field (China). They were generally men of great piety and learning, like Morrison, Brown, Martin and Williams, and did all in their power as genuine men of God to show the heathen that the stranger was not necessarily a public enemy, but might be an evangel of a higher and better civilization. These men and their co-labourers have established hospitals, schools and colleges in various cities and provinces of the Empire, which are everywhere recognized by intelligent Chinamen as centres of unmitigated blessing to the people. Millions of dollars have been spent in this beneficent work, and the result is slowly but surely spreading the conviction that foreign arts and sciences are superior to 'fung shuy' and native superstition."

The Hon. John Goodnow, American Consul-General at Shanghai, emphatically declares:—"It is absurd to charge the missionaries with causing the Boxer War. They are simply hated by the Chinese as one part of a great foreign element that threatened to upset the national institutions."

Viceroy Yuan Shih Kai when Governor of Shantung, in the spring of 1901, wrote to the Baptist and Presbyterian missionaries of the province as follows:

"You, reverend sirs, have been preaching in China for many years, and, without exception, exhort men concerning righteousness. Your church customs are strict and correct, and all your converts may well observe them. In establishing your customs you have been careful to see that Chinese law was observed. How, then, can it be said that there is disloyalty? To meet this sort of calumny, I have instructed that proclamations be put out. I purpose, hereafter, to have lasting peace. Church interests may then prosper and your idea of preaching righteousness I can promote. The present upheaval is of a most extraordinary character. It forced you, reverend sirs, by land and water to go long journeys, and subjected you to alarm and danger, causing me many qualms of conscience."

A charge which has been so completely demolished by such competent and unprejudiced witnesses can only be renewed at the expense of either intelligence or candour. Dr. Arthur H. Smith truly says that "amid the varied action of so many agents it is vain to deny that Christianity has sometimes been so presented as to be misrepresented, but on the whole there had for some time been a marked and a growing friendliness on the part of both people and officials…The convulsion which shook China to its foundations was due to general causes, slow in their operations, but inevitable in their results. It was the impact of the Middle Ages with the developed Christian commercial civilization of the nineteenth century, albeit accompanied with many incidental elements which were neither Christian nor in the true sense civilized. If Christianity had never come to China at all, some such collision must have occurred."[78]

---

78   "Rex Christus," pp. 204-206.

XXII
THE CHINESE CHRISTIANS

THE real effect of the operation of the missionary force is to be seen in the Chinese who have accepted Christianity. As the commercial force is causing an economic revolution and as the political force resulted in the Boxer uprising, so the missionary force is developing a great spiritual movement which is crystallizing into a Chinese Church. Much has been said about the character of the Chinese Christians and doubts have been cast on the genuineness of their faith. It is admitted that they sometimes try the patience of the missionary. But is the home pastor never distressed by the conduct of his members? I am inclined to believe that the Christians in China would compare favourably with the same number selected at random in America. A Chinese laundryman posted on his door this significant notice to his foreign customers:—"Please help us to remember the Sabbath day to keep it holy by bringing your clothes to the laundry before ten o'clock on Saturdays," while in another place a Chinese servant left the morning after a card party at which much money had changed hands, stating to his mistress in explanation, "Me Clistian; me no stay in heathen house!" The Chinese Christian does not content himself with church attendance once a week when the weather is pleasant or an attractive theme is announced. He does not find himself in vigorous health for an evening entertainment, and with a bad headache on prayer-meeting night. There are of course exceptions, but as a rule, the Chinese Christians worship God with regularity in all kinds of weather. A missionary told me that the attendance at his mid-week meeting was as large as at his Sunday morning service, that every member of his church asked a blessing at the table, had family prayers and tried to bring his unconverted friends to Christ. If there is a pastor in America who can say that of his people, he has modestly refrained from making it public.

But such comparisons are, after all, unfair to the Chinese Christian for he should be compared, not with Europeans and Americans who have had far greater advantages, but with the people of his own country. "At home, you have the ripe fruits of a Christianity which was planted more than a thousand years ago. The Word of God has been among you all these Christian centuries. You have in every part of the country a highly trained ministry, a gifted and devoted eldership, and a whole army of Christian workers of all ranks. You work in the atmosphere of a Christian society, and under a settled Christian government. You have an immense and varied Christian literature, and notwithstanding all defects and drawbacks, you have on your side a weight of Christian tradition and a wealth of Christian example. Under such circumstances and in such an atmosphere, what are we not entitled to expect of those who bear the Christian name? What justice is there, or what reasonableness, in demanding as a test of genuineness the same degree of attainment on the part of Christian people, many of them uneducated, who are only just emerging from the deadness and insensibility of heathenism?"[79]

The real question is this:—Is the Christian Chinese a better man than the non-Christian Chinese—more moral, more truthful, more just, more reliable? The answer is so patent that no one who knows the facts can doubt it for a moment. The best men and women in China to-day are the Protestant Christians. This is not saying that all converts are good or that all non-Christian Chinese are bad. But it is saying that comparing the average Christian with the average heathen, the superiority of the former in those things which make character and conduct is immeasurable. "The conscience of those who have been born into a new life is not suddenly transformed, yet the change does take place and upon a larger scale. When once it has been accomplished, a new force has been introduced into the Chinese Empire, a salt to preserve, a

79   Gibson, pp. 239, 240.

leaven to pervade, a seed to bring forth after its kind in perpetually augmenting abundance and fertility."[80]

The character of the Chinese Christian will appear in still more striking relief if we consider the circumstances in which he hears the gospel and the difficulties which he has to overcome. On this subject the following remarkable passage from Dr. Gibson is worth quoting entire:—

"Out there the great issue is tried with all external helps removed. The gospel goes to China with no subsidiary aids. It is spoken to the people by the stammering lips of aliens. Those who accept it do so with no prospect of temporal gain. They go counter to all their own preconceptions, and to all the prejudices of their people. Try as we may to become all things to all men, we can but little accommodate our teaching to their thought...Often and often have I looked into the faces of a crowd of non-Christian Chinese and felt keenly how many barriers lay between their minds and mine. Reasoning that seems to me conclusive makes no appeal to them. Even the words we use to convey religious ideas do not bear to their minds one-hundredth part of the meaning we wish to put into them. I have often thought that if I were to expend all my energies to persuade one Chinaman to change the cut of his coat, or to try some new experiment in agriculture, I should certainly plead in vain. And yet I stand up to beg him to change the habits of a lifetime, to break away from the whole accumulated outcome of heredity, to make himself a target for the scorn of the world in which he lives, to break off from the consolidated social system which has shaped his being, and on the bare word of an unknown stranger to plunge into the hazardous experiment of a new and untried life, to be lived on a moral plane still almost inconceivable to him, whose sanctions and rewards are higher than his thoughts as heaven is higher than earth. While I despair of inducing him by my reasonings to make the smallest change in the least of his habits, I ask him, not with a light heart, but with a hopeful one, to submit his whole being to a change that is for him the making of his whole world anew. 'Credo quia impossis-ble,' I believe it can be done because I know I cannot do it, and the smallest success is proof of the working of the

80   Smith, "Rex Christus," p. 107.

divine power. The missionary must either confess himself helpless, or he must to the last fibre of his being believe in the Holy Ghost. I choose to believe, nay I am shut up to believe, by what my eyes have seen.

"I do not mean that one sees the results of preaching directly on the spot. In China at least one seldom does. But by the power of God the results come. We have seen unclean lives made pure, the broken-hearted made glad, the false and crooked made upright and true, the harsh and cruel made kindly and gentle. I have seen old women, seventy, eighty, eighty-five years of age, throwing away the superstitions of a lifetime, the accumulated merit of years of toilsome and expensive worship, and when almost on the brink of the grave, venturing all upon a new-preached faith and a new-found Saviour. We have seen the abandoned gambler become a faithful and zealous preacher of the gospel. We have seen the poor giving out of their poverty help to others, poorer still. We see many Chinese Christians who were once narrow and avaricious, giving out of their hard-earned month's wages, or more, yearly, to help the church's work. We see dull and uneducated people drinking in new ideas, mysteriously growing in their knowledge of Christian truth, and learning to shape their lives by its teachings. We have seen proud, passionate men, whose word was formerly law in their village, submit to injury, loss and insult, because of their Christian profession, until even their enemies were put to shame by their gentleness, and were made to be at peace with them. And the men and women and children who are passing through these experiences are gathering in others, and building up one by one a Christian community which is becoming a power on the side of all that is good in the non-Christian communities around them…Everything is hostile to it. It is striking its roots in an uncongenial soil, and breathes a polluted air. It may justly claim for itself the beautiful emblem so happily seized, though so poorly justified, by Buddhism—the emblem of the lotus. It roots itself in rotten mud, thrusts up the spears of its leaves and blossoms through the foul and stagnant water, and lifts its spotless petals over all, holding them up pure, stainless and fragrant, in the face of a burning and pitiless sun. So it is with the Christian life in China

Its existence there is a continuous miracle of life, of life more abundant."[81]

Is it said that these Asiatics have become Christians for gain? Then how shall we account for the fact that out of their deep poverty they gave for church work last year $2.50 per capita, which is more in proportion to ability than Christians at home gave? The impoverished Tu-kon farmers rented a piece of land and worked it in common for the support of the Lord's work; the Peking school-girls went without their breakfasts to save money for their church, and eight graduates of Shantung College refused high salaries as teachers, and accepted low salaries as pastors of self-supporting churches. "Rice Christians?" Doubtless in some instances, just as at home some people join American churches for business or social ends. But those Chinese Christians are receiving less and less from abroad and yet their number grows.

And it costs something to be a Christian in China. All hope of official preferment must be abandoned, for the duties of every magistrate include temple ceremonies that no Christian could conduct. For the average Christian, loss of business, social ostracism, bitter hatred, are the common price. Near Peking, a young man was thrice beaten and denied the use of the village well, mill and field insurance, because he became a Christian. A widow was dragged through the streets with a rope about her neck and beaten with iron rods which cut her body to the bone, while her fiendish persecutors yelled:—"You will follow the foreign devils, will you!" And that Chinese saint replied that she was not following foreigners but Jesus Christ and that she would not deny Him!

And so on every hand there are evidences of fidelity in service, of tribulation joyfully borne, of systematic giving out of scanty resources. While sapient critics are telling us that the heathen cannot be converted, the heathen are not only being converted but are manifesting a consecration and self-denial which should shame many in Christian lands. At a Presbyterial meeting in north China, the native ministers held a two-hours' prayer-meeting before daylight. Such prayer-meetings are not common in America. Is it surprising that in that little North China Presbytery 292 baptisms were recorded that year?

---

81 "Mission Problems and Mission Methods in South China," pp. 29-31, 240.

Nor is this a solitary instance. Every Sunday the little congregations gather. Every day the native helpers tell the Bible-story to their listening countrymen.

The history of missions in China has shown that it requires more time to convert a Chinese to Christianity than some other heathen, but that he can be converted and that when he is converted, he holds to his new faith with a tenacity and fortitude which the most awful persecution seldom shakes. The behaviour of the Chinese Christians under the baptism of blood and fire to which they were subjected in the Boxer uprising eloquently testified to the genuineness of their faith. That some should have fallen away was to be expected. Not every Christian, even in the United States, can "endure hardness." Let a hundred men anywhere be told that if they do not abandon their faith, their homes will be burned, their business ruined, their wives ravished, their children brained, and they themselves scourged and beheaded, and a proportion of them will flinch.

It was to be expected, too, that when, after the uprising, the Christians found their supporters triumphing over a prostrate foe, some of them should unduly exult and take advantage of the opportunity to punish their enemies or to collect money from them as the price of protection. The spirit of retaliation is strong in human nature in China as well as in America. When the armies of the Allies, led by educated and experienced officers, and controlled by diplomats from old-established Christian countries, gave way under the provocation of the time to unmeasured greed and vindictive cruelty, it is not surprising that some of the Chinese Christians, only just emerged from heathenism, should betray a revengeful spirit towards men who had destroyed their property, slaughtered their wives and children, and hunted the survivors with the ferocity of wild beasts. In some places, the missionaries had a hard task in restraining this spirit. It was inevitable, also, that in the confusion which followed the victory of the foreigners, some "wolves" should put on "sheep's clothing," and, under the pretense of being Christians, extort money from the terror-stricken villagers, or try to deceive the foreigner with false claims for indemnity.

But as I visited the scenes of disaster, saw the frightful ruin, heard the stories of Christians and missionaries, faced the little companies of survivors and learned more of the awful ordeal through which they had passed, I marvelled, not that some yielded, but that so many stood steadfast. Edicts were issued commanding them to recant on pain of dire punishment, but promising protection to those who obeyed. The following proclamation posted on the wall of the yamen at Ching-chou-fu is a sample of hundreds:—

"The Taku forts have been retaken by the Chinese. Gen. Tung Fu Shiang has led the Boxers and the goddesses, and has destroyed twenty foreign men-of-war, killing 6,000 foreign soldiers. The seven devilish countries' consuls came to beg for peace. General Tung now has killed all the foreign soldiers. The secondary devils (the native Christians) must die. General Tung has ordered the Boxers to go to the foreign countries and bring out their devil emperors from their holes. One foreigner must not be allowed to live. All who are not Chinese must be destroyed."

It requires no large knowledge of Chinese character to calculate the effect of such official utterances on the minds of lawless men.

Word sped from a Chinese city that on a certain day all Christians who had not recanted could be pillaged. From every quarter, the lawless streamed in, eager for the shambles. Ruffians pointed out the women they intended to take. And there was no foreigner to protect, no regiment or battleship for the Chinese Christian.

Those poor people, hardly out of their spiritual infancy, stood in that awful emergency absolutely alone. Could an American congregation have endured such a strain without flinching? Let those who can safely worship God according to the dictates of their own consciences be thankful that the genuineness of their faith has never been subjected to that supreme test.

Those were grievous days for the Christians of China. Two graduates of Teng-chou College remained for weary weeks in a filthy dungeon when they might have purchased freedom at any moment by renouncing Christianity. Pastor Meng of Paoting-fu, a direct descendant of Mencius, was 120 miles from home when the outbreak occurred. He was safe where he was, but he hurried back to die with his flock. He was stabbed, his arm twisted out of joint and his back scorched with burning candles in the effort to make him recant. But he steadfastly refused to compromise either himself or his people and was finally beheaded.

The uneducated peasant was no whit behind his cultivated countrymen in devotion to duty. A poor cook was seized and beaten, his ears were cut off, his mouth and cheeks gashed with a sword and other unspeakable mutilations inflicted. Yet he stood as firmly as any martyr of the early Church.

One of the Chinese preachers, on refusing to apostatize, received a hundred blows upon his bare back, and then the bleeding sufferer was told to choose between obedience and another hundred blows. What would we have answered? Let us, who have never been called on to suffer for Him, be modest in saying what we would have done. But that mangled, half-dead Chinese gasped:—"I value Jesus Christ more than life, and I will never deny Him." Before all of the second hundred blows could be inflicted, unconsciousness came and he was left for dead. But a friend took him away by night, bathed his wounds and secretly nursed him to recovery. I saw him, when I was in China, and I looked reverently upon the back that was seamed and scarred with "the marks of the Lord Jesus." Of the hundreds of Christians who were taken inside the legation grounds in Peking, not one proved false to their benefactors. "In the midday heat, in the drenching night rains, under storms of shot and shell, they fought, filled sand-bags, built barricades, dug trenches, sang hymns and offered prayers to the God whom the foreigner had taught them to love." Even the children were faithful. During the scream of deadly bullets, and the roar of burning buildings, the voices of the Junior Christian Endeavour Society were heard singing:—

"There'll be no dark valley when Jesus comes."

Such instances could be multiplied almost indefinitely from the experiences of Chinese Christians during the Boxer uprising. Indeed the fortitude of the persecuted Christians was so remarkable that in many cases the Boxers cut out the hearts of their victims to find the secret of such sublime faith, declaring: "They have eaten the foreigner's medicine." In those humble Chinese the world has again seen a vital faith, again seen that the age of heroism has not passed, again seen that men and women are willing to die for Christ. Multitudes withstood a persecution as frightful as that of the early disciples in the gardens and arenas of Nero. If they were hypocrites why did they not recant? As Dr. Maltbie Babcock truly said:—"One-tenth of the hypocrisy with which they were charged would have saved them from martyrdom." But thousands of them died rather than abjure their faith, and thousands more "had trial of mockings and scourgings, yea, moreover of bonds and imprisonment; they were stoned, they were sawn asunder, they were tempted, they were slain with the sword; they went about in sheepskins, in goatskins; being destitute, afflicted, ill-treated; wandering in deserts and mountains and caves and the holes of the earth."

Col. Charles Denby, late United States Minister to China, declared:—"Not two per cent. of the Chinese Christians proved recreant to their faith and many meet death as martyrs. Let us not call them 'Rice Christians' any more. Their conduct at the British Legation and the Peitang is deserving of all praise."[82] Beyond question, the Chinese Christians as a body stood the test of fire and blood quite as well as an equal number of American Christians would have stood it.

One of the most trying experiences of the missionaries has been the dealing with those who did recant. Some of the cases were pitiful. Poor, ignorant men, confessed their sin with streaming eyes, saying that they did not mean to deny their Lord, but that they could not see their wives outraged and their babies' heads crushed against stone walls. Others admitted that, though they stood firm while one hundred blows were rained upon their bare backs, yet after that they became confused and were only dimly conscious of what they said to escape further agony than flesh and blood could endure. Still others made a distinction, unfamiliar to us, but quite in harmony with Oriental hereditary notions, between the convictions of the heart and the profession of the lips, so that they externally and temporarily bowed their heads to the storm without feeling that they were thereby renouncing their faith. One of the best Chinese ministers in Shantung, after 200 lashes, which pounded his back into a pulp, feebly muttered an affirmative to the question: "Will you leave the devils' church?" But he explained afterwards that while he promised to leave "the devils' church," he did not promise to leave Christ's Church. The deception was not as apparent to him as it is to us whose moral perceptions have been sharpened by centuries of Christian nurture which have been denied to the Chinese.

---

82   Letter, April 28, 1902.

When the proclamation ordering the extermination of all foreigners and Christians was posted on the walls of Ching-chou-fu, a friendly official hinted that if the Chinese pastors would sign a document to the effect that they would "no longer practice the foreign religion," he would accept it as sufficient on behalf of all their flocks, and not enforce the order. Warrants for the arrest of every Christian had already been written. Scoundrels were hurrying in from distant villages to join in the riot of plunder and lust. Two women had already been killed. What were the pastors to do? There was no missionary to guide them, for long before the consuls had ordered all foreigners out of the interior. The agonized pastors determined to sacrifice themselves for their innocent people, to go through the form of giving up the "foreign" religion. That word "foreign" must be emphasized to understand their temptation, for the Chinese Christians do not feel that Christianity is foreign, but that it is theirs as well as ours. Moreover, the pastors were made to understand that it was simply a legal fiction, not affecting the religion of their hearts, but only a temporary expedient that the friendly magistrate might have a pretext for giving his protection to the Christians. They were not asked to engage in any idolatrous rite or to make any public apostasy, but simply to sign a statement "no longer to practice the foreign religion." "So far from recanting," it was urged upon them, "you are preventing recanting."

Their decision may be best given in the words of Pastor Wu Chien Cheng: "When I thought of these people," he said, his emotion being so great that the tears were running down his face, "in most cases with children and aged parents dependent upon them, and thought of all that was involved for them if I refused to sign the paper—well, I couldn't help it. I decided to take on myself the shame and the sin."

As the Rev. J. P. Bruce, of the English Baptist Mission, who told me of this incident, truly says: "Who could listen to such a narrative—so sad and painful and yet not without much that was noble—without sympathy and tears?" In this spirit of tenderness, so marked in the Lord's dealings with sinful Peter, the missionaries dealt with the recanting Christians. With the impostors, indeed, they had less mercy. The Rev. R. M. Mateer secured the arrest of two scapegraces who, under pretense of being Christians, had blackmailed innocent villagers. Very plainly, too, did the missionaries deal with Christians, who, like some people in the United States after a fire, placed an extravagant valuation upon what they had lost. But these were exceptional cases.

On the whole, Christians in Europe and America may well have stronger sympathy and respect for their fellow-Christians in China who have suffered so much for conscience' sake. Purified and chastened by the fearful holocaust through which they have passed, they are stronger spiritually than ever before. Like the apostles after Pentecost, they are giving "with great power their witness of the resurrection of the Lord Jesus." "The Chinese Church is not yet strong enough to stand entirely alone, but it is far stronger and more self-conscious of the eternal indwelling Spirit than ever before. It has learned the power of God to keep the soul in times of deadly peril, and to enable the weakest to give the strongest testimony. It has learned by humiliation and confession to put away its sins, and to gird itself for new conflicts and new victories…Its ablest leaders are more trustworthy men than before their trials, and the body of believers has a unity and a cohesiveness which will certainly bear fruit in the not distant future."[83]

83   Smith, "Rex Christus," p. 212.

XXIII
THE STRAIN OF READJUSTMENT TO CHANGED ECONOMIC CONDITIONS

THE economic revolution in Asia, discussed in a preceding chapter,[84] bears heavily on the Chinese Christians. So far as the pressure affects the rank and file of the membership, the mission boards cannot give adequate relief. Abroad as well as at home, it must remain the inexorable rule that a Christian must live within his income and buy new things only as he can pay for them. Any other policy would mean utter ruin. Here also, men must "work out their own salvation"; and the missionary, while trying to lift men out of barbarous social conditions on the one hand, should on the other resolutely oppose the improvident eagerness which leads a blanketed Sioux Indian to buy on credit a rubber-tired surrey.

But what about the native ministers and teachers, who find it impossible to live on the salaries of a decade ago? The problem of the ordinary helper is not so difficult. Springing from the common people, accustomed from childhood to a meagre scale of living, the small salaries which the people can pay either in full or in large part are usually equal to the income which they would have had if they had not become Christians. But some native ministers come from a higher social grade. They are men of education and refinement. They cannot live in a mud hut, go barefooted, wear a loin cloth and subsist on a few cents' worth of rice a day. They must not only have better houses and food and clothing, but they must have

---

84   Chapter IX.

books and periodicals and the other apparatus of educated men. These things are not only necessary to their own maintenance, but they are essential to the work, for these men are the main reliance for influencing the upper classes in favour of Christianity. It is not a question of luxury or self-indulgence, but of bare respectability, of the simple decencies of life which are enjoyed by an American mechanic as distinguished from the poverty which, for a cultivated family, falls below the level of self-respect. But this requires a salary which, save in a very few places, cannot at present be paid by the churches. "Our pastors," writes a missionary, "are supposed to live as the middle-class of their people do, but of late years, with the great rise in prices, they are living below the middle-class."

The consequences are not only pinching poverty but sometimes a feeling of wrong, and, in some cases, a yielding to temptation. One Chinese pastor, for example, who was trying to support a wife and five children on $10 Mex. ($5) a month, shipwrecked his influence by trying to supplement his scanty income by helping in lawsuits. Can we wonder that he felt obliged to do something, almost anything?

But who is to pay the higher salaries that are now so necessary? The first impulse is to look to the mission boards in Europe and America, and accordingly missionaries and Christians are importunately calling for increased appropriations. But whatever temporary and occasional relief may be given in this way, as a permanent remedy, it is plainly impossible. If the conditions were simply sporadic and local, the case might be different. But they are universal, or fast becoming so, and they will be permanent. It is quite visionary to suppose that the income of the mission boards will permit them to meet the whole or even the larger part of the increased cost of living among the myriads of ministers, teachers and helpers in the growing churches of China. American Christians cannot be reasonably expected to add such an enormous burden to the already large responsibilities which they are carrying in their varied forms of home work and the present scale of foreign missionary expenditure. Even if they could and would, it would be at the expense of all further enlargement of the work, and at the same time it would still further weaken an already weak sense of self-reliance among the native ministers and helpers of Asia.

Moreover, the average Christian giver in America is feeling the same strain himself. The so-called "era of prosperity" has given more steady employment to the mechanic, has given better markets to the producer, and has enormously increased the wealth of many who were already rich. But the men on fixed salaries find that "prosperity" has increased the prices of commodities without proportionately increasing earnings. Millions of American church members find it harder to give than they did ten years ago, for while their incomes are about the same, they must pay higher prices for meats, groceries and clothing. True, many salaries were cut down during the financial stringency of 1896-1897, but while some of them have been restored to their former figure, few have been raised above their original level, while others are still below it. Meantime official statistics show that the average cost of food is 10.9 per cent. higher than the average for the decade between 1890 and 1899, and that there has been an increase of 16.1 per cent. as compared with 1896, the year of lowest prices.[85] It is urged that the wages of workmen have increased in proportion. But however true this may be of organized labour, it is palpably untrue of the great middle-class who are neither capitalists nor members of labour unions. They form the bulk of the church membership and to them "Mr. Wright's statement will carry no reassurance. It is they who have been hit hardest by the increased cost of living for their incomes have not kept pace with it. Indeed, they are actually worse off to-day than they were eight, ten or fifteen years ago."[86] Dun's Review, an acknowledged authority, declares that not in twenty years has it cost so much to live as now, and that March 1, 1904, the average prices of breadstuffs were thirty per cent. higher than they were seven years ago.

In such circumstances, it is clearly out of the question for the Christians of the United States to meet these enlarged demands for the support of their own families and, in addition, meet them for the churches in China.

If then, the problem of the increased cost of living in Asia cannot be solved by increased gifts from America, what other

---

85 Report of the Hon. Carroll D. Wright, Commissioner of Labour, 1903
86 The Youth's Companion, October 29, 1903.

solutions are possible? As an experienced missionary says:—"To ask for more from America seems like a step backward; but to leave matters as they are is to see our churches seriously crippled." Four possible solutions may be mentioned.

First:—Stop all expansion of the work and use any increase in receipts to raise salaries. This is undoubtedly worthy of thoughtful consideration. To what extent is it right to open new fields and enlarge old ones when the workers now employed are inadequately paid? Plainly, the mission boards should carefully consider this aspect of the question. As a matter of fact, many of them have already considered it. The Presbyterian Board has repeatedly declined urgent requests to establish new stations on the ground that it could not do so in justice to its existing work. But as a practicable solution, this method is open to serious difficulties. A living work must grow, and the living forces which govern that growth are more or less beyond the control of the boards. The boards are amenable to their constituencies and those constituencies sometimes imperatively demand the occupation of a new field, as, for example, they did in the case of the Philippine Islands, some boards which at first decided not to enter the Philippines being afterwards forced into them by a pressure of denominational opinion that they could not ignore. Moreover, the missionaries themselves are equally insistent in their demands for enlargement. Some boards are literally deluged with such appeals. The missionaries who have most strenuously insisted on the policy of no further expansion till the existing work is better sustained have sometimes been the very ones who have strongly urged that an exception should be made in their particular fields, without realizing that the argument from "exceptions" is so often pressed that it is really the rule and not the exception at all. And the churches and missionaries are usually right. God is calling His people to go forward. His voice is frequently very plain, and the boards, with all their care and conservatism, are then obliged to expand.

Second:—Diminish the number of native pastors, helpers and teachers and increase their work. In some places, this might be done by grouping congregations and fields. But the places where this could be wisely effected are so few that the relief to the situation as a whole would not be appreciable, especially as the native Christians would not give so liberally under such an arrangement. Their sense of responsibility would be weakened if they had only a half or a quarter of a pastor's time instead of the whole of it. Besides, the native force is far too small now. Instead of being diminished it should be largely increased. The great work of the future must be done by native ministers. If China is ever to be evangelized, it must be to a large degree by Chinese evangelists. To adopt deliberately the policy of restricting the number of such evangelists and teachers would be suicidal. As a solution, therefore, this method is quite impracticable, as it would be a relief at the expense of efficiency.

Third:—Require native leaders to earn their own living either wholly or in part. There is Pauline example for this method. Some of the Presbyterian missionaries in Laos have adopted it by inducing the members of a congregation to secure a ricefield and a humble house for their minister. The Korea missionaries have very successfully worked this method by insisting that the leaders of groups shall continue in their former occupations and give their services to Christian work without pay, in some such way as Sunday-school superintendents and other unpaid workers do in America. This method is deserving of wider adoption. It would give considerable relief in many other fields. It was probably the way that the early church grew.

"Two opinions," says Dr. J. J. Lucas, "have been held in regard to the basis on which the salaries of native agents should be fixed. One is that such a salary should be paid as would remove all excuse for engaging in secular work, demanding all the time of the pastor for spiritual work; another is, that acknowledging the salary to be insufficient, the pastors be expected to supplement it by what they can get from field and vineyard. If self-support is to be aimed at, at all cost, then the latter plan is the only feasible one, with the dangers of its abuse. There is no doubt, however, that a man who loves the gospel ministry and is devoted to it can, without the neglect of spiritual affairs, do enough outside to lessen materially the burden that would fall on the church in his support."

But this method of itself would hardly solve the problem. However well adapted to the beginnings of mission work, it fails to provide a properly qualified native leadership. To do efficient work, a native pastor must give his whole time to it, and to that end he must have a salary that will make him "free from worldly cares and avocations." We insist on this in the United States and the reasons for such a policy are as strong on the foreign field. The minister in Asia as well as the minister in America must have a salary. The labourer is worthy of his hire.

Fourth:—Insist upon a larger measure of self-support. The native churches must be led to a fuller responsibility in this matter. Grave as are the temporary embarrassments which the increased cost of living is forcing upon them and trying as is the permanent distress of some of them, yet as a whole the economic revolution will undoubtedly enlarge the earning capacity of the native Christians. Indeed, the new principles of life which the gospel brings should make them among the first to profit by the changed conditions, and as their wealth increases, their spirit of giving should, and under the wise lead-ership of the missionaries undoubtedly will, increase. For these reasons, the Presbyterian Board of Foreign Missions took the following action July 2, 1900:—

"As having reference to the question of self-support of the native churches on the mission field, and in view of the fact that some of its missions are proposing to increase the salaries of native preachers and helpers on account of the increased cost of living, the Board is constrained to look with no little apprehension upon the prospect of continuing and increasing demands of foreign aid in proportion to the contributions made by the churches themselves. Increased intercourse of eastern nations with those of the west has led and will still further lead to a gradual assimilation to western ways and western prices, and unless the self-reliant spirit of the churches can be stimulated to a proportionate advance, there is a sure prospect that the drafts upon mission funds will be larger and larger in proportion to the amount of work accomplished. In view of these considerations, it was resolved that the missions in which such increase is proposed be earnestly requested to arouse the churches to the purpose and the endeavour to meet this increased expenditure instead of laying still larger burdens upon the resources of foreign funds. The Board deems this necessary not merely to the interest of its expanding work but to the self-reliant character, the future stability and self-propagating power of the churches themselves."

There appears to be no alternative. And yet this policy, while adhered to, should be enforced with reasonable discretion and due regard to "this present distress." How can Christians, who can barely live themselves and pay a half or two-thirds of their pastor's present support, suddenly meet this call for enlarged salaries? For reasons already given, it is harder for them to make ends meet now than it was in the old days of primitive simplicity, while in many places a profession of Christianity is followed by the loss of property and employment so that the Christian is impoverished by the loss of the income that he already had. In these circumstances, both boards and missions must simply do the best they can, and neither allow the emergency to sweep them into a mistaken charity that would be fatal to the ultimate interests of the cause nor allow a valuable native worker to suffer for the necessaries of life.

"We need to bear in mind that the low salaries of China are not the product of Christianity, but of heathenism, and the ability to live on five or six Mexicans per month is not the result of a laudable economy unknown to Christian countries, so much as it is the result of a degradation of manhood to the level of beasts. The church is responsible for the knowledge of a better way of living. We have created the desire for a clean house, clean clothing, healthful food, and books, on the part of our educated young men. Shall we implant this desire for six or eight years and take the rest of the man's life in trying to squelch it? We have come as apostles of truth to a mighty empire, to the great and the small, to the rich and the poor, and if we had a native ministry which could appeal to a different class of men than most of them are now appealing to, would not the day of self-support be hastened beyond what we dare to hope? Is there not a feeling out for something better on the part of the well-to-do, the more intelligent, just as really as there is on the part of the lowest classes? Do not we have a mission to the man who can pay $100.00 a year to the church just as really as to the one who pays 100 cash? There is nothing so costly as cheap men. Let us have a higher grade of men and we shall have a higher grade of church-membership. Is it not true that nothing more stands in the way of self-support than some of our native clergy? We must not turn down better men because they must have a little more to live upon than poor men."[87]

---

87   Mr. F. S. Brockman, Address—"How to Retain to the Church the Services of English-Speaking Christians," Shanghai,

It is idle, however, to urge as a reason for increasing the salaries of Chinese ministers that a qualified Asiatic can earn more in commercial life than in the ministry. Such arguments often come to mission boards. But religious work cannot compete with business in financial inducements either at home or abroad. It is notorious that in America, ministers and church workers generally do not receive the compensation which they could command in secular employments or professions. The qualities that bring success in the ministry are, as a rule, far more liberally remunerated in secular life. The preacher who can command $6,000 or $8,000 in the pulpit could probably command three or four times that amount in the law or in business. Men who are as eminent in other professions and in the commercial world as the most eminent clergymen are in the ministry usually have incomes ranging from $20,000 to $100,000 a year and have no "dead line" of age either. As for others, the Rev. Dr. B. L. Agnew, Secretary of the Presbyterian Board of Ministerial Relief, is authority for the statement that the average salary of Presbyterian ministers is $700 and that for all denominations it does not equal the wages of the average mechanic. A missionary writes:—"Practically all our native pastors are underpaid." The same thing might be said of all the home missionaries and of most of the pastors of non-missionary churches at home, one-third of whom receive only $500 or less.

The churches of America cannot, or at any rate will not, do for the native ministers of Asia what they are not doing for their own ministers. The world over, the rewards of Christ's service are not financial. Those who seek that service must be content with modest support, sometimes even with poverty. This is not a reason for the home churches to be content with their present scale of missionary giving, nor does it mean that mission boards are disposed to refuse requests for appropriations. The boards are straining every nerve to secure a more generous support and they will gladly send all they can to the missions on the field. But it is a reason for impressing more strongly upon the young men in the churches of Asia that they should consecrate themselves to the Master's service from a higher motive than financial support and that while the boards will continue to give all the assistance that is in their power, yet that

1904.

the permanent dependence of the ministers of China must be in increasing measure upon the Christians of China and not upon the Christians of America. Hundreds of native pastors are already realizing this and are manifesting a self-sacrificing courage and devotion that are beyond all praise. Said Mr. Fitch of Ningpo to a Chinese youth of fine education and exceptional ability:—"Suppose a business man should offer you $100.00 a month and at the same time you had the way opened to you to study for the ministry, and after entering it, to get from $20.00 to $30.00 a month, which would you take?" And the youth answered—"I would enter the ministry." "He is now teaching a mission school at $12.00 a month, though he could easily command $30.00 a month in a business position." The hope of the churches of China is in such men. Mr. F. S. Brockman declares:—

"There is a wide-spread conviction among missionaries that the allurements of wealth alone are keeping English-speaking young men from the ministry. The facts do not bear out this belief...In order to hold them in the ministry we need not appeal to their love of money. It is death to the ministry when we do it; we have opened the vial of their fiercest passion; we are doing what Jesus Christ never did; we are working absolutely contrary to the fundamental laws of the kingdom of God...We must teach prospective ministers to look upon their lives as an unselfish expenditure of God-given power. For once make the allurement of the ministry the allurement of comfort, ease, or wealth, and we have closed up every fountain of the minister's power."

XXIV
COMITY AND COOPERATION

THE Hon. Charles Denby, then United States Minister at Peking, wrote in 1900:—

"With all due deference to the great missionary societie, who have these matters in charge, my judgment is that missionary work in China has been overdone. Take Peking as an example. There are located at Peking the following Protestant missions: American Boards American Presbyterian, American Methodist, Christian and Missionary Alliance, International Y. M. C. A., London Missionary Society, Society for the Propagation of the Gospel, International Institute, Mission for Chinese Blind, Scotch Bible Society, and the Society for the Diffusion of Christian Knowledge. To these must be added the Church of England Mission, the English Baptist Mission and the Swedish Mission. The above list shows that of American societies alone there are seven in Peking, not counting the Peking University, and that all western Powers taken collectively were represented by about twenty missions. A careful study of the situation would seem to suggest that no two American societies should occupy the same district."[88]

It may be well to examine this criticism, partly because it was made by an able man of known sympathy with mission work, and partly because it relates to the city where, if anywhere, in China, overcrowding exists. In considering Peking, therefore, we are really considering the broad question of the practicability of

---

88   Missionary Review of the World, October, 1900.

withdrawing some missionary agencies in the interest of comity and efficiency. The Presbyterian missionaries themselves opened the way for the discussion of the question by proposing to the Congregational missionaries, after the Boxer uprising had been quelled, "an exchange of all work and fields of our Presbyterian Church in the province of Chih-li in return for the work and fields of the American Board in the province of Shantung, subject to the approval of our respective Boards." The Mission added:—

"It means no little sacrifice to sever attachments made in long years of service in fields and among a people whom God has enabled us to lead to Christ, but we feel that a high spirit of loyalty to Christ and His cause, inspiring all concerned, will lead us to set aside personal preferences and attachments, if thereby the greater interests of His Church in China can be conserved."

The whole question was thoroughly discussed during my visit in Peking. Much time was spent traversing the entire ground. Then a meeting was called of the leading missionaries of all the Protestant agencies represented in Peking.

The result of all these conferences was the unanimous and emphatic judgment of the missionaries of all the boards concerned that there is not "a congestion of missionary societies in Peking," and that no one board could be spared without serious injury to the cause. In reply to the proposal of the Presbyterian missionaries, the North China Mission of the American Board wrote—

"After considering the matter in all its bearings we are constrained to say that we contemplate with regret any plan which looks to the withdrawal of the Presbyterian Mission from the field which they have so long occupied in northern Chih-li. We think that instead of illustrating comity this would appear as if comity was not to be attained without a violent dislocation from long-established foundations, and that in this particular there would be a definite loss all around...We further deprecate the proposed step because there is now an excellent opportunity for the adoption or actual measures of cooperation between our respective missions... We are ready to readjust boundaries in such a way as to remedy the waste of effort in the crossing of one another's territory...We are confident that the ultimate outcome could not fail to be a greater benefit than the sudden rupture of long-existing relations for the sake of mere geographical contiguity of the work of missions like yours and ours, each keeping its own district, careful not to encroach upon the other. In the higher unity here suggested we should expect to realize larger results in the promotion of comity not only, but also in the best interests of that kingdom of God for which we are each labouring.

"ARTHUR H. SMITH,

"D. Z. SHEFFIELD,

"Committee."

Moreover, several of the agencies enumerated by Colonel Denby, such as the Y. M. C. A., the International Institute, the Mission to the Blind, the various Bible Societies, and the Society for the Diffusion of Christian Knowledge, are not competing missionary agencies at all, but are doing a special work along such separate lines that it is unfair to take them into consideration. As a matter of fact, with the exception of a comparatively small work by the Society for the Propagation of the Gospel, the real missionary work in Peking is being done by only four Boards,—The American, Methodist, London, and Presbyterian. This is not a disproportionate number, considering the fact that Peking is one of the great cities of the world and the capital of the Empire. It is of the utmost importance that a strong Christian influence should be exerted in such a centre. Indeed, if there is any place in all China where this influence ought to be intensified, it is Peking. It is granted that Christian work is more difficult in a great city, that it is harder to convert a man there than in a country village. But, on the other hand, he is more influential when he is converted. Peking is the heart of China. Alone of all its cities, it is visited sooner or later by every ambitious scholar and prominent official. The examinations for the higher degrees bring to it myriads of the brightest young men of the country. The moral effect of a strong Christian Church in Peking will be felt in every province. If Christianity is to be a positive regenerative force in China it cannot afford to weaken its hold in the very citadel of China's power.

It should be borne in mind that the work of the missionaries stationed at Peking is not confined to the city, but that Peking is a base from which they work out on the east and south till they reach the boundaries of the Tien-tsin and Paoting-fu station fields, while on the north and west a vast and populous region for an indefinite distance is wholly dependent upon them for Christian teaching. Extensive and densely inhabited areas of the province are not being worked by any board. The Rev. Dr. John Wherry, who has lived there for a generation, says that there are a hundred times as many people in the Peking region as are now being reached, and that there are 20,000,000 in the province who have never yet heard of Christ. For this enormous field the missionary agencies now at work are really few. Hundreds of American cities of half a million inhabitants have a greater number of ordained workers than this entire province of Chih-li with a population nearly half as large as that of the United States. Indeed there is room for a great extension of the work without overcrowding.

Each denomination occupies a large and distinct geographical field in this province. For example, all that portion of the city and suburbs of Peking north of the line of the Forbidden City, with a population of about 200,000, is considered Presbyterian territory. No other missionaries are located in that part of Peking. In the country, the counties of San-ho, Huai-jou, Pao-ti, to the north and east of Peking, are also understood to be distinctively Presbyterian ground. San-ho County alone is said to have 1,200 towns and villages, while the other counties are also very populous. No other Protestant denomination is working in any of these counties. At Paoting-fu, the Congregationalists and Presbyterians have made a division of the field, the former taking everything south of a line drawn through the centre of the city and the latter everything north of that line. Each denomination thus has wholly to itself half the city of Paoting-fu and about a dozen outlying counties.

The missionaries of the three other boards concerned plainly stated that, in the event of the withdrawal of the Presbyterians, they would not be able to care for the work that would be left. They declared that they were not able adequately to sustain the work they already had and that there was not the slightest reason to hope that their home boards would find it possible to give them the reinforcements in men and money which would be required if their present responsibilities were to be increased. The large district now occupied by any given board would simply be vacated if its missionaries were transferred to other regions. The ties formed with the Chinese Christians and people in more than a generation of continuous missionary work would be broken and the influence acquired by faithful missionaries in long years of toil would be lost.

In these circumstances, would it be right for any one of these four boards to withdraw? There will, indeed, come a time when it will be the duty of the missionary to leave the Chinese church to itself. But is this the time to go, when the native church, instead of being strong and able to care for itself, is torn and bleeding after frightful persecution? These Christians look to the missionaries, who have hitherto led them, as spiritual fathers who will guide them in the future. They feel that the time has come for a new consecration to the task of evangelizing all their people. As directed by the missionaries, they may become a great influence for the conversion of their countrymen. Should they be left when other missionaries expressly state that they cannot care for them?

The question of closer cooperation, however, is worthy of careful consideration. At a conference of representatives of foreign mission boards of the United States and Canada having work in China, held in New York, September 21, 1900, the following resolution was unanimously adopted:

"It is the judgment of this conference that the resumption of mission work in those parts of China where it has been interrupted would afford a favourable opportunity for putting into practice some of the principles of mission comity which have been approved by a general concensus of opinion among missionaries and boards, especially in regard to the over lapping of fields and such work as printing and publishing, higher education and hospital work, and the conference would commend the subject to the favourable consideration and action of the various boards and their missionaries."

Christian America, which ought to set the example of comity, is distractingly divided. Should it not learn something from its experience at home and, as far as possible, organize its work abroad in such a way as to avoid perpetuating unnecessary divisions? Should it not at least carefully consider whether a limited force cannot be used to better advantage for China and for Christ? I admire the ingenuity of those at home who can find good reasons for having half a dozen denominations in a town of a few thousand inhabitants. But on the foreign field, we should adopt a different policy. In the large cities—the Londons, and Berlins,

and New Yorks, and Chicagos, of Asia, it is conceded that more than one Board may properly work. But with such exceptions, it should be the rule not to enter fields where other evangelical bodies are already established. Indeed it is already the rule. The Shanghai Conference of 1900 voted that missionary agencies should not be multiplied in small places, though that cities of prefectural rank should not be considered the exclusive territory of any one board. The American Presbyterian Board declared in 1900, and its action was specifically approved by the General Assembly of that year:—
"The time has come for a larger union and cooperation in mission work, and where church union cannot be attained, the Board and the missions will seek such divisions of territory as will leave as large districts as possible to the exclusive care and development of separate agencies."

In several places, boards and missions are moving actively in this direction. In 1902, the American and Presbyterian Boards entered into a union in educational work in the province of Chih-li by which the Presbyterians conduct a union boarding-school for girls in Paoting-fu and for boys in Peking, while the Congregationalists educate the boys of both denominations in Paoting-fu and the girls in Peking. A medical college in Peking was agreed upon in 1903, to be supported and taught jointly by the London, American and Presbyterian missions. In the province of Shantung, a notable union in both educational and medical work was effected in 1903 between English Baptists and American Presbyterians. Instead of developing duplicate institutions with all the large expenditure of men and money that would be involved, the boards and missions concerned are uniting in the development of the Shantung Protestant University with the Arts College on the Presbyterian compound at Wei-hsien and the Theological and Normal School on the Baptist compound at Ching-chou-fu. The medical class will be taught alternately at the Baptist and Presbyterian stations until funds warrant the erection of suitable buildings, probably at Chinan-fu, the capital of the province. In Shanghai, the Northern and Southern Methodists established a union publishing house in 1902, and in several other parts of China, plans for union of various kinds are being discussed.

All these enterprises met with opposition at first. There was, indeed, little objection to union in medical education, for few questions of a denominational character are involved in the training of medical students. But it was urged by some that it would not be expedient to press consolidation in educational work, as the chief object of such work was held to be the training of a native ministry and each mission could best educate its own helpers and should do so in the interest of self-preservation. The example of the Meiji Gakuin in Tokio, Japan, which is supported by the Presbyterian and Reformed Boards, was not deemed determinative as in Japan but one native church is involved, so that the cases are not parallel. Moreover, it was thought that in a large school there would not be as good an opportunity for that close personal contact between missionary and pupil which is so desirable.

These difficulties, however, are believed by many of the missionaries to be more theoretical than practical, or, at any rate, not sufficiently formidable to prevent a more effective cooperation. No plan will be free from all objections and a good effort should not be abandoned because they are found to confront it. The defects in union are less grave than those that experience has shown to be inherent in the old method of numerous weak and struggling institutions whose support requires a ruinous proportion of the mission force and the mission funds that might otherwise be available, in part at least, for the enlargement of the evangelistic work. "It certainly seems unnecessary that two missions should maintain distinct high schools looking towards a college grade side by side, when the whole number of pupils in both could be instructed more economically and perhaps more efficiently in one institution."

Nor is this all, for, wherever practicable, union of allied churches is being sought. I know we are told that Christ's words do not call for this. But when I hear the laboured arguments which defend the splitting of American Presbyterianism into more than a dozen sects, I sympathize with the child who, after a sermon in which the minister had eloquently urged that the unity for which the Lord prayed was consistent with separation, said: "Mamma, if Christ didn't mean what He said, why didn't He say what He meant?"

Premature and impracticable efforts should indeed be avoided. The deeply rooted differences of centuries are not to be eradicated in a day. We must feel our way along with caution and wisdom. To attempt too much at first would be to accomplish nothing. Work abroad is necessarily a projection of the work at home and it will be more or less hampered by our American divisions. A prominent clergyman told me that he doubted the wisdom of a union of the Asiatic churches as he feared that such a union would weaken the sense of responsibility of the home churches. He thought that a denomination in America would take a deeper interest in a comparatively small native church wholly dependent upon it than it would in an indeterminate part of a larger church. Must the unity of the foreign church be sacrificed to the divisions of the home church? Perhaps there is some ground for anticipating such objections from home. But if they are found to exist, we should not cease seeking union in Asia, but begin preaching juster views in America.

I must not be understood as depreciating the historic differences of Christendom. I am aware that each of the great religious bodies stands for some cardinal principle that is not emphasized to the same degree by others. The freedom of any given number of believers to witness to a specific truth should not be and need not be limited by union. The contention here is that the differences of the West should not be forced upon the East but that the churches of Asia should be given a fair chance to develop a unity large enough to comprehend these various forms. If they must be divided, let them separate later along their own lines of cleavage, not on lines extended from western nations. In one place, I met a swarthy Asiatic who knew just enough English to be able to tell me that he was a Scotch Presbyterian. Are we then to have a Scotch Presbyterian Church in Asia, and a Canadian Presbyterian Church, and an Australian Presbyterian Church? Is the American Civil War forever to divide communities of Chinese believers into American Northern Presbyterians and American Southern Presbyterians? Why should we force our unhappy quarrel of a generation ago upon them? The American Presbyterian Board has truly declared that "the object of the foreign missionary enterprise is not to perpetuate on the mission field the denominational distinctions of Christendom but to build up on Scriptural lines and according to Scriptural principles and methods the Kingdom of Our Lord Jesus Christ." It has advised all its missions that "we encourage as far as practicable the formation of union churches in which the results of the mission work of all allied evangelical churches should be gathered, and that they (the missions) observe everywhere the most generous principles of missionary comity." The specific approval of this declaration, by the General Assembly of 1900, makes this the authoritative policy of the Presbyterian Church in the United States of America.

In harmony with this general position, several significant efforts towards union are being made. The first movements, naturally, are towards a union of communions that are substantially alike in polity and doctrine. Already all the Presbyterian and Reformed Boards operating in Japan, Korea, Mexico and India have joined in the support of a united native church in those lands, and similar movements are in progress in other lands and in several churches, notably the Protestant Episcopal and the Methodist Episcopal. In China, the representatives of the eight Presbyterian denominations of Europe and America have met in loving conference and planned to unite all the native Christians connected with their respective missions into one magnificent and commanding Church.

And now unions of wholly different denominations are being discussed. The American Board missionaries intimated to the Presbyterian Mission in 1901 that there might be "no inherent difficulty in uniting the membership of the Presbyterian and Congregational churches in Chih-li in one common body." A similar question is being informally discussed by the American Presbyterian missionaries and those of the English Baptist Mission in Shantung. The fellowship between the two bodies there, as between Presbyterians and Congregationalists in Chih-li, is close.

The local difficulties do not appear to be serious. An English Baptist missionary frankly stated in an open conference of missionaries of various boards in Chefoo, that his mission, with the full knowledge of the home society, took the position that the Chinese Christians are not yet fit for congregational government, being, as a rule, comparatively ignorant farmers just out of heathenism; that it had been found necessary to select the best men in a local church and give them powers which, for all practical purposes, constituted them a session, and that the native church as a whole was being more and more directed by a body consisting of representatives from such sessions. An American Board missionary told me substantially the same thing regarding the churches of his mission. We should not infer too much from such admissions. Both Baptists and Congregationalists are loyally attached to their independent policy. Both referred, of course, to the temporary adaptions necessary in the present stage of mission work. As for Presbyterians, their Board's Committee on Policy and Methods declared, March 6, 1899:—

"It is inexpedient to give formal organization to churches and Presbyteries after American models unless there is manifest need therefor, and such forms are shown to be best adapted to the people and circumstances. In general, the ends of the work will be best attained by simple and flexible organizations adapted to the characteristic and real needs of the people and designed to develop and utilize spiritual power rather than merely or primarily to secure proper ecclesiastical procedure."

As a matter of fact, neither the representative nor the independent forms of church government are yet in unmodified operation on any mission fields, except perhaps in Japan, for the simple reason that the typical foreign missionary has thus far necessarily exercised the functions of a superintendent or bishop of the native churches. Undoubtedly, however, the Asiatic churches are being educated to expect self-government as soon as they are competent to exercise it.

Doctrinal differences may present greater difficulties. And yet there is a remarkable unanimity of teaching among the missionaries of the various denominations in China. However widely they may differ among themselves, nearly all agree in preaching to the Chinese the great central truths of Christianity so that most of the native Christians know little of the sectarian distinctions that are so well-understood in America. Such differences as are necessary in China might be provided for by recognizing the liberty of the local church and the individual believer to hold whichever phase of the truth might be preferred. The China Inland Mission has shown that this plan is feasible. It is composed of missionaries of all Protestant denominations, but they work in harmony and build up a Chinese church by recognizing the right of brethren to differ in the same organization.

Doubtless isolated cases of embarrassment would occur, but they would be insignificant in comparison with the embarrassments inherent in sectarian divisions. Denominational uniformity is bought at bitter cost when it separates Christians into rival camps. Unity in essentials and liberty in non-essentials are far better than a slavery to non-essentials which destroys that oneness of believers for which our Lord prayed. In the presence of a vast heathen population, let Christians at least remember that their points of disagreement are less vital than their points of agreement, that Christianity should, as far as possible, present a solid front, and let them devoutly join the Conference of Protestant missionaries in Japan in the ringing proclamation:—"That all those who are one with Christ by faith are one body, and that all who love the Lord Jesus and His Church in sincerity and truth should pray and labour for the full realization of such a corporate oneness as the Master Himself prayed for in the night in which He was betrayed."

It is true that an advanced position on comity sometimes operates to the disadvantage of the denomination that espouses it. But let us be true to our ideals even if some whom we might have reached do go to heaven by another route. Other churches are preaching the gospel and those who accept it at their hands will be saved. We are in Asia to preach Christ, to preach Him as we understand Him, but if any one else insists on preaching Him in a given place and will do so with equal fidelity to His divinity and atone-ment, let us cooperate with them, or federate with them, or combine with them, or give up the field to them, as the circumstances may require. The problem before us is not simply where we can do good, but where we can do the most good, how use to the best advantage the limited resources at our command. Givers at home have a right to demand this. Many of their gifts involve self-sacrifice, and they should be used where a real need exists. "There remains yet very much land to be possessed." I have seen enough of it to burden my heart as long as I live, toiling, sorrowing, sin-laden multitudes, who might be better Christians than we are if they had our chance, but who are scattered abroad as sheep having no shepherd. And shall we multiply missionaries in places already occupied and dispute as to who shall preach in a given fields when these millions are dying without the gospel?

PART V

THE FUTURE OF CHINA AND OUR RELATION TO IT

XXV
IS THERE A YELLOW PERIL

WILL China ever be able to menace the nations of the West? This is the startling question that many sober-minded men are asking. Some writers, indeed, make light of the "yellow peril," characterizing it "a mere bugaboo of an excited imagination," because, as they allege, China has neither the organization nor the valour to fight Europe, and because, if it had, it could not transport its army and navy so vast a distance.

But surely organization and valour can be acquired by the Chinese as well as by any other people. Their present helplessness before the aggressive foreigner is rapidly teaching them the necessity for the former. As for the latter, it is well known that the most dangerous fighter is the strong but peaceably-disposed man who has been goaded to desperation by long-continued insult and injustice. Americans may discreetly remember that they themselves were once sneeringly described as "a nation of shopkeepers who wouldn't and couldn't fight."

It is easy to be deceived by the result of the China-Japan War of 1894. The Japanese were successful, not because they are abler, but because they had more swiftly responded to the touch of the modern world and had organized their government, their army and their navy in accordance with scientific methods. More bulky and phlegmatic China was caught napping by her enterprising enemy. Despising the profession of arms, China gave her energies to scholarship and commerce, and filled her regiments and ships with paupers, criminals and opium fiends, who were as destitute of courage, intelligence and patriotism as the darky who explained his flight from the battle-field by saying that he would rather be a live coward than a dead hero. As for the men above them, a Chinese officer admitted to a friend of mine that at the outbreak of the war with Japan, the army contractors bought a lot of old rifles in Germany, which had long before been discarded as worthless by the German army, paying two ounces of silver for each gun, and thriftily charging the Government nine ounces. Then they bought a cargo of cartridges that did not fit the guns and that had been lying in damp cellars for twenty years, and put the whole equipment into the hands of raw recruits commanded by opium-smokers.

It is not surprising, therefore, that the Chinese were worsted before the onset of the wide-awake Japanese, and that the unorganized mobs with which they blindly tried to drive out foreigners in 1900 were easily crushed by the armies of the West. But it would be folly to imagine that this is the end. It takes a nation of 426,000,000 phlegmatic people longer to get under way than a nation of 43,000,000 nervous people, but when they do get started, their momentum is proportionately greater. China has plenty of men who can fight, and when they are well commanded, they make as good soldiers as there are in the world, as "Chinese Gordon" showed. Was not his force called the "Ever Victorious Army," because it was never defeated? Did not Lord Charles Beresford, of the English navy, say, after personal inspection of many of the troops of China:—"I am convinced that properly armed, disciplined and led, there could be no better material than the Chinese soldiers"? Did not Admiral Dewey report that the fifty Chinese who served under him in the battle of Manila Bay fought so magnificently that they proved themselves equal in courage to American sailors and that they should be made American citizens by special enactment? During my tour of Asia, I saw the soldiers of England, France, Germany, Italy, Austria, Belgium, Russia, America and Japan. But the Chinese cavalrymen of Governor Yuan Shih Kai, whom I have described elsewhere,[89] were as fine troops as I saw anywhere. They would be a foe not to be despised. When Bishop Potter returned from his tour of Asia, he declared that "when Japan has taught

---

89   Chapter VII.

China the art of war, neither England nor Russia nor Germany will decide the fate of the East."

It is odd that any intelligent person should suppose that distance is an effectual barrier against an aroused and organized Asia. It is no farther from China to Europe than from Europe to China, and Europe has not found the distance a barrier to its designs on China. England, Germany, France, Russia, and even little Holland and Portugal, have all managed to send ships and troops to the Far East, to seize territory and to subjugate the inhabitants. Why should it be deemed impossible for China, which alone is larger than all these nations combined, to do what they have done?

The absorption of China by Russia or any other single European power is not possible for the reason that the attempt would be resisted by all the other Powers, including the United States and Japan. The world will never permit one of its nations to make China what Great Britain has made India. A half dozen Powers are determined to have a share if the break up comes.

The real partition of the Empire, however, is hardly probable as the case stands to-day. The Powers dread the task of administering a population that is not only huge but of such a stubborn character that enormous military expenditures might be required to prevent constant rebellions. A still more potent reason lies in the fact that the European nations that covet portions of China could not agree among themselves as to the division of the spoil. There is, indeed, apparent acquiescence in Russian influence in Manchuria, German in Shantung, British in the valleys of the Yang-tze and the Pearl, and French in Tonquin. But no one nation is quite satisfied with this division. Each has thus far taken what it could get; but Germany, France and Russia are far from pleased to see Great Britain take the lion's share that she has marked out for herself. Moreover, there are important provinces that are now common ground, like the imperial province of Chih-li, or unappropriated, like several of the interior provinces. Actual partition would mean a scramble that would precipitate a general war, and such a war would involve so many uncertainties not only as to the result in China but as to possible readjustments in Europe itself, that the Powers wisely shrink from it. So they prefer for the present, at least, the policy of "spheres of influence" as giving them a commercial foothold and political influence with less risk of trouble.

Besides, Great Britain, the United States and Japan are all opposed to partition. England's chief interest in China is commercial, and it quite naturally prefers to trade with the whole of China rather than be confined to a particular section of it, for it knows that there would be little trade with any parts of China that Russia, France and Germany absolutely controlled. So England insists on the integrity of China and the open door."

The United States has the same commercial interest in this respect as Great Britain, with the added motive that partition would give her nothing at all in China; while Japan feels the most strongly of all for she has both the reasons that actuate the United States and also the vital one of self-preservation. The Hon. Chester Holcombe says that several years ago, in an interview with an influential member of the Japanese Cabinet in Tokio, the conversation turned upon the aggressions of European Powers and the weakness of Korea, which had recently declared its independence.

"The Japanese Minister was greatly disturbed at the prospect for the future. He insisted that the action taken by Korea, under the guidance of China, would not save that little kingdom from attack and absorption. Holding up one hand, and separating the first and second fingers as widely as possible from the third and fourth, he said:—'Here is the situation. Those four fingers represent the four great European Powers, Great Britain, Germany, France and Russia. In the open space between them lie Japan, China and Korea.' Then, with really dramatic force, he added: 'Like the jaws of a huge vise, those fingers are slowly closing, and unless some supreme effort is made, they will certainly crush the national life out of all three.'"

So Japan must be reckoned with in any plans which the western nations may make for China, and that Japan is a factor not to be despised, the Russians have learned to their sorrow. Japan believes that she has found the way to make her opposition so formidable that all Europe cannot overcome it. Beyond any other people in the world, the Chinese furnish the raw materials for a world power. All they need is capable leadership. This is the gigantic task to which Japan has set herself. The alert and enterprising Islanders have entered upon a career of national aggrandizement. They realize that with their limited territory and population, they can hardly hope to become a power of the first class and make headway against the tremendous forces of western nations unless they can ally themselves with their larger continental neighbour. They clearly see their own superiority in organization, discipline and modern spirit, and they see also the stupendous power of China if it can be aroused and effectively directed. The Japanese have never been accused of undue modesty and they firmly believe that they are just the people to do this work. This is not simply because they are ambitious, but because they see that unless Asia can be thus solidified against Europe, the whole mighty continent will fall under the control of the white men who already dominate so large a part of it. Accordingly the Japanese have entered upon the definite policy of not only absorbing Korea, but of cultivating the closest possible alliance with their former foe.

The Hon. Augustin Heard, formerly United States Minister to Korea, represents Japan as whispering to the sorely beset Celestials:—

"Why shouldn't we work together? I hate the foreigner as much as you do, and should be as glad to get rid of him. Together we can do great things; separate we are feeble. I am too small, and you are, so to speak, too big. You are unorganized. Let us join hands and I will do what I can to help you get ready; and when we are ready we will drive these insolent fellows into the sea. I have a big army and navy and I have learned all the foreigners have to teach. This knowledge I will pass on to you. We have great advantages over them. In the first place they are a long way from their supplies, and every move they make costs a great deal of money. Our men can fight as well as theirs, if they are shown how, and there are a great many more of them. They can march as well, will require to carry almost no baggage, and do not cost half as much to feed. Our wounded men, too, in their own country and climate will get well, while theirs will die."

To this suggestion China listens and ponders:—

"What are the objections? There is, first, the contempt which our people feel for them; but that is rapidly dying out. The Japanese showed in our last war that small men can fight as well as big ones; and a rifle in the hands of the small man will carry as far and as true as in the hands of a larger one. Then, when we have once got rid of the foreigner will Japan not try to keep the leadership and supremacy? Very likely but then we shall be armed and organized; we have as able men as they and with our overwhelming numbers shall we not be capable of holding our own—nay, if we wish, of taking possession of her?"[90]

Undoubtedly this imaginary conversation voices the ambition of the Japanese and the inclination of an increasing number of Chinese. At any rate, the possibilities which such an alliance suggests are almost overwhelming. Japan undoubtedly has the intelligence and the executive ability to organize as no other power could the vast latent forces of China. If any one doubts her fitness to discipline and lead, he might obtain some heartfelt information from the Russians. Says Mr. George Lynch in the Nineteenth Century:—

"I know of no movement more pregnant with possibilities than this now in progress which makes towards the Japanization of China. There will be great changes in the government and life of that great Empire just as soon as the Empress Dowager dies, and she is now an old woman. In the upheaval of change, if the industrious, persistent, far-sighted efforts of her neighbours bear fruit, we may witness quite a rapid transformation in the life of the Empire. That clever conspirator, Sen Yat Sen, said to me that, once the Chinese made up their minds to change, they would effect in fifteen years as much as it has taken Japan thirty to accomplish. There are some men in the East who affect to regard this rapprochement between Japan and China with alarm, as carrying in its development the menace of a really genuine 'yellow peril.'"

It certainly needs no argument to prove that if the 426,000,000 Chinese are once fairly committed to the skillful leadership of the Japanese, a force will be set in motion which could be withstood only by the united efforts of all the rest of the world.

The task to which Japan has set herself, however, will not be easily achieved. To say nothing of other nations, the Russians are not at all disposed to sit quietly by while their foes cajole the Chinese. Russia has some designs of her own on China. Half Asiatic and semi-barbarous herself, past master in all the arts of Oriental diplomacy, patient, stubborn and untroubled by scruples, she is a formidable competitor for the leadership of China. In Persia, the Russian political policy works largely through the missionaries of the Greek Church, whose propaganda is political as well as religious.

---

90   Article in The New York Tribune, September 7, 1903.

The same tactics are now being employed in China. The Chih-li correspondent of the North China Herald reports that the Holy Russian branch of the Greek Church is becoming suspiciously active in North China.

"Their work is spreading, and the methods adopted are such as to attract all the worst characters of the districts in which they operate. In a little town near the Great Wall, where in June there were about a dozen converts to the Greek Church, there are now over eighty. Any and all are welcome. Their families no less than the men themselves are reck-oned as belonging to the Church. The priest has made a round of several towns, and, though he speaks no Chinese, by unhesitatingly giving protection and assistance in any case of dispute or litigation, he has made it clearly evident that for any man in any way under a cloud there is nothing better than to join the Greek Church…The impression among European onlookers is that Russia is preparing to extend her arms over Chih-li, and is beginning to smooth her way by gaining over the people in the eastern marches of the province. It is a significant fact that the Greek Church is known among the people as a 'Kuo Chiao' (National Church), a charge from which the Protestants are considered to be entirely, and the Roman Catholics partially, free."

China, moreover, will be slow to respond to the overtures of Japan, partly because her bulk and phlegmatic disposition and lack of public spirit make it difficult for her to act quickly and unitedly in anything, partly because Chinese pride and prejudice will not easily yield to the leadership of the haughty little island whose people as well as whose territory have long been contemptuously regarded as dwarfish and inferior.

But the shrewd Japanese are making more progress than is commonly supposed. Not only have they already obtained the great island of Formosa, but they have for years been quietly making their commercial interests paramount in Korea. Their first move in the war with Russia was to occupy that strategic peninsula with a large military force and to secure a treaty with the Emperor which gives Japan a virtual protectorate over the Land of the Morning Calm. The promise to respect the independence of Korea of course deceives no one. It is probably sincere, as diplomatic promises go; but he is innocent indeed who imagines that Korea will be free to do anything that Japan disapproves. The freedom will doubtless be of the kind that Cuba enjoys—a freedom which gives large liberty in matters of internal administration, which relieves the protecting country of any trouble or responsibility that it may deem inconvenient, but which does not permit any alliance with a third nation, and which, for all important international purposes, especially of a military character, regards the "independent" nation as really dependent. It is quite safe to predict that no European power will be unsophisticated enough to assume that Korea is "a free and independent nation." The arrangement will be in every way to the advantage of the Koreans, who have suffered grievously from the pulling and hauling of contending powers and from many evils from which the abler and wiser Japanese will, in a measure at least, protect them.

For a long time, too, the Japanese have been strengthening the ties which bind them to China. The brainy Japanese can be seen to-day in almost all the leading cities of the Middle Kingdom. There is a Japanese colony of 200 souls in Chefoo and of 1,400 in Tien-tsin. Already the Japanese are advising China's government, reorganizing her army, drafting her laws and teaching in her university. Even more distant countries are not beyond the range of their ambition. The leaders of India, restive under British rule, are beginning to look with eager sympathy to Japan as the rising Asiatic power. Even the Grand Vizier of Persia has paid a state visit to Japan. Any hopes of India and Persia are likely to be vain, for Britain has a hold upon the former and Russia upon the latter which it would be Quixotic in the Japanese to attempt to break. The Islanders are not fools. But the Siamese, helplessly exasperated by the encroachments of the French, would doubtless be glad enough to enter into an alliance with Japan and China. In 1902, the Crown Prince of Siam visited Japan, where he was most graciously welcomed, and increasing numbers of Japanese who know what they are about are obtaining increasing influence in the Land of the White Elephant.

Nor is it simply by sending Japanese to neighbouring countries that Japan is extending her power. She is encouraging Chinese students to come to her shores. Dr. David S. Spencer of Japan declares that 300 Chinese are studying the art of war in Japanese barracks. Dr. Sydney L. Gulick says that 5,000 Chinese are being trained in the schools of Japan for positions of future power in their own country. It is significant that Viceroy Yuan Shih Kai, the ablest and most far-seeing statesman in China, is reported in the telegraphic despatches of February 5, 1904, as having memorialized the Throne in favour of an offensive and defensive alliance with Japan to regain Manchuria from the Russians, while the North China Daily News represents Prince Su, Prince Ching, Na Tung, President of the Wai-wu-pu, and Tieh Liang as in favour of the same policy. Mr. Holcombe is of the opinion that "the brightest spot in the outlook for China is in the increasing probability of alliance and affiliation with Japan...Together these two great nations of the Far East may, and it is confidently hoped will, safely confront those Governments whose schemes are hostile to both, and prove their right to manage their own affairs and determine their own destinies."[91]

But whatever the immediate future may be, it is not probable that so huge and virile a population as the Chinese will be permanently led by a foreign nation. Even if partition should come, it would only hasten the development of those teeming millions of people, for foreign domination would mean more railway, telegraph and steamship lines. It would mean the opening of mines, the development of the press, the complete ascendency of Western ideas. Though China as a political organism might be divided, the Chinese people would remain—the most virile, industrious, untiring people of Asia, and perhaps, after due tutelage, a coming power of the world. China's assimilative power is enormous. The black man may be dominated by the white and the Hindu by the English, but China is neither Africa nor India. It is true that the present dynasty is Manchu, but the Manchus are more akin to the Chinese than either the Russians or the Japanese. Moreover the Manchus have not tried to rule China from the outside, but have permanently settled in China, and while they have succeeded as a rule in maintaining a separate name, they have not made the Chinese Manchus, but instead they have themselves been prac-tically merged into the engulfing mass of China. "Those who imagine that the vast population of the Empire will submit quietly to the partition of their country, or that any military force of moderate size could force it to acquiesce in such a scheme, know but little of the Chinese character, of their intense love of country, or of

91   Article in The Outlook, February 13, 1904.

their unconquerable tenacity of purpose."[92] The foreign nation that gets the Chinese, or even any considerable portion of them, will probably find that it has assumed a burden in comparison with which the Egyptian trouble with the Israelites was insignificant, and it is not improbable that the conqueror will some day find himself conquered.

At any rate, portentous possibilities are conjured up by the contemplation of this mighty nation! There are upheavals compared with which our revolutions are but spasms. There are religions whose adherents outnumber ours two to one. There is a civilization which was old before ours was born. Are we to believe that these swarming legions were created for no purpose? Are their generations to appear and fall and rot unnoticed, like the leaves of the forest? Degraded, superstitious, many of them still are. But they need only to be organized and directed to do untold mischief. More than once already has a similar catastrophe occurred. Some prodigy of skill and genius has seized such enormous forces, given them discipline and coherency and hurled them like a thunderbolt upon Christendom. Sometimes the shock has been frightful, and before it the proudest of empires and the stateliest of institutions have reeled and fallen. This was the Titan-like achievement of Alaric, of Genseric, of Attila, and of Mohammed. Yet Goths and Vandals, Huns and Mohammedans, combined, had not half the numbers upon which we now look. Give the 426,000,000 Chinese the results of modern discovery and invention, and imagination falters. They have the territory. They have the resources. They have the population and they are now acquiring the knowledge. China will fight no more like the barbarians of old with spears and bows and arrows, for despite the treaty of 1900 prohibiting the importation of arms, the Chinese are buying repeating rifles and Maxim guns, while in their own arsenals they are turning out vast quantities of munitions of war. The American consul at Leipsic, Germany, reports to the State Department that an Austrian company has just received an order for so large a number of small arms for the Chinese Government that it will take several years to fill it, even with additional forces of men to whom it has given employment. This is only one of

---

92　Chester Holcombe, article in The Outlook, February 13, 1904.

many reports received in Washington within recent months that the factories of both Germany and Austria are busy supplying the Chinese with modern arms and ammunition. The armies of China will soon be as well equipped as the armies of Europe.

Incredible as it may seem, up to the year 1901, promotion in the army was often determined by trials of strength with stone weights, dexterity in sword exercises and skill in the use of the bow and arrow. But in that year, an Imperial Decree declared that such tests "have no relation to strategy and to that military science which is indispensable for military officers," commanded that they be abolished and that military academies should be established in the provincial capitals in which the science of modern war should be diligently studied. Not content with this, forty young men were sent to Europe in 1903 for the express purpose of studying the latest military and naval methods of the white man. And now Sir Robert Hart proposes not only a reorganization of China's civil service but the building of a first-class navy of thirty battleships and cruisers, and he thinks that the enormous sum of $200,000,000 a year can be obtained for this purpose by an increase in the land tax. Then, he declares, China will be enabled "not only to make her voice heard, but to take an effective share in the settlement of questions in the Far East." The London Times rather contemptuously asserts that "the entire project in its present shape is visionary from beginning to end." But Sir Robert Hart has spent fifty years in China, having entered the British consular service in 1854 and become Inspector-General of Maritime Customs in 1863. During the greater part of this long period, he has been an adviser of the Chinese Government and the most influential foreigner in the Empire. The recommendation of such a man is not to be lightly dismissed as "visionary," especially when it is made to a people who have been taught by bitter experience that a modern armament is their only hope of defense against the foreigner. As late as the beginning of the year 1904, Russia ridiculed the idea that Japan could do anything against a western power, and all the rest of Europe as well as America, while admiring the pluck of the Japanese, confidently expected them to be crushed by the Slav. Wise men will think twice in the future before they sneer at the yellow race. If Japan in half a century could go from junks and cloisonne to battleships and magazine rifles, and to the handling of them, too, more scientifically and effectively than they were ever handled by a white man, why should it be deemed chimerical that China, with equal ability and greater resources and certainly no less provocation, should in time achieve even vaster results, particularly as Japan is not only willing but eager to teach her? "We do not lack either men of intellect or brilliant talents, capable of learning and doing anything they please; but their movements have hitherto been hampered by old prejudices," said the Emperor Kuang Hsii. Precisely, and the stern, relentless pressure of necessity is now shattering some of those "old prejudices." "You urge us to move faster," said a Chinese magistrate to a foreigner. "We are slow to respond for we are a conservative people; but if you force us to start, we may move faster and farther than you like."

Some things may yet occur undreampt of in all our philosophy. We observe the changing march of world powers, the majestic procession in which the pomp and glitter of thrones are mingled with the tears and blood of calamity and war. What a pageant! Yesterday, Chaldea, Egypt, Assyria, Babylon, Persia, Greece, Rome! To-day, England, Germany, Russia, Japan, the United States! To-morrow, what? What, indeed, if not some of these now awakening nations! It is by no means impossible that some new Jenghiz Khan or Tamerlane may arise, and with the weapons of modern warfare in his hands, and these uncounted millions at his command, gaze about on the pygmies that we call the Powers! Christendom has too long regarded heathen nations with a pity not unmingled with contempt. It is now beginning to regard them with a respect not unmingled with fear. There is not a statesman in Europe to-day who is not troubled with dire forebodings regarding these teeming hordes, that appear to be just awakening from the torpor of ages, and some thoughtful observers fear that a movement has already begun which will lead to great wars whose issue no man can foresee, and to stupendous reconstructions of the map of the world. The Emperor of Germany has painted a picture which has startled not so much by its art as by its meaning. "On a projecting rock, illuminated by a shining cross, stand the allegorical figures of the civilized nations. At the feet of this rocky eminence lies the wide plain of European culture, from which rise countless cities and the steeples and spires of churches of every denomination. But ominous clouds are gathering over this peaceful landscape. A stifling gloom o'erspreads the sky. The glare of burning cities lights up the road by which the barbaric hordes of Asia are approaching. The Archangel Michael points to the fearsome foe, waving the nations on to do battle in a sacred cause. Underneath are the words—'Peoples of Europe, keep guard over your most sacred treasures!'"

Making all due allowance for the exuberance of Emperor William's imagination, the fact remains that his picture represents the thought that is uppermost to-day in the minds of the world's thinkers. All see that the next few decades are big with possibilities of peril.

> "The rudiments of Empire here
> Are plastic yet and warm,
> The chaos of a mighty world
> Is rounding into form."

One thinks instinctively of the words of Isaiah: "The noise of a multitude in the mountains, like as of a great people; a tumultuous noise of the kingdoms of nations gathered together; the Lord of hosts mustereth the hosts of the battle." Plainly, the overshadowing problem of the present age is the relation of China to the world's future. Whether recent events have lessened the danger, we shall see in the next chapter.

XXVI
FRESH REASON TO HATE
THE FOREIGNER

OF course, the victorious march of the Allies upon Peking, the capture of the city, the flight of the Emperor and the Empress Dowager and the humiliating terms of peace taught the Chinese anew their helplessness before the modern equipment of western nations and the necessity of learning the methods of the white man if they were ever to hold their own against him. But defeat, while always hard to bear, does not always embitter the conquered against the conqueror. On the contrary, there are evidences that the Chinese respect and like the Japanese far more since they were soundly whipped by them in 1894 and 1895. In considering, therefore, the effect upon the Chinese of the suppression of the Boxer uprising, we must bear in mind not so much the fact of victory by the Allies as the treatment which they accorded their prostrate foe. Was that treatment dignified and just? Did the soldiers of alleged Christian nations behave with the sobriety and fairness which so eminently characterized the Japanese troops after the China-Japan War? Have the Chinese reason to regard foreigners in the future as men who will sternly punish injustice and treachery, but who are at the same time as moral and humane and trustworthy as might be reasonably expected of the representatives of a higher civilization and a purer religion? For answer, let us turn to the conduct of the allied armies, led by experienced officers of high rank and working in harmony with diplomatic officials who were supposed to incarnate the spirit and methods of the most enlightened nations of the earth. The testimony of witnesses will be interesting.

Dr. Arthur H. Smith, who was in Peking at the time, writes:—

"Bating all exaggerations, it remains true that scores of walled cities have been visited by armed bodies of foreign soldiers, the district magistrate—and sometimes the Prefect—held up and bullied to force him to pay a large sum of money, with no other reason than the imperative demand and the threat of dire consequences on refusal. In one case the Russians kidnapped the Prefect of Yung-ping-fu and carried him off to Port Arthur. At Ting-chou the French did the same to the sub-prefect, the only energetic magistrate in all that region, bearing him in triumph to Paoting-fu and leaving the district to Boxers and to chaos. At Tsang-chou the Germans came in force, looted the yamen of General Mei, the only Chinese officer of rank who had been constantly fighting and destroying Boxers for nearly a year, drove him away and released all the Boxer prisoners in the jails of the city, plundering the yamen of the friendly and efficient sub-prefect who had saved the lives of the foreign families close by the city. Is it any wonder that General Mei complained that s on eight sides he had no face left.'...The robbery of Chinese on the way home with the avails of their day's work has been systematically carried on by some of the soldiers from Christian lands. Even foreigners are 'held up' on the street by drunken soldiers, and it is becoming necessary never to go out without one's revolver—a weapon generally quite superfluous in almost any part of China."

Bishop D. H. Moore, of the Methodist Church, who hurried to Peking as soon as the way was open, wrote:—

"You can hardly form any conception of the exposure and hardships under any but the American and Japanese flags. The English have scarcely any but the Sikhs, who are lustful and lootful to a degree. The Russians are brutal and the Germans deserve their reputation for brutality. With Lowry and Hobart, I responded to the agonizing appeal of a husband to drive out a German corporal who, on duty and armed, had run him off and was mistreating his wife. The instance is but one of hundreds of daily occurrence. The French are very devils at this sort of outrage. On the advance to Peking, beyond Tung-chou, they found married families— men, women and children—cowering in barges on the canal and volleyed into them. Every man, every cart, every boat must fly a flag. Coolies are cruelly impressed and often cruelly mistreated. The great Christian nations of the world are being represented in China by robbing, raping, looting soldiery. This is part of China's punishment; but what will she think of Christianity? Of course, our soldiers are the best behaved; but there are desperate characters in every army."

Captain Frank Brinkley, the editor of the Japan Weekly Mail, penned the following indignant paragraph:—

"It sends a thrill of horror through every white man's bosom to learn that forty missionary women and twenty-five little children were butchered by the Boxers. But in Tung-chou alone, a city where the Chinese made no resistance and where there was no fighting, 573 Chinese women of the upper classes committed suicide rather than survive the indignities they had suffered. Women of the lower classes fared similarly at the hands of the soldiers, but were not unwilling to survive their shame. With what show of consistency is the Occident to denounce the barbarity of the Chinese, when Occidental soldiers go to China and perpetrate the very acts which constitute the very basis of barbarity?"

When I asked the Rev. Dr. D. Z. Sheffield, for many years a missionary of the American Board in Tung-chou, whether this statement was accurate, he replied that it was not only true, but that it was an understatement of the truth.

Fay Chi Ho, an intelligent and reliable Chinese Christian, gives the following account of what he personally saw:—

"I travelled with a British convoy going by boat, occupying quarters on a Major's boat with his Sikh soldiers and cook. I know that the Major was not a Christian man, for he smoked and drank all day long and was constantly cursing, striking and kicking his men, especially his cook. He also gave his orders in loud tones, with fierce mien and glaring eyes, and we all feared him exceedingly. Every day at noon the Major would take four Sikhs and go to villages several miles from the river for loot, always compelling me to accompany him as interpreter. He would catch the first man whom he saw in a village and compel him to act as guide to the homes of the rich. So successful was he on these raids that by the time he reached Tung-chou, he had three new carts, three donkeys, five or six sheep, and much clothing and bric-a-brac.

"One day about noon, we reached a village from which most of the people had fled, and entering a home of wealth found there only a man about fifty or sixty years old who received us very courteously. Immedi-ately the Major demanded money, and the old man replied that though he had money it was not at hand. The Major then commanded his soldiers to bind him, while he himself went into the house to search for money. He found several weapons, among them a revolver and a sword with a red scarf bound on the handle. So he insisted that the old man must be a Boxer, and shot him with his own hand as he lay bound. As usual he impressed ten or more young men in the village to carry his loot, then compelled the strongest of them to remain and drag his boats...Later, my brother told me in detail how some Sikhs had come to the village one day, and, seizing him and several neighbours, had tied a rope to their queues, then stringing them together like mules, with men leading in front and driving behind, had taken them to the river bank to drag boats. My brother had never done such work before. Wading in mud and water, sometimes up to his waist, with the whip lash to urge him on, he had dragged until nightfall, and then, not being allowed to sleep on the boat, had lain down on the wet river bank."[93]

During my own visit in north China in the summer of 1901, I visited the hospital of the London Mission in Tien-tsin, immortalized by John Kenneth Mackenzie. I found that it was being used as a hospital for British soldiers who were suffering from venereal diseases. What a spectacle for the Chinese! What a coarse travesty of the religion of the pure Nazarene that the land from which the great British missionary came should crowd with foul white men the hospital that he had built with faith and love and prayer! In the same city, the fine Y. M. C. A. building was almost deserted by the Chinese because it was so situated that to reach it they would have to pass through the Taku Road in the Foreign Settlement, a street which was a cesspool of vice, lined with saloons, dance halls and gambling hells, and its sidewalks so crowded with fast women—French, German, American and Japanese—and with drunken, quarrelling foreign soldiers, that no respectable Chinese, or for that matter no decent foreign woman, could traverse it without fear of insult or abuse.

---

93 "Two Heroes of Cathay," pp. 154, 155, 158.

In Peking for several months after the relief of the legations, even respectable American ladies, to say nothing of Chinese women, could not prudently ride out except in closed carts, so great was the probability of indignity at the hands of foreign soldiers; while at the entrance of famous palaces, the "public is politely requested not to kick the Chinese attendants because they decline to open doors which they are forbidden to unlock"—a request that the conduct of foreigners had shown to be far from unnecessary.

In the pillaging of property, savages could not have been more lawless than the white men from "the highly civilized nations of the West."

"It is not literally true that every house in Peking was looted. There were some places in obscure alleys, and in many of the innumerable and almost impenetrable cul-de-sacs with which the capital abounds, that escaped. But persistent inquiry appears to leave no doubt of the fact that practically every yamen in the city has been rummaged, and practically there is nothing left of the contents of any of them."[94]

Words fail me to describe the beauties of the famous Summer Palace outside the city. With its gardens, temples, pagodas, bridges, lotus-ponds, statues, colonnades, walks and drives, it would do credit to the most highly civilized nation of Europe. A barbarous people could never have made such a paradise. The British and French in 1860 burned a considerable part of it, but the enclosure is so vast (twelve square miles) and the buildings are so numerous that the destroyed section appears almost insignificant. Within the grounds is a beautiful lake, fed by great springs and bordered by temples and avenues of trees and the yellow-roofed palaces of the Emperor, while near by rise the Western Hills.

This Palace is the favourite residence of the Empress Dowager and she spends long summers there. Here, too, the Emperor loves to come during the heated term and both have followed the example of their imperial predecessors in lavishing great sums upon its adornment.

After the siege the Russians occupied it at first, and when they left, the British and Italians took possession. Between the three so little was left that I found devastation reigning in that once

---

94   North China Daily News.

splendidly-furnished Palace. All the rare and costly bric-a-brac had been carried away, the mirrors had been broken and the permanent ornaments defaced. A noble bronze statue of Buddha, in the temple crowning the summit of the hill, was lying ignominiously on the floor among a pile of debris, one dark hand stiffly pointing into the air. In a stately pavilion, I saw two superb golden statues of Buddha standing upright and looking unusually dignified, but on going behind them, I found that great holes had been punched in their backs.

Even the places dedicated to science and religion were not spared. At the celebrated Astronomical Observatory not an instrument was left. Every one had been carried off by the orders of men high in authority at the French and German Legations, and the whole place was totally wrecked. What possible excuse could there have been for destroying a place for studying the heavens? At the Examination Grounds, consecrated for centuries to learning and memorable for the myriads of China's brightest men who have there demonstrated their fitness, according to China's methods, for high preferment—at these Examination Grounds, most of the 8,500 cells had been stripped of their woodwork to cook the rations of the European armies, roofs had been torn off and even stone walls had been injured in sheer wantonness.

The Temple to the Gods of Land and Grain and the Temple for Rain are sacred places to the Chinese. To the latter the Emperor comes in solemn state in time of drought to pray for rain, or, if he cannot come, he sends the highest official of his realm. It is in a spacious park and the buildings must have been stately and handsome before the Boxer outbreak. But when I saw them, they were sadly defaced. The stone balus-trades and ornaments had been broken off, the walls had been injured and one of the buildings was in ruins.

It was, of course, inevitable that much havoc should be wrought in the tumult of war. It was necessary that supplies for half-naked and famished besieged thousands should be taken from deserted grain and clothing-shops. It was expedient that certain public buildings should be destroyed by order of the allied generals as a warning for the future. But why were soldiers and thieves allowed to steal the bric-a-brac and furniture and break the mirrors of the Emperor's personal apartments, wantonly to shatter beautiful columns, deface rare works of art, punch holes in gilded statues, maliciously smash the heads of thousands of exquisitely-carved figures and lions, and wreck venerable places associated with learning and art? The world is poorer for some of this havoc, and it will be a generation before it can be remedied, if indeed, some of the edifices are ever restored to their former beauty. Can we wonder that the Chinese continue to hate and fear the foreigner? The New York Times declared that "every outrage perpetrated on foreigners in China has been repaid tenfold by the brutalities perpetrated by the allied armies. It is," added the editor, "simply monstrous that the armies of Christian nations, sent out to punish barbarism and protect the rights of foreigners in China, should themselves be guilty of barbarism. Revenge has been accompanied by mean and cruel and flagrant robbery. The story is one to fill all rational minds with disgust and shame."

The exasperation of the Chinese has not been diminished by the virtual fortifications which the foreign Powers have erected in the imperial capital since the crushing of the Boxer uprising. Most of the Legations took advantage of the panic and confusion which followed the raising of the siege, to seize large tracts adjoining their former compounds. The native buildings upon them were demolished. Massive walls were erected and cannon mounted upon them. Over the water-gate in the city wall, through which the allied troops entered the city, the Powers have cut a new gateway which they hold and guard. In addition, they have taken possession of all that part of the city wall which commands Legation Street, made barricades and built a fort upon it opposite the German Legation. Foreign soldiers patrol that wall night and day. On the other side of the Legations, a wide space has been cleared by destroying hundreds of Chinese dwellings and shops, and no buildings or trees or obstructions of any kind are allowed on that space, which can thus be swept by rifle and Gatling-gun fire in the event of any future trouble. Within, ample stores of arms, ammunition and food have been stored so that if another outbreak should occur, the Legations cannot be besieged as they were in the memorable summer of 1900.

All this, of course, is perfectly natural and perhaps necessary. The Legations would be deemed lacking in ordinary prudence if they did not guard against the repetition of their grievous experiences during the Boxer uprising. But looking at the matter from the viewpoint of the Chinese, can we marvel that it is resented? Would not a European government be stung to the quick if other nations were to fortify themselves in that fashion at its capital? Would Americans endure it for a day at Washington?

Altogether, it must be admitted that the writer of "Letters of a Chinese Official" has all too much reason to arraign western civilization as sordid, arrogant and cruel and to assert that Europeans and Americans, while pretending to follow the teachings of Christ, are really ignoring them. His words are bitter:—

"Yes, it is we who do not accept it that practice the gospel of peace; it is you who accept it that trample it under foot. And irony of ironies!—it is the nations of Christendom who have come to us to teach us by sword and fire that Right in this world is powerless unless it be supported by Might. Oh, do not doubt that we shall learn the lesson! And woe to Europe when we have acquired it. You are arming a nation of four hundred millions, a nation which, until you came, had no better wish than to live at peace with themselves and all the world. In the name of Christ you have sounded the call to arms! In the name of Confucius we respond!"[95]

And he closes the book as follows:—

"Unless you of the West will come to realize the truth, unless you will understand that the events which have shaken Europe are the Nemesis of a long course of injustice and oppression; unless you will learn that the profound opposition between your civilization and ours gives no more ground why you should regard us as barbarians than we you, unless you will treat us as a civilized power and respect our customs and our laws; unless you will accord us the treatment you would accord to any European nation and refrain from exacting conditions you would never dream of imposing on a Western power—unless you will do this, there is no hope of any peace between us. You have humiliated the proudest nation in the world; you have outraged the most upright and just; with what results is now abundantly manifest."

Whether the author is really a Chinese official as he claims to be, or a European resident in China writing under a Chinese pseudonym, there can be no doubt that he fairly represents the

---

95   "Letters of a Chinese Official," pp. 64, 65.

opinions of the old, conservative, ferociously irreconcilable mandarin class regarding the white man. Western nations, in their plans regarding the future of China, must take into consideration the existence of that spirit and the acts which, while not creating it, have intensified and inflamed it till it has come to be something to be reckoned with. Undoubtedly, one of the lessons that the Chinese have learned from defeat is bitterer hatred of the alien whose vandalisms and atrocities were so shameful as to nullify, in part at least, the benefit that might otherwise have resulted.

I am glad to report that, with the single exception of the Japanese who were universally assigned the first place from the viewpoint of good behaviour, I heard fewer complaints regarding the American troops than any other. One Colonel, indeed, lamented that his regiment "was thoroughly demoralized," and there were some instances of intemperance and lawlessness, in one case a Japanese patrol bringing in several American soldiers who had been found at midnight in a Chinese house. But as a whole, the conduct of the Americans was much better than that of most of the Europeans. That the Chinese felt the difference was apparent in the number of American flags that they raised over their houses and shops. It was significant, too, that the districts of the city that were occupied by European regiments were avoided, as far as possible, by the Chinese, while the district controlled by the Americans was thronged.

Nor need any American be ashamed of the policy of his Government. It is true that the majority of the Americans in China believe that our national policy, prior to and during the Boxer uprising, was weak and short-sighted. They spoke highly of Minister Conger and several of the American Consuls, particularly of Consul John Fowler, at Chefoo. But I was repeatedly told that our Government did not appear to realize that there were any other American citizens or properties in China than those in the Peking Legation; that it did practically nothing to rescue its citizens in the prefecture of Paoting-fu and the province of Shan-si; that, while Americans condemn the policy of the European Powers, they have been for years sponging benefits secured by them for all foreigners; and that, if it had not been for their control of the situation, not an American could have lived in China. The opinion was well-nigh universal that the Washington Administration was too much influenced by the astute Chinese Minister, Wu Ting-fang, who was believed to be an adept in "the ways that are dark and the tricks that are vain," and whose alleged success in "hoodwinking the Government and people of the United States" provoked the average foreigner in the Far East to the use of strong language.

Though I confess that I am not able satisfactorily to explain the course of our Government in some important particulars, it seems to me that these sweeping criticisms are too severe. During the dark days of the siege of Peking, I was brought into frequent correspondence with President McKinley and Secretary of State Hay, and I vividly and gratefully remember the sympathy and cooperation which they invariably gave. They were as anxious as any one, and tried to do their best in circumstances new, strange and of extraordinary difficulty. As for the Chinese Minister to the United States, of course he did what he could to "save face" for his country. That was an essential part of his duty. But while we cannot always agree with him, we should, as friends of China recognize the fact that by his ability and tact, he largely increased popular interest in and respect for the Chinese people.

Taking our Government's policy as a whole, I believe that it has been more in accord with Christian principles than that of any other nation. If our Government has erred in trusting the Chinese too much, that is, at least better than erring by trusting them too little. If it has failed to do for its own citizens all that it ought to have done, it has not wronged or humiliated the Chinese Government. There is no blood of Chinese women and children on the hands of Americans in China. No record of outrage and iniquity blackens the page on which the American part of the Boxer outbreak is written. If our nation has been unjust to any, it has been to its own. Generations will pass before the northern provinces will forget the bitterness of resentment which they now feel towards the European Powers. But already the Chinese are beginning to understand that the American Government is a friend; that it does not seek their territory; that it will not be a party to extortion; that it does not want to destroy China but to save her; that its object is not to rule her, but to fit her to rule herself, and that it desires only freedom for its citizens to trade and to communicate those ideas of religion which we ourselves originally received from the East, which have brought to us inestimable blessings, and which will, in China as in America, result in the noblest character for the individual and the most stable institutions for the state.

The Chinese keenly appreciate the fresh evidence of America's spirit of justice in connection with the payment of the indemnity. When, before the payment of the first installment in 1902, the fall in the value of the silver tael led the European Powers to insist that China should pay in gold, thereby virtually increasing the indemnity, it was the United States again which did everything in its power to moderate the demands of the European nations. If the legislative branch of the American Government would only deal as justly with the Chinese in the United States as the State Department deals with the Chinese in China, the era of good feeling would be greatly promoted.

But America is not prominent enough in China to make her example a determinate factor in the attitude of the Empire towards foreigners, nor are the people as a whole likely to discriminate in favour of a few Americans among the hosts of aggressive, grasping, domineering Europeans.

Moreover, the majority of the Chinese hear only what their scholars and officials tell them, and these worthies are careful to adjust the account to suit their own purposes, and to save the national "face." They blandly assure the credulous people that the foreign armies did not follow the court because they dared not; that the alien troops left the capital because they were driven out by Chinese patriots; and that the Boxers inflicted crushing defeat upon their foes. During my visit in Tsing-tau, the Germans were digging sewers, broad and deep, with laterals to every house and public building, and many of the Chinese actually believed that these sewers were intended to be underground passageways, down which the foreigners could flee to their boats when they were assailed by the redoubtable Boxers! The best-informed men I met in China, from Sir Robert Hart down, were fearful that the end was not near, and that an official order might repeat the whole bloody history. At a conference with forty representative missionaries of all denominations in Shanghai, August, 1901, a very large majority agreed with the Rev. Dr. Parker, of the Southern Methodist Church, in the statement: "We are not out of the trouble yet; the reactionaries are in the minority, but they are in power. They have learned nothing and they will try again to drive us out unless the Powers unseat them and reinstate the Emperor and the Reform Party."

XXVII
HOPEFUL SIGNS

THE future is not necessarily so doubtful as the facts and opinions cited in the preceding chapter might in themselves seem to indicate. It is true that the daily press often contains accounts of tumults and revolutions in China. But an Empire a third larger than all Europe, with an enormous population, a weak central Government, corrupt local officials, few railroads and frequent floods, famines and epidemics, is certain to have uprisings somewhere most of the time. A European reading in the daily despatches from the United States of strikes, riots, martial law, the burning of negroes, the mobbing of Chinese and the corruption of cities, might with equal justice get the impression that our own country is in continual turmoil. The Imperial Government in China pays little attention to what is going on in other parts of the country.

"Each province has its own army, navy, and system of taxation...So long as the provincial government sends its Peking supplies, administers a reasonable sop to its clamorous provincial duns, quells incipient insurrections, gives employment to its army of expectants, staves off foreign demands, avoids rows of all kinds, and, in a word, keeps up a decent external surface of respectability, no questions are asked; all reports and promotions are passed; the Viceroy and his colleagues 'enjoy happiness,' and every one makes his 'pile.' The Peking Government makes no new laws, does nothing of any kind for any class of persons, leaves each province to its own devices, and, like the general staff of an army organization, both absorbs successful men, and gives out needy or able men to go forth and do likewise."[96]

In these circumstances, the governors of provinces have considerable independent power in internal affairs, and a rebellion even of formidable proportions is often ignored by the Imperial Government in Peking as a purely local matter to be dealt with by the provincial authorities, much as the United States Government leaves riots and mobs to the State officials.

Moreover, to a greater extent than any other people, the Chinese are led by their officials, and some of the highest officials in Peking and the coast provinces have learned that massacres of foreigners result in the coming of more foreigners, in the capture and destruction of cities, in humiliating terms of peace, in heavy indemnities, in large losses of territory and in the degradation and perhaps the execution of the magistrates within whose jurisdiction the troubles occur.

There are, moreover, unmistakable indications of a new movement among the Chinese. One reason why they have been so ignorant of the rest of the world and even of distant parts of their own country was the lack of any facilities for transmitting mail. The only way that the missionaries in the interior could get their letters was by employing private messengers or availing themselves of a chance traveller. But now a modern post-office system, superintended by Sir Robert Hart, already includes 500 of the principal cities of the Empire and is being rapidly extended to others.

Teu years ago, there were practically no newspapers in China except those published by foreigners in the ports, all of which were in English save one which was in the German language. The only periodicals in Chinese were a few issued by the missionaries with, of course, a very limited circulation, chiefly among the Christians. There was no such thing as a Chinese press in the proper sense of the term. Now, besides a French, a Russian and a second German paper, there are nearly a hundred Chinese newspapers, many of them edited by the Chinese themselves and others by Japanese, and all, aided by the railway, the telegraph and the post-office, bringing

---

96   E. H. Parker, "China," pp. 167, 169.

new ideas to multitudes. On the basis of a joint report to the Throne by Viceroy Chang Chih-tung and Chang Pei-hsi, chancellor of the Peking University, an imperial decree has ordered the inauguration of a new system of education. The plan is to have a university in the capital of each province, with auxiliary prefectural and district colleges and schools and the whole system to culminate in the Imperial University in Peking. In all these institutions western arts and sciences are to be taught side by side with the old Confucian classics. "The Viceroys and Governors of provinces are commanded to order their subordinates to hasten the establishment of these schools. Let this decree be published through the Empire."

Nor have the new imperial decrees stopped here. A few decades ago, ambitious Chinese youths who sought an education abroad at their own expense were imprisoned on their return to their native land. One whom I met in Shantung gave me a vivid account of his arrest and incarceration in a filthy dungeon as if he had been a common criminal. But a recent edict of the Emperor directs the provincial Governors to select young men of ability and send them to Europe for special training with a view to their occupying high posts on their return.

One of the most firmly rooted customs of old China was the examination essay for literary degrees on some purely Chinese subject relating to a remote past. But August 29, 1901, to the amazement of the literati, an imperial edict abolished that time-honoured custom and directed that in the future candidates for degrees as well as for office should submit short essays on such modern topics as Western science, governments, laws, and kindred subjects. The following extracts from the examination questions for the Chu Jen (M. A.) degree in 1903 will indicate the extraordinary character of this change.

Honen—"What improvements are to be derived from the study of foreign agriculture, commerce, and postal systems?

Kwang-sg and An-huei—"What are the chief ideas underlying Austrian and German prosperity? How do foreigners regulate the press, post-office, commerce, railways, banks, bank-notes, commercial schools, taxation—and how do they get faithful men? Where is the Caucasus and how does Russia rule it?

Kiang-si—"How many sciences theoretical and practical are there? In what order should they be studied? Explain free trade and protection. What are the military services of the world? What is the bearing of the Congress of Vienna, the Treaty of Berlin and the Monroe Doctrine on the Far East? Wherein lies the naval supremacy of Great Britain? What is the bearing of the Siberian Railway and Nicaragua Canal on China?

Shuntung—"What is Herbert Spencer's philosophy of sociology? Define the relations of land, labour and capital. State how best to develop the resources of China by mines and railway? How best to modify our civil and criminal laws to regain authority over those now under extra-territoriality privileges? How best to guard land and sea frontiers from the advance of foreign Powers?

Fukien—"Which Western nations have paid most attention to education and what is the result? State the leading features of the military systems of Great Britain, Germany, Russia, and France. Which are the best colonizers? How should tea and silk be properly cultivated? What is the government, industries and education of Switzerland which, though small, is independent of surrounding great powers?

Kwang-tung—(Canton)—"What should be our best coinage, gold, silver and copper like other Western countries, or what? How could the workhouse system be started throughout China? How to fortify Kwang-tung province? How to get funds and professors for the new education? How to pro-mote Chinese international commerce, new industries and savings-banks, versus the gambling houses of China?

Hunan—"What is the policy of Japan—only following other nations or what? How to choose competent diplomatic men? Why does China feel its small national debt so heavy, while England and France with far greater debts do not feel it?

Hupch—"State the educational systems of Sparta and Athens. What are the naval strategic points of Great Britain and which should be those of China? Which nation has the best system of stamp duty? State briefly the geological ages of the earth, and the bronze and iron ages. Trace the origin of Egyptian, Babylonian and Chinese writings."[97]

The result of these edicts is that the Chinese are buying Western books as never before. Examinations cannot be passed

---

97   Report of the Society for the Diffusion of Christian and General Knowledge Among the Chinese, Shanghai, 1903.

without them. The mission presses, though run to their full capacity, cannot keep up with the demand for their publications. Dr. Timothy Richard of Shanghai reports that a quarter of a million dollars' worth of text-books were sold in that city in 1902, a single order received by the Presbyterian Press involving a bill of $328 for postage alone, as the buyer insisted that the books should be sent by mail. Mission schools that teach the English language are thronged with students, many of them from the higher classes, and every foreigner who is willing to teach Western learning finds his services eagerly sought.

China cannot be reformed by paper edicts even though they are written by an Emperor. Many reforms have been solemnly proclaimed in former years that accomplished little except to "save face" for the Government. We need not therefore imagine that the millennium is to come in China this year. But it is impossible to doubt that the reform decrees that have been issued since the Boxer uprising mean something more and are achieving something more than any other reform movements that China ever saw before. Dr. Arthur H. Smith, who knows China and the Chinese as thoroughly as any other living man, writes:—

"We behold the kernel of the reforms ordered by His Majesty, Kuang Hsum in 1898, and which led to his dethronement and imprisonment, substantially adopted less than three years later by the Empress Dowager and her advisers...The bare notation of the tenor of these far-reaching edicts gives to the Occidental reader but a vague notion of the tremendous intellectual revolution which they connote. Never before was there such an order from any government involving the reconstruction of the views of so many millions, by the study of the methods of government in other nations...It is obvious to one who knows anything of the Chinese educational system of the past millennium that the introduction of the new methods will involve its radical reconstruction from top to bottom. Western geography, mathematics, science, history, and philosophy will be everywhere studied. The result cannot fail to be an expansion of the intellectual horizon of the Chinese race comparable to that which in Europe followed the Crusades. This will be a long process and a slow one, but it is a certain one...All signs indicate that China is open as never before."

Undoubtedly the most powerful present factor in the policy of the Empire, and at the same time one of the best types of the educated Chinese, is Yuan Shih Kai, Viceroy of Chih-li and Commander-in-Chief of the Chinese army. He is not a Manchu, like many of the high officials of China, but a pure Chinese like Li Hung Chang. Born in the Province of Honan, he quickly developed unusual abilities. After a brilliant record for a young man in his native land, he was sent to Korea as the representative of the Emperor of China and for nine years he was a conspicuous member of the diplomatic corps of the Korean capital. Returning to China in 1895, he was made commander of a division of the "New Imperial Army"—a post in which he manifested high military and administrative qualities. He organized and equipped his troops after the best foreign models and they speedily became so effective that, if they had been more numerous and if he had been given a free hand in using them in Peking, the history of 1900 might have been different. I have had occasion elsewhere[98] to give some account of the soldiers who escorted me through the interior. December, 1900, he was appointed Governor of the great province of Shantung. It was here that I met him, residing at Chinan-fu, the capital of the province. As soon as possible after my arrival, I sent my card and letters of introduction to the famous Governor, and he promptly replied that he would receive me at one o'clock the following day. At the appointed hour, we called. With true courtesy, he met us at the entrance of the palace grounds and escorted us into his private room, which was neatly but very plainly furnished. He impressed me as a remarkable man. He was then forty-one years of age, of medium height, rather stout, with a strong face, a clear, frank eye, and a most engaging manner. He would be considered a man of striking appearance anywhere.

He was very cordial, and we had a long and interesting conversation. He surprised me by his familiarity with America, especially as he spoke no English and had never been out of Asia.

Partly at this interview and partly from other sources, I heard more of his plan to start a daily newspaper, a Military Academy and a Literary College. His idea was to have in each institution

---

98   Chapter VII.

two students from each of the 108 counties in the province, and thus train a body of men who would be able to carry "light and learning" into their respective districts. He appeared to feel that the only hope of averting such catastrophes as the Boxer uprising lay in enlightening the people. In answer to a question as to the teaching of foreign languages, he said that English, French and German would be taught, but that German would probably be the most useful of the foreign tongues on account of the number of Germans in the eastern part of the province.

The Governor had shown the breadth of his intelligence, and at the same time his appreciation of the high character of Protestant missionaries, by inviting one of them, the Rev. Dr. Watson M. Hayes, then President of the Presbyterian Mission College at Teng-chou, to become the President of the Literary College. I may anticipate so far as to state that Dr. Hayes accepted the invitation and began his work with every promise of large success. But unfortunately the rigid requirement of the Government that each student should worship the tablet of Confucius at stated intervals and the refusal of Yuan Shih Kai's successor to exempt Christian students made Dr. Hayes feel that he had no alternative but to resign. Whether Yuan Shih Kai, if he had remained in Shantung, would have been more lenient, it is, of course, impossible to say. I cherish the hope that he would have been, for he is a large-minded man and he discerns the signs of the times more clearly than many of his countrymen. But he is nevertheless a loyal disciple of Confucius and he might also have felt that questions of state policy were involved. It is suggestive, however, that in the spring of 1898 Yuan Shih Kai had selected a Protestant minister, the Rev. Herbert E. House, D. D., (now of the Canton Christian College) as the tutor of his own son, Yuen Yen Tai. Dr. House says, by the way, that he found the youth "wonderfully pure in his thought, high in his ambition and intense in his passion for knowledge—the most patient and diligent student I ever knew."

But to return to the interview with Yuan Shih Kai. The only other Chinese present was Tang Hsiao-chuan, a man of about thirty-five, who was in charge of the Provincial Foreign Office with the rank of Tao-tai. He had spent two years at Columbia University in New York City, spoke English fluently and impressed me as a fine man. Like the Governor, his manners were courtly and refined.

He appeared to be a man of the diplomatic type and worthy of the promotion that he will doubtless receive.

Early the next morning Captain Wang came on behalf of the Governor to return our visit. He was the translator of the Foreign Office and the tutor of one of the Governor's sons whom he was teaching English grammar, arithmetic, geography and history. I was interested to find that he had spent eight years at Philips Academy, Massachusetts, and that he spoke English with the grace of a cultured gentleman.

The policy of Yuan Shih Kai during the Boxer troubles indicated the wisdom and the courage of the man. Disturbances had already begun when he assumed office. It was not far southwest of Chinan-fu that Brooks, the devoted English missionary, was murdered by the Boxers. Yu Hsien was then Governor of Shantung but about that time was transferred to Shan-si, Yuan Shih Kai taking his place. If the notorious foreign-hating Yu Hsien had remained in Shantung, probably he would have massacred the Shantung missionaries as he did those of Shan-si, where he invited them all to his yamen, and then began the butchery by killing three missionaries with his own hand. But Yuan Shih Kai foresaw the inevitable result of such barbarity and determined to restrain the Boxers and protect foreigners. He succeeded with the foreigners, not one being killed after he took control, and all being helped as far as possible to escape. As soon as the storm had passed, he officially wrote to the missionaries who had taken refuge at the ports:—

"Everything is now quiet. If you, reverend sirs, wish to return to the interior, I would beg you first give me word that I may most certainly order the military everywhere most carefully to protect and escort."

This apparently pro-foreign policy brought upon the Governor, for a time, no small obloquy from the fiercely-fanatical conservatives who wanted to murder every foreigner within reach. Indeed the fury of the populace was so great that he was bitterly reviled as "a secondary devil," and his life was repeatedly threatened. But despite the clamour of the mob and the opposition of his associates in the government of the province, he maintained his position with iron inflexibility. Afterwards, however, the people as well as his official subordinates realized that he had saved them from the awful punishment that was inflicted upon the neighbouring province of Chih-li, and his power and prestige became greater than ever.

During my visit in Chining-chou, in the remote southwestern part of the province, an incident occurred which illustrated at once the power of Yuan Shih Kai's name and the heroic devotion of the missionaries. The day after our arrival, a friendly Chinese official brought word that Governor Yuan Shih Kai's mother had died the day before. Chinese custom in such circumstances required him to resign his office and go into retirement for three years. Now Consul Fowler and all the foreigners whom I had met in the ports had declared that the safety of foreigners in Shantung depended on the Governor, that as long as he was in power white men were safe, but that his death or removal might bring another tumult of anti-foreign fury. On the strength of his known friendship, mission work was being resumed and the missionaries were returning to the interior.

Now this man, on whose continuance in office so much depended, was apparently to retire and the future made all uncertain again. The Empress Dowager might give the post to a foreign-hater. An indifferent or even a weak pro-foreign Governor would be little better, for a strong man was needed to hold the population of Shantung in hand. The Chinese quickly take their cue from a high official and even a suspicion that he would not interfere might again loose the dogs of war. True, we had seen no signs of enmity, but appearances are deceptive in Asia. The smile of the mighty Governor meant a smile from every one. But what fires were smouldering beneath no one could know. Even in America, there are lawless men who would mob Chinese in a minute if they knew that the police were weak or indifferent.

I did not fear for myself, for my plans compelled me to journey on to Ichou-fu anyway. But I did not like to leave Mr. Laughlin and Dr. Lyon, who had come with the intention of remaining to reopen the mission work at Chining-chou. But with the true missionary spirit, they bravely decided to stay. A week later, they learned that in view of the importance of the province and his confidence in the great Governor, the Emperor had by a special dispensation shortened the period of official mourning from three years to one hundred days. During that time, the Fan-tai (treasurer) would be the nominal head of the province, though it was quietly understood that even then the Governor would be the "power behind the throne."

But as this was not known when the decision to remain was made, the heroism of the missionaries was none the less striking.

The attitude of Yuan Shih Kai is fairly indicated in the regulations which he caused to be widely published after the Boxer outbreak. Some of these were as follows:—

"In order to protect foreigners from violence and all mission property from burning and other destruction, all civil and military officials with all their subordinates (including literati, constables, village elders, et al.), must use their utmost endeavours to insure their protection. Persons refusing to submit to officials in these matters may be instantly executed without further reference to the Governor, and any one who rescues foreigners from violence will be amply rewarded.

"Any persons having been found guilty of destroying mission property or using violence to foreigners shall be severely dealt with according to the laws which refer to highway robbers, and in addition to this their goods and property shall be confiscated for the public use.

"If injury to missionaries or destruction of property occurs in any district whatever, both civil and military officials of said district shall be degraded and reported to the Throne.

"The elders, constables, et al., of every village shall do their utmost to protect missionaries and their property. If in the future there occurs in any village destruction of property or violence to a missionary, the headmen of such village shall be dealt with according to the edict issued during the twenty-second year of the present Emperor. And, in addition to this they shall be required to present themselves to the yamen and make good all losses. The constables of such villages shall be severely dealt with and expelled from office forever.

"All civil and military officials in whose districts none of these offenses named above occur in one year shall be rewarded with the third degree of merit, and three years of such freedom shall entitle the same officials to promotion.

"Rewards will also be given to village elders and constables in whose district no disturbance occurs."

These are rather remarkable words from a high Chinese official. Now their author occupies a position of even greater authority, for after the death of Li Hung Chang, he was appointed to succeed him as Viceroy of Chih-li in November, 1901. Chih-li is not only one of the greatest provinces of the Empire with a population of 20,937,000, but it includes the imperial city of Peking and the ports of Tong-ku and Tien-tsin, the gateways to the capital. The Viceroy thus controls all avenues of approach to the Throne and is, in a sense, charged with the protection of the royal family. He has free access at all times to the Emperor and the Empress Dowager with whom he is a prime favourite. It was this position of high vantage which enabled Li Hung Chang to become well-nigh omnipotent in China. Yuan Shih Kai is not such a wily schemer as his distinguished predecessor and he is not likely to use his position for self-aggrandizement to the extent that Li Hung Chang did. But he is quite as able a man and more frank and reliable. He has enemies, as every public man has, especially in Asia. Some can never forgive him for his supposed part in the virtual dethronement of the Emperor several years ago. It is alleged that the Emperor counted on the army of Yuan Shih Kai to support him in his reform policy, but that Yuan consulted with Jung Lu, who was then the Viceroy of Chih-li, and that that worthy promptly laid the whole matter before the Empress Dowager; the result being that the young Emperor awoke one morning to find himself practically stripped of his imperial power.[99] Yuan has been freely charged with treachery in this coup d'etat. Others hold that he did not intend treachery but only consultation with his superior officer as to what ought to be done in a grave crisis which was in itself revolutionary in character. Yuan was far from being a reactionary, but he was wise enough to see that China could not be suddenly transformed, and he naturally hesitated to lend himself to an enterprise which he believed to be premature and to be destined to result in certain failure. The soundness of his judgment is now generally recognized, and the Emperor himself is said to be almost as friendly towards him as the Empress Dowager, who counts him one of her ablest supporters.

In the present critical condition of far eastern politics, much depends upon the policy of Yuan Shih Kai. With exalted rank, the ear of the Empress Dowager and the command of the only real

---

99   Cf. Imperial Decree of Sept. 22, 1898, quoted in Pott, "The Outbreak in China," pp. 55sq,

soldiers that China possesses, he can do more than any other man to influence the course of the Empire. Of course, one official, however powerful, cannot absolutely control national conditions. The forces at work both within and without the Empire are too vast and too complicated. Nevertheless, the fact that such an able and far-seeing man as Yuan Shih Kai is now the most influential Viceroy in China, the Commander-in-Chief of the Army, and the trusted adviser of the Empress Dowager may be fairly included among the hopeful signs for the future.

Most significant of all is the development of missionary work since the Boxer outbreak. Not only have all the destroyed churches and chapels been rebuilt, but they are, as a rule, crowded with worshippers. In the Wei-hsien station field in Shantung, where every missionary was driven out and all the mission property destroyed, 569 Chinese were baptized last year. In Peking, the large new Presbyterian church, though erected near that great cistern in which nearly 100 bodies were found after the siege, is filled at almost every service and the churches of other denominations are also largely attended. At a single service, Dr. Pentecost preached to 800 attentive Chinese young men. Even in Paoting-fu, where every remaining missionary and scores of Chinese Christians were killed, and where one might suppose that no Chinese would ever dare to confess Christ, even in bloodstained Paoting-fu, the missionaries are preaching daily to throngs of attentive Chinese in the city, while at the spacious new compounds outside the walls the schools and hospitals and churches are taxed to care for the hundreds who go to them. In the Canton field, long known for its anti-foreign feeling, 1,564 Chinese were baptized last year by the Presbyterians alone and the missionaries are importunately calling for reinforcements to enable them to meet the multiplied demands upon them. Even the province of Hunan, which a decade ago was almost as inhospitable to foreigners as Thibet, now has half a hundred Protestant and Catholic missionaries developing a prosperous work. Bishop Graves, of the Protestant Episcopal Church, returned recently from an episcopal visitation with this inspiring message:—

"The condition and outlook of the Church's work in the province of Kiang-su are more encouraging than ever before. Hitherto we have had to persuade people to be taught. Now they come to us themselves, not one by one, but in numbers...That there is a strong movement towards Christianity setting in is evident."[100]

Not only has the old work been resumed with vigour but much new work has been opened. Within a year and a quarter after the relief of the Legations by the Allies, twenty-five new mission stations had been opened and 373 new missionaries had entered China, and each succeeding year has seen considerable additions to the number. The Rev. Dr. George F. Pentecost, who visited China in 1903, writes—

"The outlook seems to me most encouraging. I find the more thoughtful missionaries enthusiastic in their forecast for the future. My own judgment is that the cause of missions, so far as foundation work and increased power for work, has been advanced at least twenty-five years by the massacres of 1900. I think the common people are thoroughly convinced that missions cannot be destroyed, and I am equally convinced that the authorities are also convinced that it is vain for them to rage and set themselves against Christianity. The one thing which an Asiatic recognizes is power and facts accomplished, and in the rebuilding of our missions and the awakening already begun and the reinforcement of the missions in men and material means they see and recognize power. Their own temples are falling into decay and ruin and our new buildings are rising in prominence and beauty. Their ignorant priesthood is sinking deeper and deeper into degradation, while our missionaries are every where known and recognized as men of 'light and learning.'...It seems to me from all I can learn that there is no fear of another anti-foreign outbreak."

And these are but a few of the many illustrations that could be given. Everywhere, the doors are open and Chinese are now being baptized by Protestant missionaries at the rate of about 15,000 a year, while a far larger number are enrolled as inquirers or catechumens. The interdenominational conference of missionaries at Kuling, August 7, 1903, declared:—

"It is now a fact that there is not one of the more than nineteen hundred counties of China and Manchuria from which we are shut out, and before the hundredth year of our work begins, we can say that if the gospel is not preached to every creature in

---

100 "The Spirit of Missions," July, 1904.

China, the reason must be sought outside China. The opportunities of work are varied in their kind, vast in their extent. Never before have men crowded to hear the gospel as they are crowding now in the open air and indoors; in our chapels and in our guest-rooms we have opportunities to preach Christ such as can scarcely be found outside China. Never before has there been such an eager desire for education as there is now; our schools, both of elementary and of higher grades, are full, and everywhere applicants have to be refused. Never before has there been such a demand for Christian literature as there is now; our tract societies and all engaged in supplying converts and inquirers with reading material are doing their utmost, but are not able to overtake the demand; and the demand is certain to increase, for it comes from the largest number of people in the world reading one language. The medical work has from the first found an entrance into hearts that were closed against other forms of work. Its sphere of influence grows ever wider and is practically unlimited. Unique opportunities of service are afforded us by the large number of blind people, by lepers, and those suffering from incurable diseases; by the deaf and dumb, the insane and other afflicted people. In China the poor are always with us, and whensoever we will we may do them good."

Not least among the hopeful signs for the future is the new treaty between the United States and China which was signed at Shanghai, October 8, 1903, and unanimously ratified by the United States Senate December 18, 1903. It not only secured an "open door" in China for Americans, but, if the veteran "most favoured nation" clause is again pressed into service, a priceless benefit to the whole civilized world as well as to China herself. For this treaty abolished the exasperating "likin" (the inland tax heretofore exacted by local officials on goods in transit through their territories); confirmed the right of American citizens to trade, reside, travel, and own property in China; extended to China the United States' copyright laws; gained a promise from the Chinese Government to establish a patent office in which the inventions of United States' citizens may be protected; and made valuable regulations regarding trade-marks, mining concessions, judicial tribunals for the hearing of complaints, diplomatic intercourse, and several other matters which, though sanctioned by custom, were often abridged or violated.

The treaty, moreover, called for the opening of two additional treaty ports, one of which is at Feng-tien-fu, more generally known as Mukden, important not only as a city of 200,000 inhabitants but as the capital of Manchuria and with both rail and river connection with the Gulf of Pe-chi-li and the imperial province of Chih-li. The other is at An-tung, which is important because of its situation on the Yalu River opposite the Korean frontier. Of course, the Russia-Japan War has post-poned the opening of these ports, but the recognition of China's right to open them by treaty with the United States is none the less significant.

Most important of all, the treaty removes, so far as any such enactment can remove, the last barrier to the extension of Christianity throughout China. In Article XIII of the English treaty with China, September 5, 1902, Great Britain agreed to join in a commission to secure peaceable relationships between converts and non-converts in China. But the American treaty goes much farther, as the following extract (Article XIV) will show:—

"The principles of the Christian religion, as professed by the Protestant and Roman Catholic Churches, are recognized as teaching men to do good and to do to others as they would have others do to them. Those who quietly profess and teach these doctrines shall not be harassed or persecuted on account of their faith. Any person, whether citizen of the United States or Chinese convert, who, according to these tenets, peaceably teaches and practices the principles of Christianity shall in no case be interfered with or molested therefor. No restrictions shall be placed on Chinese joining Christian churches. Converts and non-converts, being Chinese subjects, shall alike conform to the laws of China, and shall pay due respect to those in authority, living together in peace and amity; and the fact of being converts shall not protect them from the consequences of any offense they may have committed before or may commit after their admission into the church, or exempt them from paying legal taxes levied on Chinese subjects generally, except taxes levied and contributions for the support of religious customs and practices contrary to their religion. Missionaries shall not interfere with the exercise by the native authorities of their jurisdiction over Chinese subjects; nor shall the native authorities make any distinction between converts and non-converts, but shall administer the laws without partiality, so that both classes can live together in peace.

"Missionary societies of the United States shall be permitted to rent and to lease in perpetuity as the property of such societies, buildings or lands in all parts of the Empire for missionary purposes and, after the title-deeds have been found in order and duly stamped by the local authorities, to erect such suitable buildings as may be required for carrying on their good work."

This gives new prestige to American missionary effort and legally confirms the opening of the Empire from end to end to missionary residence, activity and toleration. All that France harshly obtained for Roman Catholic missions by the Berthemy convention of 1865 and by the haughty ultimatum of M. Gerard at the close of the war with Japan, the United States has now peacefully secured with the apparent good-will of the Chinese Government.

XXVIII
THE PARAMOUNT DUTY
OF CHRISTENDOM

IT would be unwise to underestimate the gravity of the situation, or to assume that the most numerous and conservative nation on the globe has been suddenly transformed from foreign haters to foreign lovers. The world may again have occasion to realize that the momentum of countless myriads is an awful force even against the resources of a higher civilization, as the Romans found to their consternation when the barbarian hordes overran the Empire. We do not know what disturbances may yet occur or what proportions they may assume. It may be that much blood will yet be shed. Inflamed passions will certainly be slow in subsiding. Men who are identified with the old era will not give up without a struggle. It took 300 years to bring England from pagan barbarism to Christian civilization, and China is vaster far and more conservative than England. The world moves faster now, and the change-producing forces of the present exceed those of former centuries as a modern steam hammer exceeds a wooden sledge. But China is ponderous, and a few decades are short for so gigantic a transformation.

Meantime, much depends on the future conduct of foreigners. It is hard enough for the proud-spirited Chinese to see the aliens coming in greater numbers than ever and entrenching themselves more and more impregnably, and a continuance of the policy of greed and injustice will deepen an already deep resentment. The almost invincible prejudice against the foreigner is a serious hindrance to the regeneration of China. "This fact emphasizes the need for using every means possible for the breaking down of such a prejudice. Every careless or willful wound to Chinese susceptibilities, or unnecessary crossing of Chinese superstitions, retards our own work and increases the dead wall of opposition on the part of this people."[101]

The proper way to deal with the Chinese was illustrated by the Rev. J. Walter Lowrie of the Presbyterian Mission at Paoting-fu when, as a token of appreciation for his services to the city in connection with the retaliatory measures of the foreign troops shortly after the Boxer outbreak, the magistrate raised a special fund among wealthy Chinese, bought a fine tract of sixteen acres and presented it to the mission as a gift. The tract had been occupied for many years by several families of tenants who had built their own houses, but who were now to be evicted. Of course, Mr. Lowrie was not responsible for them. But he insisted that they should be dealt with fairly, and be paid a reasonable price for their homes and the improvements that they had made so that they could rent land and establish themselves elsewhere. In addition, he was at pains to find work for them until their new crops became available. Their affectionate greeting of Mr. Lowrie as we walked about the place clearly showed their gratification. There is not the slightest trouble with the Chinese when they are treated with ordinary decency as brother men.

At any rate, in the name of that civilization and Christianity which we profess, as well of common humanity, let foreign nations abandon the methods of brutality and rapine. If we expect to convert the Chinese, we must exemplify the principles we teach. It is not true that the Chinese cannot understand justice and magnanimity. Even if it were true, it does not follow that we should be unjust and pitiless. Let us instruct them in the higher things. How are they ever to learn, if we do not teach them? But as a matter of fact, the Chinese are as amenable to reason as any people in the world. Their temperament and inertia and long isolation from the remainder of mankind have made them slow to grasp a new idea. But they will get it if they are given reasonable time, and when they do once get it, they will hold it. Whether, therefore, further trouble occurs,

---

101 The Rev. Dr. J. C. Garritt, Hang chou.

depends in part upon the conduct of foreign nations. Justice and humanity in all dealings with the Chinese, while not perhaps wholly preventing outbreaks of hostility, will at least give less occasion for them.

But however trying the period of transition may be, the issue is not for a moment doubtful. Progress invariably wins the victory over blind conservatism. The higher idea is sure to conquer the lower. With all their admixture of selfishness and violence, the fact remains that the forces operating on China to-day include the vital regenerative element for human society. It is futile to expect that China could ever regenerate herself without outside aid. Spontaneous regeneration is an exploded theory in society as well as in biology. Life always comes from without.

The spirit of China's new system of education shows that there is imminent danger of the misuse of modern methods, even when they have been adopted. All her institutions are conducted on principles which virtually debar Christians either as students or professors. Infidelity, however, has free entrance as long as it conforms to the external forms imposed by the State. "Anti-conservative but anti-Christian," the educational movement has been characterized by Dr. W. M. Hayes of Teng-chou. Dr. W. A. P. Martin, so long President of the Imperial Chinese University, declares that "if Christians at home only knew what a determined effort is being made to exclude Christian teachers and Christian text-books from Chinese Government schools, from the Imperial University down, they would exert themselves to give a Christian education to the youth of China." A single mission institution, like the Shantung Protestant University, with its union of the best educational methods and the highest ideals of Christian character, will do more for the real enlightenment of China than a dozen provincial colleges where gambling, irreligion and opium smoking are freely tolerated and a failure to worship the tablet of Confucius is deemed the only cardinal sin.

In view of all these things, the regeneration of China becomes a question of transcendent importance, a question demanding the broadest statesmanship and the supremest effort; a question involving the future destinies of the race. "On account of its mass, its homogeneity, its high intellectual and moral qualities, its past history, its present and prospective relations to the whole world, the conversion of the Chinese people to Christianity is the most important aggressive enterprise now laid upon the Church of Christ."[102] It would be a calamity to the whole world if the dominant powers of Asia should continue to be heathen. But if they are not to be, immediate and herculean efforts must be made to regenerate them. Sir Robert Hart declares that the only hope of averting "the yellow peril" lies either in partition among the great Powers, which he regards as so difficult as to be impracticable, or in a miraculous spread of Christianity which will transform the Empire. Beyond question, Sir Robert Hart is right. It is too late now to avoid the issue. The impact of new forces is rousing this gigantic nation, and Western nations must either conquer or convert. Conquering is out of the question for reasons already given.[103] The only alternative is conversion. In these circumstances "the yellow peril becomes the golden opportunity of Christendom."[104]

And by conversion is not meant "civilization." Here is the fundamental error of the pseudonymous writer of "Letters From a Chinese Official." He evidently knows little or nothing of the missionary force or of the motives which control it. He writes as a man who has lived in a commercial and political atmosphere, and who feels outraged, and with some justice, by the policy which European nations have adopted towards China. From this viewpoint, it was easy for the quick-witted author to satirize our defects and to laud the virtues, some of them unquestionably real, of his native land. But it does not follow that his indictment holds against the Christian people of the West, who reprobate as strongly as the author the duplicity and brutality of foreign nations in their dealings with China. The West has something more to offer China than a civilization. As a matter of fact, the best people of the West are not trying to give China a civilization at all, but a gospel. With whatever is good in Chinese civilization, they have no wish to interfere. It is true that some changes in society invariably follow the acceptance of Christianity, but these changes relate only to those things that are always and everywhere inherently wrong, irrespective of the civilization to which they appear to belong. The

102 Smith, "Rex Christus," p. 237

103 Chapter XXV.

104 The Rev. Dr. Maltbie D. Babcock.

gospel transformed "the Five Points" in New York not because they were uncivilized but because they were evil. It will do in China only what it does in America—fight vice, cleanse foulness, dispel superstition. Christianity is the only power which does this. It has transformed every people among whom it has had free course. It has purified society. It has promoted intelligence. It has elevated woman. It has fitted for wise and beneficent use of power. Of those who deny this, Lowell says:

"So long as these very men are dependent for every privilege they enjoy upon that religion which they discard, they may well hesitate a little before seeking to rob the Christian of his faith and humanity of its hope in that Saviour who alone has given to man that hope of eternal life which makes life tolerable and society possible, and robs death of its terrors and the grave of its gloom."

No degradation is beyond the reach of its regenerating power. Witness the New Hebrides, Metlakatla, the Fiji, Georgia and Friendly Islands. Even England, Germany and America themselves are in evidence. Christianity lifted them out of a barbarism and superstition as dense as any prevailing among the heathen nations of this age. It can effect like changes in China if it is given the opportunity.

But it is said that the Chinese do not want to be converted. A distinguished General of the United States army declared, after his return from Peking in 1900:—"I must say that I did not meet a single intelligent Chinaman who expressed a desire to embrace the Christian religion. The masses are against Christianity."[105] It is pleasant to know that it is so common for unconverted Americans to go to that army officer for spiritual guidance that the failure of the Chinese to do so disappointed him. Most men would hardly have expected a people who were smarting under defeat to open their hearts to a commander of the conquering army. But hundreds of other foreigners in China, myself included, can testify that they have heard intelligent Chinese express a desire to embrace the Christian religion, and the fact that there are in China to-day over a hundred thousand Chinese, to say nothing of myriads of enrolled catechumens, who have publicly confessed their faith in Christ

---

105 The Christian Advocate, New York, June 11, 1903.

and who have tenaciously adhered to it under sore persecution is tangible evidence that some Chinese at least are disposed to accept Christianity.

Do they want Him? "It would please you," a missionary writes, "to see these poor people feeling after God, and their eagerness to learn more and more." It is not uncommon for converts to travel ten, fifteen and even twenty miles to attend service. The Sunday I was in Ichou-fu, I met a fine-looking young man, named Yao Chao Feng, who had walked sixteen miles to receive Christian baptism, and several other Chinese were present who had journeyed on foot from seventeen to thirty-three miles. In Paoting-fu, I heard of a mother and daughter who had painfully hobbled on bound feet thirteen miles that they might learn more about the new faith. In another city, 800 opium-smokers kneeled in a church and asked God to help them break the chains of that frightful habit. Surely He who puts His fatherly arms around the prodigal and kissed him was in that humble church and answered the prayer of those poor, sin-cursed men. It would be easy to fill a book with such instances.

But suppose the Chinese do not want Christ. What of it? Did they want the distinguished General? On the contrary, he had to fight his way into Peking at the mouth of the cannon and the point of the bayonet, over the dead bodies of Chinese and through the ruins of Chinese towns. Do "the masses" desire Christ anywhere? Mr. Moody used to say that the people of the United States did not want Christ and would probably reject Him if He came to them as He came to the Jews of old.

The question is not at all whether the Chinese or anybody else desire Christ, but whether they need Him, and a man's answer to that question largely depends upon his own relations to Christ. If we need Him, the Chinese do. If He has done anything for us, if He has brought any dignity and power and peace into our lives, the probabilities are that He can do as much for the Chinese.

"Be assured that the Christ who cannot save a Chinaman in longitude 117'0 East is a Christ who cannot save you in longitude 3'0 west. The question about missions would not be so lightly put, nor the answer so lightly listened to, if men realized that what is at stake is not a mere scheme of us missionaries, but the validity of their own hope of eternal life. Yet I am bound to say that the questions put to me, on returning from the mission field, by professedly Christian people often shake my faith, not in missions, but in their Christian profession. What kind of grasp of the gospel have men got, who doubt whether it is to-day, under any skies, the power of God unto salvation?"[106]

It passes comprehension that any one who has even a superficial knowledge of the real China can doubt for a moment its vital need of the gospel. The wretchedness of its life appals an American who goes back into the unmodified conditions of the interior or even into the old Chinese city of proud Shanghai. As I journeyed through those vast throngs, climbed many hilltops and looked out upon the innumerable villages, which thickly dotted the plain as far as the eye could reach, as I saw the unrelieved pain and the crushing poverty and the abject fear of evil spirits, I felt that in China is seen in literal truth "The Man with the Hoe."

> "Bowed by the weight of centuries, he leans
> Upon his hoe and gazes on the ground,
> The emptiness of ages in his face,
> And on his back the burden of the world.
>
> "What gulfs between him and the seraphim,
> Slave of the wheel of labour, what to him
> Are Plato and the swing of Pleiades?
> What the long reaches of the peaks of song,
> The rift of dawn, the reddening of the rose?
> Through this dread shape the suffering ages look;
> Time's tragedy is in that aching stoop."

This is the need to which the churches of Europe and America are addressing themselves through the boards and societies of foreign missions. These boards are the channels through which the highest type of Christian civilization is communicated to pagan peoples, the agencies which gather up all that is best and truest in our modern life and concentrate it upon the conditions of China. From this view-point, foreign missions is not only a question of religion, but a problem of statesmanship, and one of overshadowing magnitude. As such, it merits the sympathy and cooperation of

---

106 Gibson, pp. 11, 12.

every intelligent and broad-minded man, irrespective of his religious affiliations. Its spiritual aims are supreme and sufficient for every true disciple of Christ, but apart from them its social and educational value and its relation to the welfare of the race justly claim the interest and support of all. In this work the Church is saving both individuals and nations, and for time as well as for eternity. It holds no pessimistic views of the future. It denies that the development of the race has ended. It frankly concedes the existence of vice and superstition. But it believes that the gospel of Jesus Christ is able to subdue that vice, and to dispel that superstition. So it founds schools and colleges for the education of the young; establishes hospitals and dispensaries for the care of the sick and suffering; operates printing-presses for the dissemination of the Bible and a Christian literature; maintains churches for the worship of the true God, and in and through all it preaches to lost men the transforming and uplifting gospel of Him who alone can "speak peace to the heathen."

But some are saying that the Boxer outbreak has destroyed their confidence in the practicability of the effort to evangelize the Chinese. They are asking: "Why should we send any more missionaries to China?"

I reply: "Why send any more merchants, any more consuls, any more oil, flour, cotton? Shall we continue our commercial and political relations with China and discontinue our religious relations; allow the lower influences to flow on unchecked, but withhold the spiritual forces which would purify trade and politics, which have made us what we are, and which alone can regenerate the millions of China?"

Is disaster a reason for withdrawal? When the American colonists found themselves involved in the horrors of the Revolution, did they say that it would have been better to remain the subjects of Great Britain? When, a generation ago, our land was drenched with the blood of the Civil War, did men think that they ought to have tolerated secession and slavery? When the Maine was blown up in Havana Harbour and Lawton was killed in Luzon, did we demand withdrawal from Cuba and the Philippines? When Liscum fell under the walls of Tien-tsin, did we insist that the attempt to relieve the Legations should be abandoned? Or did not the American people, in every one of these instances, find in the very agonies of struggle and bloodshed a decisive reason for advance? Did they not sternly resolve that there should be men, that there should be money, and that the war should be pressed to victory whatever the sacrifice that might be involved?

And shall the Church of God weakly, timidly yield because the very troubles have occurred which Christ Himself predicted? He frankly said that there should "be wars and rumors of wars"; that His disciples should "be hated of all men"; that He sent them "forth as sheep in the midst of wolves," and that the brother should "deliver up the brother to death and the father the child." But in that very discourse He also said: "He that taketh not his cross and followeth after me is not worthy of me." "Go, preach," He commanded. "Woe is me if I preach not," cried Paul. Hostile rulers and priests and mobs and the bitter Cross did not swerve Him a hairbreadth from His purpose; nor did the rending of the early disciples in the arenas of Nero, the burning of a Huss and a Savonarola, the pyres of Smithfield, the dungeons of the Tolbooth and the thumb-screws of the Inquisition quench the zeal of His followers.

And in the like manner, the ashes of mission buildings and the blood of devoted missionaries and the tumult of furious men have led multitudes at home to form a high and holy resolve to send more missionaries, to give more money and to press the whole majestic enterprise with new faith and power until all China has been electrified by the vital spiritual force of a nobler faith. God summons Christendom to a forward movement in the land whose soil has been forever consecrated by the martyrdom of the beloved dead. Instead of retreating, "we should," in the immortal words of Lincoln at Gettysburg, "be here dedicated to the great task remaining before us; that from these honoured dead we take increased devotion to that cause for which they gave the last full measure of devotion; that we here highly resolve that these dead shall not have died in vain."

It may be said that this is a purely sentimental consideration. But so may love for country, for liberty, for wife and children, be called a sentiment. God forbid that the time should ever come when men will not be influenced by sentiment. The intuitions of the heart are as apt to be correct as the dictates of the head. I candidly admit that as I stood amid the ruins of the mission buildings in China, as I faced the surviving Christians and remembered what they had suffered, the property they had lost and the dear ones they had seen murdered,—as I stood with bared head on the spot where devoted missionaries had perished, I was conscious of a deeper consecration to the task of uplifting China. And I am not willing to admit that such a dedication of the living to the continuance of the work of the dead is a mere sentiment.

We are not wise above what is written when we declare that the eternal purpose of God comprehends China as well as Europe and America. He did not create those hundreds of millions of human beings simply to fertilize the soil in which their bodies will decay. He has not preserved China as a nation for nearly half a hundred centuries for nothing. Out of the apparent wreck, the new dispensation will come, is already coming. Frightened men thought that the fall of Rome meant the end of the world, but we can see that it only cleared the way for a better world. Pessimists feared that the violence and blood of the Crusades would ruin Europe, but instead they broke up the stagnation of the Middle Ages and made possible the rise of modern Europe. The faint-hearted said that the India mutiny of 1857 and the Syria massacres of 1860 ended all hope of regenerating those countries, but in both they ushered in the most successful era of missions.

So the barriers which have separated China from the rest of the world must, like the medieval wall of Tien-tsin, be cast down and over them a highway for all men be made. No one sup-posed that the process would be so sudden and violent. But in the Boxer uprising the hammer of God did in months what would otherwise have taken weary generations. Some were discouraged because the air was filled with the deafening tumult and the blinding dust and the flying debris. Many lost heart and wanted to sound a retreat because some of God's chosen ones were crushed in the awful rending. But the wiser and more far-seeing heard a new call to utilize the larger opportunity which resulted. Up to this time we have been playing with foreign missions. It is now time for Christendom to understand that its great work in the twentieth century is to plan this movement on a scale gigantic in comparison with anything it has yet done, and to grapple intelligently, generously and resolutely, with the stupendous task of Christianizing China.

But we are sometimes told that the churches should not be allowed to go on; that one of the conditions of good feeling will be the exclusion of missionaries from China. On this point, I venture three suggestions:—

First,—No administration that can ever be elected in the United States will thus interfere with the liberty of the churches. It will never say, in effect, that arms' manufacturing companies can send agents to Peking and distilleries send drummers to Shanghai, but that the Church of God cannot send devoted, intelligent men and women to found schools and hospitals and printing-presses and to preach the gospel of Jesus Christ. It will never say that American gamblers in Tien-tsin and American prostitutes in Hongkong shall be protected by all the might of the American army and navy, but that the pure, high-minded missionary, who represents the noblest motives and ideals of our American life, shall be expatriated, a man without a country.

This is, however, a problem for the nation, rather than for the boards. The American missionary went to Asia before his Government did, and until recently he saw very little of the American flag. European nations have protected their citizens, whether they were missionaries or traders. In the United States Senate Mr. Frye once reminded the nation that about twenty years ago England sent an army of 15,000 men down to the African coast, across 700 miles of burning sand, to batter down iron gates and stone walls, reach down into an Abyssinian dungeon and lift out of it one British subject who had been unlawfully imprisoned. It cost England $25,000,000 to do it, but it made a highway over this planet for every common son of Britain, and the words, "I am an English citizen," more potent than the sceptre of a king. And because of that reputation American missionaries have more than once been saved by the intervention of British ministers and consuls who have not forgotten that "blood is thicker than water." Shall we vociferously curse England one day and the next supinely depend upon her representatives to help us out when our citizens are endangered?

This is not a question of "jingoism," whatever that may be. It is not a question of making unreasonable complaints to home governments. It is not a question of religion or of missions. It is a question of treaties, of citizenship, of national honour and of self-respect. Let the nation settle it from that viewpoint. The missionary asks no special privileges. He can stand it to go on as before, if the nation can stand it to have him.

Second,—If China should ever make such a demand in repudiation of the treaties which she herself has expressly acknowledged to be valid, and if all the Powers should support her in that demand, does anybody doubt what the missionary would say? We know at any rate what he has said in similar circumstances. When Peter and John were scourged and forbidden to preach any more in the name of Jesus, friendless and penniless though they were, they ringingly answered: "Whether it be right in the sight of God to hearken unto you more than unto God, judge ye. For we cannot but speak the things which we have seen and heard." When Martin Luther was arraigned before the most powerful tribunal in Europe, he declared: "Here I stand. God help me. I can do no other." When the Russian Minister in Constantinople haughtily said to Dr. Schauffler, "My master, the Czar of all the Russias, will not let you put foot on that territory,"—the intrepid missionary replied: "My Master, the Lord Jesus Christ, will never ask the Czar of all the Russias where He shall put His foot." Scores of missionaries have not hesitated to say to hostile authorities: "I did not receive my commission from any earthly potentate but from the King of Kings, and I shall, I must go on."

Some will say that this is madness. So of old men said of Christ, "He hath a demon"; so they said of Paul, "Thou art beside thyself." If magnificent moral courage and unyielding devotion to duty are "madness," then the more the world has of it the better.

The effort to minimize the significance of the missionary force in China will be made only by those who, destitute of any vital religious faith themselves, of course see no reason for communicating it to others, or by those who are strangely blind and deaf to the real issues of the age. In the words of Benjamin Kidd, "it is not improbable that, to a future observer, one of the most curious features of our time will appear to be the prevailing unconsciousness of the real nature of the issues in the midst of which we are living."

"No more did the statesmen and the philosophers of Rome understand the character and issues of that greatest movement of all history, of which their literature takes so little notice. That the greatest religious change in the history of mankind should have taken place under the eyes of a brilliant galaxy of philosophers and historians who were profoundly conscious of decomposition around them; that all these writers should have utterly failed to predict the issue of the movement they were then observing; and that during the space of three centuries they should have treated as simply contemptible an agency which all men must now admit to have been, for good or evil, the most powerful moral lever that has ever been applied to the affairs of men, are facts well worthy of meditation in every period of religious transition."[107]

Does any sane man imagine that the Church could cease to be missionary and remain a Church? It has been well said that the Christian nations might as well face the utter futility of any hypothesis based upon the supposition that they can remain away from the Orient. The occurrences of recent years have made changes in their relation to the world which they can no more recall than they can alter the course of a planet. It is idle for doctrinaires to tell us from the quiet comfort of home libraries, that we should "keep hands off." We can no more keep hands off than our country could keep hands off slavery in the South, no more than New York could keep hands off a borough infected with smallpox. The world has passed the point where one-third of its population can be allowed to breed miasma which the other two-thirds must breathe. Both for China's sake and for our own, we must continue this work. If this is true in the political and commercial realms, much more is it true in the religious. Chalmer's notable sermon on the "Expulsive Power of a New Affection" enunciates a permanent principle. When a man's soul is once thrilled with the conviction that he has found God, he must declare that sublime truth,

"To doubt would be disloyalty,
To falter would be sin."

I confess to a feeling of impatience when I am told that all missionary plans for China must be contingent "upon the settlement of political negotiations," "the overthrow of the Empress Dowager and her reactionary advisers," "the reestablishment of the Emperor on his rightful throne," "the continuance in power of Viceroy Yuan Shih Kai," "the mainte-nance of a strong foreign military and naval

---

107 Lecky, "History of European Morals," Vol. 1, p. 359.

force in China," "the thwarting of Russia's plans for supremacy," and several other events.

All these things have been said and more. Is the Church then despairingly to resign her commission from Jesus Christ and humbly ask a new one from Caesar? Not so did the apostolic missionaries, and not so, I am persuaded, will their modern successors do. They cannot, indeed, be indifferent to the course of political events or to their bearing upon the missionary problem. But, on the other hand, they cannot make their obedience to Christ and their duty to their fellow men dependent upon political considerations. For Christian men to wait until China is pacified by the Powers, or "until she is enlightened by the dissemination of truer conceptions of the Western world," would be to abdicate their responsibility as the chief factor in bringing about a better state of affairs. Is the Church prepared to abandon the field to the diplomat, the soldier, the trader? How soon is China likely to be pacified by them, judging from their past acts? The gospel is the primary need of China to-day, not the tertiary. The period of unrest is not the time for the messenger of Christ to hold his peace, but to declare with new zeal and fidelity his ministry of reconciliation. To leave the field to the politician, the soldier and the trader would be to dishonour Christ, to fail to utilize an unprecedented opportunity, to abandon the Chinese Christians in their hour of special need and to prejudice missionary influence at home and abroad for a generation.

But the numbers at work are painfully inadequate. To say that there are 2,950 Protestant foreign missionaries in China is apt to give a distorted idea of the real situation unless one remembers the immensity of the population. A station is considered well-manned when it has four families and a couple of single women. But what are they among those swarming myriads? The proportion of Protestant missionaries to the population, which is commonly quoted, needs revision. There is one to about every 144,000 souls. But that, too, requires modification, for it counts the sick, the aged, recruits who are learning the language, wives whose time is absorbed by household cares, and those who are absent on furloughs, the last class alone being often about ten per cent. of the total enrollment. The actual working force, therefore, is far smaller than the statistics suggest.

Of China as a whole, it is said that "some of the missionaries and some of the converts are to be found in every one of the provinces, both of China and Manchuria. But in the 1,900 odd counties into which the provinces are divided, each with one important town and a large part of them with more than one, there are but some 400 stations. That is to say, at least four-fifths of the counties of China are almost entirely unprovided with the means of hearing the gospel."[108]Of all the walled cities in the Empire, less than 300 are occupied by missionaries. There are literally tens of thousands of communities that have not yet been touched by the gospel. Plainly, the missionary force must be largely augmented if the work is to be adequately done. The home churches have gone too far to stop without going farther. "Those who undertake to carry on mission work among great peoples undertake great responsibilities. We have no right to penetrate these nations with a revolutionary gospel of enormous power, unless we are prepared to make every sacrifice and every effort for the proper care and the wise training of the organization of the Christian community itself which, while it must become increasingly a source of revolutionary thought and movement, is also the only body that can by the help and grace of God give these far-reaching movements a healthy direction and lead them to safe and happy issues."[109]

Grant that the work of evangelization must be chiefly done by Chinese preachers; there is still much for the missionary to do. Allowing for those who, on account of illness, furlough or other duties, are temporarily non-effective, 10,000 missionaries for China would not give a working average of one for every 50,000 of the population. In these circumstances, the union conference of missionaries at Kuling, August 7, 1903, was surely within reasonable bounds when, in urging the Protestant churches to celebrate in 1907 the one hundredth anniversary of the sending forth of Robert Morrison, it declared:—

"...In view of the vastness of the field that lies open before us, and of the immense opportunities for good which China offers the Christian Church—opportunities so many of which have been quite recently opened to us and which were won by the blood of the martyrs of 1900—we appeal to the boards and committees of our respective societies, and individually to all our brethren and

108 "China's Call for a Three Years' Enterprise," 1903.
109 Gibson, p. 277.

sisters in the home churches, to say if we are unreasonable in asking that the last object of the Three Years' Enterprise be to double the number of missionaries now working in China."

The time has come to "attempt great things for God, expect great things from God." When in 1806, those five students in Williamstown, Massachusetts, held that immortal conference in the lee of a haystack, talked of the mighty task of world evangelization and wondered whether it could be accomplished, it was given to Samuel J. Mills to cry out: "We can if we will!" And the little company took up the cry and literally shouted it to the heavens: "We can if we will!" "A growing church among a strong people burdened by a decadent Empire—the spirit of life working against the forces of death and decay in the one great Pagan Empire which the wrecks of millenniums have left on the earth—surely there is a call to service that might fire the spirit of the dullest of us."[110] The obstacles are indeed formidable, but he who can look beneath the eddying flotsam and jetsam of the surface to the mighty undercurrents which are sweeping majestically onward can exclaim with Gladstone:—

"Time is on our side. The great social forces which move onward in their might and majesty, and which the tumults of these strifes do not for a moment impede or disturb—those forces are marshalled in our support. And the banner which we now carry in the fight, though perhaps at some moment of the struggle it may droop over our sinking hearts, yet will float again in the eye of heaven and will be borne, perhaps not to an easy, but to a certain and to a not distant victory."[111]

In a famous art gallery, there is a famous painting called "Anno Domini." It represents an Egyptian temple, from whose spacious courts a brilliant procession of soldiers, statesmen, philosophers, artists, musicians and priests is advancing in triumphal march, bearing a huge idol, the challenge and the boast of heathenism. Across the pathway of the procession is an ass, whose bridle is held by a reverent looking man and upon whose back is a fair young mother with her infant child. It is Jesus, entering Egypt in flight from the wrath of Herod, and thus crossing the path of aggressive heathenism. Then the clock strikes and the Christian era begins.

---

110 Gibson, p. 331.
111 Speech on the Reform Bill.

It is a noble parable. Its fulfillment has been long delayed till the Child has become a Man, crucified, risen, crowned. But now in majesty and power, He stands across the pathway of advancing heathenism in China. There may be confusion and tumult for a time. The heathen may rage, "and the rulers take counsel together against the Lord." But the idol shall be broken "with a rod of iron," and the King upon his holy hill shall have "the heathen for 'his' inheritance and the uttermost parts of the earth for 'his' possession."

For a consummation so majestic in its character and so vital to the welfare not only of China but of the whole human race we may well make our own the organ-voiced invocation of Milton:—

"Come, O Thou that hast the seven stars in Thy right hand, appoint Thy chosen priests according to their order and courses of old, to minister before Thee, and duly to dress and pour out the consecrated oil into Thy holy and ever burning lamps. Thou hast sent out the spirit of prayer upon Thy servants over all the earth to this effect, and stored up their voices as the sound of many waters about Thy throne...O perfect and accomplish Thy glorious acts; for men may leave their works unfinished, but Thou art a God; Thy nature is perfection...The times and seasons pass along under Thy feet, to go and come at Thy bidding; and as Thou didst dignify our fathers' days with many revelations, above all their foregoing ages since Thou tookest the flesh, so Thou canst vouchsafe to us, though unworthy, as large a portion of Thy Spirit as Thou pleasest; for who shall prejudice Thy all-governing will? Seeing the power of Thy grace is not passed away with the primitive times, as fond and faithless men imagine, but Thy kingdom is now at hand, and Thou standing at the door, come forth out of Thy royal chambers, O Prince of all the kings of the earth; put on the visible robes of Thy imperial majesty, take up that unlimited sceptre which Thy Almighty Father hath bequeathed Thee; for now the voice of Thy bride calls Thee, and all creatures sigh to be renewed."[112]

---

112 Milton, "Prose Works."

INDEX

International Eastern Co., 133
Inventions, 112
Inventions of Chinese, 39sq.
Iron, 18, 136
Irrawaddy, 105
Italy, 172-174 175, 212; soldiers
ofw 325
JAPAN, 17, 36, 101, 105, log, 111,
114, 167, 172, 173, 179, 182, 194,
212, 307, 308,309, 314, 337, 350;
Churches in, 299, 301
yapan WeekEy MviS, 125, 322
Japanese, 29, 44, 117, 118, 119,
305, 306, 312, 313, 317, 320,
321, 328, 329.
Jenghiz Khan, 318
Jerusalem, 105
Jewelry, 23
Jews, 4xsq., 217, 218
Johnson, Dr. Chas. F., 68, 91~ 229
Jones, Mr. A. G., 62
Junks, 130
KAI PING, 130
Kameruns, 108
Kansas 22
Kan-su 22, 66
Kao-liang, 46
Kaomi, 57
Kassai, 107
Khartoum, 104
Kai-feng-fu, 133, 217
Kentucky, 21, 22
Kerosene, sr3
Kiang-si, 21, 336
Kiang-su, 22, 336
Kiao-chou, 53, 57, 97; Bay of, 176
Kidd, Benjamin, 33, 364
Kien Lung, Emperor, 80
King of Siam, 114, 119

BIBLIOBAZAAR

The essential book market!

Did you know that you can get any of our titles in large print?

Did you know that we have an ever-growing collection of books in many languages?

Order online:
www.bibliobazaar.com

Find all of your favorite classic books!

Stay up to date with the latest government reports!

At BiblioBazaar, we aim to make knowledge more accessible by making thousands of titles available to you- *quickly and affordably*.

Contact us:
BiblioBazaar
PO Box 21206
Charleston, SC 29413